Redemption

Redemption

G.R. Thomas

To Kristen, Thomas and Ava,
May these books inspire you to reach for your own dreams.
You have inspired me to realise mine.

*"I drew this gallant head of war, and cull'd these fiery spirits
from the world, to outlook conquest and to win renown
even in the jaws of danger and of death."*

WILLIAM SHAKESPEARE
King John. Act V, scene 2

Prologue

The Gods' breath chased away the night's blanket. Verdant hues curtained the horizon, guiding three excited children away from the comfort of their beds.

"Stop wriggling, Cobaya," Inkasisa said. "My little flower, we are almost there."

Inkasisa snuggled her treasured pet closer to her chest as she climbed the rocky trail. The dawn air was crisp and fresh but always unsettled the scruffy guinea pig.

"Quiet down now, and I shall find you a snack once we have spoken to the Cloud Gods."

Inkasisa's eyes rose and widened at the sight of the aurora. She smiled until the impatient rodent disturbed her. Cobaya wriggled until Inkasisa's calm voice and warm body settled it. It squeaked a little and nodded off.

"I don't know about you, little one," Inkasisa said, "But I think my brother and sister need to come here more often." She stopped and turned, shielding her eyes as she glanced down the steep hill. Far below, the birthing sunrise outlined two shapes scrambling up after her, "They are too lazy, and now they suffer for it."

Inkasisa giggled as she watched them catch up.

"I think the alpaca has more strength than you, Manko," she called through a chuckle.

Manko scowled at her, his mouth as tight as he could squeeze it. "You made me wake early to drag this smelly thing up here in the dark. What do you expect?" he stamped his foot, startling the alpaca.

Inkasisa furrowed her brows at her younger brother. Her olive complexion reddened with annoyance. She flicked her thick black hair over her shoulders out of the tangle of her beads. The wooden spheres were a comforting reminder of her long-passed grandmother, gifted to Inkasisa on her death bed.

"Manko. We are here to honour the Gods who protect us!" Inkasisa said. "You know how much they mean to us. They protect us from the world's unseen evils. If you cannot manage to bring them one alpaca once a year so that they may drink milk and weave clothing, shame on you," she wagged a finger at him.

He glanced at the ground as the chestnut alpaca wriggled and pulled on the woven rope halter. It pulled its head back and spat in Manko's face.

Inkasisa stumbled with laughter, "That will teach you for being so unpleasant."

Manko hissed at the indifferent animal, which blinked its long lashes without a care, as he wiped the slime off his face, "I'd rather roast you for dinner."

"Oh, calm down," Inkasisa said. "What is your problem today? We are nearly there."

He grumbled and grit his teeth, trying to regain a little dignity as he pointed at their smallest sibling. "Achik has whined the whole way too. Why do you not scold and laugh at her?" Manko asked as he tried to hide tears of embarrassment.

"Because, brother, she is five years old. You are ten and should know better. Why, you are practically a man," Inkasisa looked past him towards her youngest sibling. "Are you alright, Little Light?"

She adored Achik and her two long black plaits. Her name meant *light,* and she was indeed the light of Inkasisa's life and constantly made her smile.

"I am tired," Achik said. "My legs hurt. I am hungry. I want water."

Manko bristled and stamped his foot again, "See? She has whined like this the whole way, and she has not pulled this stubborn creature!"

"Manko, enough," Inkasisa said. "We are nearly there. Come, Achik. I will carry you the rest of the way."

Achik ran with a giggle to Inkasisa, who handed her Cobaya. The guinea pig squealed at being disturbed.

"Oh, quiet, Cobaya. Now, Little Light, hold on to my baby so I may carry you," Inkasisa hoisted Achik onto her hip, her beads clinking around her arms and neck. Achik fiddled with the adornments and twirled them around her stubby fingers.

"Now, Manko, see that my workload is more than yours. Honour Father and Mother and stop complaining. Are you not the son of a king? Start acting like one," Inkasisa trudged off with her brother grumbling behind.

When the sun was half its width above the horizon, they reached their destination. Atop the peak, the three children gazed at the huge lake in awe.

Inkasisa sighed, "See, Manko? We are almost there."

He grunted, unapologetic but relieved to be mere paces away.

Floating islands of brush weed rested by the shoreline. The vast body of deep water made the islands bob in a way that relaxed Inkasisa.

The alpaca cooed. Its gentle voice carried across the water and startled some birds into the air. As Inkasisa's eyes drew away from the beat of their wings, she saw her favourite place in the world.

In the distance, like a mirage, a palace sat above the waters. As white as the hair of the Gods who dwelled within, it sparkled in the amber and pink dawn light.

The children picked their way towards the shore. Even Manko was reverent at the sight.

Achik yawned, "Will they come?"

"They always come when I visit," Inkasisa said. "They call me in my dreams. Mother tells me never to come unless the Gods call; we are not to disturb them. Last night, Copacati called to me. She said the Gods have an urgent message."

Achik's eyes widened, "What does the Lake Goddess want?"

"Probably more alpacas," Manko said, "and I suppose I will have to bring them."

"Hush, or you will find a giant frog in your bed when you least expect it."

Achik giggled, "Oh, yuck! That would be horrible. Eww, their saggy skin is so yucky! Be a good boy."

She giggled again as Inkasisa placed her down by the shore, where their bare feet sunk a little into the mud.

They gazed at the palace. The swirls that decorated the window frames matched the pretty marks of white light that glowed on their Gods' faces. Inkasisa touched her cheek. She wished every night since she had first met Copacati that she, too, could be one of them.

"How long until she comes?" Manko yanked the alpaca still as it foraged the few strands of grass.

"I do not know, but we will wait."

Achik made shapes in the mud as Cobaya scarpered around their feet, sniffing for a morsel. The air was still and quiet. A smattering of fluffy clouds dotted the sky, which became more cerulean by the minute.

Hypnotised by the serenity, it was only when Manko tugged on Inkasisa's hair that she noticed the water lapped a little faster at her feet. She focused on the dark water as a light appeared within its depths. It glided forwards like a smooth moving fish and made its way towards them. Inkasisa habitually gripped her beads. Never had the sight failed to make her gasp.

"Look, Little Light. Look!"

As the muddy-faced girl glanced up, the surface broke. Someone emerged in a fluid, ethereal motion. White hair, long and smooth, preceded a face of heavenly beauty. The pretty swirls of light that enveloped Copacati's face lit her rainbow eyes and warm smile. She glided over the water in a simple white dress and with wings of light. Copacati's wings were smaller than Inkasisa knew them to be, otherwise, Copacati's power would blind them. The full morning sun behind her made Copacati all the more otherworldly.

Achik clung to her sister's leg as she scooped up Cobaya. Manko, who had seen the Cloud God only once, was equally mesmerized.

Inkasisa bowed her head as the stunning woman approached.

"Child, I have told you many times that you need not bow to me," Copacati smiled. "Let me see your pretty face."

Inkasisa obeyed, even though she always felt unworthy.

"There now. My day is all the better for seeing you. And who have we here? Manko? I have not seen you in so long. You are so big, very much a strong man."

Manko puffed out his chest, never one to shy away from a compliment.

"Hello," Achik called.

Inkasisa moved to silence her, but Copacati hushed Inkasisa and moved closer. She kneeled to Achik's level.

"You, too, have grown. Did you walk all the way up the mountain yourself?" Copacati brushed stray hairs out of Achik's face.

"Nearly," Achik beamed. "Sister had to carry me for the last part."

"Well, a fine effort for all of you," Copacati stood and stroked the alpaca's neck, entwining elegant fingers through its silken coat. "This is a beautiful creature. Thank you. She will provide us with much milk and wool."

"And next year, I will find you a white one," Inkasisa said, excited. "A beautiful white one to match your hair."

"Dear child, your heart is full and pure. I wish for you and your family to stay so. I am afraid, however, that we shall not need another animal. This is why I have called you early this year," Copacati was solemn.

Achik grabbed Inkasisa's leg again. Manko clenched his fists. Inkasisa tugged at her beads and looked between herself, Copacati, and her siblings. Had she done something to offend Copacati? Her chin quivered.

"I have an important message for your parents, which they must share with all your people."

Inkasisa looked at Copacati with trepidation, "Have we displeased the Gods?"

Copacati smiled, "Child, I have told you more than once that we are not gods. We are your protectors. You could never displease us. You live well. You live happily and peacefully. You bring us the few necessities that make our lives more pleasant. That is all we wish for."

"Then… what do you wish of me to tell my family?" Inkasisa sheepishly kept her eyes on the tall woman.

"I am sad to say that we must leave you."

"What?" Manko and Inkasisa gasped in unison. They grabbed their faces in disbelief.

"But why?" Inkasisa asked. Tears weighed down her long lashes. "Why would you leave us?"

"Do you remember the stories I told you about the evil ones that walk the Earth?"

They nodded and paled. Achik held Cobaya closer.

"They have found us. The energy we create with our home, and when we communicate with you and the other people of this land, it has drawn them to us, and this puts you in danger."

Achik whimpered.

"Do not cry, little one. We will retreat and thus cut off the signal that attracts them. The last thing we want is for the evil ones to find your home. We will still be here, but you will no longer see or hear us. We will come when we can if you need protection, but for now, we must leave. I want you to tell your family and friends this story. We want you to continue the peaceful lives that the great Creator intended for you. Remember all we have taught you, and it is my hope that all shall be well."

There was a sudden and thunderous explosion. Inkasisa glanced around her goddess, past the mesmerising light of her wings, and saw the palace crack and crumble. The giant diamond, which was a beacon to all, fell as the great building crumbled and disappeared into the lake's depths.

Inkasisa cried, "No!"

Copacati bent down and kissed the children's heads, "Now, close your eyes and think of sweet things." Copacati took the alpaca's lead rope, "Do not open them until you have counted to twenty." Copacati placed her hand on the alpaca's head and put it into an instant slumber.

The children counted between sobs, eyes squeezed shut and tears streaming down their cheeks.

Copacati disappeared in a blinding flash of white light.

"Eighteen… nineteen… twenty," Inkasisa opened her eyes. The shoreline foamed as the last of the towering palace sunk away.

The children watched in silence until the lake was still and the reed islands had settled once more. Gone was the comforting glow over the lake. Dulled was the sun. The ground beneath them trembled.

Achik screamed. "Sissy, pick me up. I'm frightened," she jumped up and down.

"Hurry," Inkasisa said. "We must get to Mother and Father."

Inkasisa scooped up Achik and ran over the steep, barren terrain. Desperation drove her even under Achik's weight. Even Manko did not complain.

As they entered the village, drenched in sweat, Inkasisa handed Achik to Manko, "Carry her the rest of the way and follow as quickly as you can. I must get to Mother and Father."

Dodging the early morning traders along the neat stone streets, she pushed herself towards the royal palace — her home.

The straight lines of one hundred wide steps loomed ahead. Hefty guards pitched their blades into the steps at regular intervals. Her familiar presence didn't distract their intense focus as Inkasisa loped past them. Her legs burned; she cried from pain and fear. After many minutes, stopping only to cough and catch her breath, Inkasisa made it to the peak, where the royal chamber was nestled.

Once she had regained her composure, she stifled a scream. Biting her fist, she hid behind a tall pillar and peeked around.

Dark fluid stained the creamy stone platform and drizzled towards the steps she had just ascended. Four guards lay stabbed in the heart with their own spears. A strange mist rose from within the palace and floated around them. Inkasisa gagged at its foul stench.

She had never seen such a sight. They had guards as a precaution, but there had never been a need to worry about an attack as the Gods protected them. They had maintained peace between them and their neighbours from the south.

Unsure of what to do, Inkasisa only moved forwards when someone screamed within the temple.

"Mother. Father," she whispered breathlessly. Her shaky hand clamped over her mouth to prevent too much sound from escaping.

She checked her surroundings. No one else was present, only the murky mist that thickened by the second.

Inkasisa inched towards the ornate entry to the royal chamber with her hands pressed against the smooth wall. As the shouts became louder and more desperate, she flattened herself against the warm stone, her head resting under a carving of a puma. She was careful not to step in the crimson stains as she sidled towards the doorway. The guards' faces horrified her. Their mouths were agape and their eyes bulged. Flies buzzed around them, looking for a meal. She couldn't stand to look twice.

Two fires burned either side of the doorway to indicate that the royal family was home. The light flickered across splatters of blood marring the entrance. Inkasisa threw up as silently as she could just outside the looming door. As she wiped her mouth clean, her father's voice rang loud.

"No. We will not bend to your evil ways. We follow the Cloud Gods; you are from the underworld. Return to where you belong," her father was a brave man, but his voice trembled.

Inkasisa crept into the dark corridor on quivering tiptoes until she reached the first pillar within. She squished down into an insignificant ball and gaped in horror.

Her parents stood against the wall behind their ornate thrones. The room was full of strange people and frightening creatures. Curved horns grew out of the head of a tall, imposing man. People that appeared dead but alive surrounded him. Inkasisa blinked. Maybe she was in a dream? She bit her lip and felt the pain of being awake. The dead-but-alive people gurgled and snarled and smelled terrible, like meat that had been left too long in the sun. A tall woman with long red hair and pale skin roamed among them. A handful of children, who were as pale as she, followed and begged her for something. She slapped at them until they hushed.

"We need not know of your Gods," the horned man said. "They are nothing to us. Know this though; *we* are your Gods now. You will serve us. Our needs are few, but quite a bit different to your Cloud Gods'." He looked at the woman. They laughed together as though it was funny.

The king gripped a white stone around his neck, "What do you want then?"

"Nothing much, really. Just a little something for our protection of you and your people."

"What is it will you protect us from that Copacati did not?" the king asked.

The woman cackled, her blood-red lips thick and glistening. The horned man surveyed the room and clicked his fingers. Five men just like him emerged from the shadows. All but one carried glowing weapons.

"Why, we will protect you from us," the horned man laughed again, as did they all.

The king stood in front of his wife, "What do you mean by this?"

"Shall I demonstrate, my queen?" the horned one asked.

"Oh yes please, my king," the pale woman clapped. Her children squealed with excitement.

"Asbel, bring one to me," he commanded.

"Yes, Master Yeqon."

Asbel dragged a struggling guard into the middle of the room and threw him at Yeqon's feet.

"Please, show mercy!" the young guard quivered. His skin glistened with sweat.

"Of course, human," Yeqon said. "I shall make it quick."

Yeqon slashed open the guard's neck with a three-pointed weapon. The guard gargled and fitted as his blood spurted everywhere. The air thickened as the dead-but-alive things became agitated and the children whined impatiently.

Inkasisa swallowed hard and tried not to faint. Her fingers quivered and tingled; she bit them to quell the trembling. She feared for her parents and hoped that Manko and Achik did not make it up the steps after all.

"The price for my protection is blood. My queen and my children, my army, they all require fresh blood to sustain them. On every new moon and the beginning of a new year, you shall provide the blood of your people. I will await you on these days atop this palace. If you fail, this sacrifice will happen not only to you and your own children but to your entire city," he turned to nod at the pale woman with red hair.

She smiled and pushed her children, "Dinner, my lovelies. Eat your fill."

The children screeched as they descended on the fallen guard. They slurped and sucked every drop of blood from his greying body. They even licked the thick clots off the floor.

Inkasisa vomited again. Her throat burned and she moaned out loud. One of the dead-but-alive things appeared out of nowhere and dragged her out of the shadows. She screamed as she kicked and struggled to free herself.

"Daughter!" her mother cried.

Yeqon smiled, "How fortuitous."

The dead-but-alive thing delivered Inkasisa to Yeqon's side. He was even more enormous close up. Bigger than Copacati. His black eyes glared as he twisted her face this way and that, his fingertips were warm and scratched her skin. He had wings of light like Copacati, but his were a dirty grey. They made her cheeks sting and her eyes water. His evil eyes examined her, lit by the same swirls as Copacati's. Inkasisa's body tremored more than before.

"The Gods will save you, daughter," her mother called. "Have faith."

Tears sprung into Inkasisa's eyes. No one knew about the Cloud Gods' retreat yet.

"It is true then," she whispered.

"What is true, small one?" Yeqon asked, narrowing his eyes until they were slits.

Inkasisa looked up at his handsome face, "Copacati spoke the truth. She said the evil ones are near, and that is why they must hide."

Yeqon bellowed, throwing his head back as his full laugh echoed around the chamber.

"They have hidden again? These are your Gods?" he laughed again, as did the other five. "Your Gods have deserted you, Your Highness. Deserted you and left you to us," Yeqon shook his head and clicked his tongue. "Well then. How easy was that? They left you with the slightest threat. Pathetic. I promise you this; I will not abandon you. I will build you an even greater empire and protect you from your southern enemies. All you need to do is offer me a blood sacrifice, and all will be well."

The queen paled. The king curled his fingers into fists. Inkasisa struggled in Yeqon's grasp.

"The first sacrifice shall be tonight, for it is most fortuitously a full moon. A perfect way to regulate your offerings. Until then, I shall keep this little one to myself as an enticement for your cooperation."

The queen fell to her knees, screaming. The king roared, and Inkasisa slapped at Yeqon. Her fingers stung against his firm chest; her useless nails did not even graze the smooth skin. While her fist was poised for another blow, he knocked her out like Copacati had done with the alpaca. The room of invaders vanished, leaving nothing but the remnants of the foul mist.

The king and queen clung to each other. The unearthly light had blinded them, their faces blistered raw from the heat.

Guards arrived with Manko and Achik.

"Your Highness, what happened?" the guard looked horrified as he smelled blood and saw the bodies. He gently touched the king's tender skin. "You are injured, my Lord. Call the medicine woman," he bellowed to the others behind him.

The king's eyes swelled shut and blood ran from the inner corners. His cheeks peeled in white sheets. His body shook before he managed to regain composure. The guard guided him and the queen back to their thrones, where they sat in silence as healers tended their burns.

The king, with Manko and Achik crying at his feet, banged his fist on the stone armrest, "Organise a tournament for the people. The loser shall be brought to the temple roof at midnight. This is my order and that of your new god Supay, the God of Death."

Chapter One

Embers danced on the breeze as I walked away from the manor. Vengeance was a comforting echo in every thump of my heart, a warm hug that tantalised the darkest of thoughts. A high I'd never allowed myself to court numbed my skin in a way that felt like a barrier between myself and the rest of the world.

But disappointment doused the thrill of destruction. I hadn't found Nephr'reus and Anjou'elle. I'd failed to kill them.

Snow squelched under my feet and soothed the burns I'd ignored. When I reached the Blackthorn trees, I turned around to survey my work. A smouldering blot behind Chateau Pouancé was all that remained of the manor, the place of Jaz' torture. Black smoke curled up from its centre and entwined with the clouds. Sirens sounded in the distance. Humans were on the way. I didn't know where to go, so I transferred to the first place that came to mind.

Frozen gravel dug into my now stinging and blistered soles. I rounded the corner of the old priory house. The air was fresh, a virginal wintery cleanliness that filled each breath. It tempered the hot anger prickling beneath my skin and cleared the heavy fog in my head.

My ears pricked up at the odd chitter of birds and the rush of a river. My eyes hurt. I pinched the bridge of my nose; the pounding ache abated a little. I hurried, peering over my shoulders for any sign I'd been followed. Nothing, but every hair rose across my body anyway. I crossed my arms and rubbed at my unease. In the cold silence, I walked along a pebbled drive towards the thousand-year-old church atop the abandoned Katoika sanctuary in Tewkesbury.

I began to shake. A time-ravaged gravestone held me up, its rough surface the only thing that felt real in a situation that was rapidly feeling like a nightmare. My nails split as they dug into it. I squeezed my eyes shut; they felt hot and wrong. The memory of my reflection in the burning manor punched the air from my chest. I fell to the ground, gasping and holding onto my soul stone for dear life.

My lips quivered. Tears mingled with snot and dribbled into the grooves of my fists. I hunched over like it would protect me from what I'd done. I was cold, hot, angry, terrified.

Birdsong broke through my sobs. A raven sat on a naked branch, its head tilting like it was trying to set its black eyes more on me; eyes as black as mine.

The quiet became an ominous threat. I clambered up and pulled the heavy church door shut behind me. The clean smell of winter gave way to a musty interior that reeked of every one of its thousand years. The small decommissioned church was empty of course, it felt empty of body and spirit. No energy, other than my panicked one. I slumped on the closest pew and healed the stinging blisters on my heels—just enough that the fluid-filled sacks retreated into light pink skin that was sensitive but not too painful.

Ben's pleading face flashed through my mind. *Don't do it*, he'd begged. Jaz' dying body drowned him out. Anger drummed in my head, and it felt easy to let it overwhelm the pleas for morality crying in the far reaches of my mind. My eyes watered as the throbbing intensified. I blinked the pain away….and noticed the font on the altar. I was beside it and holding the lid's tarnished brass handle before I realised I'd moved. It had an inch of stagnant water in its base. Shining black eyes that couldn't possibly belong to me stared back. My hair fell forwards, a veil to protect me but it didn't do its job.

Ashes and spice cut through the dank air.

"Like what you see?"

I settled the lid back over the water. The metallic clang echoed throughout the church.

"Turn around," Ben said.

"No," the word tasted bitter.

Another presence lightened the pressing atmosphere further.

"Turn around, Sophia," Lorcan's voice was as flat as Ben's.

My wings stung as they released, "Leave me alone."

"We can fix this," Ben said, his voice a little closer.

My bloodied nails held onto the font for dear life. I took a short, sharp breath, trying to quell the flutter in my heart.

"Nothing can fix this," I said. "They've won."

"That's not true," Lorcan said. "Don't let them beat you."

My fingers dug in harder as though I might fall if I let go. I closed my eyes and held my breath. The taste of blood mingled with a desirable vengeance, a feeling that stayed tantalizingly close to the surface.

A hand touched my shoulder. My instincts reacted so fast it wasn't until the dust settled that I realized what I'd done.

The right-hand pews were splintered and upturned. St Peter, mere rubble, scattered across the marble floor. A dust plume blotted out the pale sunrays streaming through an arched window by the door.

Lorcan lay among the rubble. Ben tried to pull him out, but Lorcan slapped him away. He climbed out and swore to himself, "Get off!"

Ben backed away; his eyes heavy on me.

My shaking hands were white hot. My memory of the attack — nothing but black-out rage. My face tingled with a strange and pleasurable high. I peered towards the door, pictured other places, anywhere but here with them. Flight or fight were parrying in my mind. My body numbed, and my gut pulled towards the nothingness.

"Soph, stop!"

I transferred.

Water rushed, muted to a dull hum under a thin ice layer. A smattering of melting snow bearded the Avon river. Fish darted along the current and drew my eyes to a dishevelled hut. I remembered it from when I'd first arrived in England. For some reason I was drawn to it and I padded along the bank; the closer I came, the more it intrigued me. An energy came from it. Ben and Lorcan were screaming into my mind, but I blocked them out.

I stopped about twenty feet away from the hut under a willow tree. Its naked branches raked the river banks. I held onto its cold trunk as though grasping it would connect me more to the moaning in the ether. It was getting louder, its energy familiar but not enough to pinpoint who or what it was.

I closed my eyes and honed my senses to the nearby rhythmic pulsations of someone of A'vean heritage. I gasped, and a shock of freezing air hit my insides. Was it the sisters? Did they have some other poor sod underground, torturing them as they had done to Jaz? My mark burned like fire ants marching under my skin, and my pounding eyes flew open.

"Bitches," I ripped bark from the tree, crumpled it in my palm. I walked towards the wooden structure with death on my mind.

A flash got in my way.

"Leave me the hell alone, Lorcan," I clenched my fists and suppressed a rush of energy.

He stepped to the left when I did and folded his arms, "Can't do that."

I stepped to the right. So did he.

"Stop it!"

My wings gnashed towards him like teeth. Lorcan swerved to avoid their bite.

"You want to draw something out of the Pits with those? You're leaving your very precise calling card all over the place whilst you have a temper tantrum. I'm surprised Yeqon isn't here already," Lorcan checked over his shoulders as though to look for him.

A part of me screamed to stop what I was doing, but a more enticing voice coaxed me to let raw emotion rule the show. A tremble began in my hands and rushed up my chest and into my head. I threw an orb at him, its release a relief of explosive tension. Of course, it made no contact. He did a backflip, and my orb obliterated a small sapling on the offside of the building that held my interest. Birds screeched and took flight, disappearing in a chaotic smudge across the grey sky.

"Do that again, Soph and I'll have no choice but to…"

"To what? You know you can't hurt me," my coarse voice sounded alien, even to me.

"Cut it out! This isn't you!"

Lorcan's words were an annoying, muffled garble that interrupted the chaos in my mind. I struggled to hide my shaking, to hide my vulnerability. I needed to escape, I felt trapped; exposed. I shuffled back and searched my memories for somewhere else to go, somewhere I could hide to pull my messy self together.

Lorcan rushed me, "Uh-uh! No you don't!"

I wound my arm back, ready to strike again, but he clamped it behind me. My other arm soon followed. A sting glued them together at the small of my back. I struggled against the burn and fell to the ground, twisting like a fish out of water. I rolled over to find Ben standing above me.

"You're not going anywhere," Ben's arms were firmly crossed, his face stony.

"Get these off me!" I screeched; my teeth clenched.

I spun around and kicked towards Ben, but my furious thrashing only dug a niche into the cold ground. The river seemed louder, or maybe it was panic; the shackles stopped me from transferring. I struggled until I rolled over again and tumbled down towards the frozen banks. I stopped right on the edge.

"Help me up, you idiots!"

"Name-calling will get you nowhere," Ben said. "Calm down and I'll help you."

I struggled against the biting shackles, tipping over onto the river's smooth ice. The cool shock eased the burn of the binds, but the humiliation of the situation only whipped my already frightening anger into a frenzy.

"I'll kill you both! Do you know *who* you're dealing with?"

I slipped along the ice, the river louder than ever beneath me.

Lorcan and Ben stood on the edge of the bank, doing nothing to help.

"Did you hear that, Daimon? Fame has finally got to her head," Lorcan said.

"Knew it would happen eventually. And don't call me *Daimon*, pretty boy," Ben snapped back.

I wriggled towards the river's centre, "Let me go, damn it! I just want to kill the sisters, that's all!"

"It starts with one murder, then another," Lorcan said. "Before you know it, you're Yeqon," he shrugged and raised his brows.

"You kill those two with a dark heart and you're lost, just like they are," Ben said.

"I don't care! They need to die!"

There was a subtle crack under me. I held still.

"That's every Daimon's excuse. Someone hurt their feelings, so they kill who they like. Not how it works, Soph." Lorcan tilted his head. "We defend ourselves and the weak. We don't hunt for personal retribution."

"Are you two serious? Look what they did to Jaz!" Another crack. "Get me off this!"

Neither of them moved. They exchanged a knowing glance like they were best-damned-friends now.

Lorcan cracked his neck, "You won't drown."

Water seeped against my neck. I rolled carefully onto my side so I could see them better.

"Get me…"

The river swallowed me. Black arctic water dragged me quickly away from the hazy white of the surface. I panicked initially. The urge to breath made me convulse; I slammed into a rock, and it jolted the desire out of me. The current was strong, like hands gripping my ankles. Debris hit me from all sides as I whooshed along. I forced myself to relax; this was an opportunity to get away, to try and get the damned shackles off. I closed my eyes and let myself go with the current. For a second, there was a calming darkness and a hushed bubbling.

Arms grappled around my torso and pulled me out of the frozen river. Ben set me down below an evergreen with a wide canopy. I kicked out, and he backed away.

"Get off me!" I coughed up some brackish water.

The shackles burned hotter. I grunted and cursed to myself as I wriggled up until I could lean against the tree trunk.

Ben squatted in front of me, Lorcan to my right.

"You know there is only one outcome, don't you?" Lorcan said.

"Yes! Let me go."

"No," Lorcan answered. I narrowed my eyes at him.

"I'll remove your shackles if you promise to behave," Ben said. His eyes held no anger, but shone with pain.

I nodded, desperate to be rid of them.

They exchanged a look and Lorcan disappeared.

"Where did he go?"

Ben indicated for me to turn around. The burn released; I fled up the river bank and away from him.

He chuckled in my mind, *"He's waiting for you."*

I soared high into the clouds without a plan, just a need to flee.

I pumped my wings twice before I was descending back towards the ground, once more wrapped in Lorcan's arms.

"Lorcan!" I screamed.

"You're too predictable."

His laughter infuriated me. My wrists stung again.

"Get them off me!"

We curved through tingly clouds as Lorcan slowed and headed back the way I'd come.

"Nope," he said. "Not until your head's screwed back on right."

We landed under the same tree. Behind Lorcan's and Ben's satisfied expressions, I caught a glimpse of the church steeple below the crest of a hill.

Ben nodded at Lorcan, who pulled something from his pocket. His fist concealed it, and my heart thrashed with panic. Ben slid in behind me, threaded his arms through mine, and pulled me against his chest. My mind clouded. The cold air pressed in on me. Lorcan kneeled in front of me; I jerked and kicked at him.

His fist rushed towards me too quickly to understand what he was up to. Pressure thumped into my chest. My eyes flew back into my head. A million stars came at me, innumerable pinpricks of pain. Every nerve ending was on fire. Silence enveloped me as heat built up, an uncomfortable temperature paired with a vile smell. Chills ran down my spine as things I couldn't see rushed around me, touched me and prodded me. The darkness reddening until it was a sickening ruby.

Screams, horrified and high-pitched, ended the silence. Something grabbed my wrist. I looked down and saw the bony protrusions of a hand and a tortured face. The Afflicted looked sorrowfully at me before the River of Blood in Oblivion swept her away. Human and Daimon souls flew by in a never-ending circle of torment.

Ben's face flashed into my mind. "This is your destiny if you let the darkness consume you."

I scrambled to reach the surface, but two souls collided in front of me, their screams soul-destroying moans. The current thrust me towards them, my body breaking their embrace. I spun with the flow as they struggled for each other's comfort and realised they were Nephr'eus and Anjou'elle.

I was pulled from Oblivion and into a milky calm. A long smear of starlight across an endless horizon formed one great sheet so bright I thought it might blind me.

A voice, a touch; a feeling of great comfort and safety cocooned my thrashing heart.

"There, there. Shh."

"Enl'iel?" I screamed. Was I dead?

"Let the pain go, dear. Let the light back in."

"Where are you? Help me!"

The hypnotic whiteness pulsated in tune with my pulse.

"There, there…" her voice drifted away.

The light faded, and blackness took over.

I never felt the transfer but awoke in my room in Kaymakli with a thumping pain in my chest. I sat up with a start and ran my hands over my body, finishing with a reassuring slap to my face. I was alive, in pain and confused, but alive.

Brennan sat on a chair and leaned it back against the door, "Well, that tantrum was up there with the best of them. So, how was the dark side?"

I swallowed hard; my throat dry. The duvet felt too heavy as I kicked it away. I reached for a full glass of water by the bedside and gulped it like I hadn't drunk in days. I coughed, too greedy for its soothing taste. I poured the last mouthful onto my hands and wiped them across my face, breathing deep as I did so. Leaning forwards, I gripped the bed's edge, reached for my pendant…

And noticed the black-purple bruise across my chest. A large blister just under my collar bone. I ran my fingers over it.

"What the hell happened?"

"Hmm, let me see…" Brennan steepled his hands against his lips.

"Just tell me what's going on," I said.

I rubbed the aching bruise. Had I had a psynostris cycle? "How did I get this?" Were my memories a nightmare? I was exhausted; I didn't feel like I'd slept.

Brennan quirked an eyebrow, his expression a cross between annoyance and empathy.

"Let me tell you a story," he said. I sighed and flung back onto my pillow.

"There was once an angel who knew a daimon. They hated each other, like, *really* hated each other. However, there was another angel, who was so very, very good, but…" Brennan stood, hands clasped behind his back, and let the chair fall. He paced between the bed and the door. "The very good angel was tempted by the devil, who had tasted her pain. Of course, this was a great pain," he shook his head sorrowfully. "Everyone wanted to help her, but she was too stubborn. So, despite hating each other, the angel and daimon put aside their personal feelings for a short time. They searched until they found the very good angel, who was now ungrateful and spiteful. She wasn't thinking clearly, so they outmanoeuvred her and used a powerful soul stone to purge the evil from her. Evil doesn't give in easily and she was left with an awfully large burn across her chest," Brennan peered at the bruise I was trying to sooth. "No pain, no gain as they say. They saved her and brought her home. The end."

Brennan lifted the oval mirror from the wall and held it to my face. I was pale, shocked. But I had blue eyes... and a whole lot of shame.

I was transfixed with my reflection, at the memories of Pouancé Manor, the inferno I created, and the urge to cause mayhem and death that had turned my eyes to demonic black. I gulped. It was a bitter flavour.

"Be kind to Ben and Lorcan," Brennan said. "They just saved you from yourself. Now, get back to your mission."

Two

Lilith feasted on a platter of red apples and a goblet of fresh blood. An Afflicted lay drained by the pool she was bathing in.

A mountain rumbled in the distance. The cries of babies echoed from dark tunnels.

"You took your time," she said to her visitor. "I expected you well before now."

"I've had a few interruptions," her guest said. "Every movement is a risk."

Lilith nodded and looked him up and down. "You look well, at least. I, too, had a setback; not unexpected however," she rose slowly from the pool and enjoyed her own nakedness, gazing upon her rises and falls that were shadowed seductively by flame and orb. Her hands smoothed across her breasts and along the pale bump. Water drizzled across the taught skin and into the natural rock pool.

"Hmm. I am restored," Lilith rejoiced.

He watched her with guarded eyes, "You have been fortunate to have another birthing cycle."

Lilith smiled to herself and ran her hands more slowly over her skin, enjoying the attention. "Yes, my dear, and what a gift it shall be for the world," she flicked her wet hair behind her shoulders and smoothed it back. "And wont it bite, so to speak?" her laugh was short and sharp.

Her visitor grinned.

She stepped out of the dark waters. The gestational swelling of her belly retracted quickly as the last of labour's blood dribbled down her thighs. The wails of nearby infants and toddlers echoed along the raw recesses of the cave. She cocked her head to listen.

"The children hunger?" her guest asked.

"Don't they always?" Lilith squeezed water from her hair. "It is why they are such divine beings. Feed them well, and they are my greatest creation and weapon. They serve their parents with unwavering loyalty."

She winked at him and clapped twice. An Afflicted entered from a dark fissure behind her. She draped Lilith in luxurious white muslin, which clung to her physique.

"Feed the children," Lilith said. "Be quick about it or you will be their next meal."

The servant's eyes flashed with fear. She bowed, backed away, and disappeared into the niche. She reappeared with a bound and gagged man, who writhed and bucked as he sought freedom in the last place he would find it. His eyes fluttered, gibbous with terror.

Her guest's nose flared in disgust, "A human?"

"Judge me not. It is a means to an end for our benefit. It's best we get them used to the flavours of everyday now, don't you think?" Lilith kneeled and took a hand full of the human's hair. He screamed around his gag and urinated.

"Oh, disgusting!" Lilith dropped his head onto a rock. He fell limp.

Lilith rubbed her hands clean and made her way towards her guest. She brushed his face with the edge of her hand, running a finger along his jawline until it rested on his lip. A lusty growl rumbled in his throat. He leaned towards her, but the human roused and began thrashing again. The infants screamed for food once more.

Lilith pulled away, "Best whet their appetite so they can serve their parents well."

Her guest sat and retrieved an apple from her platter. "Indeed. A plentiful supply awaits," he took a bite.

"I long to forget the taste of the half dead," Lilith said. "It's like eating dirt. I would not like to inflict it on my next generation. It lacks a certain kick," she dressed herself. The Afflicted was still there; Lilith rolled her eyes. "Hurry up. Take it away," she pointed at the bound man. "You will be fed when my children have quieted."

The Afflicted sped away with the body, towards the hungry calls. She stopped at the tunnel's mouth to throw an orb up to light her way. Its glow highlighted a drag mark along the ground made by the man's body.

Squeals of delight echoed, quickly followed by a few seconds of agonised screams. Lilith and her visitor smiled.

"It warms my belly when I know they are sated. I suppose it's impossible for you to understand that satisfaction?"

"It's not a feeling I understand, but I am their father, and it pleases me that they are well kept," he took another bite of the apple before flinging it away. "How many have you birthed this time?"

"Fifty, all unsullied and mine to do with as I wish. I have plenty older, more experienced children. Yeqon's offspring are still loyal to me first, as yours will be too," Lilith slipped on her long, red boots.

"Fifty will do as a start. Here, as requested," he held out a tinkling bag. Lilith took it. "It should keep your Afflicted obedient for quite a while."

Lilith's eyes danced, "And…?"

He placed a small stone into her palm. She held it aloft; the overhead orb backlit its orange hue.

"Wonderful," Lilith said. "This will make tuning into the goings-on much easier."

He nodded, "Have you heard from Yeqon?" He sneered as the name crossed his lips.

"No. He hasn't dared set foot back here since he left," her voice, hitched and she changed the subject quickly. "What news of the Earthborn?"

His lips curled in disgust, "She continues to whine over everything. I'll be glad to hear an end to it. She knows nothing of our suffering. I doubt she'll find the time to finish her quest with all her agonising."

Their eyes met; a knowing exchange of all things secretive.

He drummed on his thigh, "Her heart still blinds her head."

Lilith clapped and laughed, "She shall be blinded by not only her human fallibilities, but by a strike she will never see coming."

Chapter Three

"Where is he?"

I'd come to the cells to thank Ben only to find an almighty mess and Ben and Belial nowhere to be found. There were hurried footprints and a guard rubbing the back of his head. A few scorch marks defaced the walls.

"How did he get out?" I asked no one in particular.

Panic erased my urge to say *thank you*. Ben had taken Belial, released that maniac into the world, but he wouldn't have been out of the cells at all if he hadn't had to come save me from myself. I'd created an opportunity for him to betray us.

I wandered into his cell, then Belial's. They were definitely empty, neat even. They'd pulled up the blankets on the beds, and Belial had even cleaned the plates off the floor. I flung one across the room, and it cracked against the door.

My fingers dug into my hips. I sighed and let my head fall back. I heard Lorcan's footsteps, smelled the ocean breeze that always preceded him.

"What?" I snapped without looking at him. "I thought *you* were watching him?" I threw my hands in the air, confused, hurt, bruised, and frustrated.

"Don't even go there," Lorcan said. "I have other duties, too, Sophia, one of which was swallowing my pride and saving your backside with him last night," he pointed at me. "This one's on you," Lorcan sighed, his shoulders dropped, he rubbed his temples. "After we got you home, I left him here and went to clean up," he grumbled. "I didn't expect him to leave after what he did to help you."

I felt terrible. My fault, his fault… what did it matter? Ben and Belial were gone.

I walked up behind Lorcan and touched his arm. "Sorry, you're right," I could barely look at his face. "And thank you. I'm so sorry for… I just…"

He shrugged. "You made a mistake. Don't do it again. You're not like him," he poked around inside the cells. "Didn't even hang around to see if you were okay."

"Where would he have gone?"

"Back to that animal," Jude's booming voice made me jump, snapping me out of a fog of thoughts. He circled us, his arms wide and his sneer even wider. "And with all the intel he's gleaned from us, too!'" Jude looked me up and down, "You sorted your shit out?"

I lowered my eyes and nodded.

"Good," and that was all he had to say on the matter. He sniffed around the two cells.

I shook my head, "He wouldn't go back to Yeqon."

It felt so wrong to defend Ben, but he had just saved me from falling into the darkest place. I trailed Jude. Ben's energy lingered in his cell like a slap in the face. He hadn't been gone long.

Jude flipped the cot. "Why not? It's where he belongs," he sniffed a cup and flung it to the ground.

"Yeqon beat him to a pulp last time," I winced at the memory. "He's probably running from everything."

"He hasn't got the right to do that," Lorcan said. "He owes you — after all, he was Yeqon's eyes on you, remember?" Lorcan helped the guard up and sent him to the Stasis room. The guard limped away, hurt by Ben or Belial or both. Lorcan was right, Ben had a lifetime of redemption ahead of himself, so running *was* cowardly.

I'd been a fool. I hadn't trusted him completely, and this had proven why. He'd helped me to get just enough favour to pull this stunt.

"Are you happy now?" Lorcan asked.

He was on the floor before I realised I'd punched him.

"No, Lorcan, I'm far from happy!"

He rolled over and pushed himself up, gingerly rubbing his jaw. Jude chuckled to himself, which stirred the anger in my gut. I watched that feeling more carefully, not wanting it to get out of hand again.

I stepped around Lorcan, "Be at the training room in twenty minutes. It's time to weapon up and get the hell out of here."

My hand hurt. Lorcan's face probably didn't feel too good either. I twirled my fingers around my pendant and thought of Jaz. I'd avenge her the right way… by completing my mission and restoring this world to what it should be.

Enl'iel met me on my way to the training room. She reached for my hand, a barely hidden *I told you so* in her eyes.

"How can I help?" she asked.

"Just look after Jaz and Kristen. I'll fix this," I stopped a moment and leaned into a vine cluster a small distance from my bedroom door. "Sorry," I squashed green snippets between my fingers.

Enl'iel reached towards my bruise, her face ashen. "I'm sorry for your pain," she pulled a soul stone from her pocket. "This is the largest soul stone we have. They had to use it to purge you of the darkness."

My eyes and mouth widened as I looked at the glittering stone. I reached for it but pulled away and shook my head.

"I deserved it — all of it."

Enl'iel pocketed the stone. With the same hand, she soothed my bruise away until only a pale green-yellow hue remained.

"Don't be so harsh on yourself," she said. "It will do you no good at all. We all make mistakes. It's how we move on that counts," she answered softly. She held my hand to her chest. "Just breathe," her soft eyes hooked mine, just like they'd done when I was a little girl afraid of the dark.

"I'll make this count," I said.

Enl'iel nodded, kissed my hand, and let go.

We returned to my bedroom. The posted guard moved aside as we entered. He nodded politely before speaking.

"It was good to see your friend," he said.

I restocked my weapons belt. "What friend?"

"Jasmine."

My dagger clattered to the ground.

"What?" Enl'iel and I asked simultaneously.

"She was here just a little while ago, but I sent her away," the guard said. "No one may enter without you, as per my orders."

"Jaz was here?" The words were breathy. I blinked at the guard as though that would clear my confusion.

"You must have confused her with someone else," Enl'iel said. "Jasmine is gravely unwell."

The guard bowed but looked confused himself, "With respect, no one forgets that human. She was not quite herself, but it was her, Ma'am."

"This is rubbish," Enl'iel said. "Take my hand."

My gut swirled as she transferred us back to the Stasis room. The dimmed evening hue set a hushed and calm tone as the Alchemae did their rounds. A guard stood by the new door. We shuffled past the beds to the intensive care veil. Kristen slept nearby. She looked well with just a small dressing over her wound now.

"What time is it?" I asked.

"A little after midnight," Enl'iel answered.

The veil hummed and tingled as I passed through. Jaz was exactly the same. The pasty pale of impending death, a glowing soul stone over her heart, and herbs smoking around her bed. My heart sank at her stillness.

I circled her bed, "Where are her carers?"

"They should always be here," Enl'iel said, annoyance in her voice.

"That guard is mistaken," I rested my head on Jaz' chest and hugged her tight. Her heartbeat was slow and faint.

Enl'iel pulled me into a hug, "Perhaps he is tired, standing around for hours can be monotonous. I'll organise a change of duty."

I pulled away from Enl'iel and kissed Jaz' forehead. Her skin was horridly cold. She felt absent, a soul evaporating without hope for return. A tear landed on her skin and rolled into her hair.

Keep your cool girl. Focus. I twisted memories of vengeance into a renewed focus. One, that in the end would see peace for Jaz, in one realm or another.

"It's time to finish this, Enl'iel."

She nodded and crossed her hands over her belly, "Be careful. The world is more dangerous today than it was yesterday, and tomorrow that shall increase tenfold. Follow Enoch's words. They are there to protect you."

A quick peck on her cheek, a sorrowful glance back at Jaz, and I welcomed the elemental pull that took me to the training room. Lorcan, Jude, and Brennan were armed and furious.

"Not a word, any of you," I walked to the weapon bank on the far wall. A few extra daggers were a welcome weight on my belt.

Lorcan looked away when I caught his eyes. His swollen chin shamed me. It wasn't acceptable.

"Sorry for that," I said.

"That's two apologies today," Lorcan muttered in response.

"Hmm," I snorted. My annoyance for him rose again.

"Save your passion for the Rogues, Sophia," Jude ran his hand along the flat side of a longsword. He didn't make eye contact, "How is she?"

"The same," I answered softly.

He stopped and looked at his reflection in the blade. His hand blazed with white energy, which flowed along the chromious.

He sheathed the sword, "No mercy, young one."

"That I can promise you," I gulped. It had to be the only way from here on.

Brennan had swapped his blunt weapon for a newly sharpened one. "Where to?"

"The Isle of Capri," I said. "Specifically, a place called the Blue Grotto. It's where Tiberius fooled around with Daimon. I'm sure the last clue referred to it. Ben knows this, too, so I assume Belial does also. If you see them, kill them."

They stared at me with surprise, but left it at that. I retrieved new armour and slipped it onto my torso. Jude tightened it down my back.

"Do any of you know the Blue Grotto?" I asked.

"I know the general vicinity," Brennan said.

"Same," Lorcan added. He didn't meet my eyes; he hadn't forgiven me.

Jude slapped the last clasp shut, "I know Capris, but I've not been to the grotto."

"Let's just get going and work out the rest once we're there," I shook my arms out to dissipate the tingle of nerves that was flooding me. "I don't know Italy. You'll need to guide me through the transfer," I said.

We gathered into a small circle of grim determination. Enl'iel watched on from the door across the arena. She blew me a kiss. I closed my eyes and took Brennan's and Jude's hands in mine.

"I'll see you soon, Enli'el,"

We transferred in one almighty flash.

Cool ocean water lapped around our feet, whispering rhythmically across the sand. Seagulls flapped about the jetty lights, unsettled by our sudden appearance. Mountains rose before us, vast shadows against the stars. Classic Italian buildings skirted a choppy sea and hugged by a hilly vista. There were no people, just the distant regular thud of a night club nestled somewhere amongst the ancient town of Capri.

"Where to from here?" I asked.

I stepped through soft sand. A flickering streetlight caught my eye. Moths fought to plunge to their deaths in its intensity, and it felt a little like what I was doing. The truth of it was nauseating.

"It's on the north-west coast," Brennan said. "We should go on foot though; it would be more dangerous to spike the E'lan any further. We'll save any elementals for when absolutely necessary."

"We can follow the cable car tracks over there," Jude pointed up to the left. "There's good coverage overhead and plenty of trees for camouflage."

Cables ran up the steep hills and into the night. Carriages sat in quiet solitude at the base, awaiting tomorrow's passengers.

I peered into the darkness at the steep landscape, "How long will it take?"

Brennan pointed to a street sign that said Via Grotta Azzurra, "It's only a couple of miles this way."

"Let's conceal and get going," I said.

Within minutes, we were sporting regular clothes and hair colours and walking along the road, a group of sleepless backpackers picking their way through the town. I hadn't gone for my standard rainbow locks but a mousy brown; the less attention the better.

"Do you know what you're looking for?" Jude asked.

"The third of three chests that Enoch referred to," I said. "Hopefully, it will have all that I need to open the portal. I bet it won't be sitting around with a bow and a card saying *take me* though."

"I would imagine not," Jude added, almost, but not quite smiling.

"So, I think two of you should act as lookouts and one of you should help me."

"I'll go with you," Lorcan said.

"Actually, I'd like Jude to come with me. You and Brennan fight well together. He and Jude… well, you know. I have to be able to trust that my lookouts won't attack each other," I said.

Lorcan peered at the ground and sped ahead. And there was insult number three for the day.

"I wouldn't lay a hand on him during a mission, Sophia," Jude grumbled. "You underestimate my integrity."

"That's good to know, but I'd feel better if you stuck with me."

"As you wish. You buffoons can stand guard," Jude scoffed.

"And that just makes my point." I exclaimed. Jude winked at me, and his mouth curved a little. I snorted. How much of his behaviour was for show? We trudged on ahead, side by side.

The off-road terrain was rough. This little island off the west coast of Italy made us work hard for the destination. Those few miles were taking longer than I'd anticipated. The sky had tinted a lighter blue with dawn encroaching on the night. When we reached the north-western side, cliffs fell away to a wild and foaming sea. The salty air warmed a little. We veered off the access road and navigated low-lying scrub until we reached a small building. It bore a weathered sign that read Grotta Azzurra Informazione.

"Well, this looks about right," Brennan tapped on the modest structure. "This wasn't here last time I passed by," he yanked on the padlock and let it clatter against the door. "That was hundreds of years back though."

A map in a plastic casing pointed to the grotto. A large red spot read, 'You Are Here.' I peered beyond it at the aquamarine sky.

The sun had yet to breach the horizon, but I saw the pale rock outcrop that formed an arch down into the sea and over the grotto's entrance.

"As things seem quiet up here and the E'lan is calm, I think you should wait until the sun rises further so you can see better. It says here," Brennan pointed to the information board. "The sun shines through into the cave, lighting up the water. It will be safer, quicker and easier for you to find what you're looking for."

"The fool speaks intelligently for once," Jude said.

"Again, you prove why you need to come with me, Jude," I looked for that smile again, but it wasn't there anymore. I rolled my eyes.

"Thanks Brennan, that makes perfect sense. We'll rest for a bit and then by hell or by heaven, I'll find what's down there."

Chapter Four

Enl'iel clasped her hands beneath her chin, her brows knit tight in thought.

"I'm sure I'm not mistaken Enl'iel," the guard said. "I did see her," he bowed his head and stamped his sword into the ground. He looked past her towards the Zythros stone.

Enl'iel paced in front of him, "I don't doubt your sensibilities, good soldier, but the human girl was in here as well? By herself?"

He glanced at her, defensive tension holding his body tall and alert. "Yes, just like earlier outside Soph'ael's room. I'm not mistaken. I've only just completed a psynostris cycle; I am very well rested."

"Yes, I am aware," Enl'iel looked up into his stoic face. She sighed; her voice more empathetic. "We are down to the bare bones of staff with so many out hunting Yeqon and his like. I am concerned you are all over-taxed. I, for one, am exhausted," she pinched the bridge of her nose.

"I am not fatigued," the guard said. "My eyes and mind are clear. I am aware of the human girl's condition now, but it was without a doubt her. I swear upon the Throne that I saw her as clear as I see you in front of me."

Enl'iel rubbed her chin, her face taught, "And that's all that has been out of the ordinary?"

"All has been quiet since last meal, only the cooks and cleaners finishing up. I ran into Soph'ael's brother, and then…"

Enl'iel's head snapped up. "Excuse me? Rik was here? By himself, at night?" she narrowed her eyes. "Are you sure?" Enli'el wondered why Rik would wander the tunnels alone? He was a nervous wreck at the best of times. Had he had another breakdown? Her head ached a little harder.

The guard cleared his throat, clearly offended at the constant questioning of his merit, "Yes, Enli'el, I thought it odd too. He is under Jude's tutelage and usually shadows him."

"Jude is currently away," Enl'iel pulled at her pendant and rubbed the charm. "Go on, soldier."

He cleared his throat again, "Initially, I didn't notice that he was behind the Zythros stone until he moved around the front of it. He seemed a little… you know." The guard tapped his temple, indicating his thoughts on Rik's mental state.

Enl'iel pursed her lips, "Go on, and more respectfully please. He is, after all, the Earth-born's brother."

The guard coughed uncomfortably. "Apologies," he inclined his head. "The lad was very forthcoming when I approached him. He finds it hard to sleep, so he takes comfort in the stone's murmurings. The voices help him rest."

Enl'iel twirled her pendant. "That makes sense. His upbringing has severely damaged his psynostris cycle. I have asked him to come to me for remedies, however, he has chosen to remain quite distant," she furrowed her brows and bit her bottom lip. "And you say that's when you saw Jasmine again? Near the stone?"

"Yes. She wandered in, headed straight for the stone. When she saw me, she turned and ran straight back out, knocking into Rik as she fled."

Enl'iel wandered over to the Zythros stone and placed her hand on it, relishing the comfort of the wisdom within. She circled it, noting the guard's eyes on her when she returned to him.

"This is all very strange. I'm not saying I don't believe you saw someone who looked like her, but Jasmine is languishing on her death bed as you saw for yourself. I cannot understand this. I wonder if her soul could be wandering, confused as it lingers between the realms of life and death?" Enl'iel stared off into space, deep in thought.

The guard's brow creased in confusion, "She looked purposeful, not confused. Her appearance was opaque, I can assure you she was not an apparition."

"Thank you for alerting me," Enl'iel said. "Stay on duty. If Rik returns, follow him for me. He is unwell, and I'd prefer for him not to be wandering the tunnels alone. As for whomever you have seen, if you do so again, apprehend and question them."

The guard nodded, and Enl'iel headed for the door.

The walls rumbled. The Zythros stone came to life, glowing a bright peach, and its whispering grew louder. Enl'iel spun back to it and grabbed her pendant anew. The guard drew his weapon. His face lit with the power in his veins, which coursed towards his hands. Enl'iel's own modest mark equalled the intensity of the guard's.

The stone flashed twice. Elmas and Mehmet arrived hand in hand and breathless.

"Elmas? Mehmet?" Enl'iel ran to them, and they shared a rushed K'ufili with her.

"We may have to evacuate the locals from Nevşehir," Elmas spoke urgently. "There have been too many attacks to hide from the humans, and we are too few to defend them. Our aging bodies bely our will to intervene. Look at this," Elmas passed Enl'iel a local newspaper.

The headline blazed in Turkish. Mehmet read it out loud.

"Serial Killers on the Loose. Bloody Attacks on Twelve Locals. Federal Forces Arriving this Week to Investigate," his fingers trailed the print.

Enl'iel clapped her hand to her chest and gasped. A greyscale picture above a lengthy article showed several bodies under plastic sheets. Streets were cordoned off and teeming with local law enforcement.

She shook her head, "It was only a matter of time. Ben most assuredly has drawn them to us."

"This isn't the work of Rogues or Afflicted, Enl'iel," Mehmet shook his fist. "It's the bloody murder of vampires."

Enl'iel's eyes widened. Her fingertips reddish-blue as they twisted the chain of her pendant tight.

"Vampires? Are you sure?" Enl'iel's fingers tremored, her heart raced faster.

"The kills were clean," Elmas said, her face pale. "Not the vile mess Rogues leave behind. The bodies were drained and left in neat order, as though they had lain down for sleep."

Mehmet pulled Elmas into his side to comfort her. She rested her hand against his chest and her head on his shoulder.

"What is going on?" Enli'el looked to the guard who had not moved a muscle.

"Gedz'iel did warn us that Yeqon had released his children," the guard said.

"Yes, yes he did," Enl'iel put her face in her palms. "Oh, dear I'el, please don't let it be so."

Elmas took Enl'iel's hand in hers, "That's why we are here. We aren't safe anymore, and we haven't warred in a long time. We cannot protect the locals any further I'm afraid. We have other brothers and sisters following along soon. You have room I hope?"

"Of course we do," Enl'iel took a deep breath and gathered her thoughts. "How many?"

Elmas glanced at Mehmet and smiled, "Fifteen in total."

Enl'iel clicked her fingers towards a wide-eyed cleaner who had wandered in with a bucket and duster, drawn in by the fuss, "Make up extra cots on the stasis level, please. Tell the kitchen to prepare extra meals."

The man nodded and rushed quickly away.

Enl'iel returned her attention to Mehmet and Elmas. "You may be required to fight if things become any more dire. We will protect any of your minors or infirm here. Please, find your way to the weapons depository and gear up with whatever fits and suits your strengths. I do hope this won't be the case but it's best at this time to be as prepared as we can be," Enl'iel said, her eyes glistened with worry.

"Of course. We'll do our utmost to help," Mehmet replied. He held Elmas' hand tighter and gently rubbed her wrinkled skin with his other hand. She looked up into his face, and their eyes returned to the native azure. Love and fear glistened in their lashes as well.

Enl'iel shared another K'ufili with them. She pulled away and straightened her shirt.

"Now, have you put anything in place to divert the humans from the true perpetrators?" she asked.

"Yes," Elmas said. "One of us works in the local police force. He has entered a number of false reports about a van of tourists seen in the vicinity of each murder. They're looking for a specific vehicle carrying four men."

"Well done," Enl'iel said. "We will fabricate a chemical spill if anything else occurs. That will make evacuation of the humans easier if need be. I'll send more sentries out on patrol. Now, freshen up and prepare. We may be breached ourselves at any time," her mark stuttered at the thought.

The ground shook as though in response to her fears. The Zythros stone glimmered intensely. Dozens of Keepers rushed through the door.

"Help our refugees!" Enl'iel ordered them.

Thunderous footsteps pounded through from the corridors, the night watch not far away. The Keepers buzzed around the stone, ducking up and down against it, listening to its chatter. The E'lan roused and plucked at Enl'iel's loose hair.

"Guard every entry, both old and new," she told the guards as they entered. "Seal the European link tunnels with extra chromious," she pointed to the Zythros stone. "Close down that stone the very second the locals arrive so it cannot be used as an access port. Allow only Sophia, Jude, Lorcan, and Brennan back in."

Two guards ran towards the stone.

"What of master Gedz'iel?" one asked.

"He does not require the stone's assistance," Enl'iel responded.

Enl'iel transferred into the Stasis room followed by a handful of Keepers. She stopped by Kristen's bed. The girl was awake. She smiled at Enl'iel, who forced a smile through her anxiety.

Cael spun around, "I heard and felt that. Not a tremor?"

"Not a tremor," Enl'iel slowly let out a deep breath through pursed lips. "Everybody, remain on alert. We may be under attack. This room is in lockdown. All humans who don't need to be here must go to the sublevels for safety. If you must stay here, load up your weapons."

Thomas kissed his sister's forehead, "I'll be back for you soon. Please, don't try to be brave today, just be safe," he ran from the room.

Enl'iel nodded at Cael, "You should consider going downstairs with the humans. You can be on communications and keep the hotter heads in check."

"Probably wise," Cael tapped his wheelchair. "This chair doesn't limit all of me, just some of me," he smiled and transferred.

The Alchemae threw white and red orbs either side of the door where they hovered ready to attack. Two Alchemae heaved a slab off the floor under the preparation bench and pulled out a cache of weapons. The stone slid back into place with a grinding *thud*. They took up places either side of the barricaded entrance, their faces aglow.

Enl'iel hurried through the isolation curtain.

"No change?" she asked the Alchemae on duty.

"None at all. She is fragile. I feel barely anything of her life force."

Enl'iel lay her hand on Jaz. It came away wet with sweat. She readjusted a damp cloth on Jaz' brow.

"And someone has been with her at all times?"

"Yes. She's only been alone a few minutes at a time whilst we mix her new balms and poultices."

"So, she has been alone?" Enl'iel glared at the Alchemae, resting her fists on her hips, "You were to watch her at *all* times."

The Alchemae slapped her armful of cloths onto a small table. "What are you suggesting, Enl'iel?"

Enl'iel lifted Jaz' eyelids one at a time and peered in. Jaz' eyes were white, rolled back in a state of constant seizure. Her breaths were barely audible. She stood back and stared down at her.

The Alchemae moved around the room, jostling her equipment unnecessarily loudly.

Enl'iel waved at her, "Please calm yourself. I'm frustrated, not accusing you of anything. Some extremely odd things have occurred overnight. Call in extra staff so that Jaz is always accompanied, it is best given the current circumstances. You may continue your duties. I will sit with her a while."

"As you wish," the woman bowed, lips still pursed, and joined the hustle outside.

Enl'iel pulled up a seat and sat by Jaz' side. Her skin was dull and cold. She inspected every fingernail, chipped and packed with grime. Her hand ran through Jaz' hair, the short strands a melody of black and white. Jaz' expression was one twitch short of an unconscious grimace.

Enl'iel placed Jaz' small hand back down across her chest and patted it softly, "Your energy is not right, young lady. What in the heavens have they done to you?"

Chapter Five

I sat on the edge of the cliff. Gulls circled overhead, waiting for a morsel, but I had nothing to offer them.

"I can't believe we've been here this long and there's been no sign of Yeqon," I said over the sound of the crashing waves. I was relieved that he'd not made an appearance but had expected him well before now.

Brennan gaped at me, "Why in I'el's name would you say something like that out loud? You're practically inviting fate in!"

I was grateful that the anger I'd felt from him earlier had waned.

I jostled into his shoulder, "Oh please, don't be ridiculous. Just be grateful that we've had a clear run for once."

"Well, you've put it out there now, Princess. I can feel it in my bones that you've just asked the universe for trouble. I'll blame you if anything goes pear-shaped."

I breathed in the salty air, enjoying the unadulterated breeze for just a moment.

On my other side, Jude stood up and stretched his arms. His muscles and bones cracked. He pointed to the curve of sun on the horizon and peered down at me.

"Are you ready?" the coarse angles of Jude's almost perpetual scowl softened. "I've got your back, kid. Let's get going before the scary monsters arrive." he made a face at Brennan, and I took the hand he offered me.

Dawn's orange glow warmed away the cool night. It glanced across the rocky ground, which canopied the cave far below. I scanned the waters through the smooth hole that gaped down into the Grotta Azzura. It seemed calm, a soft rhythmic slosh against the walls the only sound. There was just enough light to see that it was crystal clear through to the seabed.

I shook off my concealment, as did Jude. The others kept their guises up.

Lorcan turned away to watch for anything approaching from the scrubland, "Call if you need us."

Brennan winked at me under his Elvis-style quiff, "Be careful down there."

"Likewise," I said.

"Scared?" Jude asked with a devious smile. He took my hand again and squeezed it.

I took one more look down. The rhythmic tide was almost relaxing.

"Never."

"Good. Let's go then."

Our wings opened into the glow of the morning, brighter than the first rays creeping along the ground behind us.

We swan-dived into the cave. I gripped his fingers tighter as we fell and hit the water. The cool shock knocked the breath out of me. Our hands separated when our heads broke the surface. I cleared my nose and throat, filling my lungs before I spun around to see where I was.

We floated in an intense cerulean blue. Sunlight bathed the umber interior. Through the cave's mouth, the Tyrrhenian Sea washed against layers of coffee-and-ginger stone.

"Wow! It's stunning!"

Jude floated towards the entrance, buoyant on his wings, "Pretty isn't why we're here. Get busy whilst I keep a look out."

I inspected the rocky outcrops that formed the large cave. Nothing of interest jumped out. All my visions had been underwater, so I plunged headfirst towards the sand. I needed to find the Vitruvian Man in one form or another.

Whilst it was pretty and calm on the surface, there was a wilder current below. The white sand sailed along with it in little gusts. It was warmer too. I glanced up to get my bearings; Jude's legs dangled into the water whilst he waded on his wings. My pendant floated in front of my face, a different force than the current tugging at it.

I was definitely in the right place.

Schools of small, thin fish darted amongst lime-green seaweed, which reached for the light above. A smattering of scattered, rocky protrusions provided a bed on which barnacles and algae proliferated. My wings guided me like a rudder as I allowed the current to sweep me around the bland walls.

Prodding and poking into cracks and fissures proved fruitless, so I sunk towards the rocks on the sea bed hoping for better luck. The first one was lumpy but smooth to the touch, its shape strangely orderly. I dug into the sand down to my elbows—this rock was buried deep. I moved up its length to a rounded protrusion covered in thick, slimy algae. My fingers slid through the muck, digging through an indentation and over another rise. I flicked the sludge away where a small school of fish had been gobbling it up. I picked away some hardened sand…and revealed what looked very much like a nose.

Excitement had my pulse racing. I plunged back to the base and dug faster, tolerating the water's sting where the sand scoured my skin. I floated back up to look at it once I'd revealed a good chunk of the rock.

It was a head. A few more sweeps across the top, and part of a Romanesque face appeared. Orb-like eyes devoid of pupils, chubby cheeks, and short curly hair were embedded with clusters of sea snails. A good wedge was missing at the back of the head where more ocean slime coated it. Further digging revealed a neck, and after a little more, the top of the torso appeared. Before long I had exposed the top half of a figure. Two arms reached up, one ending where a hand should have been.

I nearly drew in a lung full of water as the image registered. It was exactly like my underwater vision, the one which Rogues had entered into.

I thrashed about like a panicked fish until I remembered that I was alone with this old, sunken statue.

Come on Soph, I coaxed myself along. Jude's glimmer above reassured me.

I moved back towards the walls with a flick of my wings. Their light made every groove and crack easy to observe. I pulled myself along the sand bed and up the walls, but nothing else revealed itself.

I floated back into the middle, swam amongst thicker seaweed to find another rocky cluster. I repeated my excavations and found another two half-submerged eyeless effigies, both with one arm pointing up. I scooted around the figures, pulling and tugging at them, but they didn't move. Were they some sort of secret entrance to another cavern?

What was I missing?

I let go and bobbed around, deep in thought. There was no Vitruvian clue; my excitement died away. I rose to the surface and took a beautiful lungful of air. Despite not needing to breathe, it didn't feel normal not to. I shook the water from my face and wiped salt from my eyes.

Jude swam over to me, "No luck?"

"Not really. It feels right, but nothing is sticking out just yet," I banged a little water from my ears.

He swam back to the cave's entrance, "Put your head into gear and hit the pedal. We don't have the luxury of time as you should know by now."

"I know, I know. I'm thinking on it," I answered, resting back, I floated on my back, trawling through my visions for something I might have missed.

"Do you know what you're looking for?" Jude asked. "Sophia?"

I squinted at the ceiling. My eyes widened, and my jaw dropped.

Jude coasted back to me, "Hello? Are you with me?" he tapped my shoulder.

"Ahhh," I was too entranced for words.

My concentration was elsewhere. My attention was magnetised to the cave's ceiling. I rotated my wings and revealed a gemstone image that took my breath away… a crystalline Vitruvian Man surrounded by four Angels pointing at it.

"Look," I pointed up.

"That looks like a damned big clue to me," Jude muttered.

I peered back down towards the seabed and the figures that were pointing just like the ones above.

"Follow me."

We broke through the current and sent the fish scattering.

"Dig out those rocks over there," I whispered into Jude's mind.

He was efficient, quickly revealing a third statue and helped me with a fourth. We floated back to examine our finds—four silhouettes unearthed from the distant past, reaching up from the sand, pointing to the centre of the sea bed. A guiding hand from long ago. A mirror image of Vitruvian man above.

Jude cocked his head, *"Well? What do you make of it?"*

Dawn had come and gone, leaving strong morning rays to bounce across the water. A faint spray of gemstone glittered across the sandy bottom. I sunk down and reached for one, but my hand came up empty, they weren't gems but thousands of reflections. I peered up towards the surface through thick fingers of sunshine. The Vitruvian Man appeared warped through the water, but its dazzling display mirrored the one in the sand.

"Go up a little," I whispered to Jude. *"Tilt your wings so they shine on the ceiling."*

Jude floated up. His light refracted off the Vitruvian Man and back down, amplifying the image onto the sand. Its prismed lights were the centre of the statues' attention, their arms pointing directly at it.

Jude rushed back down, leaving a flurry of bubbles in his wake.

We dug right in the centre of the Vitruvian Man's reflection. Sand sullied the clear waters amidst our fervour. Bleached coral shards and shells scattered as our fingers clawed faster.

A dull *thud* stopped me. Something smooth and hard was under the last slap of my hand. My pendant yanked at my neck, drawn to the treasure like a magnet.

Our eyes met. Jude's glinted with the thrill and swirled with something akin to excitement. His was a battle-weary face, hardened by time, yet a sadness was also etched within those eyes.

"Well, don't stop now!" he urged impatiently, crushing my little moment of wonder.

Uneasiness took hold of my insides. What if this was the moment that would draw me to my journey's climax? The road to my demise? I held my stomach as I floated above the tiny wedge of metal shining up through the sand. I argued with my natural desire to flee from what would most assuredly lead to a confrontation with Yeqon. I stared hard at it; my fingers clung to my sides.

Jude cupped my elbow with this hand, *"Do you need help?"*

I shook my head.

"Are you sure?" his question was softer in my mind.

The current's tepid tendrils hugged me as though it was encouraging me.

"Got this," I relaxed from his grasp and eased in closer, gently brushing away the sand until a larger silver glimmer revealed itself. I continued until I had unearthed the upper casing of another box with delicate etchings, concentric circles, and lustrous swirls around its edge. I rested my palms across it. The vibration under my touch confirmed it to be what I was searching for. Its energy had the same rush as the others. My pendant matched its rhythm and danced to the pulse rushing through me.

I wiped the rest of the sand off it.

Swirling script revealed itself across the lid. Fine lettering twisted with intricate twirls resembling the markings on my face spanned the metal. I touched my cheek; it was cool from the water but warmed by the sight. Its light shimmered across the beautiful surface. I wanted to read the words and admire the images, but this wasn't the place to decipher it. I tugged and dug around the edges, but it was much bigger than the other box—a good two feet—and it was jammed tight.

"I'm right here, you know?" Jude whispered.

"I need to do this myself."

I pulled at the lid, but nothing moved. I dug a little deeper to release its base. In my determination to retrieve the box myself, I only succeeded in scraping my arm on a crag of rock concealed under the sand.

Blood trickled into the current.

"Oh crap," I panicked. I dug faster and deeper, but the damned thing didn't budge.

Jude's eyes flashed with concern. *"And that's why I offered to help,"* he squeezed the gash on my arm and sealed it with a flash of energy.

The E'lan shifted from a gentle hum to chaotic static, *"Okay, sorry! Help now…please?"* My gut surrendered to a clawing fear.

"Bit bloody late," Jude pushed me aside and pointed; the box was wedged down by another larger rock under the sand. He smashed it with an energy pulse, and we twisted the box free. We hoisted it onto the seabed.

"How will we get it out of here?"

"Bloody quickly, that's how!" Jude grabbed for me, ready to transfer home, but the current changed direction at the same moment. Its warmth dissipated into chilling lashes that no longer felt comforting. It jostled us roughly in opposite directions. An unsettling silence replaced the bubbling of the water. Sand churned and floated up rather than down, biting my skin as it swirled faster. It obliterated the sunlight and replaced it with a dank grey hue. Slimy seaweed clawed around my wrists. I smacked into Jude. He grabbed my waist and pushed through the rush.

"Get out! Get out now!" Lorcan yelled into my thoughts.

Jude yelled, *"Grab the box!"*

"I can't get a hold of it!" my hands slipped as the current tugged me from every direction.

Jude held onto one corner and reached for my hand, but the current sucked me back. Something heaved me forwards, slipped into my hand, and pulled.

"Got ya, Princess!"

Brennan steadied me until all three of us had a hand on the box and were connected with one another.

We powered up our wings as the ocean pressed in, a desperate, ominous foe trying to imprison us. Sand bit at my eyes as it churned faster. The pull in my gut strengthened for the transfer…

I lost my grip on the box, and Brennan's fingers slid from mine.

I sunk rapidly backwards, the bony grip of a Rogue pulling me down.

Even angels can't scream under water. My visions were coming to a vivid and horrific reality. I kicked at the garish limb and it crumbled away, disappearing into the maelstrom of ocean detritus. I kicked back up towards the others through the chaotic current.

Large bubbles gurgled up from below. Numerous holes pockmarked the seabed. Some of the bubbles popped as they rose, carrying the garbled snarls of Rogues inside them.

I reached for Jude and hooked a few fingers under the box.

Brennan dipped his hand into his wings. His arm arched forwards in watery slow-motion, releasing needle-like jets from his fingers. They impaled a skull that had chewed itself out of the sand.

An explosive rush of lava shot up from the holes. It slowed and blackened as it quickly cooled in the water. The undead clawed their way out around the pillars of pumice. The water surged and tossed us about.

Another flash of light, and the current jostled Lorcan around too.

Jude heaved the box away from me and into Lorcan's waiting arms. He swayed under its weight, thrashing his wings to keep balanced.

"Get it outta here, now!" Jude bellowed.

Lorcan nodded and transferred the precious box to safety. Jude grabbed one of my hands, Brennan the other, and we readied for transfer. I closed my eyes, relishing the oncoming safety, but instead fell back in the wrong direction. Something pulled me away from them and towards the gaseous hell holes.

Jude swooped in from the left, Brennan from the right. I reached desperately for them, and their light revealed my skeletal kidnapper. Brennan took me by the waist whilst Jude sliced his wings underneath us. They moved smooth and precise, cutting through the water, slicing through my captor in two.

We rose, but a new wave of bubbles preceded another eruption of lava.

"You get her outta here," Jude yelled at Brennan. *"I'll make sure none follow!"*

"No, leave them," I yelled back. *"Let's go, Jude! We're a team!"*

His eyes widened, and he glanced below. More limbs appeared amongst the glow of cooling lava. He reached for me—

But the ground exploded underneath him. It ripped me away from Brennan. Everything went dark as I tumbled through the hot and cold soup. My chest bubbled with a scream that wanted to escape as I banged into hard things, soft things, slimy things; things that scratched and clawed at me. Gritty salt water rushed into my mouth as I spun and hit something solid.

I clung to the familiar feel of the rock and crawled along the wall the only way I thought was safe: up. The water boiled beneath me as I felt for the next handhold. Where were Jude and Brennan? I headed for a light above that cut through the murkiness. I pushed off the wall and surged into the maelstrom. This light shone down like heaven as darkness drew me back from below. I swam harder, faster as my visions came into reality. Relief ran through me... the light was Brennan's wings.

We smashed together and tumbled sideways. Brennan started to transfer.

"Wait for Jude," I whispered frantically.

Sunlight pierced the water, and it calmed a little. The pull in my gut intensified.

Something yanked at my head. Brennan lost his grip on me, and I plunged down again. Fingers dug into my scalp. My wings slashed at the unseen assailant, but something propelled me back to Brennan.

"Got you!" Jude held me tight. He grabbed for Brennan as we burst above the surface and straight into a transfer home.

We arrived at the Zythros stone a soggy, messy heap. Its orange glow was an instant comfort. All three of us were panting hard. I slapped my arm over my eyes and calmed my breathing.

The same guard who thought he'd seen Jaz ran our way and called for backup.

"Soph'ael, are you alright?" the guard kneeled in front of us, his eyes searching for injury.

I patted my arms and legs, which seemed reasonably unscathed, "I think so. You okay?" I asked Jude and slumped more heavily against the Zythros stone.

He nodded.

I put my hand on his, "Thank you."

Jude wiped sand off his face and slicked water from his hair, "No need to thank me."

He stood and left without a further word. I was too tired to question it and let my head fall back. The stone's whispers were insistent, but I didn't listen in.

To my left, Brennan chuckled, "That was awesome, eh?"

"Awesome? Are you mental?"

"Some say eccentric," he elbowed me and pointed at my hair. "You've got a little something in your, um…"

I reached back and screamed. A Rogue hand still clung to my hair. I flung it away past the silvery shine by my side. Revulsion dissipated quickly as a smile weaved its way across my face.

I had the last box.

Six

The third box rested at the foot of the Zythros stone, its bright shine a perfect mirrored sheen as it dried under the stone's gentle glow. As I finished towel-drying my hair, I noticed guards posted heavily by the door. The rhythmic pounding of people running through the tunnels outside left me with a blood-curdling sense of dread that cut through my initial relief. I dropped the towel into an Alchemae's waiting hands and squatted by the box. My body was aching, but there was no time to heal.

I touched the lid, "We need to pull the rug out from under Yeqon, create a diversion so I can follow this through to the end."

Koi kneeled next to me. "She's right," he ran his fingers over the concentric circles around the box's edges. His mark fired up, highlighting a swelling on his chin.

Gedz'iel, Koi, and the Eloi had returned to restore their weapons. They'd beelined to the Zythros room upon hearing about the box. They were filthy, their eyes heavy with battle fatigue.

Gedz'iel rested his elbows on a table and he chewed slowly on some fresh-baked bread. The Eloi, whom I'd never seen do anything so human as eat, also indulged and whispered amongst themselves. They were a little less stiff since Pathos' betrayal and more present with us underlings.

"I think I should draw Yeqon out," I said. "I could return to his realm. We can set a trap there," I said.

"That's ludicrous," Lorcan said. He'd been lounging against a wall but stood now, "Aren't we done saving you? You think you can just wander in and…"

"Do what needs to be done? Yes I can," I said.

If I hadn't been so tired, I'd have punched him again. He meant well, but I was no damsel, and I didn't need saving.

Lorcan's jaw twitched.

Enl'iel twisted and turned her pendant, "You should be opening that box and ending this, not heading back to the slaughterhouse. It's not safe, Sophia."

I stood and grabbed some bread. "Nothing and nowhere is safe Enl'iel."

The floor rumbled. I stood still, waiting. But the shudder settled, and I breathed in relief that nothing had penetrated into the safety of the sanctuary.

Gedz'iel stood and cleared his throat. His morose expression put shadows where there once hadn't been any. A greyness underpinned his normally bright eyes. The silvery battle scars along his arms and chest were more pronounced. Welts blazed where they shouldn't have. My breath hitched to see this great Watcher so affected.

He made his way to the box and looked at it for a moment.

"I agree with Sophia," Gedz'iel said.

"We are running in circles trying to keep Yeqon off our backs, and we are failing," Gedz'iel ran a hand over his face. "There have been hundreds of ascensions this past week. Yeqon will not desist whilst Sophia breathes, whilst the Kaladai remains up for the taking, no matter the cost to us, humanity, or himself."

I nodded in appreciation of his support. Gedz'iel gathered his hands in front of him and looked into my eyes. His head tilted towards the box.

"I ask you to reveal the contents of your find. It might be all you need to see the last of this wretched torment," Gedz'iel kneeled and reverently ran his hand along the box. He closed his eyes and took a deep breath before standing again, "Double security for this room."

The guards' wings blazed as they raised their hands towards the doorway. The familiar buzz of electric fortification snapped and sizzled as they sealed the door with white bars. They took positions either side of the arch and jabbed their swords into the ground, their marks bright and ready.

Deep breath in, deep breath out.

I could do this, and I knew it.

"You got this, Princess."

I smiled at Brennan. He sat nearby, hunched over a plate of food, his cheeks pocketed full like a squirrel.

Gedz'iel turned back to me and swept his hands towards the box, "When you are ready, Sophia."

All eyes were wide with anticipation; everyone seemed to hold their breaths.

I edged closer, drawn to the box's magnetism like there was a secret language between us. My fingers trailed the ornate design around the lid. Each curve and flick married into the next, creating a seamless connection of metallic swirls that reflected the unique marks on our faces. Every indentation I touched sent a buzz through my skin.

The harsh lines around Gedz'iel's mouth softened into a mild smile. "At your leisure, Sophia, but not too long either, please?" he kneeled next to me, his voice low and kind. "You are not the sacrificial lamb Yeqon would have you believe. You are our inspiration," he patted me gently on my back and nodded in encouragement.

"Thank you," I said.

I focussed everything on what I hoped would be the last leg of this almighty journey.

"So, what will it be?" I muttered. "Blood, sweat, tears, or all three?"

The metal grew warmer and shinier as I examined the smooth sides. As usual, there was no latch or lock, no handle to crack open. I drew my diamond dagger.

"This is too much bloodletting," Enl'iel whispered.

"It is I'el's wish," Gedz'iel said. "She has faced worse."

The nick in my palm stung like salt sprinkled into a fresh wound. I made a fist and squeezed crimson droplets onto the box, they slid into the crevices. The tense silence of expectation weighed on me, so I leaned in closer and urged my life source to weave its magic. Instinct drew my light-filled palms to grasp the chest. My blood smeared along the rim, fresh and bright with its iridescence. The box awoke under my touch, and my hands trembled with its rising vibration. A halo emerged underneath it, a luminosity so intense that my hands dissolved into its brilliance.

The expected click of a lock yielding didn't occur.

I fumbled along the edges, feeling for a latch or anything hidden, but there was nothing — quite literally nothing. No uncooperative lid, just handfuls of emptiness. I gasped and waved my arms through the haze. My skin prickled with uncertainty.

"Where is it?" my voice wavered, but panic didn't take over.

Gedz'iel leaned over my shoulder, "What is it, Sophia?"

"I don't know. Just... wait a moment."

I focussed on the pulsing energy in front of me. Nervous droplets drizzled down my forehead and steamed on my mark. The salt tempted its way into my mouth just as the light flickered like an old black-and-white movie and halted.

A cool chill raced its way up the length of my arms and ran down my spine.

"Hurry, Sophia," Gedz'iel said.

Deep breath in, deep breath out.

I cracked my knuckles and drew out a hotter energy than the one blazing in front of me. It stirred the butterflies in my stomach and scorched my fingertips as it blanketed the light of the box. The sizzle and snap of the two became louder until I heard a *pop*. My light faded, as did the box's.

Lorcan rushed to the empty divot in the ground where the box had been and ran his hands over the earth.

"It's gone!" Lorcan looked up at me…
His mouth dropped open.
"By the blessings of the angels," Lorcan muttered.
Excitement tingled through my hands.
I held a second, larger cog of the Kaladai.

Chapter
Seven

Everyone crowded around me, silent with intrigue.

"Read it," Gedz'iel instructed. He indicated for the Eloi to gather by his side. Matias, Theus, Amais, and Serail joined him. "We leave imminently," he added.

Ornate words were perfectly engraved around the Kaladai cog.

"It looks kind of familiar, but…" my heart skipped a beat, and I glanced up at Gedz'iel. "I can't make it out."

"The Earth-born can no longer read the prime language?" Matias blurted out rather abruptly.

"Soph?" Brennan's voice was heavy with concern.

My hands became sweaty. Had one blow too many to my head stunted my abilities? I squinted, but it made no difference. The letters were just… wrong in some way.

Brennan squatted next to me and rested his hand on my shoulder. "Can you read it?" he asked.

I shrugged him away, "I'm not sure. Just give me a moment."

The weight of his concern and the blood-draining thought that I couldn't read the writing was too much. I felt like I might faint.

"It's alright," Brennan whispered. He tilted my chin to face him and smiled, "You got this, as always."

He backed off and stood next to Enl'iel, who was twirling her pendant more ferociously than ever. They whispered between themselves — actually, lots of whispers had flourished where there was silence a few moments ago.

My heart hammered. My skin burned hot and cold. What the hell was going on?

Gedz'iel loomed closer, "Decipher his words quickly."

His shadow stretched past me. I gazed at it, lost in the way it fell across the Zythros stone's steps. It was larger than he, a phantom representation of who he really was. This box was like that too. It somehow was a part of who I was, and right now, its mystery dwarfed me like Gedz'iel's shadow dwarfed him.

He moved a little, and I snapped out of it. I peered over my shoulder, caught his expectant stare, and picked up my dagger again. I drew it across my skin, almost immune to the pain by now. I let the dagger fall to the floor and rubbed my blood across the neat script.

"Well?" Gedz'iel asked.

Nothing changed. It was still gibberish.

"This can't be right," I muttered. My knuckles paled as I gripped the stubborn device harder. Blood dripped from my hand and back onto the dagger.

"How much more do I need to bleed?"

I reached for the dagger again, and a reflection in the blade caught my eye. I laughed, clutching the blade to my chest.

"Soph?" Lorcan asked. But I just kept laughing.

"She clearly has a malady of the mind," Matias mumbled.

"I'm not mad! It's just so clever!" I waved the others closer and had them kneel next to me. "Look!" I caught the cog's reflection in the blade. "Leonardo da Vinci… he's the human who prepared the Kaladai," I explained.

Gedz'iel kneeled next to me, "Go on."

"He was well known for concealing his writings in mirrored script. This is penned backwards."

Gedz'iel's eyes widened as he looked at the words that now appeared the right way around in the reflection.

I chuckled and nodded to myself, "Clever old Leo."

"Indeed," Gedz'iel straightened. "You can read it now, child?"

"I can!"

My heart fluttered with excitement, not dread. I bit my lip, but it didn't stop my smile as my eyes lingered on the words. The thumping in my head eased as my fingers followed the script. The smooth metal warmed against my skin, its silent reverberating song dissolving through my hands. With my next heartbeat, its power exploded through my body, and I felt an immense sense of calm.

Despite this, the cog was heavy and awkward to hold. Holding the blade just the right way to read the script was difficult. I tilted it up with one hand whilst angling the blade. I turned the cog so the orb light shone on it, but the dagger was too small. It was difficult to read the words along its faceted length. It slipped from my hand and clattered to the ground.

"Damn it!" I snatched the dagger back up, angling it again towards the script.

Gedz'iel put his hand on my shoulder again, "Pass me the Kaladai and your dagger. I can assist you."

He swung the cog up as though it were made of feathers and rested it against the Zythros stone. I watched as he studied it. Everyone was quiet, their energy heavy in the air. Our anticipation caused the orb light to strobe. Static tugged at my hair and tickled my skin.

Gedz'iel leaned into the stone and touched it with one hand. A soft orange hue emanated behind the cog and brightened when it rattled against the stone. I dug my nails into my palms. Light haloed around the cog and Gedz'iel stepped back, holding the dagger out in front of the cog. An arc of light shot out from its centre. Gedz'iel caught it with the blade. He moved his hand to the left to catch another strike before the power abruptly switched off.

He polished the dagger against his leg and placed it into my hand. It was piping hot.

Gedz'iel gestured towards a wall, "Use your light to illuminate the words over there."

He turned me around, held my hand up, and pressed my fingers around the handle until the diamond blade glittered. Hundreds of little scratches marred the clear perfection. He angled my hand just so and lit his palm behind it.

"See?" his breath was on my ear. His strength gave me strength. He shone his own light through the blade, and we projected the words onto the wall.

"That's amazing!" my voice was breathy with wonder.

He leaned closer and whispered softly as his hand fell away, "I regret it is all I can offer. The rest is up to you, young one." Gedz'iel straightened, tall and foreboding behind me, "Now, please read for us."

The sweeping words, accented with lines and dots, were as easy to read as plain English.

Enl'iel threaded her arm around my waist, "What does it say?"

I read.

Behold! Mine life's love regards the way.
Beneath mine atlas, two souls unite.
I'el doth balance upon the truth, then fly by wing of beast.
To the child who dwells between
the veil, preserved by devil's poison.
Redemption's truth is abundant.
Earth's mirror within
the lion's keep where old angels' dwell.
Ichor of devil and purity of angel.
A'vean's light shall rise over the moon and across the sun.
Thy livid creator shall turn into A'vean's embrace.
Death of the flesh, birth of the light, unto A'mageddon's fold.

The A'vean words were comforting as they fell from my lips, familiar in a way I still didn't understand. My eyes ran over the words again. My hand was shaking and blurred the script a little.

Someone cleared their throat.

"Well, that's about as clear as mud," Brennan said.

Lorcan hovered beside him and rubbed his chin, his eyes tight as he examined the words.

A glance over the room revealed a bunch of confused expressions as everyone contemplated Enoch's convoluted message. My arm fell to my side and the light faded, but the words burned bright in my mind.

Relief flashed across Gedz'iel's face.

"A'maggeddon is the awakening of the Earth and its people. This is the final step," he explained.

"But what does it really mean? Hellfire and the dead rising?" I asked.

Gedz'iel chuckled, "Not quite the way you've heard of it. I'el's instructions are seldom straightforward, often misunderstood and convoluted over the ages. A'maggeddon is a burden we all bare, but more so you, Sophia," his eyes swirled, their rainbows bright and intoxicating. Emotion might have moistened the lower lids, but he blinked it away.

"When we first met, your untapped power affronted me," he held me at arm's length, his fingers squeezed gently into my shoulders. I swallowed hard, overwhelmed by his presence, both thrilled and awed by him. I held his gaze, I didn't look away, something I would have done not so long ago.

"However, I know now that it was fear that you would not realise your potential," his eyes softened. "You have grasped it and accepted it. You have risen to challenges many of us would have feared. Many forks in your path will test you, but you have my trust that you will end this dammed war."

He leaned in, a K'ufili sharpened my courage. The warmth of pride ran though me — I had honoured him and my legacy.

A rush of footsteps interrupted the moment, and a small contingent of soldiers entered.

"Go now, Sophia, as must we," Gedz'iel pointed the Eloi to the Zythros stone.

I was horrified to see that it was Thomas who led a few other humans, armoured to the hilt.

"They will not face Yeqon head on but sweep the older sanctuaries," Gedz'iel said, "Or what's left of them. They will have plenty of support," he assured me, obviously seeing the worry in my expression.

Thomas, along with his battalion, pulled down his protective face shield. They gathered around the stone, activated by Gedz'iel's touch. Every human was cocooned under the wings of a Watcher to protect them from the transfer's effects.

The walls rumbled. Sand rained down. Someone coughed in the back of the room.

Gedz'iel pointed above us, "I have dispatched two fresh battalions from Africa to deal with whatever is going on up there. You have my blessing to do what you must. Fear not your instincts or your methods as Yeqon offers no mercy. You will be judged upon your intent, not your means of our salvation. Watch your back, and do not take unnecessary risks" he bowed before me, and I returned the gesture. "Your time runs short, yet your battles become more difficult. This is the time to show us who you really are," Gedz'iel looked to the ceiling. "Return, Jude!"

Jude flashed into the room. His eyes thinned at Brennan before his attention fell on me.

"Stay here with Koi," Gedz'iel said. "Join me once you are satisfied that the sanctuary is safe."

They both nodded.

"Lorcan, Brennan, as Sophia is to us, so you are to her. Be her shield and her guide."

They nodded. Gedz'iel and the Eloi readied for transfer.

"Hell is upon the Earth. Let's put out its fire."

I leaned into the Zythros stone. It was rife with urgent chatter, and I listened this time. Whispers of discontent were making it to the mainstream media. Humans were panicking. Riots increased in the face of mass murders that couldn't be explained. One phrase repeated over and over, *"We are losing control of the Daimon. We cannot protect our humans."*

It was time to multitask. In my former life as a nurse, multitasking was my specialty — it would just be a little different from balancing medication rounds and dressings. Instead, I would subdue a demonic enemy and save the world. I could do that.

The whispers receded, and Enoch's words scrolled through my mind. I dug my fingers into the stone as I ran over the few sentences. My hand slipped into a missing piece of apricot stone. The rock in this area was dull and lifeless where the palm-sized chunk had fallen away; a dead zone free of murmurings.

"Look at this?" I said.

Brennan furrowed his brows and poked at the hole, "That shouldn't be there. Wonder if the quakes have damaged it?"

Lorcan waved Koi over.

"That's no accident," Koi's face was taught as his eyes ran over the rest of the rock.

Jude wandered up the steps as well and examined the darkened area. He rubbed his fingers together, sniffing the soot that blackened the tips, "Hmm, this smells of a Daimon."

"Daimon?" I asked.

Brennan dabbed at the rock, "This is bad news."

Jude glanced at me as he came around the far side of the rock. "Why are you surprised Sophia? Daimon follow you everywhere," he headed to the guards at the door, but his comment stung.

"Why's it been tampered with, Koi?" my mind blurred. Who else could have breached the sanctuary? This place was so heavily guarded.

"It's a powerful communication tool, Sophia," Koi stood back, hands on his hips as he assessed the stone from a distance. "It could be used to tap into our communications," he clicked his fingers at a guard, who ran onto the dais, "I want this stone surrounded twenty-four-seven."

The guard gestured behind me, and four guards circled the stone within seconds. Their wings elongated, cutting off all access to it.

Brennan's mouth thinned. His hands fell to his weapons, and he scanned the room. Lorcan settled in next to me, his wings rippling in front of me as a shield. In that uncertain moment, it wasn't unwelcome.

"Another spy?" I asked through my teeth.

Anger dizzied me as Pathos came to mind, but he was long descended. I couldn't think of a single person here who warranted suspicion, which worsened the dread. Were people coming and going without our knowledge?

"A spy is highly likely," Koi said. "These stones do not yield like this to earth tremors. All who enter this room will need the highest security clearance from now on."

Enl'iel shielded her mouth with her hand. Her worried eyes slid between Koi and I.

I recalled three individuals who'd been seen around the stone. Someone who resembled Jaz, Rik, and the shadow that had rushed past the door. The owner of the shadow had to be the culprit, but who was it? Had they impersonated Jaz? Nausea spilled into my guts.

"Open the stone," I picked up the cog up and stepped around Lorcan, who shadowed me up the steps.

"Extra security on the doors, please!" Koi called. He urged the guards to step away from the stone and slid the rock aside with Brennan under the watchful eyes of its new guards. It yielded easily, and Brennan passed me the other cog.

"You know what to do?" Koi asked.

"Not really," I answered.

I sat on the bottom step and lay the pieces on the ground. The first, smaller cog was more vibrant than previously. Its hum strengthened when I brought it close to the new cog. It seemed natural to sit the smaller one upon the larger, like the internal workings of a clock. They teetered on each other, and a faint light sandwiched between them.

The smaller cog began to move. It turned clockwise until it clicked, then turned anticlockwise until it clicked again. It dropped a few millimetres into the larger wheel. They moved like a combination lock. The central hole moulded itself into an oval and stopped.

"Wow!" Brennan said.

"Is it complete?" Enl'iel asked.

"I don't think so," the prophecy had too much to say for this to be all it was.

"Put it away," Jude grumbled from afar.

"He's right," Koi said. "Until you know how to use it, we must keep it under the highest security."

I tucked it back under the Zythros stone.

"What more does it need?" Lorcan asked.

"Well," I said, "As much as I don't want to entertain the thought, I think it needs Yeqon's blood and mine."

Enl'iel gasped.

Jude swore like Jaz, "Why would I'el want that?"

"To make sure Yeqon's dead?" I shrugged. "The prophecy clearly said *ichor of devil and purity of angel*. Perhaps it requires the purity of my blood and the darkness of his to negate the curse?"

"You may be correct," Koi tapped his temple. "These two forces create a powerful equilibrium when combined. It is how the universes balance, how things move forwards. Too much of one or the other and the physics of all things dysfunction."

"Like yin and yang?" I asked.

Koi paced beside me, "Yes."

"I've got to get to Yeqon then," I said

"That is a deadly and stupidly dangerous undertaking," Jude said.

Lorcan moved closer to me, "Couldn't we just grab one of his offspring?"

Jude shook his head, "They're monstrous hybrids. Their blood could well destroy the last portal, and that's if you could actually catch one."

"Vampires," I touched my throat, recalling the sting of Lilith's bite.

"I'm sure I'el never designed this game for their blood," Jude said. "So we…"

"Not we," I interrupted, stepping out from behind Lorcan's protection. "Me. It means quite clearly that I'm in the driver's seat, and

I need to get to Yeqon," my soul stone bracelet jingled as I tapped my chest.

Jude held up his pointer finger, "Not necessarily. One of us could conceal as you, fool him. Then you remain safe and can continue your work."

"He isn't that stupid," Lorcan said. "Yeqon knows her, he would sniff out an imposter," he threw his hands in the air.

Jude pumped his fists and bit his lip, "Pretty boy does have a point. Yeqon is no fool, neither are his brothers. They've all been close enough to know her E'lan signature."

"What if I conceal myself as someone else and leave just enough bursts of my energy to attract him?" I asked. "That way the honey trap is laid but the prize is not what he will expect?"

Lorcan shook his head and breezed back in front of me. I urged him away.

Koi tapped his lips. He glanced between me and the others.

"And you can stay out of the firing line?" Brennan asked.

"I can't guarantee it, but I can promise that I wouldn't run straight for him!"

Enl'iel grabbed me from behind, "No, I won't have it. You've put yourself in harm's way too often. I will conceal myself as you, I know you far better than anyone. You stay here and watch over Jaz."

She pushed me closer to Lorcan, and his wing curled around my shoulder.

Brennan's eyes bulged, and he rushed to Enl'iel, "What are you saying, Li Li?"

He cupped her chin in his hand. Their eyes connected, and she caressed his cheek. Her mouth opened as if to say something, but she stepped out of his reach.

"I'm as good as anyone, aren't I?" Her hands sat on her hips, "Koi? Jude? It's true, isn't it?"

Jude nodded, "As long as you're not required to fly."

She pursed her lips. That shouldn't be a problem. Young Rik can come with me. He's strong enough now. He can pretend he has fled back to Yeqon with Sophia," Enl'iel emphasised my name and made quotation marks with her fingers. "If I'm a prisoner, I will be bound and therefore unable to fly."

Brennan's face flushed. He was about to interject, but Enl'iel raised a finger to shush him.

"My life is as good to risk as any," Enl'iel said.

I took her hands in mine, "I can't let you."

She squeezed my hands and let go, "You can and you will. We are in this together."

"Koi? You're quiet on the matter?" her arms folded.

"It is not an unreasonable plan," Koi said. "It would make sense to Yeqon. It is plausible that Rik could fall back under his tormentor's spell. Given Rik's traumatic past, Yeqon could use his hold over Rik and take advantage of the chaos," he pointed at Brennan, Lorcan, and Jude. "I insist on plenty of back up, however."

"We will shadow her closely," Jude said.

I made my way back to the Zythros stone, leaned in and felt the energy within it. I turned and faced them all. My mark burned as I looked at Enl'iel. "I've been there, and you haven't. I know the place. I've run through its stinking tunnels. I can guide everyone concealed as a Rogue or Afflicted or whatever," I slapped my hand against my chest. "I can hang in the background, leaving morsels of energy to fool him," my pendent hummed, but I wasn't sure if it was with encouragement or warning.

Enl'iel's eyes fogged and swirled like a mini cosmos framed by her modest glimmering mark. Her shoulders slackened, and she sighed.

"Your voice is no longer an echo, Sophia. The universes hear your song," her lashes lowered.

My heart ached, and I stepped back down to her.

I took her hands in mine again, "I'm sorry. I don't want to hurt you either, but I have to do this myself."

"You are every bit my daughter," she brushed a lock of hair back behind my ear. Her warm palm stayed on my cheek, and she smiled with tears in her lashes. "You will not put yourself in harm's way, do you hear me?" her chin quivered, but her voice remained steady.

"And neither will you?" I said.

We embraced, and her vanilla-lavender perfume took me back to a time when warm scones and knitted blankets had still comforted me. A carefree time with a bright and certain future. A time with Ben.

I jerked back. The memory blackened the warm moment.

"So, how will we ask Rik to go back there?" I asked.

"I'll make him do it." the voice caressed and choked my heart.

Ben and Belial had returned.

We drew our weapons, ignited with the E'lan. Their power lit the room. Red orbs hovered overhead and aimed at the doorway behind the white fortification beams. I crouched front and centre, Kea's sword aloft and ready to cut them down. Jude, Lorcan, Brennan, and Koi flanked me.

I glowered at Ben's unreadable face. My heart pounded against my ribs. Step by step, we moved towards them. They waited, unmoving, without any weapons drawn.

"What are you doing here?" Betrayal burnt my throat, but my voice lacked the flavour of anger I felt.

Jude pointed his sword at Ben, "You'd better talk while you're on that side, Daimon. Once those bars are gone, your time will be done."

The urge to strike was overwhelming. My wings burned as their power surged, and I drew a length of energy from them into both hands. My breath was heavy and slow, my head dizzy with rage. Koi touched my arm, which calmed my primal desire to destroy. It settled that darkness that I knew could so easily rise. My head cleared a little, but I didn't take my eyes off Ben. My knuckles tightened around my weapons.

Koi ushered more guards to the door, "How did you get through security?"

"We followed the couple from Nevşehir before you shut down the Zythros stone," Ben answered.

"Why have you returned?" I hissed, furious at myself that my voice remained shaky. I wanted to be strong, needed him to know I was strong.

Ben shook his head and looked at his feet, "We have returned with help."

"Liar!" Lorcan shouted.

Jude threw a small orb at the door in warning. Dust and light erupted between the guards. Ben and Belial remained still; eyes focused only on me.

"What do you really want?" I asked.

"To help you, Soph."

Lorcan lashed an energy cord at them, "Don't speak her name!"

The cord whipped through the bars and nicked Ben's right cheek. Ben barely flinched, only groaned. He ignored the blood that drizzled towards his chest.

Inside myself, I was screaming. I couldn't tell if my heart was hurting with hate or love or both. "I'm here to help you," Ben said.

"You both disappear and claim you've returned to help us?" Lorcan drew another sizzling rope, ready to release it. He laughed hard, "You think we are fools?"

"It's another ploy," Jude said. "You buttered Sophia up purely to help yourself, you scum," he made sure I was behind him as he stepped closer to Ben. "Just to grease the wheels enough to follow your true plan!"

Lorcan coiled his arm back. "You still want her. You still serve him!" he approached the door, but Jude pulled him back.

It struck me how white Ben's hair was under the light of Lorcan's wings. His eyes were dark, but not black as they'd once been. Weary shadows underpinned a vibrant Mediterranean blue. I lowered my arms. The angelic white of his hair, the huge risk of returning here... Was it real?

"I serve no one," Ben said. "I'm not what you think I am, not anymore," he sighed and ran his hand through his hair. His voice was fatigued, but his stance was proud. He was strong, powerful and not stupid enough to let his guard down too much.

"You can choose to believe me, or not," he added.

I moved one step forwards. Brennan shadowed me, keeping close by my side.

"How on earth has you leaving helped me?" I asked. "Why not say anything? That reeks of underhandedness."

"I hardly expected a royal escort, not without an orb in the back," Ben said. "You would never have believed us if we'd told you our plan. You might have let me go, but I needed Belial for this, and you wouldn't have released him. We have brought you someone who can help," Ben glanced back over his shoulder.

Belial turned as well.

Shouts travelled down the corridor as more sentries came to our aid. Jude shouted for them to keep their distance.

Belial was talking to someone, but the E'lan crackled over their voices. He pulled this someone into the glow of the bars, a hooded figure, hands clasping a posy of herbs and metallic trinkets.

I raised Kea's sword, "Who is that?"

I feared it was Yeqon in disguise.

Enl'iel emerged from behind us and walked up to the door, "Belial? What have you done?"

Belial moved closer to the bars, "The only good thing I've done since the day you were born."

Brennan left my side to shield Enl'iel, but she raised a hand to stop him.

"Leave me Brennan," she said.

"Li Li, what...?"

"I'm fine," her tone tinged with annoyance.

Brennan backed down but hung close behind her. He lowered his sword and grabbed her shoulder, "What's going on?"

Enl'iel shrugged him off, "Just give me a moment, Brennan, please?"

He glanced back at me and then at Koi, his face pale.

My attention was torn between Enl'iel and Ben. His bright eyes were crushing me. There was something different about him, but in the stress of the moment, I couldn't see what it was. It was unfathomable to understand what he might still be or not be.

"So, what have you done?" Enl'iel asked Belial, much too familiar for my liking. She pointed at the hooded person. "Who is this? You're back to kidnapping, are you? We don't house the abducted here," Enl'iel clenched her arms and tapped her foot.

"I have brought you my son," Belial said. "The Great Healer."

I gasped. Jaz' face flashed in my mind.

Enl'iel swayed enough for Brennan to move in and support her.

Belial pulled back the stranger's hood. The heavy brown fabric fell back onto wide shoulders, revealing a face as beautiful as it was familiar. Silvery hair, shaved in the style of a monk, covered a scalp full of unfamiliar symbols, tattooed in dark blue. His eyes and mouth, though sombre, appeared soft and kind. Even the guards were magnetised, their stony stares drawn to him.

Enl'iel moved away from Brennan, one step at a time, "It can't be."

"What the hell is this?" Brennan dragged his sword along the floor, following Enli'el.

Enl'iel reached for the man twice but pulled back both times.

"Say hello," Belial said, "To your brother, Devon."

Chapter Eight

I had no words. Only the crackling E'lan chattered overhead.

Enl'iel was trembling. Tears streamed down her blotchy face.

Koi turned her towards him, "Enli'el? What is this?"

Enl'iel looked from Koi to Brennan and back again, then glanced at me. She wrenched from Koi and screamed.

"Open the door!"

Guards moved in front of it. She pushed at them, punched their chests.

"Open it!" she screamed. "Now!"

The guards crossed their arms, but she thumped at them anyway.

Jude and Lorcan rushed towards her.

"Calm down, Li Li," Brennan pulled her back, but she struggled against him. "It is a trick," he was still pale; his movements slow like the air itself pushed against him.

Enl'iel elbowed out of his grip. "Open the goddamn door!" she stumbled towards the silent stranger, who stared at her with vacant curiosity.

I'd never seen anyone show anger towards Enl'iel before, never seen her so out of control. I flipped my sword between my hands, not sure what to do or what would happen.

"Stop this, now," Koi demanded.

"No! Open the door!" she thumped the patient guards again.

"What the hell is going on?" Jude pushed in between Brennan and Koi. "Has she lost the bloody plot?"

Jude grabbed Enl'iel's arm and pulled her away, but Brennan muscled in Jude's way and shoved him heavily backwards. He fell onto the first step under the stone.

"Hands off!" he bellowed, Brennan pulled Enl'iel under his wing and held her tight.

I ran to Jude and pulled him up. He brushed me away, pointing at Brennan.

"Deal with her then!" he thundered back to Brennan and punched his chest armour. "Do that again and you'll eat more than dirt."

The two glared at each other, their marks blaring with threat.

"Stop it!" I finally managed to get words out of my dry throat. I bustled between them and moved to Enl'iel. My eyes were drawn to this man who looked just like her.

"What's going on?" my mouth was numb, as though the question invited answers I didn't want to hear.

I slid my arm around Enl'iel's shoulders, which quivered in shock. She leaned into me. "What is Belial saying Enl'iel? I don't understand?"

Betrayed by a weary sigh, I knew this was too much for her, yet her gaze didn't leave the stranger. Her eyelids twitched, and her lips trembled.

"It's true," she began to sob. "Belial is my father and… I thought my brother long dead."

I froze. I let her go as though her admission forced me away.

Her slender hands covered her eyes. Her shoulders jerked as she tried to quell her tears. A rumble of shocked commentary swept the room.

Jude spat. His nostrils flared as though she smelled offensive, "*You are Daimon spawn?*" his top lip peeled back in disgust as he eyed her up and down.

Enl'iel's head flung up, eyes red and brimming with a fear I'd never seen in her. She backed away from him, and from me. Her misty eyes flitted between everyone and fell on Brennan, who stood paralysed as he stared at her. She backed into a table, and her fingers dug into it. Devon watched on, passive and silent.

Enl'iel sniffed and wiped the tears from her eyes. She shook her arms out, straightened, and tossed her head back.

She turned to Jude. "If you wish to vulgarise it like that, then yes, Jude, I am a spawn of evil, a filthy under-worlder," she averted her eyes from Jude's florid mask to her brother.

Koi stepped between her and Jude. "Why have you never told us?" he shielded her from Jude with his wings.

Enl'iel looked to the door, where Belial was waiting.

"Why do you think? Would you have taken me in? Accepted me? You would have thrown me to Yeqon's Pits," her mouth tightened as she fought a new wave of tears. She tugged at her pendant and looked at the ground.

"Stop, Li Li. Please?" Brennan whispered. He held a hand up to her. "Don't say anything else," he looked nervously at me, his expression mimicking hers. He shook his head when their eyes met.

He'd known.

I shuffled through a thousand memories with them, rubbing my temple as though it might unblock something I'd missed, but nothing would have given away this kind of secret. No matter how hard I looked at them, I couldn't see the deception, couldn't see anything dark in her. Koi's even voice snapped me from my thoughts.

"Did you allow us the opportunity to hear your truth, sister?" Koi spread his arms, indicating everyone present.

Enl'iel cleared her throat and peeled her attention away from Brennan.

"No, and it is unforgivable," she blushed and twirled her pendant faster. "In my defence however, I was very young and ever aware of the danger my heritage could bring," her eyes misted anew. "When this community adopted me, I felt safer than I ever had. I felt home," she clasped her heart. "I have tried to repay the kindness with unwavering loyalty and servitude. I was afraid of rejection, of losing that love," she glanced at Brennan, and her voice hitched. "The fear built over the years until the burden was too heavy, the wall of the lie too high. I could not find my way out from under it," her head fell into her hands as she began to sob again.

Brennan shuffled, his hands fidgeting as though he wanted to rush to her, but he held back, his face dark with pain.

"You have lived with us under the guise of this lie," Jude said. "You were privy to what a Daimon should never know," he stepped around Koi and pointed at Enl'iel. "She must be confined and tried for treason!" Jude's eyes flashed at Brennan, and he spat at his feet. "Another reason to hate you — you lay with a Daimon!"

Enl'iel nodded, glancing between Devon and Brennan.

I pointed my sword at Jude.

"Do *not* speak about them like that. Calm the hell down!" my head felt stuffed with cotton, dulling all but a confused muddle. I was trembling; Enl'iel was in danger, from *us*.

Jude puffed his chest out. "Don't point that at me and ask me to calm down when the child of our enemy has been hiding in the heart of our community. It is treason. She was in charge of your welfare, for I'el's sake! Perhaps she led him to your side!" Jude pointed at Ben.

Enl'iel screamed. "I would never endanger my child!" she clawed through her hair, her eyes pleading with Koi and me. "I wouldn't, Sophia. You know that?" she stepped towards me, but Brennan put a hand out to stop her. She held it tight like it was her lifeline.

Our eyes locked. I smelled the vanilla of her perfume, the lavender of her soap. I felt the love emanating from her.

The fuzzy feeling in my head cleared.

I turned to Jude, "How dare you. You don't know her truth. She is my mother; I know her better than anyone."

Jude's mark blazed to life, "Open your eyes, you foolish girl."

I saw red; I threw an orb at his feet. He somersaulted backwards, summoning his own as he landed on his feet.

Koi swung around and stepped up to Jude, "Put that down! Do you not recall my story? Did you not understand and forgive me?"

"You were never a Daimon, Koi," Jude growled through his teeth. "You did not live among us under the guise of lies. She has made it quite clear what her truth is, as you like to put it!"

I put myself between Enl'iel and the muscly ball of rage that was Jude.

"Brother, stop and breathe," Lorcan said. "Let's keep our heads here."

"You can back the hell off too!" Jude raised his sword at Lorcan, who responded in kind.

"Don't be an idiot!" Lorcan snapped.

"You're all fools!"

Jude shoved Lorcan to the ground. Lorcan flipped back to his feet and punched Jude's chin. Jude's arm wound back to strike, but Koi's wing struck his weapon from his hand.

"Enough! You've made yourself quite clear! She is in our world and surrounded," Koi pointed at the armed guards. "What do you think she will do?"

Jude was panting. He flushed. He retrieved his sword, pointing sharply towards her.

"*She* needs confining until we know exactly who and what she is!" Jude demanded, breathing heavily still.

Koi held up his hands, "No one will be confining anyone just yet."

Jude threw his arms up, "Really?" His sword arched over his head, his anger shimmering through his veins and into the sword until it shone like a beacon. He looked at me, "I'm fighting for you. But you're siding with a Daimon? Again?" The weapon now pointed back to Ben.

I shook my head. "We're fighting for each other," I extinguished my weapon. "Let's calm down to work this through, like Lorcan suggested."

Jude huffed like a bull about to charge. He growled to himself, spun on his heels, and flung his sword across the room where it pierced the far wall. He stomped away to retrieve it, uttering foul insults the whole way. Lorcan was about to follow, but Brennan grabbed his arm.

"Leave him," Brennan said. "You're safer by my side at the moment. His temper is quicker than his reasoning. He will calm down shortly," Lorcan nodded as Koi cleared his throat.

Koi folded his hands in front of his belly, "Enl'iel, this is a difficult and uncharted situation we find ourselves in."

She hung her head. "You have known me all my life. I am nothing like him," her arm flung towards Belial. "Not one atom of my being is called to him or his like. I live by I'el's light, not Yeqon's darkness, but I cannot change whom I was born to."

Her posture's proud poise slipped away until her surrender weighed her down. She sunk onto the stool next to the table. I sat by her side and took her hand. Her fingers were limp.

A lump stuck in my throat. Shame threatened to swallow me that I had doubted her, even for a moment. Her motive for keeping her secret could only have been self-preservation. My fingers curled around hers, and she clung to mine.

"How do we even know this person is related to her?" I asked.

I didn't want to believe my beloved guardian was part Daimon, didn't want to admit a Daimon could be good and whole, because that would have forced me to look at Ben in a completely new light.

"His energy mirrors hers," Lorcan said. "His blood and hers are the same."

Enl'iel let go of my hands and offered hers to Koi. She kneeled and bent her head.

Brennan kneeled with her. "Please don't, Li Li," he stroked her hair.

Koi waved for her to stop, "Stand. Do not kneel at my feet."

"It is necessary," Enl'iel said. Her voice was thready, "If it were someone else, I would insist on it. Bind me and call Gedz'iel back. I submit to your judgement and mercy."

"You can't lock her up," I said. "She's innocent. She's my mother," I pulled her back to her feet and into my arms. She clung to me.

Koi rubbed his temples. "Despite all the emotion that needs to settle, this does need to be treated with the seriousness it requires, Sophia," he pointed at the guards corralling Ben, Belial, and Devon.

"Bind those three and open the door. Everyone else, leave immediately, except you," he indicated a female guard. "Come here, please. Afford Enl'iel all the respect she deserves."

The guard marched towards us, her eyes on Enl'iel.

I jumped in front of her, "Koi! What are you doing? Brennan, stop him!" I stepped left and right, getting in the guard's way.

She screwed up her face, unsure what to do, "Master Koi?"

"No harm will come to her, I promise," Koi peeled my fingers away from Enl'iel. The fuzzy feeling surged back into my head.

Relinquishing Enl'iel's hand as the guard took her aside was like a moment of slow-motion, my mind couldn't quite fathom what reality was dishing up. I had been slapped in the face by it.

Brennan was ashen. He stepped back, allowing the guard to take Enl'iel's arm.

"Brennan, help her?" I yanked his hands, pulling him towards her, but he was immovable.

"I cannot," his shoulders fell. His hands ran through the length of his hair, pulling hard on the ends as though his own physical pain might help.

I turned back to Koi.

"Koi? Please don't do this?" I begged, grabbing his hands hopefully. Koi placed one hand over mine. Its warmth spoke of empathy, but it didn't quell my despair.

"Sophia, I must inform Gedz'iel," he said. "I am sorry. It would be the same for any of us. This is not a secret she should have kept. You understand that, don't you, Enl'iel?"

She nodded, "Fear overrode my common sense and good judgement. I was selfish. I did not want to lose my daughter."

I glanced at Ben, who was shackled once more, "So, you'll just toss her in the cells with those two?"

"No, of course not," Koi said. "She will remain in her room until Gedz'iel can assess her."

Enli'el looked surprised by this.

"What does that even mean?" I asked.

"It means, Sophia, that I must submit to a perlustration. I will do so willingly."

The guard escorted Enl'iel to the door.

"A what?" I didn't like the sound of that.

Brennan pulled me into his side. He shivered like he was in shock.

"It is an examination of the inner soul," Koi said. "Only Gedz'iel, an unadulterated Watcher, or a higher angel such as yourself is able and allowed to perform such a task."

I clung to Brennan a little harder.

Koi's eyes softened, the irises swirling with conflict, "I think for now, given all that must be done, we focus on the issues at hand. Please, take Enl'iel to her rooms. Ensure she has no visitors until Gedz'iel arrives. It may take time; he is overwhelmed trying to control the mayhem above ground. I'm sorry, Enl'iel, my hands are tied."

"Enl'iel…?" I could do nothing to stop this. I was outranked, my lack of cultural knowledge laid bare.

"Focus on your mission," Enl'iel said to me. "Yeqon must be stopped. You are so close, my beautiful daughter, and I am no shrinking violet. I will be fine," her eyes firmed into a determination reminiscent of when she'd been my nan, "Now, do as you are told, young lady. I'll hear nothing more about it."

She followed the guard into a corridor as dark and foreboding as my emotions. The glimmer of her hair, dancing at the small of her back, disappeared behind Ben, Belial, and her brother.

Belial's eyes followed her. He looked about to say something, but Ben elbowed him and mumbled out of the corner of his mouth. It was faint, yet I heard his words, "You've done enough damage."

I leaned into Brennan and watched as the three were marched in. I grimaced at Belial, stared at Devon and was transfixed by Ben.

I finally understood what was different about Ben. His hair was now almost pure white. Just a few strands of black streaked through the fringe. He looked like us, like a human-watcher hybrid; like a Eudaimonian.

He was no longer a Daimon.

Devon's eyes travelled the room, briefly settling on each of us as he took in his new surroundings. He held his hands close, unbothered by the shackles. The more I stared at him, the more I saw the resemblance to Enl'iel. There was a softness to Devon's mouth, a kindness in his eyes.

I gripped Brennan's hand so tight he squeaked.

"Careful there, Princess," he whispered. "I may need that hand."

"Your name is Devon?" Koi asked. Devon nodded. "Where have you been living?"

Devon swallowed, but his mouth stayed closed. Koi acknowledged their unseen communication with a nod.

"Why isn't he talking?" I asked, desperate to know more about him.

Devon looked at me and pointed to his mouth. He inclined his head at Koi and shrugged, which made his trinkets jingle.

"Show them," Koi said.

Devon opened his mouth.

I clamped my hand over my mouth in shock.

"What the hell?" Lorcan muttered.

Jude grumbled in disgust but moved in for a closer look. "Even I wouldn't do this," he retreated again.

Devon had no tongue, only a scarred stub.

He continued to look around the room with interest, unfazed by our reactions.

"What happened?" I asked.

Empathy tugged at my heart, but I kept my emotions in check. Despite his link to Enl'iel, Devon was a stranger to me. Even more so, his relationship to Belial frightened me.

Devon smiled apologetically as though it was his fault he'd been brutalised.

"It was cut out when I was a child," he whispered into my head.

"Why would someone cut out your tongue?" I shielded my mouth as though it could happen to me.

"As a child, I lived with humans for a time. I knew not what I was, and I spoke of strange things—of angels and daimons, of spirits and the like. It scared them. They did not wish to hear my words. It was a time of dark religious superstition, which had dreadful consequences more often than not. I was lucky to avoid the pyre."

Koi waved Devon towards the Zythros stone, "We can use the stone to communicate communally. Come."

Devon followed Koi, jingling with every step. Koi removed his shackles and activated the stone. As it glowed its soft apricot hue, he encouraged Devon to lay his hands on it. The stone pulsed, acknowledging receipt of his energy.

"Speak about who you are so everyone present may bear witness," Koi said.

Devon's pale brows furrowed. He removed his hand, examined it, and placed it back down. He closed his eyes and his voice radiated from within the stone.

"My mother named me Devon. A place close to her heart, so I'm told," Devon jumped backwards, breaking the connection. The sound of his voice amplified through the stone seemed to startle him. His eyes were wide with surprise.

"Please continue," Koi said. "You are quite safe."

Devon walked around stone, then nodded to himself and placed his palm back down.

"I was born sometime in the seventeenth century, though I am unsure when exactly."

His smooth voice echoed through the empty hall.

Koi's brows were tight in thought, "Who was your mother?"

"I do not remember," Devon crossed his arms over his stomach.

"Her name was Mary," Belial mumbled.

The guards bustled closer, weapons high and ready for Koi's word.

"Let him speak," Koi said.

The guards relaxed. Belial drew a deep breath, his attention on Devon. He swallowed, shifted his feet, and moved his hands against his shackles and then he spoke.

"Many years ago," he sighed again. He almost sounded bereft. "I found a human woman named Mary about to drown herself. For some reason I pulled her from the water to find she'd been battered within an inch of her life," his face twisted into a deep-creased grimace. "She was married to a vile human who had beaten her senseless. A Rogue I was travelling with had sniffed her out, hungry for a fresh meal. Our chance meeting brought nothing but pain and regret in the end," Belial wiped his shackled hands roughly across his eyes. "You, Devon, were born in 1685. You were the product of our affair."

"Oh God!" I muttered, shocked. He didn't acknowledge me, but stared on ahead, blinking his eyes with each slow draw of breath.

"Quiet, Sophia, I wish to hear what he has to say," Koi said

Belial continued, "Devon was the first born of our communion. Enl'iel followed much later. Mary passed you off as her husband's offspring for your safety and hers. We secretly met in their guest house for many years. Sometimes we travelled the countryside of Devon throughout the night. It was her only release from a miserable existence. When it became evident that she would not be safe with me in her life, I ended the relationship. Daimon follow Daimon, and they often do not respect boundaries. I could not risk others harming her. Impossible as it is to imagine, she was safer with her husband."

His eyes became a deeper shade of black with the memories. As much as I couldn't stomach the idea, I wondered if he had actually truly loved this woman.

He threaded his fingers together, his knuckles white, I could smell the shackles burning his skin... he didn't flinch.

"Mary was with child when we parted. She wanted to come with me, but that was impossible. No human could live a such a life. But she was foolish in her desperation and told her family and anyone who would listen, that an angel had impregnated her," he closed his eyes and shook his head. "Of course, Devon's hair was white, he did not look like her husband. The weasels that were her family thought her an insane or possessed adulteress," Belial swallowed hard. "They threw her and Devon into Bedlam, an asylum. That vile place sent her insane. It is my life's shame that I left her there."

I let go of Brennan, "You deserted them?" I wasn't scared of Belial in this environment, "You left her to suffer after you turned her life upside down?" Anger tightened my jaw. The injustice of her life sent an angry growl to my lungs from the pit of my stomach.

"I protected her from a worse fate. She and Devon could have burned on the pyre."

His steely eyes were uncomfortable, but I refused to look away.

"And Bedlam was a better fate?" I could only imagine the trauma of being locked in such a place.

"Than being burned as a witch or repeatedly assaulted by other Daimon? Yes, Sophia, it was a better option," Belial said. I cringed at hearing him say my name.

"I cannot control them all. It was better than letting my children suffer an unfathomable death," he said.

"What happened to Mary?" Koi asked.

Devon stared at no one in particular, fiddling with his herbs and trinkets.

"Mary escaped with him into the township of Devon where Enl'iel was born. She wanted to throw herself and her children off the cliffs into the sea. I tracked her just in time to rescue them, but as I held my children in my arms, she jumped. I know where her bones lie at the bottom of those cliffs to this very day," Belial answered.

The moisture in his eyes seemed real, but I couldn't accept that he had real emotions.

"How, then, did they not grow up together?" Koi asked. "How did they not know of each other?"

Belial looked towards the Zythros stone as though it were an enemy. "It seemed best to separate them. They would have fed each other's power, possibly marking themselves on the E'lan. Enl'iel was an infant; I hoped she would never remember him and that would keep them both safe," he said.

Koi moved closer, tapping his chin in thought, "So, what did you do?"

Belial glanced at Devon, "They needed to be invisible, and for that, I had to place them with humans. As a Daimon, I could not approach the Watchers and they certainly could not stay with me. I left them with human families as foundlings. It worked for Enl'iel until someone in the Hidden community took her in after her surrogate parents were killed by the plague. Her power ignited when she wept by their graves, paving their way to find her. Devon was not so fortunate. He was mistreated," Belial lowered his head as though he was sad. I hated that it didn't fit my view of him.

"Is this the truth, Devon?" Koi asked.

Devon looked to the ceiling in thought and nodded.

"As much as I can recall, yes. When I was around fifteen years old, I ran away after one beating too many," he clasped a silvery trinket around his neck. It had a white stone in its centre — a soul stone. "I didn't know it then, but I could detect the E'lan. I thought its murmurings were the voices of angels, and I followed its call. Eventually, I found a Hidden community near Tewkesbury. They took me in, no questions asked, and brought me back to health. They taught me about my true heritage."

No one spoke. Devon examined us without apparent judgement, without a spike in emotions.

Koi's eyes thinned, "And what about your claim, Belial? The Great Healer is a myth for those who regret their actions using the drug. A tease to those who are on the brink of descending."

"He is who I say he is. Devon has lived among the Afflicted and devised a method to heal the addiction. I brought him here to help Jasmine if at all possible."

The room pressed in on me. Every time someone mentioned her name, my stomach flipped. Mourning feelings had already been swirling through my thoughts, trying to accept her fate, but now, there could be hope. This didn't seem real. The source of hope for Jaz was gut-churning, but did I grasp it? Could I accept help from someone I so reviled?

Hell yes.

I stepped a little closer to Belial, "You can help her?"

His appearance offended every part of me. With his black eyes and devilish, broken horns, he was everything revolting. But, if he held hope, I'd risk it. He stood shoulder to shoulder with Ben, and it took all my effort to ignore Ben's overwhelming attention.

Jude rushed over and shuffled me behind him, "It is a trick, mere rubbish. No one survives Thanratos." A dagger flashed in his hands, "You'll go near her through this!"

Devon placed his hand on the stone and bowed, "I would never minister to anyone without their consent."

Jude's brows arched in surprised. He lowered the weapon.

"You could help Jaz if we gave you permission?" I asked.

I smiled at the memory of Jaz dancing on a table. What I wouldn't give for her to live her best life.

"Perhaps. Most still pass I'm afraid. I discovered the treatment after my guardian fell victim to Thanratos. I witnessed her wither away. It took me the better part of a century, but I solved her addiction, eventually," his eyes lowered in reverence.

Hopeful intrigue sparkled in Koi's eyes, "How do you cure the addiction?"

"It is a delicate balance of weaning her off the drug whilst teaching her body and mind to reject it. I use chromious," Devon jingled his charms. "It makes the body nauseous at the taste of it. I combine that with elemental pulsation therapy to ease the pain of withdrawal. It is not a pleasant experience. Often, they must be heavily restrained with chains. They scream with the agony. It is hard to witness, but herbal remedies sometimes dampen the pain."

Screaming? Chains?

Had I tapped into Devon in the past?

"Do you still live in Tewkesbury?" I asked.

He nodded.

"I felt you! Near Katoika sanctuary. Is that where you live?"

"Beneath an old boat shed," Devon said. "The Avon provides sustenance and its noisy rush an effective barrier to keep my work secret."

"Brennan! Remember that night? I said I could hear screams when we went running?

Devon had been there. It must have been him that I'd been hearing in the farthest reaches on my mind. I tugged on Brennan's arm, realising also it was Devon who I'd sensed when I'd lost the plot after torching Pouancé manor. I'd ended up at the Avon River near the ramshackle shed. Brennan's eyebrows quirked up. His eyes glimmered as he monitored Devon's every move.

"You're right, I remember that," his eyes narrowed at Devon.

Koi's eyes glinted with interest, "You have resided by Katoika?"

"Yes," Devon bowed. "It gives me comfort and strength to be near my kin. Since it was abandoned, I have sat in solitude, perfecting newer therapies in silent contemplation."

"It makes no sense," Jude said. "Why not share this? Why hide? You could have saved thousands of us."

"I have been alone for a long time," Devon said. "Studying the addiction in secret suited me," he twirled the vials and implements hanging on his rope belt.

"But you must have known how many people needed you?" Koi asked. "You've been a myth, a fantasy the desperate dared not dream of," Koi pressed him a little harder.

Devon reached for the trinket with the soul stone. "I have become scared of the wider world. I know what dwells upon and within it. I have seen pain and, perhaps to my shame, want to avoid more. The Afflicted have always known of me. They come to me when they are ready and able. The result of successful treatment is amnesia; therefore, the mythical understanding of my existence no doubt rests upon this side effect. I never hid, I just did not advertise myself."

Devon raised his soft eyes to Koi, who steepled his fingers under his chin.

"Did you know about Enl'iel?" I asked. "Your sister could have supported you."

Jude muttered a foul insult that sounded something like *Daimon spawn*. I glowered at him.

I moved closer to Devon. His fine nose and the rise of his cheeks were Enl'iel's, but it was his eyes that had it. We all had blue eyes of varying tones, but his had the exact same softness as hers, not the stark bright blue of many. The way he twirled his soul stone between his fingers and stared past me towards the door from which Enl'iel had left was so very Enl'iel, so very me.

His eyes rested back on me. "I did not know her. It is a shame," a wistful smile then brightened his face. "To have known my real family would have been all I could have wished for. To have gathered strength from kin would perhaps have helped my own maladies."

Jude twirled a dagger in his palm, "You're not buying into this tripe, are you?"

Lorcan edged in behind Jude. "Let's test him, see if he's the real deal," he leaned back on one foot and crossed his arms.

"How do you propose we do that, pretty boy?" Jude pointed his dagger at Lorcan. "You going to volunteer?"

Lorcan flushed against his fiery mark, its loops and swirls clawing around his face. Even his hair shimmered at Jude's constant insults.

"If you would just take your head out of your arse, you'd think clearly enough to remember that we conveniently have an Afflicted holding onto life in the Stasis room."

Jude's face darkened, and he shoved his dagger back into his belt. I suppressed a smile. I'd never seen Lorcan stand up for himself like that.

"It's a perfect opportunity for him to demonstrate his magical powers," Lorcan wriggled his fingers sarcastically towards Devon, who didn't react.

"Settle down, both of you," Koi said. "That's an excellent idea though, Lorcan."

Jude's mouth puckered, "And what about those two?"

"They'll go back to the cells," I said.

Koi agreed, "Yes, that they will."

Ben nodded and elbowed Belial, who glanced at Devon before bowing his head as well.

"That's a good idea, given the circumstances," Ben said.

"It has an opinion now?" Jude scoffed and wandered towards Ben. "Any other nuggets of wisdom for us?" Jude crossed his arms.

Ben waved him off, "Look, either descend me or lock me up, but can you just shut the hell up?"

I held my breath. This wasn't good.

Jude straightened and cracked his neck, spinning his dagger again. "Sounds like you wanna take it outside, mate?"

Ben held up his bound hands, "About the only way you could take me, *mate!*"

"Oh shit," Lorcan stammered.

Koi stepped between them both, spread his wings, and cast a derisive glance at Jude.

"Until we assess Devon's ability, you are both confined. We will reassess Ben's intentions afterwards, as we will Enl'iel's. Belial, you will not be allowed free under any circumstances. Do you understand?"

Belial nodded; his weary eyes blinked hard. His head fell forwards, and his shoulders slumped. Two horn stubs jutted out above his dark waves. I didn't pity him; his face brought Esme's to mind every time I saw him.

His eyes were on the ground, unable or unwilling to look up, when he called out to Devon.

"Help them, my son. Perhaps one day, you and your sister will find some small measure of forgiveness for me. I hope you see the redemption from I'el that you both deserve."

Koi waved at some guards, and they took Belial and Ben away.

Chapter Nine

I stood outside Enl'iel's guarded door, hot tea steaming on a tray. I took a breath before I knocked and reflected on what I'd just witnessed.

I had followed Devon to the stasis room. He had been placed with the Afflicted woman under heavy guard and had quickly settled into his work. I observed him for half an hour, and it was fascinating. He began by pounding herbs into pastes, into which he sprinkled Thanratos using ancient bronze tweezers. His chromious trinkets had warmed under the heat of an unusual orb, which had hovered just inches above the trinkets on a preparation bench. Jaz had stabilised at the crossroads of death, and I hoped to I'el he could do something. If wishing were terminal, I would have died right there. I was hoping so hard that there was some remote possibility this wasn't a hoax.

I looked just as hopeful at the guard outside Enl'iel's door.

"I am sorry, Sophia, but even you cannot enter."

I was about to plead but held my tongue. I didn't want to make things more difficult for her by causing trouble.

"Give this to her, please? She loves her tea."

As I offered up the tray, my heart broke a little more. How much would be left at the end of this quest?

The guard took the tray with a smile in her eyes. Her armour squeaked with the movement.

"Enl'iel will be okay. She cared for my mother when she was Awakening. There's a soft spot in my heart for her. I believe her soul is good, but I'm just a guardian; I must do my duty. This will be sorted in her favour, I'm sure."

The guard took the tea inside and let the door thud shut behind her.

I walked a few feet away and leaned into a cool section of vine below a clutch of A'vexia. I needed a moment to process everything and reached up for a fruit. The leaves were soothing against my skin, which had so often burned with fear and anger.

"Sophia?"

"Enl'iel?" I ran back to her door. "I'm here!" I leaned my head and hands against the door, "Are you okay?"

"Yes, dear," she sounded tired.

I dug my nails into the wood. It was warm and forgiving, I pressed my body closer to it.

There was a long intake of breath and a small *thud*, she was leaning against the door too.

"Now, you go along to the Empyrean realm. Bring Yeqon down; do not just take a piece of him. Bind that Daimon within an inch of his life and descend him into his own Pits. Do *not* let him prevail!" her voice quivered with the fever of her emotion.

There was a brief silence.

"I will. I'll beat him, I promise, Enl'iel. Then I'll get you out of here."

The door fell away from my cheek, and the guard reappeared. "Sorry, that's enough of that now. You'd best move along," the guard waved her hand for me to leave. The door clicked shut, and I left.

Brennan met me at the juncture between corridors, "Is she okay?"

"She's fine."

I plucked a fruit as we distanced ourselves from Enl'iel's room. I took a bite and shared it with him. He took one bite and returned it.

I peered up at him, "You knew about this, didn't you?"

Brennan took his time to swallow his mouthful, "For a long time. She told me as soon as we... you know," he shrugged.

"Fell in love?"

"Yes," his voice strained. "It was a hard thing to keep to myself," he stopped as some guards marched by, then turned me by my shoulders to face him. "I've encouraged her to reach out to Gedz'iel, but she's been too terrified," Brennan's wide eyes were pained.

I squeezed his arms in support "I can't imagine her fear."

"Perhaps it's for the best," Brennan said. "This way, she's not in harm's way."

"Well, that's true," I agreed.

We wandered a little farther towards Rik's room in silence.

"So, Leonardo da Vinci?" Brennan snatched the notebook which was poking out of my pocket. "'Beneath mine atlas,'" he chuckled and flicked through the pages I'd scratched notes on. "You reckon Leo has a clue in a book of maps?"

"That's what I'm thinking, too," I said. "But I really have no idea what map that could be. What I do know, though, is that many of his works are in Milan. We might find something there?" I plucked the notebook back. "I'll need your phone again."

Brennan pulled it from his pocket, "Solid plan."

His phone sparked to life, and I typed quickly.

"Before we snoop around Italy again, I have to stop Yeqon."

"*We* have to stop him, Princess. This one's definitely a group effort. You're merely... the bait," he grimaced.

"That's nothing new," I shrugged; although, on the inside, I cringed. "Is it as dire as Gedz'iel said?"

He sucked in a long breath as we turned the final corner.

"Humans think terrorism is exponentially on the rise," Brennan said. "Everyone is blaming one another. Sanctions are in force between many previous allies, and the human economy is bottoming out. Food production is affected, transport and communication are compromised. There's global panic."

We stopped just short of Rik's room. Brennan ran his hands over his face. His eyes were heavy with fatigue and dark circles hollowed them.

"Are we losing the fight for humanity?" I asked. The question chilled my skin.

He sighed, "Our sleepers are struggling to contain the fallout. If we let Yeqon's attacks continue, a full-blown human war will develop; there'll be nothing left to protect because they'll annihilate each other."

I pinched the bridge of my nose. How much worse could this get?

"What do you think his reaction will be?" I pointed my thumb at Rik's door.

Brennan whistled and threw his hands in the air, "With him, well… even I don't know. Let's see, hey?"

He knocked. The door opened quickly, as though Rik had been standing right behind it. He eyed us both, leaving the door open just a crack.

"What do you want?"

"Can we come in?" I asked. "I need to ask you something important that might help bring Yeqon down."

Rik's fingertips gouged into the door as he glared at me.

"Please, just hear us out, and then we'll leave you be, I promise."

Brennan pushed the door open, forcing Rik to retreat into his room. "C'mon mate?" Brennan said and blurted out why we were there before I had the chance to set the scene and soften the blow.

Rik's hands began to shake, and the cup he'd been holding shattered at his feet.

"You want me to go back there? With you?"

He staggered back into a chair, swore, and flung it across the room. His lips quivered. He paced, wrenching his shaking hands into submission. A light sheen sparkled over his skin from head to waist. Orb light danced over the new and old scars that criss-crossed his torso. He tugged a shirt from a hook and slipped it on.

"Rik, please calm down?"

His eyes narrowed at me, "This your idea? Or his?" He scoffed at Brennan and kicked at his unmade bed.

Uneasiness crept along my skin. I wasn't at all sure if he would get violent. I stepped back and held up my hands, "I know you don't have warm feelings for me, but this is bigger than us. We need to bring your tormentor down."

Rik tugged at his shirt and mumbled to himself.

Brennan pumped his fists together, "You can help us destroy him, see him kneel at your feet for a change."

Rik's fingers delved into his short crop of hair. He crouched forwards, mumbling incoherent worries to himself. The sight of him broke my heart. I moved a little closer again. When my shadow crossed his, he jumped up and backed away until his bed stopped him. His fingers drummed at his sides. He looked behind me as though he was eyeing the door.

Those eyes settled on me, "And when one of your *special* friends finds themselves in trouble, you'll dump me again? That the plan, sister? Am I bait?"

"Of course not!"

I was horrified that he saw me in that light, but there was truth to his accusation, and the shame made me pause. My mouth was dry. I peered at Brennan, who nodded with encouragement. I stepped closer to Rik again. He leaned harder against the bed, and it forced him to sit. I stopped and held my hands up in peace.

"*I* am the bait, as always." I wrung my hands as I sought the right words. "I know it hurt when I let you go. I'm sorry," my bottom lip quivered.

Rik pushed himself up and paced at the end of the bed. He shook his head and ran his hands through his hair.

"Easy words to say," he jabbed his finger into his chest. "I've been promised a lot throughout my miserable life," he pointed his finger at me, and I felt the weight of its incrimination. "The only promises that are guaranteed are the painful ones," Rik's foot connected with the discarded chair so forcefully that it slid across the room, only just stopping before it hit me.

"Careful there, mate," Brennan kneed the chair away from me and put his hand on my shoulder. "You okay?"

I nodded.

I moved closer to Rik and slunk onto the bed, "I'm sorry, Rik."

Untouched food—a few days' worth, judging by the amount, cluttered his bedside table.

"You're not eating?" I asked.

"Worry not, sister. I'm stronger than I've ever been. I could barely even speak when we met. Look at me now," he waved his arms across his body and moved to the farthest corner. He crossed those arms and rested against the wall. His waif-thin frame contradicted him, yet his muscles did seem more defined than the broken body I'd found just a few weeks ago. I remembered that he could barely put two words together, he had progressed quickly.

"You've gotta eat man. No point self-destructing," Brennan said. Rik kicked the wall a few times with his heel. Blood nipped the air.

"Please stop that?" I begged.

He kicked again, rendering a deep gash along the edge of his bare foot.

"Rik! Stop it!" I stood, my heart hammering.

"Better my pain comes from me than anyone else, sister."

His garish smile and wild eyes made him look completely unhinged. He reached down to wipe the blood from his foot, then moved towards the bed again. Brennan stayed close; his energy tinged with nerves. Rik leaned onto the opposite side of the bed and smeared the blood across the linen before he sat down and pulled a boot over the open wound.

"You think he's alright upstairs?" Brennan whispered.

"Of course he isn't?" I snapped back.

"And if I say no to your request?" Rik asked.

His scarred mind and body were every reason to refuse. I should never have asked, but we wouldn't fool Yeqon without him.

I rubbed my sweaty hands dry on my hips, "I'll understand. I won't insist. I just thought it would be more believable if you fled with me to gain Yeqon's favour."

"Favour?" Rik's head shot up, and he stared at us. "You think I want his approval?" Rik's bloody hands scrunched the linen into a tight wad.

I shook my head. "No, of course not. That's not what I meant," I tried to think of the right words; I really wasn't good at this. "Wouldn't his ego expect that though? He demands total submission. He would never expect the strength you have now or our trust in you. His conceit would never let him accept the incredible force you've become."

Rik's eyes were wide, and his mouth hung open a little. He snapped it shut and took a sharp breath though his nose. He picked at his nails, looked at me and shook his head.

"He'll kill me on sight," he jumped off the bed and crouched against the wall, slamming his head into it.

"Over my dead body," Brennan sunk down next to him. "There'll come a point where you'll have to trust someone," he leaned against the wall, too, and shrugged. "We all have our demons. You, unfortunately, have the worst."

Rik rubbed the back of his head, and his hand came away red. He seemed mesmerised by his own blood; rubbing it between his fingers before wiping it onto his trousers.

He peered at Brennan. "There's no such thing as trust," Rik glanced at me, and it was as good as a stake in my heart. "Just when you think you know someone, their true agenda rises. Trust no one."

The passion in his voice took my breath away. My pendant hummed against my skin; I twirled it a few times and tapped it against my lip.

I squatted in front of him. "I can't force you to believe us, I understand betrayal is part of your identity," I reached for his hand, but he pulled it back. He didn't even look at me. "I hope to show you that there is goodness in the world, that you can feel the love and warmth of those around you, but that won't happen if Yeqon brings this world down."

I clenched my hands and closed my eyes, willing things to ease, begging I'el to give me a break.

I rose. Brennan did too.

"Brother," I smiled at the word. "I promise on my soul that I won't let Yeqon hurt you again. All you have to do is be yourself. That's all he'll expect."

Rik pushed away from the wall and glared at me, his lips quivering.

"You can't guarantee that," Rik pointed at me, then tapped his temple. "He gets into my head. He'll probably have me descend myself for deserting him. He's tried it before when I displeased him."

Brennan and I blanched. My jaw was tight with anger.

"I'm sorry he did those things to you," I said.

I crooked my head towards the door, and Brennan followed me towards it. I stopped and glanced back.

"This was a mistake. We'll find another way."

The door clicked shut. A white flower, shrivelled around its edges, dangled above his door. A little like Rik, a beautiful thing damaged by the world it lived in. I stared at it until my eyes glazed over.

"What else can we do, Bren?" I headed back towards the Zythros room, Brennan by my side. "Should I just spring myself on Yeqon and hope for the best?"

"That would be a no," Brennan said.

A bang had us spin on our heels.

Rik stood outside his door, securing a belt crammed with weapons around his waist.

"I've had no purpose my whole life. Let me have one now."

Ten

Gedz'iel's feet landed lightly on the wide streets of Del Rio, Texas. Pale dust settled between his toes. His nostrils flared as he drew in the tepid air. Amais arrived seconds later. Gedz'iel put his finger to his lips and tapped his temple as both of them concealed themselves seamlessly into dark attire, fitting in with the federal forces that had shut down the town. A light February drizzle wet his knuckles which he cracked impatiently. Gedz'iel plucked at the police tape that closed off the immediate area.

"They think this will help?" he shook his head, his mouth a thin, grim line.

Amais pointed to signs warning of a non-specific hazard that were placed at regular intervals along the length of yellow and black barricade.

"Undercover for now," Gedz'iel slung an automatic rifle over his head. The night sky flashed red and blue above the modest townscape. A white spotlight cut through from an overhead chopper that scanned the farther edges where the town met barren countryside. Gedz'iel's eyes flashed as he tracked two dark forms that cut across the sky.

"Amais?" Gedz'iel pointed up. Both of them watched the movement streak quickly overhead, two hazy smudges that disappeared into the evening horizon.

"This way," Gedz'iel jumped the cyclone fencing that surrounded the local high school, the centre of the latest atrocities. A hundred feet to their left, human military personnel manned the site, the sounds of their muffled radio conversations easy for the duo to listen into. They walked towards them, listening intently, their eyes alert and sweeping the area.

"Fifty civilians taken in a week! This has become unmanageable, Gedz'iel," Amais said.

"That's why we can't ignore this. One or two, that's easily a human issue. Fifty, that gets a lot of attention, and not just amongst humans," Gedz'iel added, waving Amais on as he sped up.

Amais ran his hand along the chain link fence as they moved along, shaking his head, *"They've no idea what they're dealing with."*

"That's why we are here. I need to see for myself what exactly is going on. It's not normal Rogue behaviour," Gedz'iel looked to the sky again, but it was clear, no movement other than thin wisps of cloud bearding the moon. His fingers clenched tighter around the rifle, *"It's new, it's desperate and creating the panic any enemy of ours would want. We need to end it."*

Amais nodded in agreement as a blinding spotlight shone their way. Gedz'iel saluted towards the guard on the outside.

"You're either a fuckin' brave son of bitch or a moron!" a soldier called to him.

Amais smiled at Gedz'iel and they made their way towards the young soldier.

"Get back outta there!" the soldier picked up his radio and leaned his mouth towards it, ready to call it in. Gedz'iel strode over quickly.

"Special forces!" Gedz'iel put a finger to his lips, stepped further into the spotlight and raised his firearm. His eyebrows twitched up.

The soldier hesitated before he holstered his communications. He stepped closer to Gedz'iel and Amais.

"Didn't know you guys were here yet. There's some sick shit going on in this place. Don't know what it is, but they say you don't see it coming!" he ran his finger across his neck. "It's all silence and then, goodnight before you can scream!"

"We are well aware. Stay at your post soldier, and keep alert," Amais dismissed the soldier with a firm salute. The soldier resumed his post, rifle out-front.

The two Watchers turned away.

"I want to see what's out back. The E'lan feels disturbed over there," Gedz'iel pointed towards the largest building on the school grounds. They moved towards the shadows and out of sight. Their rifles then resumed their true forms; long, sharp A'vean swords.

Moonlight draped the surrounds in a silvery hue that exaggerated the intensity of the E'lan. Its tickle was a burn, and that burn tugged at Gedz'iel's skin, drawing light to his face. They headed to the rear of the school. That was where the sightings had been; where human blood had been shed.

"Whatever we saw overhead was headed that way. If anything is here, we need to interrogate it first," Gedz'iel whispered. *"Then descend it,"* he added.

Amais nodded. He sniffed the air.

"The E'lan is stronger over that way," Amais pointed towards a sign that read, 'Gymnasium.'

A large basketball image adorned the gable over double entry doors. Faded writing peeled away underneath it. A blue light hung from the eave, flashing intermittently.

"Alarm is faulty," Amais commented after poking at the control panel.

Gedz'iel pulled at the double doors, *"Locked."*

Wheels grinding over gravel interrupted their investigation. They sunk into the shadows of nearby bushes. Two motorbikes were being wheeled along, gears in neutral, motors off.

"Are all humans this stupid?" Amais groaned as two teens elbowed each other before scaling the fence into the school. They landed in crouches, holding out their phones, recording their adventure.

"This is going to go so viral if we get anything!" a girl crouched at the base of the fence, grinning, eyes wide with excitement.

"Totally Blair Witch!" a boy said loudly, holding his phone out, its light brightening his freckled face.

"Shut the fuck up! If it's in here, it'll hear you, you stupid dick!" she shushed him just as loudly.

The boy slapped a hand across his mouth.

"Shit," he mumbled behind it. He looked left and right nervously, and then directly towards the bushes where Gedz'iel and Amais hid. They sunk back further until they hit the wall of the building. The teens didn't seem to noticed them.

The girl nodded, "Follow me." In a crouch, they tiptoed their way towards the entrance of the Gym.

"Just kill me now Gedz'iel. Are we really trying to protect this level of evolution?" Amais ran his palm across his mouth and shook his head.

Gedz'iel sighed impatiently, *"Unfortunately, yes. Not all of them possess enough of this."* he tapped his head. *"Hopefully they will get bored quickly and leave. Let's finish our search whilst they get their thrill,"* he tilted his head, cocking his ear up. *"It seems the E'lan is settling. They'll probably be picked up by the guards anyway."*

Amais and Gedz'iel emerged from the shadows just as a tree rustled nearby. They melted back into the darkness and watched on.

The teens ran towards the noise, their phone lights catching a bird chase a flurry of bugs for a midnight snack.

"You *so* shit yourself!" the girl teased, slapping the boy's back and grabbing her belly, trying to keep her laughter low. She dragged her friend in the opposite direction around the corner of the building.

"Perhaps the humans have done our job for us? The army patrols may have frightened them away. This place seems quiet," Amais said.

"Perhaps," Gedz'iel replied. *"Let's sweep the grounds though. I want to see if there is evidence of the cause of the disappearances. I need to know how to handle this with the White House. The last thing we need is miscommunication and inuendo causing humanity firing up their war machines at each other."*

They retreated back towards the bushes when there was a heavy thud in the direction the teens had gone. Someone or something groaned. The cyclone fencing nearby wobbled noisily. Amais stared hard at Gedz'iel. The patrols outside remained as they were, oblivious to these subtle events. The chopper had circled further away, leaving the place darker than before.

Gedz'iel sniffed the air. *"Do you smell that?"* he asked. Amais nodded, his mouth narrowed and he brought his sword out front. Gedz'iel pointed to flank the building from the other side. Veins of power flooded their skin, igniting their bodies. They shook away the last of their concealment. The moonlight paled under the shimmer of their wings as they rose silently. More birds were startled from their nests as the two Watchers sped past.

The unmistakable flutter of a dying heart travelled along the E'lan. Gedz'iel hastened, his own heart rushing faster. A small blue light shone up from a tuft of un-mowed grass. Gedz'iel and Amais moved in swiftly. The shadows were faster. The rush of hurried footsteps preceded a low growl. Gedz'iel and Amais moved faster as they sensed the unmistakable buzz of pterugia wings.

"Quickly!" Gedz'iel said. He sent power along his arm, fusing it with his sword.

The two Watchers came to a halt where an elemental signature lingered strong and fresh. Under the soft light of their wings was a bloody mess on the ground below.

Gedz'iel approached, kneeling and dipping his fingers into the blood.

His mouth clenched. In the darkness beyond, nothing was to be seen, no perpetrator to be apprehended, no victims to save.

"Fledglings?" Amais asked, his eyebrows drew close.

"Perhaps so," Gedz'iel reached to his right and picked up the head of the girl. Her expression forever in abject horror, mouth agape, eyes plucked neatly from the sockets.

"For the love of I'el!" Gedz'iel's shoulders fell a little. "Where is the rest of her?" he whispered out loud.

They both scanned the darkness.

"Over there," Amais pointed a few feet away towards another tuft of grass.

As he picked up the phone, it buzzed, lighting up briefly.

"Here, I don't understand these things," Amais passed it to Gedz'iel whose fingers slid adeptly across the screen.

He opened a voicemail and held the device close, both of them leaning into it.

"Harley? Harley, I got one!" the boy yelled excitedly; his words spilled out breathlessly. "It's, it's …" his voice muffled. "Oh…" more muffled sounds like he was scrambling to hold the phone. "My god, oh my fucking god, I got one!"

The unmistakable sound of feet pounding the ground followed, the boy's breaths were exhaustive and rapid, "Get… round… back!" He made a low gurgling sound and the phone went dead.

Gedz'iel sighed. *"Something was here and it's swift."* he felt the E'lan again, it remained unsettled.

"This is worrying," Gedz'iel licked a finger, he raised it into the air. Closing his eyes, he concentrated.

"Nothing. Whatever it was, it was so fast that its signature has vanished already," he said, turning around and looking out across the immediate area. He held up the light of his sword and widened his wings, squinting at something on the ground.

"Ash the remains. Let's find what's left before anyone else does," Gedz'iel waved to Amais who quickly burnt the girl into dust. He joined Gedz'iel; both flew low and slow, scanning the grounds.

"Over there," Gedz'iel turned towards the far side of the gymnasium, banking back towards a car park.

The night lightened as clouds released the moon, letting her cast her fingers across the gravel, revealing clotted splashes of crimson. A finger floated in one red puddle, a left foot in another, its shoe still in place. Clumps of hair sat atop a second phone.

Amais picked up the phone between two fingers, flicking the clutch of hair to the ground. He passed it to Gedz'iel who turned the phone on, touching the camera icon. He held it up for Amais to see. They watched the few seconds of footage.

A shadow, tall and fast sped through the grounds, quickly followed by another.

Gedz'iel held the phone steadier as fury tempted his fingers to shake. The image shook and blurred as the teen rushed to follow the movement. Deadly quiet ghosts with the mark of A'vean singed like blackened veins across their cheeks. Most telling was their smoky wings. They saw the light of the teen's phone and that was the end. They moved like lightning, rushing straight towards him. The phone fell to the ground, its camera recorded a few seconds more where it lay. Flashes of movement and blood-chilling moans.

"She's breeding again?" Amais murmured. Both he and Gedz'iel glanced worriedly at each other.

"Brother, I thought she may be long past this," Gedz'iel sighed, slipping the phone in to his pocket. He smoothed his palm across his eyes.

"They look different to the others," Amais commented as he knelt by the shredded torso of the boy. Disembowelled, his flesh flayed to the bones. "What a waste," he spoke out loud now as he sat back on his legs and just stared at the remains.

"Yes," Gedz'iel stared at the grizzly sight, recounting all he'd seen in his long life. This was new. "The question is, who is she breeding with? She has never produced winged vampires before," he scanned the smattering of stars above.

"They're quick," Gedz'iel said.

"This is a mess," Amais grimaced. "Reminds me of Satanos."

"Indeed," Gedz'iel's expression was grim. "We will have to change our plans. Many have never come to blows with the children of Lilith," he rested the tip of his sword on the ground. Gedz'iel breathed long and deep and pulled the phone from his pocket again, replaying the scene.

"Yeqon may not be our biggest threat," Amais said.

"We must warn Sophia and everyone else," Gedz'iel said as he kneeled by Amais who held his hand over the corpse. "The soul remains intact?"

Amais nodded.

"Retrieve it," Gedz'iel said.

Amais rested his palms over the temples of the second decapitated head. "Come now," he urged. A sliver of mist snaked out of the slack mouth. "Come to me. You're safe now," Amais wriggled his fingers. The soul brightened, moving quickly out of the fleshy shell until its entirety swirled and weaved through Amais' fingers. He brought his other hand protectively over the boy's soul.

"I will guide him on. Shall we meet back at the sanctuary and regroup?" Amais asked, standing up, cupping the soul against his chest.

Gedz'iel nodded and his hand burst into a fiery light, incinerating the remnants of the body.

"If we don't stop this now, there will be nothing left worth saving."

Chapter Eleven

I tightened my boot laces and ensured my dagger and Kea's sword were secured in my belt.

"You sure, Rik?" I asked. "You can handle seeing him?"

"It isn't whether I can handle it," the muscles in Rik's neck strained as he wriggled his jaw, cracking its joint. His eyes met mine, "It's whether you can stop me from killing him."

He rammed another dagger into his belt. A new shade had fallen across his skin, and thinly veiled tension caused his chin to twitch.

Lorcan slid his own blades into his belt, "Don't see how that's a problem."

"Killing Yeqon would be the easy, gratifying option," Koi said. "In truth, we must catch him and bring him before I'el."

My head shot up, "What?"

"His punishment will be best served by I'el. All we require of you is to bring Yeqon to his knees, to stop his murderous rampage."

My neck tightened. I hadn't considered escorting him to I'el. I'd only had visions of his limp body at the end of Kea's sword.

"However," Koi said, "I will not hesitate to fight to the death if required, as many of us may need to. I'el would not look unkindly upon us." Koi nodded at me, almost encouragingly.

All I needed was a drop of Yeqon's blood. I could convince myself to be satisfied with that, but it would be a lie. There was no way I'd let him live if I had the chance to squeeze the life out of him.

"Right, we ready to move out then?"

Nervous anticipation clenched my stomach. Would Yeqon already be there and catch us off guard? Would *he* trap *us*? Even if he did, I was stronger than ever with way too many lives on my conscience. My fear was a secret, but Rik was struggling to mask his.

"Everything is secure," Jude grumbled.

I pulled him aside, tired of his caustic mood.

"Jude, I need you. I need your strength and experience, but I also need you to cut out this macho rubbish," I waved my hands up and down in front of him. "I know you're mad and sad about Jaz."

Jude drew a sharp breath in.

"I know you have a lot of pent-up rage, but I need you at your best," I grasped his shoulders, he glared at me, dead on, lips pressed white. "You're behaving like a human. Cut it out or I don't want you with me," I squeezed his shoulders, let go, and turned away.

Jude didn't need me to humiliate him, he just needed to hear the truth and make a choice.

I felt him by my side, and we watched the others finalise preparations. Jude's arm brushed against mine; his armour clanged against mine. "I am not human. I will honour you as I should," he said.

Relief ran though me.

Koi motioned Jude over.

"Activate the stone," Koi said.

Jude obliged, no smart remarks, no filthy looks. He placed his fiery fingertips on the orange rock. Koi drew his sword, and we all copied. Jude, Brennan, Lorcan, Rik, and I touched our chromious weapons to the stone with a light metallic scrape, letting our energy flow along the weapons and into the Zythros stone.

I nodded at Rik, "Take us back."

Rik closed his eyes, and that familiar pull yanked at my insides. The room dulled, sounds ebbed away, and the vacuous nothingness of the in-between dragged me away.

The Empyrean realm wasn't what I'd expected. Not the volcanically unstable, fiery tunnels that reeked of Rogues and misery. We found ourselves cloistered into a small room, roughly dug into the stone. A hearth fire warmed a wooden bed. Shreds of linen lay askew over its end. There was a sweaty odour tinged with the taste of fear. Rik looked around with disgust. He rubbed his hand across his chest as though it pained him to be here.

Koi scanned the space, "What is this place?"

Jude leaned his head against a heavy door and listened.

The ground rumbled, an angry call from the mountain that dominated the Empyrean landscape. Heat radiated up through the ground, and sulphur marred the air, eclipsing the more domestic smells.

"This is where I have lived since I was a young child," Rik's voice was tense, his hands tapping against his thighs. His eyes darted to the door, and relief softened their fear when he saw that Jude guarded it.

Dozens of rotten apple cores lay scattered over the ground. Upturned wooden plates, glossed with a dark residue, piled atop a small table. A roughly made stool sat next to the bed. Scuff marks disturbed the loose layer of topsoil on the ground… a distinct, large shoe print. Over the stool, deep gouge marks disfigured the brackish walls.

Rik pointed at the stool. "He would sit there and watch me sleep. I heard him murmur to me whilst he thought I was sleeping. I smelled the blood on him, felt his rage," he gulped, the pallor of his face lighter again.

A painful knot wadded in my chest. I envisaged the scene, and it broke my heart.

"Were you alone?" I asked. "Apart from him?"

"Ben visited me," Rik whispered.

The knot tightened.

Jude cracked the door open and inched out. He poked his head back in and waved for us to follow, "All clear. Let's go."

The door yawned wide with invitation. I was relieved to get out of this horrid place and walked into a dank and dark tunnel, flanked by them all. Drips and hisses in the dark encouraged a quick pace. Scurries and scratching, howls and cackles chilled my skin. Thin lines of lava veined the walls. It reminded me of the cave where Ben had held me captive. The sounds were like the now-dead Asmodai, and I feared he might have had friends.

I surged ahead of everyone, "I want to get out of here."

I rushed until the tunnel widened towards a bright light. It opened to a vast and dry plain far below.

"I know this place," I said from behind my hand.

The smell was the overwhelming tang of decomposition. I pinched my nose and looked around me. It was the same tunnel I'd run from before. I'd been here, near Rik, and hadn't realised it. It was only then that I noticed dozens of tunnel entrances pock-marked the immediate area. I wondered whom or what else may lie behind us, hidden away in Hell's domain.

"I was there," I pointed towards the barren landscape with the mountain rumbling in the distance. I knew from experience that its emptiness was a mirage, that it was teeming with nightmarish creatures.

"As have I been," Koi said.

Jude cracked his knuckles, but his voice was even, "Many of us have been here at some point."

Lorcan stared wide-eyed, "It's deserted."

"It's far from that, trust me," I stepped out of the cave and into the glare of a pearlescent sun. I urged Lorcan to join me, "Look down there. Let your eyes rest into a stare."

He did so and groaned with disgust as the mirage gave way to the scurrying of evil things.

Brennan squinted next to his brother and mouthed a series of curses. Jude glowered at the monsters and ghouls, which moved with a disturbingly normal pattern. They carried baskets of goods between places, marched along trails through the bustle of the demonic daily grind. A disturbing kind of normal. A loping creature, reminiscent of a gargoyle, pushed an onion-laden barrow. Rat-like creatures nipped at its heels, and he flung an onion to the ground for them to devour.

"We have to fly," I said. "I'm not walking through that again," I peered down the shale-strewn mount that led up to the cave. It was teeming with bugs and those rat creatures, "Overland isn't an option."

"I'm with her," Brennan said. "Rather not get rabies before we face Yeqon," he stared at the horrid vista in disgust a little longer, wiping sweat from his eyes as the heat bore down from the Empyrean sun.

The mountain rumbled, and the ground spewed a new gaseous offering into the air.

Rik's eyes darted between the mountain and the avenue of dead trees that led to a pumice platform to its left. His hand sought mine, his arm rigid, his fingers nearly cut off the circulation to mine. I didn't move, not wanting to break this moment of trust.

I looked at Koi, "I need to plant my energy signature to draw Yeqon out. Flying will do that, won't it?"

"Without doubt," Koi said. "If it goes pear-shaped, conceal yourself and retreat. Rik, hold onto her and stay close to her. She needs you."

Rik swallowed. Resentment clouded his eyes when he looked at me, but his hand squeezed tighter.

"You sure you're okay?" I asked. "I know this is hard."

"Never better, sister," his thumb twitched against the back of my hand, fear palpable in his pulse.

My eyes held his for a moment, imploring him to not look away. He gulped, and his mouth clenched. His eyes moistened, but he blinked his tears away and broke the eye contact. He stared at our still-locked hands. I felt his relief.

I squeezed his hand, "I've got you, Rik. I won't leave you again, I promise."

"Ready?" Koi asked. Everyone nodded. "Let's go then," he said.

Energy surged behind us. Everyone except Rik and I concealed into a debauched crowd of Rogues.

I pointed past the avenue of dead trees, "To the Thyros henge. They're just behind the pumice."

Rik and I stretched our wings, and I pulled him into the air.

The mountain rumbled anew and spewed its displeasure from its top. We banked away to the left to avoid the thickest cloud of poisonous gas, but we didn't evade the sting of its odour and coughed on its vapours.

Rik's flying was raw. We wobbled and dipped as I struggled to keep him level. The back draught of noxious gas and ash unbalanced us further. His face flushed from the struggle, and it reminded me how far I'd come in such a short while.

My wings hummed with robust energy, their shadow small and distorted upon the ground far below. The sun burned into my back, a nasty heat with extra bite. I dipped to avoid it. Horned, bipedal beasts roared with fear and rushed across the plains, diving into their cracks and fissures and leaving their wares behind—my presence had been duly noted.

We approached the tall, stygian stones of the henge, where dozens of vulture-like creatures bunkered into nearby cracks. They were featherless with wrinkled skin, their beaks lined with rows of razor-sharp fangs. They peered up at us, black eyes watching our descent. We landed, and dozens more eyes squinted out of the thin crevices. Excited chittering matched another rousing explosion of the mountain.

The others surrounded Rik and I.

Brennan prodded at his repulsive disguise. "If he's not here now, it won't be long," he turned and growled at the vulture creatures, which returned the gesture with a snake-like hiss. They retreated into their lairs and hissed more once hidden.

I grimaced at Brennan when he dribbled, "You're quite scary, you know?"

He smiled toothlessly. "Might use this get-up for Halloween," he winked with the one eye he had.

"How do we enter?" Koi looked down at his Rogue disguise. "I imagine Rogues wouldn't have a free pass."

Koi tilted his head at the many eyes upon us.

I let go of Rik and pointed at the pillars.

Rik looked up the length of them, squinting in the few sharp rays of light that bore down from the sun. The burning slivers sliced through the enormous obelisks. Their light glistened across the sweat of Rik's face, highlighting the dark rings under his eyes. He mumbled to himself, rubbed his hands together and seemed to hesitate. I reached for him, thinking that he was about to fall apart, but he grabbed my hand in a flash, a tremble in his grasp. He pulled me close. He pressed his other hand to the black stone and whispered, *"Time to play,"* Rik's voice stuttered in my mind.

Rik growled out loud, "Time to visit Father!"

The boys chittered and jeered, playing along, although none of this sat comfortably in my gut, and I guessed, not theirs either.

Rik pressed my hand against one of the pillars. Its power turned my stomach immediately. A groan rumbled in my chest as the nausea rolled over and over in my stomach. I lurched forwards, gripping my gut.

Rik dropped my hand and backed away.

"What are you doing?" he asked, his eyes darted nervously.

"It hurts to touch. It makes me sick," I felt breathless.

But I pressed harder against the pillar again, searching for the right energy to draw us into the tunnels. I closed my eyes, but that made it worse. My mouth was wet with bile, but I couldn't swallow it, I had to spit it away. My tongue burned until it felt like a rock was wedged in my throat. The feeling was the polar opposite of a healing soul stone, the negative to the Zythros stone's positive. Sweat dripped from my nose onto the red earth. The thick air was hard to breathe back out once it was inside my lungs, like I was allergic to this darkness — just like I used to respond to Ben. The darkness repelled me, but I also felt its desperation to draw me into it.

Brennan pulled my hand off the rock.

"Green isn't your colour, Princess. Let's not hurl in front of the spectators — not a good look for the Earth-born," he grunted at Rik and pointed at him to help me.

I coughed as the feeling quickly dissipated. Rik took my hand again, his eyes seemed unsure.

Koi's shadow blotted the sun from my skin, *"Be careful, Sophia."*

"Thanks," I smiled at him and squeezed Rik's hand, *"How do I get in if I can't touch the stones long enough?"*

"Follow me," Rik said. "Fall behind and Oblivion will eat you alive," he snapped sharply in his guise as my captor.

The boys played along as we followed Rik through the henge away from curious eyes. He stopped at a central pillar, which was taller than the rest. Its surface was etched with a myriad of concentric lines, like the circles at the sanctuaries. The vultures followed and perched on the stones overhead where they stretched their leathery wings and settled down, eyes bright and focussed intently on us.

Rik leaned into the central pillar. He pulled me closer too. Suddenly and roughly, he grabbed a handful of my hair. He forced my face hard against glyphs and patterns.

"It's time you bled for my father."

The monolith's negativity stung my skin with barely a touch. I struggled in Rik's firm grip, half freaked out and partly trying to put on an act for the prying eyes around us. The vultures danced along the top of the henge, excited by the goings-on, their claws tapped on the stone.

"You'll not take me back to him!" I tried to sound terrified.

"You'll do what I say, sister," Rik's voice rose into an all too believable rage. He snatched my diamond dagger from my side, and my heart beat faster. He fell into this quite well.

I screamed and stamped on his foot. Rik let go, and I backed away.

"Brennan! Catch me!"

I turned to run, but Brennan scooped me up and threw me over his shoulder, pretending to stop my escape. I punched and kicked, but he dropped me at Rik's feet. I heaved, spitting dirt. Rik grabbed my arm and yanked me back up.

"I said, you will bleed for Father! You owe me, *sister*."

The anger in his face was so believable that blood rushed to my head and my wings widened in defence. Rik yanked my arm until I fell to my knees. He dodged a deliberately ineffective swipe of my wings… and plunged the dagger into my palm. My scream sent the creatures scattering and circling above. The mountain rumbled as I bled onto the bone-dry ground. I was shocked by the pain of it, by how hard he had struck. I pulled back, but my knees were weak.

The boys gathered close; their discomfort almost palpable.

"It's as simple as this, sister: you bleed, we win."

Rik slapped my hand onto the hot stone. The crimson flow trailed along the etchings, and my head began to swim. I heard the others' unsure chatter in my mind, but I was already entering another realm, and their voices faded. My guts twisted with the wicked power emanating from the pillar and the pull of an uninvited transfer.

Chapter Twelve

e landed on a soft ground in a hushed and dim chamber beneath the henge. Ash floated like motes in the air, it clung to my sweaty and itchy skin. I wiped away as much as I could, reducing the irritation to tolerable.

An amber hue softened the darkness as rivulets of lava etched a path towards a tunnel. The familiar ambient glow a sinister highway of light. The walls glowed like the tip of a cigar. Pungent sulphur was thick in the scorching air. It was all too familiar, and it chilled me to my core.

We had all arrived in one piece. I relaxed my wings, and Rik let go of my arm. His face was ashen, and his hands glimmered under a slick red stain of my blood. Gone was the vengeful scowl, gone was the confidence.

I healed the throbbing gash with my other hand, "Look, Rik. I'm fine."

He sighed with relief but didn't look any of us in the eyes. I took his hand and pulled him along.

"Do you think that worked?" I asked.

I walked alongside the lava towards the far end of the room. Another dank corridor awaited, the path that led to Yeqon's chamber. The others were close behind us.

Brennan slapped Rik's shoulder, "You did good, kid."

"I've not drawn blood before," Rik whispered. "Not on purpose, anyway."

Jude stuck his head out into the dark, "Well, it may not be the only time today, so suck it up, sunshine."

"It's okay, Rik. I've got your back," I squeezed his sweaty palm. "All you need to do is what you just did. Convince Yeqon you've kidnapped me so he'll lower his guard. We can take him by surprise. I'm counting on his ego to bring him down."

Rik bit his lip, his eyes narrowed in thought, "Okay."

His voice shook more the closer we came to the tunnel. My insides shook just as much. Rik opened his wings and urged me up. We flew out, the others running after us as Rogues would do.

We glided above the lava rivers, which covered a large portion of the ground, and quickly arrived at the decrepit lair Yeqon called home. I landed in the middle of the cavern and tucked my wings away. Empty thrones sat on the central dais. I smelled old blood and even tasted my own — the memory of Yeqon beating me was that powerful. It took my breath away and rendered me unsure of what to do next. I was trembling. Rik dropped my hand, wide-eyed and looking equally fearful.

"So, do we whistle for the dog or just wait for the mongrel to arrive?" Jude whispered.

He paced the room but stopped at a scorch mark on the ground. His Rogue face fell when he kneeled to rub the black dirt between thumb and forefinger. He brought the substance to his nose and smelled it.

"This is where Kea died," he rested his palm on the spot and lowered his hand for a moment.

Adrenaline surged in hot pulses through my body, and a sheet of heat draped my skin. My eyes and cheeks flushed with anger.

Brennan kneeled in the same spot and hung his head. He ran his fingers over the dark stain and punched the ground. His energy rose when he stood. I felt him concentrating to keep his disguise up.

I took my dagger off Rik's belt and sliced another score into my palm. I was too numb from the rush of vengeance scourging my system to feel the sting. Thick droplets fell onto the foul Daimon territory. I climbed the stairs and watched the shadows behind me, knowing there were numerous fissures for anyone to enter. I leaned in and smeared my hand across Yeqon's throne and into the grooves where he smashed things and people in anger.

The ground rumbled as the mountain roared. Lava pulsed to the surface, orange pinpricks leaving the ground impossibly hotter.

"That'll do it," Lorcan whispered into our minds.

He paced along the lower step and cocked his hairless head left and right to listen. Koi did the same. We were all on guard, yet only the mountain's murmurings disturbed the E'lan, which was a draining and sinister force here — a nothingness with bite.

A pale face, a galloping heart, and that telling bead of saltiness that drizzled down Rik's temple told me something had changed. Rik became very still. The small finger of his right hand twitched, and his other fingers followed suit.

The cloak of fog wasn't immediately apparent, but I smelled the approaching decomposition of real Rogues. My guts churned when I spotted the fog creeping along the ground. Ghoulish shapes emerged from within it. Rogues coasted through the foul vapour like zombie surfers, their decrepit faces wary. They kept their distance from what they thought were their own kind. Brennan, Lorcan, Jude, and Koi encased me and hissed at the newcomers.

An orb exploded into existence above us. Rik ducked as though programmed to fear such things. Its intensity exaggerated his ghostly hue. I worried he would fall apart and give us away. I licked my lips nervously, watching him intently. His rigid form didn't move from the bottom step of the dais as footsteps sounded closer in the recesses behind the thrones.

My blood turned to ice when Yeqon appeared.

Yeqon strode to his seat shadowed by his fallen crew. Pineme, Asbel, Ged'erel, and Kasadya. He sat with one leg over the arm rest and dabbed a finger into my blood smears. The others sat in their own places, Pineme giving me an extra hard look. A chill ran down where my wings would normally have burned. I moved in front of the gurgling spectres that were Koi, Brennan, Lorcan, and Jude. They hissed convincingly at me, and I legitimately shuddered.

Yeqon's cold eyes focussed on Rik. He clicked his fingers, and a Rogue who looked like a mere child produced a tray of apples. Yeqon pulled a short blade from his knee-high boot and peeled the skin away. He chewed as his gaze bore into Rik.

Rik jumped when Yeqon's booming voice filled the cave.

"The son returns! And with a gift no less," he pointed the dagger at Rik and raised his eyebrows, but his black eyes still didn't reach me.

Rik nodded.

Yeqon cupped his ear, "Lost your tongue, boy?"

Rik fell to his knees, leaving me exposed to the beast. "I have not, Father," his voice was shaking.

"Then speak of your adventure, my son," a callous smile spread across Yeqon's face as he ate the last of the apple skin and discarded the rest to the ground.

"I… I…"

Yeqon slammed his fist onto the arm rest, "I, I, I… what? Speak, you fool!"

Rik jumped again, nearly falling down the steps this time.

I'd made a huge mistake. I'd delivered a victim into the hands of his abuser.

The boys shuffled against me as they, too, felt my uneasiness. How could I stop this without Yeqon killing Rik? Backing out was impossible. I froze, scared that the smallest move would bring Yeqon's wrath upon my brother.

Yeqon rose and walked down to Rik, "What is it that you have you brought me?"

Even a few feet away my body reacted with violent revulsion. It was all I could do to not vomit or run away. I needed Yeqon's blood. I needed him descended. I needed us all to survive this.

I willed strength to Rik, and he stood taller before Yeqon. Rik stretched his neck side to side, shook out his arms. He moved towards me, bold and expressionless. He grabbed my arm and shoved me to my knees at Yeqon's feet.

I yelped in shock. My knees stung. Quick thoughts, muddled thoughts, but I reminded myself to play along; Rik was only doing what I'd asked.

Although, it felt very real.

The others growled and groaned, slapping their corpse feet closer to us.

"He's too cool and calm for my liking," Jude whispered.

I agreed, but begged them to keep their disguises up. Pins and needles numbed my fingers. I dug them into my thighs to keep myself balanced and calmer than my instinct dictated.

Rik took a handful of my hair and forced me to bow my head.

"Respect… for… Father," his words were slow, calmer, but there was still a slight hesitation to his voice.

"Are you okay?" I asked.

I told myself that he didn't reply out of fear.

"Now's a good time, Sophia," Brennan whispered.

"Stab the bastard and let's get outta here," Jude snapped.

It had to be hard for them to witness this, but I didn't want to risk Rik being hurt again. He was too close if an early move went wrong.

"I don't want to act too soon. Let Rik smooth Yeqon's ego."

Yeqon's heavy footsteps fell close to me. I braced myself, every muscle tense.

I just needed one drop.

Rik pulled my hair again, forcing me to raise my head and look at Yeqon. He stopped two steps above me, tall and powerful, but his attention still wasn't on me. Instead, he peered over Rik's head at the boys.

Yeqon stepped around me. Rik pulled me along as we watched him circle the boys. They played their roles well, cowering and gurgling before Yeqon's looming presence. I willed their concealments to hold.

"Where did you find these?" Yeqon sniffed them, "You can't trust fresh ones, boy. They need to be trained to yield. They're wild, desperate cretins who will turn on you in a heartbeat. You, my son, don't yet have the skill to bend their souls to your will."

Yeqon moved towards Koi, who averted his milky, dead eyes and feigned fear as Yeqon yanked out a clump of his hair. Koi screeched, and I wondered if it had really hurt. Yeqon rolled the hairs between his fingers and held them up to his nose. His attention rested on Koi as his nostrils drew in the scent. His pupils darkened further. Koi hacked through a fake coughing fit, putrid drool pooling in the corners of his pustular lips.

Yeqon flicked the hair to the ground and grabbed Koi's head. His fingers curled through Koi's remaining hair, dull with death and falling from his scalp with every forceful tug. Koi winced and snivelled, his pain a mask for the seething rage that had to be boiling beneath his disguise. Yeqon shoved him away.

His eyes flickered to me but fell back on Rik, "I said, boy, where did you get them?"

"I-I…"

"If you stutter once more, I'll rip out your tongue."

Yeqon moved through the group. They cowered together as Rogues should.

"I'd heard talk of a cemetery near the place where the Watchers held me," Rik said. "I sneaked out once they trusted me and found these Rogues after a few nights living off rodents and scrabbling among the headstones. I returned the next night to bribe them with bloodied bandages I stole from the sick. I promised them more if they did what I said. They made a good diversion when I kidnapped Sophia," he lied so eloquently under distress.

As soon as Rik said my name, Yeqon couldn't resist any longer. He turned on his heals to face me. His Rogues spluttered and shuffled closer for the show.

I looked straight into his eyes without blinking. He was so close I saw the pulse in his neck drumming rapidly. I imagined slicing it open.

Yet the room felt like it was closing in. These thoughts were just my imaginings, things I needed to make happen. I just had to wait for the right time, but we hadn't devised when that would be or how I would attack him. I had to wing it, and that felt all levels of dangerous.

Yeqon circled around me, "Well done, my son. You did your job well."

"Thank you, Father," Rik yanked me up, nearly scalping me in the process. His cheek rested against mine, "Well played, sister. You have been such a good actress."

Rik's low laugh caught me off guard as he shoved me into Yeqon's chest. I kicked and elbowed Yeqon as he spun me around, only to see the excited blush on Rik's face. Yeqon leaned into my ear, his pulse thrumming against my skin. He whispered with a barely restrained thrill.

"And that, my dear, is a well-trained soldier."

Chapter Thirteen

Enl'iel kneeled before Gedz'iel, her hands out front.

"Forgive me. I have deceived all who have trusted me for my own selfish needs," her voice wavered. Rules made sense to her; breaking them was an uncomfortable departure she only resorted to in the direst circumstances.

Taking up the entire door frame, Gedz'iel recalled his wings and nodded at someone behind him to leave them.

Enl'iel trembled as the heavy door closed with a *thud*. She lowered her eyes in deference to the benevolent leader whose trust she had shattered.

"Look at me, Enl'iel."

His face blurred through her tears. Shouting from the floor below reached up through the ground. Gedz'iel shuffled and tilted his ear to it.

She held her hands higher, awaiting the bite of shackles. His energy weighed on her from above, its goodness too much to bear. She felt insignificant, a failure. A distrustful outcast who no longer deserved her privileged position.

"Please descend me. I deserve nothing less."

Gedz'iel kneeled before her. He gently cupped her chin and raised her face.

"Why would I descend you, young Enl'iel?"

Confused, she looked into his eyes. They were soft, his mark calm. She sniffed and bit her lip to quell its tremor. Was this a test? Her fingers worked their way up to her pendant, and she twirled it. A tear rolled down her cheek.

"I am a daughter of evil. I lied about it for my own gain."

He wiped her tear away and pushed errant hairs away from her puffy eyes. She struggled to not look away from his intense gaze.

"I beg you not to punish Brennan. He trusted me. I used his love against him and promised I would reveal the truth, but I became too much of a coward as the years passed."

Gedz'iel's silence accelerated her nervous fiddling. The ground shook under her knees.

"I thought my heritage could help me to subvert Belial. I can sense his presence, which has helped me many times to divert him from us and to protect Sophia."

Gedz'iel held up a hand to quiet her and stood as the sounds from below intensified. The ground tremored again. He moved towards the door. Looking back over his shoulder, he threw her a weapon from his heavy belt. Enl'iel's eyes fell upon the sword, confused.

"It seems there's a disturbance in the Zythros room," he said. "You'll probably need this."

The door whined open, and he held his arm out for her to follow. Guards thundered past.

Enl'iel glanced from the weapon to him, too scared to move.

"I don't understand."

"I have always known what you are. It is why we chose you to care for Sophia."

Enl'iel's hand flew to her chest, "What?"

"You rose above your heritage's temptation when you could have used it as an excuse to choose a dark path. Your secret was hidden from all but me. Now, pull yourself together. I have precious few soldiers of worth available and you, dear Enl'iel, are not someone I can do without."

Enl'iel's hand fell onto the sword. She rose. The relief made her feel light, almost giddy. She felt the sword's power, let it take the shame away….and ran to Gedz'iel.

Gedz'iel took Enl'iel's hand and transferred them to the Zythros room. Chaos met them. Tables were upturned against the doorway. Dozens of Keepers buzzed in circles overhead. Someone was screaming. An accented, desperate, and expletive-laden rant bellowed over the rushing guards. An orb exploded, followed by demands for someone to calm down.

Just outside the doorway, Kristen leaned against the wall, her bloodied fingers grasping for balance. Her breaths were laboured. Gedz'iel kicked in the tables to free up the doorway and ordered guards through.

"See to her, Enl'iel," Gedz'iel said.

"Kristen?" Enl'iel scooped her up and sat Kristen out of the way under a clutch of vine below A'vexia blossoms.

Kristen groaned; her head flopped back into the foliage. Disarrayed bandages hung from the wounds on her neck, the pink tissue only just healed. Fresh blood drizzled down from a deep gash across her forehead.

"What happened? Why are you here?" Enl'iel's hands glimmered with diagnostic energy. She smoothed them over Kristen's body to search for more serious injuries. She sighed with relief. Kristen was physically intact, and a quick pulse cauterised the head wound.

Kristen pointed shakily towards the room from where Enl'iel could hear fighting. Cold rushed down the back of her neck, and the E'lan stung. The energy that snapped overhead confused her. Above the shouts of the guards, she heard a familiar yet misplaced laugh.

Thomas rushed past in battered battle gear.

"There you are!" he squatted and kissed Kristen's cheek, "You shouldn't be here."

There was an explosion in the Zythros room, and another contingent of guards thundered past.

Thomas pulled Kristen close. "Stay safe," he kissed her cheek again and looked at Enl'iel. "The Alchemae have been reading Kristen's thoughts to communicate with her. She knows what's going on," he stood, pulled an arrow from his quiver, and cocked it in the bow, "All I know is that Jaz has disappeared."

He sped off after the guards towards the violence.

Enl'iel shook her head. "She's been kidnapped? Again?" she cupped her mouth and puffed into her hands. None of this made sense. Enl'iel turned back to Kristen. "Is this true?"

Kristen nodded; her eyes half closed. She held Enl'iel's hand against her temple, grunted, and shook her head. Enl'iel shut her eyes. She drew on the weary energy of Kristen's brain, her fingers tingling with the synaptic activation as she drew out Kristen's episodic memories.

A shape had rushed through the Stasis room, leaping over beds and knocking Alchemae to the floor, killing some of the gentle healers with red orbs.

Through Kristen's eyes, she saw the perpetrator. Enl'iel felt Kristen screaming in her own head. Kristen had grabbed a broom as a makeshift weapon when she'd seen a sweet face screwed up in hatred. She swung the bristles back and forth as Jaz had sauntered towards her.

"Stupid human," Jaz had said. *"Get out of my way before I squash you."*

Kristen had swung the broom. Jaz lashed out, and her fist connected with Kristen's head. The memory blurred; Kristen had fallen to the floor. In the dimness of Kristen's vision, Jaz had leaned down, her cheeks flushed with excitement. She blew her short black hair from her eyes, her cherubic pout pulled into a malicious grin.

Jaz had laughed, *"Cat got your tongue?"*

Kristen had tried to jostle with her, but Jaz pinned her arms to the floor.

"Hmm, pretty. Behave yourself, and I might find a use for you once we rise."

The memory blurred again when Jaz had slapped Kristen's face. Kristen had struggled harder, her breaths short and sharp, but a flash stilled her. Jaz had held a hand above Kristen's face, her fingertips glimmering with the dying glower of an orb.

Cael had fallen out of his wheelchair, motionless beside Devon.

"Who am I, you ask?" Jaz' delighted grin had spread. *"Who do you think I am?"*

Kristen heaved her torso, shaking her head defiantly as the mark of A'vean had seared across the familiar face, *"It has not been at all fun. Not until now. You can blame that stinking healer thing. I would have waited a little longer if he hadn't started poking at me. It feels so lovely to stretch!"* Jaz surveyed her handiwork in the upturned Stasis room as she sat astride Kristen. *"Freedom awaits!"*

Jaz stood, dusted off her simple patient gown, and smoothed a hand through her pixie cut.

"Stay still and be a good human, or move and be a dead one... your choice."

The memory faded, and Kristen rolled over.

Enl'iel's hand jerked back from Kristen, her mouth dry. "Stay... here," she swallowed for moisture. "Don't move until someone comes back for you."

Enl'iel ran into the Zythros room. The E'lan's lightning crackled across the ceiling. Guards encircled the orange stone, wide wings bright. They were armed and pointed their swords out front. The Zythros stone had been pushed aside. Jaz balanced atop it, a bag dangling from her hand. Her eyes were dark and crazed, her mouth an evil grin.

"Stand down," Gedz'iel called with forced calm. "Surrender before you are hurt," he stood outside the circle of guards without a weapon and with his hands by his side.

Jaz held the bag out and jiggled it above Gedz'iel's head, "Are you mad? I have it in my hands! I'll destroy it here and now!"

She flicked her hand to draw an orb and held it close enough to singe the bag.

Enl'iel squinted, trying to see the energy within the concealment. "Who are you?" No one heard Enli'el in the confusion. Whomever it was, they were strong and they weren't Jaz.

Gedz'iel pushed forwards, "What do you want, Anjou'elle?"

Enl'iel gasped. Her heart missed a beat. If this was Anjou'elle, Jaz was dead. She'd known there was something wrong with the girl, but this… anger surged beneath her pain.

Anjou'elle shimmered and shook away Jaz' image.

Gedz'iel sharpened the edges of his wings into laser-like blades. "What have you done with the human girl?"

Anjou'elle laughed. She stretched to her full height, perfectly balanced on the tip of the stone which hummed with the sheer power in the room.

"Oh, I like a man with big pterugia!" she patted her heart and blew him a kiss.

Enl'iel stepped closer to Gedz'iel. "Where's Jasmine?" her voice sharp, her furious mark pulsing.

Gedz'iel shook his head at her. Enl'iel complied. She wished to string Anjou'elle up, but after recent events, Gedz'iel's word was her command.

Gedz'iel's eyes followed the swinging bag, "Where is Jasmine?"

"Ah, such a fun human," Anjou'elle tapped a finger to her lips and batted her lashes. "Such sass! Entertaining despite her dirty mouth. Such language from a young lady!" Anjou'elle wriggled a finger, sighed, and swung the bag onto her shoulder. "What wonderful help she was in the end though. You people are so willing to save humans that you don't see danger right under your noses," she shook her head and shrugged.

"I will ask you a final time, where is the human girl?" Gedz'iel's energy was reaching its steely zenith.

Enl'iel, along with the guards, stepped back.

Anjou'elle rolled her eyes and waved off the question. "Oh, she's somewhere, I suppose. Whether it's this realm or that, I honestly couldn't say now, really," Anjou'elle preened herself and blew a kiss at a guard. "I wanted to keep her, but sister is such a bore," she huffed.

"Elmas?" Gedz'iel called without taking his eyes off Anjou'elle, who watched as Elmas pushed through the anxious crowd.

Elmas bowed, "Yes, Master Gedz'iel."

"You know Jasmine?"

"Yes, I recall her well."

"Take a small group to Pouancé. Search the manor."

Elmas called Mehmet and took his hand. With three other guards, they utilised the power of Gedz'iel's touch to transfer.

Anjou'elle screeched with maniacal laughter, "Good luck! Sister has probably fed her to a Rogue by now. I believe she keeps a few spares somewhere."

Two guards stepped towards her. One looked over his shoulder at Gedz'iel.

"Uh, uh, uh!" she waved her finger. "You want this?" she poked the bag and raised her eyebrows. "Let me leave peacefully, and I'll leave it with you."

Gedz'iel held up his hand for the guards to halt. "Go then."

Enl'iel rushed forwards. "I don't understand," her mouth hung open as she glanced between him and Anjou'elle and the precious cargo Anjou'elle had hijacked. "But…"

"Be my guest," Gedz'iel said. "You are free to leave."

Anjou'elle's eyes widened, then thinned.

"Rubbish," she sneered at the guards. "Your dogs will stop me."

Enl'iel hoped this was the case. There were plenty to chase Anjou'elle down. Did Gedz'iel plan to let Anjou'elle leave and follow her to Nephr'eus?

Gedz'iel quirked his eyebrow. "They won't. I need them elsewhere to fight a more powerful enemy… Yeqon. You are merely a boil on my arse."

Anjou'elle's face darkened. Her mouth puckered as she glared at Gedz'iel. She huffed, and a smile tugged at her lips.

"Send them out then," she pointed at the guards, then to the door.

Gedz'iel flicked his hands, and just he and Enl'iel remained in the room. Anjou'elle's laughter echoed around the room.

"Go," Gedz'iel said. "You're wasting my time. Take your prize as well if you wish. We'll find another way."

Enl'iel's mouth dropped again, but she forced herself to trust him, as he had trusted her.

Anjou'elle hugged the bag to her chest, her eyes wide.

"I have your word that I can leave of my own accord?"

She looked at the ceiling. Gedz'iel looked up as well.

He raised his hands towards it, "Why are you still here?"

Anjou'elle leaned forwards to double-check the empty doorway. She looked down her nose at Gedz'iel and shook her head. Her wings unveiled, and her mark crept across her cheek and whorled beneath her eye. The E'lan stuttered as she prepared to transfer.

She cocked her head to the side, "Well, we shall call this a bargain. I'll grant you leniency, perhaps, when Sister and I rule, hm?"

"I don't bargain with Daimon, but I won't fight you," Gedz'iel pointed sharply. "Get out of here."

"I'll remember your insult," Anjou'elle began to fade in and out, a bright light encapsulating her.

Everything Sophia had sacrificed was about to vanish with the Daimon.

"Gedz'iel? Are you sure?" Enl'iel asked.

She couldn't help it; doubt invaded her thoughts. Gedz'iel tilted her face towards Anjou'elle.

Anjou'elle shot up towards freedom, her laughter trickling down to them.

A heavy *thud* followed.

Enl'iel jumped. Gedz'iel squinted at the ceiling. Something clattered to the floor in front of his feet and rolled on its side. He smiled whilst Enl'iel flushed with surprise.

"Oh my…"

A few feet from her, the Kaladai cogs spun to a stop. A lingering light shone in Gedz'iel's hand from the orb he'd fired at the Zythros stone, completely disabling it, the moment Anjou'elle had leapt.

Fluid dripped onto Enl'iel's head. She reached up to wipe it away, and her fingers came away red. More droplets spattered onto her cheeks. She dabbed at the iridescent blood striping down her shoulders.

Enl'iel raised her eyes to a dark stain on the chromious lined ceiling. Clumps of flesh fell away until Anjou'elle's remains plummeted to Enl'iel's feet.

Chapter Fourteen

ik lounged on a throne and picked his fingernails with a dagger. He concentrated on his hands whilst Yeqon squeezed me against his body.

My blood boiled. I felt a new wave of nausea as I watched Rik relax. Had he fooled me or was he playing the game too well?

Yeqon chuckled and pulled my hair, "Could the lot of you be more predictably pathetic?"

Koi, Jude, Lorcan, and Brennan returned to their true forms, ablaze and ready to attack. The orb that Yeqon held over my heart had their full attention. Brennan's eyes were like saucers.

"Hold on, Princess."

Koi's eyes followed Yeqon's orb as he moved it along my body.

"Any chance you have, take it," Koi whispered into my mind.

"We could say the same of you, Yeqon. You're a rabid animal to the bait," Koi said with an impressive calm. "We seeded the scent and, of course, like the dog you are, you sniffed it out. Release Sophia and live out your final days here in your Pits, or face I'el and die for good. Your choice," he arched his brows.

Yeqon's laughter rumbled through my hair, hot and foul.

"But it is I'el I wish to face and destroy! You are mere excrement underfoot."

He dragged me closer to his throne. I gritted me teeth when my body jostled against his; however, the movement freed one my arms and brought it within reach of my weapons. I fumbled for the dagger, but Kasadya's black eyes were on me and so unfeeling that they chilled me to the bone. I held my fist against my hip to hide my arm's freedom.

The cavern grumbled. Debris misted the room and clogged up my lashes. Red dust peppered the boys until it covered their white hair.

"Your kingdom is falling, Yeqon," Koi said. "Let her go. She will open the portal, whether you choose freedom or death," he kept the others at arm's length.

"I want both; freedom for myself and death for I'el. Vengeance is all I have, Koi. You of all people should understand the pain of deceit."

A vein under Koi's eye twitched.

"You, too, have felt that warm, satisfying rush of hate."

Yeqon leaned down so his lips brushed my ear. He rubbed his cheek against my hair, and his stubble scratched my skin. I wanted to vomit, felt the knot in my throat. The orb was right under my neck, its heat threatening.

"That's right," he whispered in my ear. "Let it be as it should be," He straightened and turned to Koi. "There is a finite amount of suffrage to be expected from anyone, even I understand this of my own parasitic army."

Yeqon looked to Rik. I squirmed around to see him too. He was still draped across the throne, polishing an apple on his trousers.

"Rik? What are you doing?" I whispered into his mind.

He didn't answer.

Yeqon drew me closer, and I no longer saw Rik. My spine cracked a little with the pressure, but I wriggled my free arm closer to the diamond dagger. It warmed against my thigh.

I was positive I could bring Yeqon down when he was at his egotistical best. I also had my eyes on his lackies, who were keenly watching the boys.

Koi edged closer, "How do you think you'll overwhelm the Throne? Are you that fundamentally deluded to believe you will breach even the first defences? The Knights of A'mageddon are impenetrable."

A tiny, almost imperceptible call was tapping at my thoughts, raking through the molasses that was this dark realm's elemental voice. My pendant picked it up and pulsed against my chest. Koi's eyes darted between Yeqon and I. Did he sense it too?

Yeqon pushed me forwards, and I stumbled. His orb heated my chest guard enough that my skin burnt underneath. We stopped a few feet from Koi, who stayed protectively in front of the others.

I concentrated on the close proximity of my brethren rather than Yeqon's foul tide of negativity. Koi's bravery and self-control buffered me. Brennan's fierce power was a loving, heavenly light. Jude oozed strength and confidence. Lorcan was my ever loyal and brave friend.

I moved my hand ever so slightly again. The dagger's handle grazed my small finger.

"I don't have to win to exact my vengeance," Yeqon growled. "I want to cause chaos, to rip the carpet out from under them, smash the Throne so it will take I'el eons to regroup. I'll take a world for myself, be my own king! This world or another, I don't really care."

His hot breath rolled down my neck, but I hooked my little finger around my blade.

Koi snorted, his eyes keen and sharp, "Your delusions are impressive."

"Surround them!" Yeqon bellowed.

Ged'erel, Asbel, Pineme, and Kasadya moved around them. The little voice grew louder, telling me help was coming.

And my dagger was now tight in my palm.

"Descend them!" Yeqon barked.

Pineme aimed his multi-arrowed crossbow up, and the boys widened their wings.

I plunged my blade backwards, right into Yeqon's thigh. He howled and dropped the orb, which exploded at our feet. I slipped out of his arms and somersaulted to the right, bowling Pineme over and discharging my own orb. His arrows flew everywhere but at us.

I blasted the ground into a small wall of flame between us and them.

Yeqon's bleeding leg drew Rogues from the crevices. They ran at him, lapped his blood from the dust. He kicked at them as he hurried to heal himself, growling viciously. Spittle bubbled in the corners of his mouth.

I moved in front of my friends. A red orb pulsed ready in my hand. My dagger had Yeqon's blood on it; I had what I'd come for. Time to leave.

"Stop!" the voice from the ether called.

In a blinding white haze, Gedz'iel and Ben arrived with… me!

"Do as I say and run when you can," the other me called into my mind.

I drew another orb, protective of the boys, not sure if this was an hallucination.

"Gedz'iel?" I quirked my head in his direction. My attention flitted between my doppelgänger and Ben, who was focussed on Yeqon. His fists were tight, vengeful hammers, his eyes bright A'vean blue.

"Gedz'iel, what is this?" my voice was edgy.

Everyone had frozen, confused as to their next move. I looked the other me up and down, and she returned the gesture. Yeqon and his offsiders seemed every bit as unsure as we did. Rik, however, remained disinterested in the background.

The ground cracked with another seismic cry. I stumbled and fell into Jude.

He pushed me back up. "This is bad shit," he whispered. "Be careful."

I gestured the boys back, "Back up. I don't know what the hell this is."

Thick lava bubbled up from a gaping fissure that separated us from Yeqon. Hissing steam rained its boiling wrath down on us, drenching us. The other me and Gedz'iel seemed unperturbed to be on the other side with Yeqon. Ben flanked Gedz'iel like an equal and moved only in response to subtle movements of Gedz'iel's hands. They seemed to be communicating, glancing between each other, us, and Yeqon.

"What is this?" Yeqon thundered.

He glared at Ben but stole glances at me and the other me. His chest muscles rippled in anger. His lackies crouched and swung their weapons in anticipation.

"Boy!" he pointed at Rik, who was paying more attention now. He sat up, looked around the room without emotion on his face, and tossed Yeqon his trident. Yeqon rammed it into the ground. White jets exploded from its points, breaking shards off the ceiling. Yeqon aimed it at me, then the other me, Gedz'iel, and finally at Ben, who remained unmoved by Yeqon's aggression. Yeqon's attention finally settled on the other me.

"This is the end, Yeqon," the other me said. "I'm tired. Enough have died. I can't find the last elements for the portal, so I'm here to give myself to you. All I ask is that you stop attacking humans and leave the Watcher communities to live in peace in their sanctuaries. You can either do what you wish with what lays above ground or find the portal yourself to have your vengeance. Here," she threw something at his feet. Metallic clatter rung through the air and pinged against the rock. Silver shimmered under the blaring light. The brilliant discs of the Kaladai came to rest.

My head hurt; my lungs dry," Who are you?"

Koi's eyes were as wide as mine and Yeqon's.

"You!" Yeqon pointed at a Rogue, "Pick it up."

The bony Rogue shuddered. He moved towards the Kaladai cogs, yet his bloated face spoke of abject terror. Drool bubbled from his loose jaw. His bones crunched when he bent down and his shaking fingers clutched the metal. Smoke charred his bones, which held on tighter despite the Rogue trying to fling it away. What skin remained, bubbled and roasted, the smoked travelled up his arm. He screamed, a pitiful high-pitched squeal, and the chromious' power turned the Rogue to charcoal.

"Grab the dammed thing!" Yeqon pointed at another Rogue. He cowered but moved towards Yeqon as though compelled by an unseen force. His eyes darted to the remnants of the last Rogue.

"Hurry," Yeqon yelled.

The Rogue sped up, head bowed at Yeqon's feet and heaving coarse breaths. Yeqon ripped the Rogue's clothes from its body, "Use this." The now naked Rogue wound the cloth around one hand and scooped up the precious artefact from the ashes.

Its silver reflected across his eyes as he held it up in greedy paws. Yeqon roared, his laugh deep. "You give in this easily, after such little blood spilled?" he smiled at his brothers. "One wonders if you really are the Earth-born. No angel of worth would be swayed by so few sacrifices."

Ged'erel moved towards the other me. "Enough of your antics. Let's kill her and be done with it," he wriggled his finger at the other me. "Come then, prove your worth. Die for your cause."

The tune of her heart, the smell of vanilla and lavender… she reached for her pendant and twirled it. My blood froze in my veins.

It was Enl'iel.

"Koi?"

"Hold your position. I don't know what she's doing."

Enl'iel offered her hand to Ged'erel. The gentleness with which he handled her was anachronistic, like it would negate his intent.

I couldn't watch. Why weren't the others stopping this? Why were they so clueless?

"Get her away from him, Koi! She can't do this!"

I rushed towards the fiery division, but Brennan pulled me back by my arm. He shook his head, his eyes red-rimmed. Orbs burned in my palms, but I wasn't sure what to do.

I screamed, "For I'el's sake, this is madness!"

The Kaladai was in Yeqon's hands. Enl'iel was in his grasp. I couldn't see a way out without a huge massacre, without utter failure.

Brennan shoved past me. Tension oozed from the boys behind me. Sweat beaded down Brennan's arms and mixed with the steamy drizzle.

From within Ged'erel's clutches, Enl'iel watched on passively with wide eyes.

I lunged at Brennan, shook his armour, "What are you doing?"

He paid me no attention; he was too focussed on Enl'iel. His eyes sparkled with intrigue, widened with shock, then fell with despair.

"What are you telling him?" I called to her.

Enl'iel's poise and serenity in Ged'erel's arms was incredulous. My heart twisted until it hurt.

Her eyes… my eyes… shifted to me.

"You can stop the charade now, Enl'iel," she called. "I can't have you getting hurt too."

She was every bit my no-nonsense Enl'iel, but in *my* skin. Ged'erel sniffed her hair, his eyes flickering to me and back to her. Pineme, Asbel, and Kasadya closed in on him.

Ben and Gedz'iel didn't intervene.

I thumped my palm against my chest, "I'm the real me!"

I knew what she was up to, she thought she was saving me, but she'd dumped us into a heap of trouble. They still didn't trust me. She still didn't think I could help myself. If only she knew that I had the blood I'd come for. I was every bit as angry at her as I was terrified for her.

"Get her outta there!" I shouted at Gedz'iel, but he stared past me.

He knew the plan. Why was he ruining it?

Yeqon's eyes were slits, his fist tight around the trident. He limped over to Enl'iel and flicked at a lock of her hair with its points. His glare was darker than sin.

He growled at Ged'erel, "What is this trickery?"

Ged'erel edged away from his leader and dragged Enl'iel with him.

Yeqon spat at his feet. "What are you doing?" he stabbed his trident into the ground. "Step away, Ged'erel, or wear my trident around your throat," Yeqon raised it like a spear, poised to impale him.

Asbel, Pineme, and Kasadya held their weapons higher, their Daimon markings lit with excitement.

"We do what needs to be done together, Yeqon," Ged'erel said in a grating tone. "Enough of your ridiculous games. We have worn them down as you instructed, and now it must end. She is willing to sacrifice herself for her people. Are you willing to sacrifice your ego for us?"

I didn't dare move.

Yeqon flushed beet red. He jutted forwards, his trident shaking.

Enl'iel laughed, "You want to have a civil war now, when you have me? You're more stupid than I thought."

Yeqon pointed the weapon at her. His teeth grated together.

"Let them go," Enl'iel said. "Do you want to waste your energy on them, or get on with whatever you need from me?"

Enl'iel was scarily relaxed; ridiculously calm. She was convincingly me.

Ged'erel nodded. Yeqon's right eye twitched as he stared her down.

New steam vents choked the air, and more lava spilled across the floor.

"Your world is crumbling," Enl'iel said. "Take this opportunity while you have it," she lowered her head in submission.

I threw myself towards her. Brennan and Lorcan caught my arms, preventing me from getting to her.

I stamped on Brennan's foot, "Let go!"

"Settle down, Princess."

Nothing made sense. I wanted to release my wings, to slap the boys down with them, but I didn't want to hurt them.

I elbowed Brennan, "Why are you allowing this? That's your soul mate!"

I caught Ben's eyes, but he quickly looked away.

Gedz'iel bowed, "I trust we will never meet again."

Yeqon's eyes narrowed to suspicious slits as Gedz'iel retreated across the molten crack towards us. Gedz'iel's steely eyes were on me.

"I cannot believe you!" I said. "She's sacrificing herself for nothing! And you gave him the Kaladai?"

Gedz'iel grabbed me and looked into my eyes. "Enl'iel, we must accept that we must sacrifice for the greater good. There has been far too much loss," he turned me to face the boys. "Keep quiet," he whispered into my ear.

I yelped at a painful *thud* against my back.

When I was half collapsed from the fading pain in my spine, Gedz'iel held me up.

"Enl'iel came to buy us time as we hunted for the last piece of the Kaladai," he said to Yeqon. "That time has expired."

I twisted, "No! Stop, this isn't true, It's me! Listen to me! I have what I need!"

Gedz'iel tightened his grasp until I released the two orbs I'd called upon. They exploded at our feet and knocked us back. I recovered first and lurched towards the lava current, slightly deafened and unsteady.

"Don't touch me!" I turned on both he and Brennan who moved at me again. They halted as I drew another orb. My head swivelled back and forth between them and the others. Ben hovered on the other side of the fire, far enough from Yeqon, but not close enough to me.

"Ben, you know who I am. Tell him *I* am me!"

He stared at Enl'iel.

I slammed an orb down near him, "Don't you bloody do this to her! She loved you, defended you!" Another orb left my hand.

Ben tumbled to the left and commando-rolled before his head would have touched the outer edges of the boiling river. He stood; his face screwed up in annoyance.

The other me sobbed, "Please, Enl'iel, Ben has no part in this. He belongs in this realm; he can't stay with us." Fake tears billowed over her fake eyes. She pointed Ben towards Rik, "Go on now."

I didn't believe her. Ben would never return to this place of torture. He clenched his fists and sneaked a fleeting glimpse in my direction. His eyes glimmered like he was trying to tell me something. He moved with a disjointed lack of commitment as he stepped over the narrowest part of the lava and squatted near Rik, who eased forwards and offered him an apple. Ben flicked it away. It bounced down the steps and split in two, just like I had.

"This isn't right!" I screamed over and over.

Yeqon's filthy henchman raised their weapons higher. Supercharged with the darkness of their souls, they burned bright and deadly. The boys jostled and hissed, threatening Yeqon's crew for getting too close.

Yeqon lowered his trident as though he was listening, as though he was caught off guard by the dissent.

"Look, I'll prove it's me," I yelled, desperation hitching my voice. "Open your wings, Enl'iel. Go on."

I dared her to do what I knew she couldn't. It was a risk, but I needed to end this. Fear flashed through her eyes.

"Don't do this," she whispered into my mind.

"You can't, can you? You weren't born with any. Here, look at mine."

The Daimon mumbled amongst themselves, sly smirks on their faces. Even Yeqon smiled, his eyes sparkling with dark delight. Was he measuring his next move? He wouldn't be satisfied with an impersonation of the Earth-born. He still believed he needed my blood, and I knew he wanted me for more than that. His knuckles were white around my precious artefacts. I would get them back and save Enl'iel from her stupid loyalty.

Energy coursed from my belly and sung up my spine.

Nothing happened.

I tried again. Nothing.

I turned around and smacked Gedz'iel's chest, "What did you do to me?"

He grabbed my wrists to hold me back.

I balled my hands into fists, "What... have... you... done?" I clenched my teeth so tightly I thought they might crack.

Yeqon roared with laughter. I glanced over my shoulder and saw a soft white energy surrounding Enl'iel. Strong wings rippled around her.

Words were lost on me, I even started to doubt that I was even me. That snaking doubt that harboured deep in my gut uncoiled with a vicious snap. I squeezed my eyes shut, "I don't understand."

My arms went limp.

Gedz'iel let me go and pushed me behind him.

"Enough!" Gedz'iel yelled, "What's done is done."

I didn't know what to do. Did I fight back? Did I acquiesce to this madness?

"Yes! I agree! Enough!" Yeqon lunged at Ged'erel and grabbed Enl'iel's neck. They locked eyes, "Yield, Ged'erel!"

Enl'iel's cheeks bulged and reddened.

Ged'erel sighed, "Make it quick."

He shoved Enl'iel into Yeqon's greedy arms, and my vision went black for a moment. Yeqon hoisted her to the top step, away from us.

Gedz'iel tugged at my shoulder, "It's time to go."

"No, no, *no*!" I writhed, a new orb threatening just beneath my skin.

"I agree with her," Yeqon said. "Stay, why don't you?"

A horde of Rogues gathered around us.

Yeqon dipped his trident's points into a lava stream oozing from the wall and held it to Enl'iel's face. She closed her eyes but didn't pull away. He nicked her cheek. She winced and bit her lip. Her chin quivered, but she didn't make a sound. A droplet emerged from the open flesh. Yeqon smeared it away with his thumb, rubbed his fingers together, and pursed her face between his crimson fingers. His face was terrifyingly close to hers. She didn't flinch; she was poised and defiant.

"I'll not look a gift horse in the mouth. It was only a matter of time before you relented to all the death," Yeqon said. "I knew you were weak. The journey shall end, and you and I shall complete this quest together."

He kissed her temple and hugged her possessively into his side. He inhaled her scent. His hand clawed around a fistful of her hair and pulled her head backwards. He licked her throat and finished with a kiss on her ear.

Acid coated my throat. Brennan clenched his fists, and his mark blazed. Every muscle in his face twitched. I was furious that he did nothing. I was furious that I didn't know what held him back.

"First order of this new day, a little entertainment," Yeqon said.

He pressed his trident into her cheek again. Her nostrils flared, and a tear slid down her blistered skin.

It was only then that I noticed the orb forming in her free hand. I felt like I could breathe again.

Yeqon and the others were too distracted by their perceived victory to notice, but Asbel watched from behind the thrones, intrigued. He rubbed a shiny silver scar on his neck as though it pained him.

"Descend them all," Yeqon yelled. "Feed their bones to the Rogues!"

Rogues charged out of the crevices of the cavern. Yeqon pulled Enl'iel away towards the fissure that led to Oblivion. Rik followed at a run, not so much as a glance back at us, as though I meant nothing at all. Asbel kept his distance but followed them. He disappeared amongst the gnashes and cries of the undead as Ged'erel, Pineme, and Kasadya launched at us.

Chapter
Fifteen

Gedz'iel thumped me in the back again and hauled me away from Kasadya's blade. He rose into the air with me dangling under his arm, the same pain as before zinging up and down my spine.

The cavern filled with a putrid fog, and the boys disappeared into its soup. Shadows flitted through it as the Rogues searched for a meal. If we fell at the wrong moment, one of us would be easy pickings. Brennan rose then dove headlong back into the stench. They dodged and attacked Pineme, Kasadya, and Ged'erel, who moved with the fog's tide and hid amongst the Rogues. Orange fireballs, stinking Rogue remains, cut through the fog. The Rogues were easy victims to a roomful of A'vean wrath.

I wriggled against Gedz'iel, "I don't care how important you are — you've made a big bloody mistake!"

"Hush," he dodged an arrow. My stomach flipped from the movement and the unmistakable feeling of a transfer.

"Don't you dare take me away!"

"You have a quest to finish."

The pull in my gut strengthened.

"Quest? You gave him my artefacts! What's left to finish?"

My elbow connected with a rib. Gedz'iel didn't flinch. My back burned, but the sting was comforting; he'd given me my wings back.

"Do you really think I would offer him victory?" Gedz'iel asked. "They're fake, Sophia. Enl'iel is a distraction that gives us time to get ahead of him with less carnage to the human world."

My arms flailed as the room faded in and out, clawing for the here and now.

"Don't sacrifice her," I pleaded. "We were meant to catch him."

"You have his blood on your dagger, that's all we needed. We do what needs to be done for the greater good; it's her sacrifice to offer."

His voice seemed fainter, as though we were fading away. I heard Jude scream, saw the blur of Brennan, Lorcan, and Koi darting below. Stars and blackness whizzed by in a dizzying spiral. I closed my eyes and recalled Enl'iel being led away, seeing Ben, Rik, and Asbel slink towards Oblivion, but the transfer pulled me the opposite way. I felt like I was going to rip in two. Gedz'iel told me to stop resisting, so I resisted even further and willed myself away from him. His warmth disappeared; his voice drowned out by the silence of nothingness.

My feet sunk deep into cool, soft sand as I landed at a run. I stumbled forwards, panting. Every hair stood on end. My eyes were so wide with caution that they hurt. Water rushed in the darkness. Small cries for help pin-pricked an otherwise vacuous quiet. Above, there was a black void. To my left, ran the wild Blood River of Souls, which carried the dammed along its current.

I patted myself down. Everything was where it needed to be, so I waited. Yeqon would come this way, the portal back to the earthen realm lay here, and he would want to take Enl'iel to the elusive portal he thought she could find. I'd surprise him, save her, and never look back.

It wasn't long before I heard something. Measured breaths; a slow strong heartbeat followed by a rapid one. There was nowhere to hide along the expansive beach, so I did the only thing I could.

I entered the Blood River of Souls.

The current's impossible cold didn't mask the frigid stab of terror that tried to coax my bravado away. I waded past its constant passengers. A hand tried to grab me, but the current was too strong and pulled it away, its familiar eyes wide with horror as it sailed away amongst a thousand other corpses. Pathos had met his fate. Pity crossed my mind for a moment, then I blanked it and left him to his destiny.

The river begged me to give in to it, tugging at my fears. Images of spiders flashed through my vision. I blinked them away, remembering the rivers' hypnotic powers. I closed my mind. I had focus and purpose; I would not flee this time.

I waited, submerged up to my nose. This gave me a clear view of the lunar-like beach. The desperate souls that bobbed around my head provided a handy camouflage as someone arrived overhead. Their shape was a mere blot in the inky darkness above. The sweet and sour voices of lost souls that drifted around them, turned vicious when the newcomers didn't heed their calls for escape. I cracked my knuckles as I watched and waited for the right time to strike.

Yeqon landed fifty feet or so away atop a rock. Enl'iel, still looking like a compliant me, dangled under his arm. The fake Kaladai was firm in his grip. Rik and Ben landed behind him, whilst Asbel stayed aloft.

Yeqon paid no heed to any of them, his focus obsessive over the prizes in his grasp. Enl'iel's hand pulsed behind her, its secret shimmer reflected in Asbel's eyes. He lowered a little, his attention shooting between her, Yeqon, and then back to the void above. His hand fell to his sword but pulled away again. Ben had noticed and watched as Asbel shook his head like he was having a conversation with himself.

Yeqon paced towards the lapping shoreline, and I tensed… ready to attack…

Then Asbel flew towards Yeqon, sword high above his head.

"There is a weapon!" he roared.

Ben and Rik raced forwards, cutting up the sand from different directions, both headed towards Yeqon and Enl'iel at the same time.

Yeqon spun, Enl'iel a rag doll in his arms. He didn't see Enl'iel's orb, but he saw Rik's dagger.

Ben fell on Rik and rammed his face into the sand. Rik's arms flapped, unable to break free, and he dropped the dagger.

Asbel pulled up and hovered high above Yeqon.

"Stay down, dog!" Ben grunted as Rik bucked underneath.

"Do something about these cretins," Yeqon barked.

Asbel ran a finger across the scar on his neck, his narrow eyes on Enl'iel's orb. He just hung there, doing nothing whilst Ben and Rik cursed and struggled on the sand. Blood stained the chalky white.

Enl'iel pulled her arm back. Her fingers moulded the orb, ready to strike. I froze, but Asbel shook his head, beat his wings, and soared down towards Enl'iel, "It is her, not the boy!"

Yeqon followed Asbel's attention and spotted the glow by his side. He flung his arm around his body and punched Enl'iel's face with the Kaladai. Her light died, and she went limp.

Kasadya burst into the cavern, his transfer igniting it like a lightning bolt. I froze. His fatigued eyes dilated in anger when they focussed on Ben and Rik. He plunged towards them. Yeqon roared at the sight. Asbel lurched out of the way, uncertainty blanching his face again.

Ben and Rik dove out of Kasadya's way, and he skidded across the sand. The heat of his wings scorched the sand, leaving glass shards in his wake. Rik fell on Ben again, shoved him in the chest. Both were bloody-nosed and spluttering.

Yeqon circled, a cruel smile on his lips.

"I was trying to save her, you fool!" Rik screamed at Ben.

Ben coughed and spat sand. His head snapped up, "Duck!"

Kasadya buzzed towards them. He arced his sword low and missed Rik by inches. Ben somersaulted and kicked Kasadya in the chest, which knocked him into a slump on the river's edge.

Yeqon began to retreat towards the river. I poised my energy for him; the other two would have to look after themselves.

Asbel's eyes cleared from the indecision that seemed to haunt them. He rose high in the air, stretched his wings wide, and circled his sword above Ben and Rik. Their eyes met, and they nodded at each other.

Rik shot straight up and plunged the point of his wing through Asbel's heart. Asbel erupted into flame. His agonised soul zoomed for the river, where it fell into its eternity.

Yeqon dragged Enl'iel into the shallow water. I turned my back on my brother and my… and Ben. When Yeqon was waist deep, Enl'iel roused as the freezing current lapped at her face. Fear showed in her eyes, but she stayed slack and reignited her hand.

I ducked under the wicked water. Liquid howls stroked along the flow and bit at my calm. Vile things poked and prodded me, threatening my balance. Taking one step at a time was precarious in the thick sludge. I held my pendant and focussed on beauty, such as Grey and my long-lost Shadow. It swept the tarantulas into the depths of my memories until I felt only sand under my feet.

Souls darted away from Yeqon and Enl'iel, revulsed by her orb's positive glow. Yeqon kept moving, unaware or uncaring.

I fought my way through the onslaught of the dead, trying not to startle him and risk Enl'iel. Her fingers teased the orb out until it filled her hand. Once she was chest-deep and her head barely above the writhing red, she struck.

Her arm whipped through the current, aiming for the side of Yeqon's chest. A headless torso barrelled into them at the same moment and she missed. She seared his ribs before his arm came down on her head and the chromious cogs knocked her unconscious again. The river screamed with delight as her blood dribbled into it.

I pushed on through more insistent tugs at my body. I wouldn't allow death to take my Enl'iel.

Yeqon's angry growl travelled through the water. His impatience quickened his pace, but I slithered closer by the second. In his hurry, Yeqon hadn't noticed that Enl'iel looked like herself again.

Yeqon stopped in front of the small, shimmering portal. A large skeleton barrelled into him where the current was fastest, but he knocked it out of the way… and saw Enl'iel for who she was. He dropped her and clawed at his head; his bared teeth clenched. He kicked at her. She sunk to the bottom, but he pulled her back up and stared at her face. His moment of his confusion was my moment.

I struck. My wings cut through the river, and he spotted me when I was just feet away. A second of astonishment washed over his face. He turned away as if to flee to the portal, which gave me the moment I needed. I sliced across his spine. He sunk to his knees and dropped Enl'iel, who coasted away from me and disappeared with the current. Yeqon rolled on the sand. The water's inhabitants schooled around him, hungry for his blood. They rushed at his face, pawed at his spine, whilst I wondered what Enl'iel would want me to do.

I conjured a red orb whilst Yeqon struggled to push himself up. The current now separated — nothing wanted to touch me or my orb's luminous pulse.

Yeqon grimaced at me as he rolled on his side and hauled himself up, swatting the excited dead out of his way. I flew towards him. He scrambled for a weapon, but the hungry creatures hampered him and I rammed him into the rock wall. My orb exploded and I hurtled backwards until I crashed into a school of skeletons. Clambering through the mash of bones, I found Yeqon a few feet away. He was wobbly on his feet, dazed and bloody. The river seemed to rush faster, either excited or terrified by our disturbance. It blurred the distance between us. I sliced my wings though the distortion and landed ankle-deep in the sludge in front of him. His fractured jaw hung open, and his free hand threw an orb at me. A blood-thirsty soul got in its way, its bones blasting into a million shards that washed away on the hungry current.

Yeqon's lips peeled back, another orb in his battered but still strong hands. I had re-ignited too. Without Enl'iel in front of my target, I could release redemption upon him.

I locked into his bloodshot eyes. He aimed an orb at me, but I was too quick and he was unprepared for my fury. With a flick of my wrist, I lengthened my orbs into long blades. We crashed into each other and spun though the maelstrom. I beat my wings hard, flung him away, and plunged the burning blades into his belly, pinning him to the underworld. Yeqon's head smacked into rock and his face grimaced with agony, yet he didn't drop the fake Kaladai.

My only option was to end him; the bloodshed wouldn't stop whilst he drew breath.

I buried two more shards in his arms. My heart didn't skip a beat when I curled my right wing around, preparing it for his neck. His luminous blood spilled from his head. His eyes rolled white, then slid back into Daimon black. My wing swung for his jugular.

The damned stampeded towards his blood and knocked me back, their blood lust stronger than their fear of my power. Hundreds of souls rushed in, smothering him, trying to feast on him. Yeqon had wriggled one blade out of his arm and worked on the other, but it only added more blood to their frenzy.

I pushed through the hordes of teeth and claws and pulsed my wings wide again. I reached back to pull a new blade from one—

Sharp pain exploded across my face. There was laughter in the back of my mind. I tumbled back. Spots danced in my hazy vision, and I tasted my own blood. My chromious chest guard had dented inwards and pushed into my sternum. I rolled over, and sticky mud sucked me down. My limbs were heavy and awkward in the daze. I crawled towards Yeqon, but the current pounded into me now that it had tasted my blood as well. As I swatted away a skull and a strange blob with teeth, I saw that Yeqon had nearly extinguished the other blade.

A ghastly smile spread across Yeqon's battered face when he saw me. He righted his jaw. It's click echoed through the water, and I shuddered.

I shook my head clear in the river's molasses and pulled two shards from my wings. Summoning all that I had, I beelined for Yeqon and rammed into him.

I thrust one blade into his chest, the other fell from my grip. I pushed myself against him to hold him down. I felt his stubble on my face, heard his head bang against the rock. The hatred I felt from him could never be redeemed. I fumbled against his chest, found the slipperiness of a wound, and shoved my hand into it. He arched in pain. With my other hand, I clawed at his face and smacked it back. He bucked and ripped at the base of my wings. The bite was unbearable. I screamed in my mind and drew the agony's heat to my hand. I shoved my nails deeper into him, tearing at his insides. He seized and his hands jerked, yet he didn't relent. He dug his fingers into my face. I grabbed his hair.

The opalescent portal behind him gave me an idea. I edged us towards it and we fell to our knees, neither ready to relent. I kicked his chest wound with my knee, and he doubled over. I drove a new blade into the back of his neck. He didn't make a sound, but I felt the energy of his pain. Agony strained his face as he grabbed for the weapon. I lunged forwards with another, but he grabbed my legs and flipped me onto my back. He pulled himself up, a bloodied mess.

His eyes travelled all over me as he took a slow-motion step forward. Every muscle in his face twitched. I dragged myself through the sand. He pulled the blade from his neck, closed his fist around it, and leaned back to strike.

I double-barrelled his chest with my feet. He fell backwards into the portal, eyes wide as it swallowed him.

I wanted to roll into a ball and cry, but I dragged myself up, elbowed my way through the corpses, and went after Enl'iel.

Chapter
Sixteen

Snow fell over Pouancé, the manor roof crumbling charcoal under the light dusting.

Elmas pulled her shawl tighter around her shoulders, "Are you sure this is the way?"

"Yes," Matias answered.

Mehmet chuckled and squeezed Elmas' cold fingers, "The Eloi know north from south and east from west, my dear. Have faith."

Mehmet patted Elmas' hand and ducked around a Blackthorn tree. He eased himself and Elmas over the fence onto a gravel drive. They tiptoed through knee-high weeds, their eyes alert.

Being out of their coffee shop was unsettling. Elmas had been comfortable in Turkey for so long that venturing out of just her main street undermined her confidence as a protector of the Earth. Her life had been relative peace.

"It is ruins," her voice a hushed whisper. The breeze picked up her shawl. The vibrant red-and-gold cotton snapped like a whip, and only stayed in place with the golden hair clip that secured it to her umber crown.

Matias raised his hand and they pulled to a stop outside the burnt remains of a stately old home. Blue-and-white tape around the perimeter sectioned the populace off from the charred stones. A warning sign was tacked to a tree in the centre of the front garden. The wet smell of a recently doused fire sour.

Matias grumbled to himself. He drew a deep breath; his chest rose and fell as he tested the air for the elements. Elmas had never felt proficient at this and watched him carefully.

"There is still energy here," Matias said. "I cannot tell if someone resides in this destruction or if it is the remnants from when they departed. It is weak, however. Tread with caution. I will watch for danger out here. Do not hesitate if I call you to retreat, it will be for good cause. Hurry, the E'lan is very disturbed." Matias pointed at the burnt-out ruins.

Elmas dug her fingers into Mehmet's hand

"Fear not," Matias said. "Your age wearies your signature; I will be found before you," he nodded, and she bowed.

Elmas and Mehmet hurried forwards. She glanced back at Matias twice, who stood stone-still as he guarded their small adventure.

Mehmet ducked through a shattered window, "I do coffee better than reconnaissance, my love." Mehmet helped her through the frame, making sure it didn't hurt her. "But I shall do my very best."

"I only hope we find the dear girl," Elmas said.

She wondered how a single human could make any difference to anything? She looked around the degraded surroundings, smelled the charred air, and doubted they would find Jasmine at all, let alone alive.

"As do I," Mehmet shook his head. "So many innocents… It is just not right."

They padded through the moist deluge left by the fire trucks. The still-warm smell of freshly burned furniture mingled with the damp. Drips and cracks shattered the silence. They stopped, listened for a breath, a heartbeat, and moved on when they heard nothing.

"Down there," Elmas pointed to a corridor. "I feel a disturbance that way," her hand fluttered at her chest. Her eyebrows gathered close as she listened harder, "I'm sure it's a heartbeat."

The pale sun shone through an opening in the roof. Tiles and rafters littered the floor, covering most of the parquetry.

"Do you hear that?" Elmas stopped half-way down the entry hall, "It's definitely a heartbeat, don't you think?"

Mehmet tip-toed through the mess and jumped in front of her. He cocked his head to the side, "Yes, there is life here somewhere."

Elmas pointed to her feet, her pulse racing, "Down there. They said she was in a basement room."

Mehmet kneeled and pushed splintered beams out of the way. He touched his ear to the floor, his eyes closed. The corner of his mouth quirked a little, and his brows furrowed. He sat back up and dusted off his hands before running them over his face.

He sighed, "There is someone directly underneath us, but they sound weak. It could well be the girl."

"Let us be careful," Elmas said. "I dread to imagine what could return here."

Mehmet pushed back his long linen sleeves. His palm began to glow against the floor. Elmas held her breath in case the rush of it through her lungs might hide someone's approach. She trusted Matias, but her sheltered life hadn't prepared her for such adventure.

"Just a little, my darling. Just a little," she whispered. Mehmet circled his palm over the floor. The wood gave way to his angelic fire as he burned a hole into the basement. A smooth orange rim cooled to charcoal. A moan carried on the basement's stagnant breath; it rose and lulled, a pained, mourning ululation. Elmas' eyes held Mehmet's, which widened with curiosity. A lustrous trail curled about his cheek as the E'lan came to life.

"Be careful, my love," he said.

"Always, darling."

They dropped into the darkness. Elmas rolled an orb into existence, dull but bright enough that her aging hybrid eyes could pick through the dark towards the desperate call. Damp dungeons overwhelmed the burned smell. The freezing air was still along a corridor lined with old doors.

Elmas sloshed through a puddle. The moan stopped, started again, then stopped once more. Her eyes widened, and she held a hand to her mouth, looking to Mehmet for strength.

"What is that sound?" she asked.

Confused and nervous, Elmas nudged closer to Mehmet. The moan hadn't been human, but she still heard the heartbeat.

Mehmet held up his hand outside a heavy wooden door with an ornate wrought-iron handle. He leaned his ear against the oak. The door rattled. He sprung back, surprise washing across his dark face.

"Careful!" Elmas urged.

The door shook again and more violently.

"Get out," came a throaty whisper.

Elmas grabbed Mehmet's clothes with shaking fingers.

"What is it?" she asked.

Mehmet stood back and examined the door, "Not the source of the energy, but perhaps the source of the whining."

He reached for the handle, but the door shook so hard that the aged bolts screeched out of the filigree hinges. The oak panels bulged, snapped and warped. The wood moved like snakes slithered within it and splinted. It pulsed and writhed into a yawning mouth that screamed unearthly sounds.

A ghoul stretched out of the wood.

Elmas gasped and hugged Mehmet tighter, "For the love of I'el!"

"Get out of my home," the entity said.

Its hiss echoed down the corridor. The door crumbled further with every movement of the revenant. They watched agape and stepped back.

Elmas hid behind Mehmet, her heart racing, "I've not seen one before."

Mehmet crossed his arms and watched the spectre have its tantrum. "Neither have I."

"What do we do?"

Elmas bit her knuckle and peered over Mehmet's shoulder.

"I think we ignore it," Mehmet said. "They cannot hurt us, only intimidate."

Two fists emerged from the door's base. Woody claws unravelled from it and reached towards them.

Elmas' fists shook as she balled them tighter into Mehmet's back.

Mehmet put his hands on his hips, "Desist, spectre. We are not here to disturb you."

He pulled Elmas to his side. A small spattering of his aging wing light brightened the darkness. Elmas took a calming breath and called upon her own wings. They drew forth their full marks, Elmas' dainty and compact whilst Mehmet's plunged around his strong jaw. Their eyes faded and re-emerged in the bright blue of their Watcher heritage. Elmas reached for Mehmet, and he held her hand.

The claws froze, and the mouth closed. An ornately dressed gentleman with a powdered wig and rouged cheeks stepped out of the shattered oak. Moaning, soft like a kitten, echoed from the room behind him.

The ghost bowed. "Sir William," he eyed them up and down. "You are different to M'lady." Sir William's French lilt was heavy with a native English accent.

Elmas was no longer afraid but fascinated.

"He speaks of Nephr'eus no doubt."

"You know, M' Lady?"

Sir William floated closer, grey lips pursed and brows furrowed. His delicate middle-aged face puckered with interest.

"We do," Mehmet said. "Unlike her, we are not here to ask servitude of you. We are here for a human girl. Do you know her?"

Sir William threw his arms in the air and pulled a lace kerchief from his ornate sleeve.

"Oh please, rid me of that wretched thing, I beg you. The whining is going to kill me — or it would if I were not already…" He flicked the kerchief across his nose and pointed it into the void behind the door. "In there. Take it away. It's stinking up my beautiful home. Well, what's left of it!" he dabbed non-existent tears from his eyes.

Elmas grabbed her chest with relief, hoping they'd find a salvageable human. She bowed her head. "Thank you," she said awkwardly as they dashed past.

Sir William hovered within the safety of the corridor. Large droplets of water dribbled from overhead through his apparition. He dabbed at them as though they were real tears.

The darkness tried to swallow them, but their light chased it away. Mehmet threw two light orbs to the ceiling.

Elmas gasped, "What happened here?"

A glass cabinet lay upturned, its contents smashed and floating in an inch of stale water. Crystalline fingers veined the whitewashed walls; the burn marks of angelic weaponry. They stepped around a shredded chaise longue, meandering through broken glass and shattered vials.

Sir William shook his head and spun a garish gold ring around his pale finger. "M' Lady did this….and then another burned the rest to cinders just the other day. After all my service, she allows this to occur. Just look at it… all gone!" he sobbed into the damp lace cloth.

Mehmet raised an unamused eyebrow. Elmas rolled her eyes and looked around for Jasmine. The heartbeat was closer but fainter, too.

"There now," Elmas said. "Nephr'eus ruins all that she touches, dear spectre, but be comforted by the knowledge that you are now free of her," she followed the soft pulsations away from Mehmet, leaving him to deal with the forlorn spectre.

Sir William glanced up, "I am?"

"If you wish to be," Mehmet said. "Go to the realm of the dead before she returns for you."

"But... my home?"

"Your home is not here, you know that. You've had your mortal life. It is time for the next level of existence."

Sir William began to slowly spin and mumble to himself.

Elmas rummaged through the detritus, pulling back drapery and rolling back rugs. Mehmet turned over chairs and lifted an armoire that spilled a dozen dresses onto the floor.

"Where is she?" Elmas asked.

"Over there, behind the bed and under the floor," Sir William pointed to a bed at the end of the room. It had been turned on its side.

A flick of her wing and Elmas landed on its other side. Charred floor boards revealed a gap leading to the footings of the manor. Elmas pulled them up and gasped.

Balled in a heap, naked, in her own waste, and wheezing, lay Jasmine.

"Oh Mehmet, I think we are too late."

Mehmet joined her. Sir William hovered above them, more concerned with a broken crystal ornament.

Elmas gathered Jaz into her lap. She felt for a pulse and listened closely to her rasping breaths. She retracted her hand with the shock of Jaz' cold skin, her bloodless pallor a stark contrast to Elmas.

Elmas wept, "You poor child."

Jasmine groaned the agonal breaths of impending death. Her mouth gasped like a fish out of water.

"Quick, grab something to warm her."

Mehmet pulled a thick tapestry off the wall and helped to cocoon Jaz within it. Elmas wanted to warm Jaz with a gentle pulse, but she was too scared her power would kill the girl. She tucked the tapestry tighter around Jaz and held her close.

"Look at her lips, Mehmet. Nephr'eus has fed her the drug."

"This is terrible business," he took Jaz gently into his arms. "Let us return her so she can pass in peace."

Seventeen

had searched and searched for Enl'iel, but the current had stolen her and refused to bring her back. I followed its foul course, dodged a thousand desperate souls that begged for my help and called for my blood. I coasted along the surface, sank into its depths, and trudged along the muddy bottom to no avail. Enl'iel was gone.

I stood on the riverbed and elbowed bony bodies away. I came to a stark realisation as the current pushed on relentlessly. Yeqon was merely inconvenienced; I had to move forwards. I had to return to the real Kaladai and solve this quest before he could regroup.

I had to leave Enl'iel behind.

I forced myself back upriver towards the portal. With each unwilling stroke of my wings, my resolve strengthened and my heart hardened. Enl'iel would have told me to keep going.

The portal's shimmer was just a little to the right; I had made it back to the beach.

The greedy current's drawl gave way to voices up ahead.

"Enl'iel!" Ben cried.

I breached the surface to see Ben kneeling in the sand with Enl'iel draped across his lap. He had unravelled his wings to cocoon her. She was still and pale. His hands, aglow with healing energy, rushed over her body. I held my breath as I watched him treat her with the care befitting a Watcher.

"Come on!" Ben called over to me, "She needs you!"

I rushed out of the river but noticed someone a good fifty feet to Ben's right. Kasadya was still there, no longer a crumpled heap on the shoreline but standing over Rik, who was unconscious. Kasadya made his way towards Ben, his sword dragging behind him through the sand.

"I warned Yeqon about you from the beginning," he said with pleasure in his tone.

He ran at Ben, who hesitated with Enl'iel in his arms. Kasadya shot into the air; weapon poised to strike. Ben rolled into a ball and wrapped Enl'iel in his protective embrace.

I threw an orb at Kasadya and knocked his sword from his hands. He swopped away, recovered the weapon, and hovered high above Ben.

Kasadya raised it, charging it alight. I flew full pelt at him. Kea's sword was swift and light and met his with equal force. I held him back and glared into his black eyes.

Kasadya shoved me back, "Stronger, aren't we?"

I fluttered away to give myself enough room to attack again. Ben placed Enl'iel out of the way behind the only rock on the beach.

"Don't you dare!" I called down to him. "You keep her safe or you'll follow this one!"

"I'll take my chances!" Ben said.

I screamed in frustration and slashed up as Kasadya lunged down. I rolled aside and saw that I'd caught him across his chest, the cut so fine I hadn't felt the contact. He laughed as though it were a mosquito bite. He chased me and I pumped my wings hard, circling up and down around him only for his speed and experience to outwit me. He stabbed deep into my left thigh, and I let out a guttural scream. The pain shot all the way down to my toes. I fell to the ground with a bruising *thud*. His energy sped towards me. I rolled to the left, catching flashes of Kasadya's weapon and Ben, who was still near Enl'iel. I rolled right to avoid another slash. Sand sprayed into the air as I fought to regain my footing whilst my leg throbbed and spasmed. I crawled towards Ben. He ran towards me, his wide wings and bright. Kasadya grabbed my hair and yanked me to my feet. He fired an orb at Ben, who flipped backwards out of its way. I slashed a wing behind me and caught Kasadya's weapon hand. He dropped his sword, threw me over his shoulder and pushed me against the edge of the cave. His hand closed around my neck. Blood pooled in my head, and I gasped. The delight on his face was sickening.

He fired another orb at Ben to keep him at bay.

"Do it!" I rasped. "Go on, you coward!" I kicked at him, but he didn't flinch. "Hiding under Yeqon like a snivelling rodent all these years…" I drew in a wheezy breath, "You wouldn't dare touch me if he were here!"

Colour rose to his cheeks. Kasadya's mark seared white-hot. My lips quivered over my clamped teeth as I forced myself to match his insidious glare.

"Oh, you are so far out of your depth, young one," Kasadya said. "Your power may be great, but your youth is most definitely your weakness."

He hauled me up by my hair and spun me around until he let go. I was flung like a frisbee. I hit rock. There was a crunch and a painful crack. I slumped, sure that every bone had broken.

Ben screamed, "Sophia!"

I raised my head and blinked sand from my eyes. Through a curtain of hair, I saw Kasadya fire at Ben and hit his shoulder. Ben fell to his side and curled into a ball.

Kasadya laughed. He turned around and sauntered back towards me, cracking his knuckles.

"Yeqon will be jealous of my good fortune."

A *thump* cut him off. Kasadya lurched forwards, the smell of burning flesh fresh and vile. He roared and turned away from me. His right shoulder blade was exposed, skin and muscle flapping around it. He spread his wings and rushed away.

I clawed my way up and saw that Ben was fine. He and Kasadya circled the cavern, alight with orbs. The noise of fists plunging into each other's flesh echoed off the walls.

I edged back, desperate to help but so broken. It hurt to breathe. Down my right side, my skin was ripped and swollen. The pain of my dislocated right kneecap breath-taking. I sat in a pool of my own blood, which excited the souls in the river. They screamed louder as the current swept them along. It was a great motivator to heal, but it would take me some time to do it properly. I wrapped my wings around me to accelerate the process while watching Ben and Kasadya through a small slit in their light.

They raged a war of repressed hatred. Thrashing, punching, and burning each other. Kasadya was larger, older, and much more practiced than Ben. He wore him down until Ben fell heavily into the sand. Kasadya pounded into Ben. Blood sprayed from Ben's nose and poured from his mouth.

After all he had done, after all the pain he had caused, my heart shattered at the sight. My gut clenched, and my skin crawled to see him so undone. I urged more power to my wings, called on everything I had to heal myself so I could help him. My ribs had knitted and some of the flesh along my side was restored, but my kneecap was still out of place. I heaved myself forwards, one hand over the other, hoping that Kasadya wouldn't see me coming. I felt the vibrations of every thrust against Ben.

When I was within easy range, I pushed myself up and fired an orb straight into Kasadya's back. It knocked him off Ben's limp body. He roared but rolled onto his feet and pulled Ben up the scruff. His retaliatory orb flung me back into the sand before I could protect myself.

I spat sand as I tried to catch my breath. I could exist without it, but my human past made the reflex hard to ignore. My dented chest guard was lava-hot, my re-broken ribs in agony. Kasadya pulled Ben towards me, his sword dragging through the sand on his other side now.

He glared down at me, "Don't bother trying to slither away. Let's make this quick." Kasadya raised his sword.

I had nothing left; my energy depleted. I closed my eyes and thought of what death would feel like. Would it hurt?

Kasadya's energy spiked. I exhaled my last small breath. Something hit me in the chest. It hurt. It wasn't sharp, it was heavy and stayed there as I waited for death to take me away.

Death didn't arrive.

I opened my eyes. Kasadya was gone. I lifted the thing off my chest… and screamed.

It was Kasadya's head.

"Shall we call that even, sister?"

Chapter Eighteen

I sat next to Enl'iel by the real Jaz' bedside. I leaned into my clasped hands and shook my head. I didn't know how to prevent her death. I took her cold hand in mine, and that cold tingled all the way up my arms. I swallowed my tears and squeezed her fingers, hoping she would know that I was there, just like everyone else was.

Kristen and Jude hugged either side of me. Brennan fussed over Enl'iel, who had recovered quickly and batted him away as he insisted she sip one of her own teas. Cael was recovering from Anjou'elle's attack by holding a poultice to the bump on his head. She had merely knocked him out. Devon looked battered as he held a smoking potion under Jaz' nose. His face was bruised and tired, yet his eyes were sharp and focussed as he held his palm over Jaz' heart. Ben stood hunched over in a corner. Like a sadist, he chose to let his shattered body suffer a natural healing again. His face and torso were a mess. Rik kept his distance, too, and watched through the haze of today's healing embers.

"She will die," I whispered.

I pulled up the thick tapestry Elmas and Mehmet had brought Jaz back in. The creases straightened as I tucked it under her chin, revealing a black-haired woman woven into it. Jaz' irregular breaths were increasingly disconcerting. As a nurse, I'd seen the death rattles many times.

I rested my hands on her chest, afraid every breath would be her last. My palms circled over the woven image as I tried to rub life into her. The picture smiled at me; her face familiar.

"What is it you're doing?" I asked Devon.

He ignored me.

After a while, a finger touching my cheek brought my eyes back to focus. Devon inspected the tear he'd wiped from my skin.

"This may help," he whispered in my mind.

He mixed my tear with a few grains of Thanratos and dipped it just inside Jaz' blue bottom lip.

His gentle eyes smiled at me, *"A little bit of good, a little bit of bad."*

"How do you know this will work?" I asked.

"I do not," he plucked a pin from his robes and wriggled his fingers, asking for my hand.

Hesitantly, I held it out. He pricked my finger.

He squeezed the drop into a shallow dish.

"I have had success with our own kind," he said. *"Pure blood reacts with the drug when treated just the right way. It changes it so the effects are reversed when ingested."*

"Have you ever tried it on a human?" Enl'iel asked. Her eyes were bright with hope and curiosity in what her brother was doing.

He glanced at her and smiled. *"I have never needed to. I can only hope that, if it brings along her death, it is less painful than the drug's torture,"* Devon's apologetic eyes rested back on me and then returned to Jaz.

I squeezed Jaz' hand tighter. I didn't want to let go, "When will you know?"

He put the new mixture under her tongue. Jude tensed but remained quiet.

"It absorbs faster this way," Devon said. He closed her mouth and tucked the blanket in at her sides. The movement straightened the tapestry so that its image was fully exposed.

"Will you look at that?" Brennan said. "Mona Lisa. Leo seems to be haunting you."

I studied the woman's coy expression, biting my lip in thought.

"It can't be… But maybe, just maybe, it is?"

I pulled my dagger out and shone a light underneath it. The prophecy glowed into existence on the wall. I read the first line twice to myself— *"Behold! Mine life's love regards the way."*

"Didn't Leo spend many years painting the Mona Lisa?" my attention bounced between Jaz, the script and the tapestry image.

Enl'iel stood as well and stared at the prophecy with me, "I believe he did."

I stared long and hard at the girl who'd sucker-punched anyone who had looked at her the wrong way. Was this the last time I'd see the pixie face that masked a mini superhero?

I leaned into her ear. "I'm sorry, I have to go. Stay strong, but… if you need to go, you do that. Don't fight for anyone but yourself," I kissed her forehead. My heart skipped a few beats, one for Jaz, another for what I needed to do next.

"I think the next clue is at the Louvre," I said.

Enl'iel grabbed Brennan's arm, "Go with her."

Brennan's face lit as it always did when adventure was on the cards.

He pecked Enl'iel's head, Jaz' as well, "Ready and waiting, Princess."

I rested my hand on Jude's shoulder, "Look after her."

Jude squeezed my hand and bowed his head. For once he had no retort or opinion. For once, this hulk of a Watcher seemed vulnerable.

He took Jaz' hand in his other one. My heart cracked just a little more.

"Is this place secure?" I asked.

I picked up my weapons from the hooks by the door. The frame was off centre since the Rogue attacks outside the perimeter had upset our foundations. The floor had also cracked, but none had breached the outer chromious lining or the Watchers who surrounded our perimeter for miles.

"Matias is with us," Cael said. "Ged'erel and Pineme are unaccounted for. Matias will personally make sure those two don't come sniffing around. Otherwise, it's been quiet since you returned.

We've pulled back a few battalions to widen the exclusion zone around us. At night, the human regiments are drilling chromious bollards into the surrounding landscape to ward off any unwanted guests."

"And Gedz'iel?" I asked.

"He's taken Lorcan and the Eloi to other hot spots," Brennan said. "The vampire activity is still on the boil in the US," his eyes slid towards Ben, and I nodded.

"Sounds like you guys are on top of this," I said. "Right, I'll make this quick if I can."

Brennan and I walked towards Ben. He looked up from his hands.

Brennan passed him a sword, "Are you coming with us?"

Ben's eyes widened.

"You saved Enl'iel and Sophia," Brennan said. "You brought her brother home twice. You have my trust."

Ben ran his hand through his pure white hair, which retained just one strand of ebony. His blue eyes rested on Jaz before landing back on me.

He balled his hands, "I don't know that I can trust myself."

I held my hand out for him, but he hesitated. I wriggled my fingers impatiently, "Haven't got all day, you know."

He reached out with his less injured hand, but pulled it back.

I grabbed it before he could change his mind and took Brennan's with the other.

"Let's pay a visit to Mona Lisa."

We waited in the niches of the Louvre's steep roof until after midnight. I hadn't anticipated time differences and security; waiting for the city to quieten and for the guards to move to another wing wasn't easy when my patience was thin.

The City of Lights glittered like an earthbound celestial body. Fewer cars than I'd expected hooted below. There was little foot traffic, and a number of emergency vehicles screamed by whilst we waited. The Eiffel tower observed it all, a queen guarding her beloved city.

"Are you sure about this?" Ben asked. He'd been short on words but plenty long on brooding during our thirty-minute hiatus.

"I'm sure I've read that this painting was Leo's greatest love. I took an art history elective in high school and we studied him. Apparently, he carried it around for years, and everything points to all things Leonardo... my dreams, the chest, his Vitruvian Man."

Ben perked up, "Vitruvian man?" The moon cast deep shadows and masked most of his face. "You know what that really is, don't you?"

"The perfect man, apparently," I said. "It was our guiding light, so to speak, at the Grotta Azzurra."

Brennan preened and ran his hands down his body, "It was modelled on myself."

"You're an idiot," Ben mumbled.

Brennan smiled, "Absolutely."

"It's I'el," Ben said. "It's his architecture of humanity. It's an image of him, or one of his many forms."

Brennan whistled, "Deep. Is that true?"

Ben picked at a loose tile. "What kind of Watcher are you? *You* should know that; I'm just a half-breed as I'm frequently reminded."

I glared at Ben; thankful it was Brennan rather than Jude he was insulting. Last thing I needed was an all-out fight on top of the Louvre.

"I'm the kind of Watcher who keeps his head on straight, his conscience clear, and his morals intact," Brennan smirked at Ben and pulled me closer, "It's quiet enough now I think, Princess."

A helicopter flew overhead, quickly followed by another. They panned the streets with powerful spotlights and headed towards the Arc de Triomphe.

"Military," Ben mumbled.

"Best get on with it then," Brennan said.

We held hands and transferred into a wide hall. The place was rigged to the hilt with security. The incessant buzz of hidden lasers was as loud to me as the sirens outside.

"Just remember where we are, kids," Brennan whistled low. "Nice and easy now," he twisted around a corner like a cat. "Let me just..."

Brennan shot out all the motion sensors we could see, "That's this lot, but the whole place will be hot. Not sure how high the lasers reach, but it will be safer at the ceiling, I imagine." Brennan pointed up.

We flew up and coasted through several halls. Brennan disabled the alarms in each new area.

"You're rather good at criminal trespass, Brennan," I whispered, impressed with his many hidden talents.

He winked, "Oh, I've had a bit of fun in my time, Princess."

We passed a large window. Moonlight cast a soft path, gleaning off the pure white of the Venus de Milo and past Nike's bronze statue before it was cut off by another room; the resting place of what we were here for.

The room was dark apart from soft floor lighting that shone upwards at a wall in the middle of the room.

I sighed in awe.

"You're not lifting it, are you?" Brennan asked, a little too much intrigue in his eyes.

"If I have to."

I bit the inside of my cheek. Stealing the Mona Lisa to save the world seemed proportional.

We floated down, keeping a few feet above the ground. The painting illuminated under the light of our wings. Glare bounced off a thick protective perspex covering. It was smaller than I imagined but no less beautiful. The woman peered past us, amused by something only she and Leonardo knew about.

Ben leaned in close, "What do you think you'll find?" He ran a finger along the edge of the outer casing.

"Well, the prophecy stated that his life's love regards the way. That's a French derivative of the word *look* or *see*," I quietly thanked Madame Babineaux for forcing me to do my homework. "Something about where she is looking?" I floated in for a closer look.

Brennan came up next to me, "Maybe that's why she looks like she's up to something, because she's got a bloody big secret."

I pulled out my dagger to re-read the prophecy. Smears of Yeqon's blood were on it. So much blood… It seemed to be the ultimate gory answer to everything.

"Well?" Ben asked.

"I think we need to take her down and quickly. I'm pretty sure I need to touch the painting, and we won't be able to stop the alarms on her. You two," I pointed them in different directions towards the two entrances of the room. "Keep an eye out for security."

They nodded and took up spots either side of the room.

"Never thought this would be on my to do list…"

I shook my head and ran my suddenly sweaty palms down my sides, in awe at what I was about to do.

"Hang on," Ben whispered into my head.

Footsteps clicked close by. Two flashlights drew around the corner as two guards entered. I flew to the highest and darkest corner of the room and dulled my wings.

The guards argued in French.

One guard swung his flashlight left and right "I saw something," he said.

I held my breath.

The other guard stepped past him and swept his beam across the parquet, "There's nothing here, you idiot."

"I saw a light, I'm sure of it," the first guard insisted.

The second guard elbowed his partner, "It would have been from a car or streetlight you fool."

"There aren't any windows in here, Miguel. You're the idiot."

"Look quickly then. I need a coffee," Miguel sighed.

I squished as tight as I could into the corner.

Miguel's radio went off. *"Unit 252, emergency evac…"* He switched it off.

"What if it's important?" the other guard asked.

"It'll just be another practice drill," Miguel replied. "You want to go out into that cold? I prefer being in here than out in the streets with all that weird shit going on. It can wait, don't worry."

The other guard hesitated but turned his radio off too.

The two burly guards swept the room, checked on Mona, then headed towards the farthest exit. I was about to breathe a sigh of relief when for no particular reason one of them turned around and swung his torch into my corner. I froze.

"Miguel. What… is… that?" his torchlight quivered.

Miguel's jaw dropped.

The torch clanged to the ground. The guard scrambled for his radio. Before he could switch it back on, Brennan and Ben swooped in and pulsed both guards into a deep sleep.

I raced over and felt the guards' pulses.

"Hopefully, they'll remember nothing," I sighed. "Put them back in the main security room, and keep an eye out for others. I have a feeling we won't be leaving here quietly."

I hurried back to Mona, charged my dagger with blood and E'lan, and worked away at the bulletproof casing. The edges were thick and armed inside with all sorts of foreign protective wires.

All was well until I hit the third corner.

An alarm screeched through the Louvre. The piercing sound was disorienting. Lights turned on and blue beacons flashed, catching me red-handed with the world's most famous portrait. Heavy gates rolled down and barred the exits.

I put more energy into the dagger to melt away the last covering. It fell to the floor with a *thud*, but there was another complicated system of alarmed attachments behind it. I worked through a dozen wires, searing through them one by one, careful not to damage the canvas. My fingers trembled as I snapped the last red wire.

It triggered a trap of prison bars, which flew down from the ceiling, entrapping me with Mona Lisa in my clutches. Police sirens had already been blaring outside, and more joined the cacophony now. Multiple feet rushed towards the room. Shouts over radios were just audible under the piercing alarms.

I wiggled the little painting off its hooks. The gilded frame fit snug against my chest. I turned away from the wall and wrapped my wings around her.

A flurry of guards entered the room, weapons raised. They saw me floating high above them, aglow and in possession of their charge. I hovered a few moments to let them see me, and it worked. Their mouths dropped in shock.

They dropped their weapons; ignored their radios. One fell to his knees with his hands in prayer.

I smiled at them, gave them their moment of awe, then called the boys.

"Let's get outta here."

The guards roared in a new wave of shock when Ben and Brennan appeared. Brennan saluted them. We transferred back to Kaymakli while they swooned below us, the Mona Lisa safe and sound in my arms.

Chapter
Nineteen

Enl'iel rushed to me the second I returned, gawking at the painting in my grasp.

"You stole the Mona Lisa!"

"*We* stole the Mona Lisa," Brennan interjected, looking proud of himself.

"Our hand was forced," Ben added soberly.

Kristen rushed to my side, her hands hiding her gaping mouth.

"She says Paris will be in meltdown," Enl'iel translated Kristen's thoughts to me.

Kristen giggled, but her smile faded when my attention slid back to Jaz. Devon still hovered over her. Jude remained by her side, and Rik sat on a stool behind him.

I tucked the painting under my arm and walked over to Jaz. Her lips had changed from blue to a pasty yellow.

My fingers dug into painting's frame, "She looks worse."

"*She has not improved,*" Devon waved over the Alchemae for more herbs and ground some new concoction.

"At least keep her comfortable?" I asked.

I grazed her cool arm with the edge of my hand. She was so far from the girl who'd chased me around the tree at school to beat me up. She was far from the girl who'd become my most trusted ally.

Devon smiled mildly, "*Her comfort is something I can promise you.*"

The room buzzed with an incoming transfer.

"Gedz'iel is on his way," I said.

I'd become accustomed to his strong elemental signature. He snapped into view seconds later, Lorcan by his side. They bore the raw and bloody wounds of yet another battle.

Gedz'iel took the painting from me, "I heard about your find, and not too soon either." He looked it over and handed it back, "I hope this is the final element. Chaos is spreading through the Americas like wildfire. It is only a matter of time before the whole world succumbs."

Gedz'iel pressed a bloody swelling on his temple with the back of his hand and leaned into the large preparation table. He accepted a drink from an Alchemae and hung his head.

"Emergency services are down across two continents," Lorcan said as he too gulped a drink down. "Vamps are doing fake call-outs and killing the responders, so the police and paramedics refuse to attend. Communities are afraid," Lorcan took a second cup and drained it. "Looting and violence are spreading quicker than we can suppress it," he sniffed and wiped grit from his eyes with his thumb. "We can't control it, Soph. There are too many humans. You need to find the portal or Earth will destroy itself," Lorcan clenched his jaw and leaned back into the table looking exhausted too.

Gedz'iel peered around the room at all of us, "For the first time ever, we must put ourselves first. I'm pulling everyone back. I won't play to whoever is running this game."

I grabbed my pendant. This went against everything I believed in, but he had a point.

"I've seen how vampires kill," Rik said quite unexpectedly. "It's an awful death."

The E'lan lulled as we took in that statement. I felt the painting's weight, stared at Jaz, thought about Yeqon and Nephr'eus who were still out there somewhere. For every step forward, I took ten back.

Enl'iel fiddled with her pendant, "This is horrific."

"Yes. It is horrific. Humans are terrified and so are our own people," Gedz'iel said, "Humans as usual react to fear with aggression and greed. This situation will worsen the longer the portal remains hidden," Gedz'iel straightened and hardened his eyes. "It is time for the soldiers of A'maggedon to come through," his attention landed on me, eyes heavy. "Open the portal, Sophia."

I transferred to the Zythros stone, retrieved the Kaladai cogs, and returned to the privacy of the intensive care area.

It was time Mona and I got to know each other. To my right, I had a live stream of the BBC on Brennan's smart phone. Sequences of mob protests and disorder across the globe flashed by as the over-enthused journalist barely drew breath.

"The bloody attacks we've seen over the past two weeks are becoming more frequent and random. Authorities are at a loss to explain the perpetrators' motives or whom they might be. Several theories regarding a new form of terrorism have been touted, but political leaders are unwilling to discuss them at this stage despite growing protests online and across all major cities."

The journalist re-aligned her notes with a tap on her desk. Her eyes flitted off camera like she was looking for someone. The screen behind her cut to those brave enough to hit mostly deserted streets, holding signs and demanding action.

"The public are urged to stay indoors to minimise further attacks. Across London, armoured cars will be delivering essentials to homes. The public are advised to not approach the personnel but to wait until their care packages have been left. All personnel have a shoot-to-kill order if approached."

Her flushed cheeks and bright eyes sparkled with the fervour of the story, or was something else shining through? She touched her earpiece. Her tone and pitch changed suddenly.

"A general call-out to all protective guardians: Retreat to your closest sanctuary and await further orders. Do not engage with the Unseen under any circumstances. This is by order of Gedz'iel."

Her smile was static as those words rung in my ears. Her eyes flashed once more, and the broadcast died. After a few moments of fuzz on the screen, a message rolled across it warning everyone to stay indoors.

The world was literally going to Hell and I had to stop it.

I shook my head and sighed, "So, it's you and me, Mona. What are you smiling about?"

Her soft eyes stared past me, framed by that famous curtain of luscious dark hair. The back ground was almost non-descript, such was the way she commanded your attention to her expression. I twirled my pendant, ran a finger around her jawline and traced it up to her eyes. Destroying such an icon of human history was no trivial matter, but I drew my dagger anyway. Leo had created her for a reason, and this was her moment.

My dagger was so bloody from the recent fighting that the prophetic script had turned black. Mona's eyes magnified under the blade as I held it this way and that. My pendant pounded into my chest, so I angled the blade in a different direction. My hands froze. I hovered my dagger close over Mona's eyes, adjusted the angle to catch some imperfections in her eyes, and they revealed the reason of her knowing smile to me. They weren't imperfections at all.

A longitude and latitude in each eye.

"Brennan!"

He ran inside within seconds, as though he'd been hovering right outside.

"Are you okay?" he leaned over my shoulder; his mark alight as I pointed excitedly at the painting.

I nodded towards my dagger, "It's directions, Bren, isn't it?"

He squinted at the tiny numbers.

"You bet your beautiful angelic arse it is!" he squeezed my shoulder and kissed the top of my head.

"Get the others ready," I said. "I want to follow this now. Bring Ben too."

He ran out; quiet ruptured as footsteps rushed around and the E'lan crackled, its tingle shivering across my skin.

I stood, ready to join them…

And felt a heart stop.

I raced out of the room, my arms and legs like jelly. I was back at Jaz' side, her stone-cold hand in mine. Devon had retreated, his hands clasped over his chest. Jude was ashen next to me.

"Do something!" I screamed.

"I cannot."

I pulsed energy into her heart. What I'd whispered to her before meant nothing now that death had come for her. I didn't want her to go.

"Don't you dare be a selfish bitch and leave me!"

My head was filled with cotton. Her lips were colourless, her mouth slack, her milky skin a sour yellow. Death's touch had kissed her fingers blue.

I choked, "Jaz! Please?" Jaz jerked with every pulsation.

She had no pulse.

"Devon!" I screamed.

"I am sorry," Devon replied softly. *"She was too weak and too human."*

I looked up, "What's that supposed to mean?"

Jude pulled me away from Jaz. His bottom lip quivered, "Enough now," his voice was soft and broken.

Brennan sobbed, "Oh, Mini Princess."

I looked a while longer into Jude's eyes, which fought against the tears. He squeezed my hand, and I slumped down and lay my head onto Jaz' still chest.

I'd seen death. I'd lost Esme and Kea, but this was my best friend, my link to the past, the one who made me brave.

Something stirred under my agony. In between sobs, denial rose strong and loud.

"Not today!" I jumped up and pulsed her heart again, over and over. Her flaccid arms twitched with every life-sustaining effort.

Enl'iel begged me to stop, but I continued. I flung Jaz' shirt back and put my hands on her skin, tried with all that I had to draw energy back into her heart. I started CPR, pressing on her sternum over and over and over. I was back in my zone, just me and her, the world could wait. Intermittently I blasted her heart like a defibrillator, yet she remained cold and dead. Jude grabbed my hands when one of her ribs cracked.

He glared at me, his eyes red and dry. "That's enough!" Jude pulled the covers back over her.

The quiver in my chin spread until all my limbs shook. Jude let go.

I sunk to my knees and lay my head on Jaz' chest. The cold of death was shockingly immediate. Enl'iel sobbed next to me, others to themselves. I smelled the Alchemae before they arrived. They slipped herbs and a soul stone onto her to ease her soul onwards.

I felt a hand on my shoulder, smelled the ocean breeze though my tears.

"I'm sorry," Lorcan whispered.

I turned my head away from him, and he retreated. I remembered what he'd said about Jaz just being a human and didn't want to look at him.

Heat filled my skin. It grew, burning into my cheek until it was almost unbearable, but I held on to her. The murmurings grew stronger but faded at the same time. I felt secluded with my best friend, entombed in the power of my grief. I clung to her, because the moment I let go, she would be gone forever.

An immense flash of light brought me back from my all-consuming misery. I jolted, and my head raised and lowered. It raised and lowered again. The energy in the room spiked. My head raised and lowered once more. *Thud, thud, thud…* a regular, rhythmic pounding inside my head. I held on to Jaz, but something was different. The E'lan was excitable, as were the murmurings.

Something threw me off Jaz. I scrambled up off the floor.

Jaz was resting on her elbows. "Um, what the fuck is going on?"

Chapter Twenty

I couldn't take my eyes off Jaz or the pale swirls around her right eye. I was transfixed by the blueness of her eyes and the shocking white of her hair. Petrified, I sat a few feet away from her bed, hoping I wasn't dreaming.

Jude sat at the foot of her bed with his chin resting on steepled fingers. He looked like someone who'd been in a car wreck and survived.

Jaz was eating off a tray table across her knees. She flicked meat out of her meal, only eating the vegetables, and asked for more. She had no idea what she was. I'd had no idea.

But someone had known all along.

Ben sat next to me. Shoulder to shoulder, we watched the Alchemae and Enl'iel fuss over Jaz.

"This is why I protected her," Ben said. He ran his hands through his hair and rested them against his chin just like Jude, "The irony is, I actually intended to kill her."

I gawked at him, "Why?"

"Orders, Soph." he kept his eyes on Jaz. "I'd sensed her and hunted her down, but when I found her choking to death in a house fire, just an innocent child…" Ben shook his head. "I just couldn't do it," he glanced my way, his eyes pained at the memory. "So, I took her in and brought her up. Her parents were dead, and there was the smell of

Rogue about the home. She was safer with me. Her parents never knew what they were either, hence the strange life they led. They were terrified of themselves and of things they could feel but not see. They tried to hide Jaz, but in the end, they had no idea how to protect themselves," he sighed like the memories fatigued him.

Brennan pulled up a stool next to us, "Who'd have thought it? Mini Princess was one of us all along. I say she gets her grit from me!"

"Shh!" Enl'iel lay a platter of fruit in front of Jaz, her eyes a shade of worry.

"What did you just say?" Jaz asked. Her cheeks were pouched with food, and she kept stuffing in more.

"How do we explain this to her?" I asked as Enl'iel stopped next to us as well.

Jaz whipped her attention to me with eyes I'd never thought I'd see again, and certainly not in that shade.

"What if it's too much of a shock?" I whispered.

Enl'iel tapped her lips in thought, then padded over to the prep table and jostled underneath it. She returned to Jaz and passed her a hand mirror.

"Have a look at yourself, dear."

"Hmm, okay," Jaz dropped her fork and snatched the mirror.

After a glance, she pouted and slapped the mirror onto the bed, but her hand smacked back to it within seconds, and she slowly picked it up. Food bulged in her cheek as she stopped chewing. She shoved the tray to the floor, swallowed the ball of food, and coughed. Her slender fingertips prodded her face, tracing the modest silver-white scrolls that adorned her right eye. She leaned into her oval reflection, then held it out. She turned her head, tugged at her hair, and smacked her lips together.

"Well, fuck me, Soph! I'm a goddamned bloody angel!"

Ben cupped his head with his hands. Brennan held his belly in laughter. There were more than a few uncomfortable coughs and a chuckle behind me, but my heart felt like it was exploding with joy.

Jude leaned in, "How do you feel?"

She wiped her mouth with the back of her hand and blinked as though she was just noticing him.

"Well, hello, Freak!" Jaz' eyes travelled up and down Jude with a delighted glimmer. "Want to give me some crap *now*, do you?" she grinned.

Jude laughed and took her hand. Her eyes rested on the point where skin touched skin and then met his.

I thought I might implode from the tension.

"Full of ourselves, aren't we?" she murmured. Her classic come-hither eyes flashed back into existence. Her thumb slid across his hand.

His smile toughened, "You're still disrespectful."

"And I always will be," she bit her bottom lip.

I was all levels of uncomfortable.

Enl'iel shuffled into Jude's space and passed Jaz a tonic, "Okay then. Nothing more to be done here. She needs rest after her rather unexpected Awakening. The Alchemae, Devon, and I can take things from here." She nudged Jude's shoulder, urging him up, "Go on with you. Sophia needs you more than Jaz does."

Jude glared at her. Enl'iel placed her hands on her hips, cocked her head to the side, and scowled. He screwed up his face. Jaz smiled behind her cup and kicked playfully at him.

"Need you, buddy!" Brennan said.

Jude pushed back on the stool, its wooden legs screeching in protest. He dwarfed Enl'iel, but she looked up at him with every bit of *don't mess with me* that she could muster.

"Very well," he retreated to Ben.

Devon took his place by Jaz' bedside and reached for her forehead.

She smacked him away, "What are you doing?"

He cupped his hand in his other and smiled at her.

"Fear not, new-born," his voice now travelled through a soul stone wedge in his palm. "I am calling your energy to join the E'lan."

Jaz quirked one brow and pulled the covers higher up her chest. "You need consent to touch my… whatever it is!"

I laughed.

She looked Devon up and down, "Soph, who is this weirdo?"

"He's here to help."

Her blue eyes held mine for a moment. I couldn't stop smiling. The relief and surprise to see her like this was incredible. She smiled back.

"Fine!" Jaz flopped back onto the pillow and allowed him to put his hand on her forehead.

The E'lan picked up, tingling like the touch of mid-winter frost. Her mark glowed brighter as it received the power and brought out the fullness of its curls across her skin.

Jaz cried out. "Oh God! My back is stinging!" she writhed in the bed. "What've you done to me?"

Devon's eyes narrowed with concern, "Sit up."

She leaned forward, her face florid with pain. Jude instantly returned to her side.

There were undulations all down her spine.

I gasped, "Oh… my… Jaz!"

Enl'iel clapped, "By the blessings of A'vean."

"What is it?" Jaz' voice stained with worry. She leaned back, her eyes darting to each of us.

Jude crossed his arms and nodded, satisfaction on his face, "This explains a lot."

"I'm pretty sure I knew it," Brennan gushed.

I elbowed him, "You did not."

"No one could have guessed," Ben said, his face bright with surprise. "Her parents were too weak."

"However weak her parents were, they've thrown a powerful offspring," Enl'iel said. "It seems it took your power to bring it to the surface, Sophia. She could have lived an ordinary human life and never known her true heritage."

Devon nodded, tucked his trinkets away.

Jaz slapped the bed, "Can you all please share whatever it is you're on about?"

"You're fine," I said. "Trust me, you're more than fine."

I encouraged her to lean forwards again. We inspected her back, which blazed red-raw with new pterugia leaflets, just waiting for wings to emerge.

Jaz grabbed Devon's arm, "Am I dying? What the hell is it?"

Devon eased her back onto the pillow, "You are experiencing the rise of your pterugia, Jasmine. Your A'vean heritage is stronger than we suspected."

"What? My terwhatia?" Jaz looked at me, utterly confused.

I gripped her hands with mine, "Wings, Jaz! You've got wings!"

Her mouth fell open. "You're totally shitting me!" she tried to peer over her shoulders.

I grinned. Enl'iel passed her the mirror again, followed by a smaller one. We held them in a way that, when Jaz sat forwards, she saw the faint glow running down her spine.

Enl'iel's fingers cushioned Jaz' chin. "There was always a strange strength about you, dear. How did I not see it? What an absolute joy."

"I saw it," Brennan said. "Always did call her Mini Princess."

Enl'iel scoffed.

"This is profound," Devon said. "It means that A'vean blood can strengthen again over time. Perhaps there are more out there like her, more to protect and serve, to raze evil from the earth?"

Jaz' eyes were large azure dishes. They darted all over her own reflection again.

A blush filled her cheeks as a tear fell from each eye.

"Mum? Dad?" she whispered. She held her head and shook it. "I was so awful to them. I've said so many horrid things about them."

Enl'iel stroked her hair, "Now, now, you weren't to know, and they clearly didn't know what they were. How on earth could you ever imagine the truth of your heritage if they did not? There's no time to waste on misplaced guilt, dear. They are at peace in the Cavern of Souls and all their questions answered, I assure you."

Jaz blinked and wiped her nose, "They're safe?"

"Yes, dear," Enl'iel glanced at me and straightened, letting Jaz go. "But it will not last if Sophia doesn't get herself out of here and back to portal hunting."

Jaz dried her tears and licked her lips, "Does that mean I get to kick Daimon arse now too?"

The glow to her cheeks both chilled and thrilled me. Jaz would never be an unwilling member of this community like I'd been. Her eyes swirled with anticipation and landed on Ben.

"You!" Jaz rushed to get up, but Enl'iel grabbed her wrist. "What is he doing here?" Jaz yelled.

Ben gulped. He was going to say something, but I shook my head.

"Let her vent," I whispered into his mind.

Jaz wrenched free from Enl'iel, "You goddamned piece of filth! Why is he here, Soph?"

Jude hurried between her and Ben, arms crossed. Jaz was on her feet, albeit wobbly, and tried to get past, but Jude was faster.

"You serious? Get outta my way!" she wound her arm back to punch him but lost her balance and fell. Jude scooped her up before she hit the floor and put her back on the bed.

"Stay there, and calm down," he said firmly.

I edged next to him whilst Jaz pulled herself onto her elbows.

"You need to take it easy," I said. "A lot has happened since… well, since I saw you last."

"No shit, Sherlock," Jaz grumbled, her eyes narrowed at Ben. She picked at the bedlinen, a little paler.

I kneeled next to her, "It's a long story, another unbelievable one, and there's no time to explain now. Just trust me. He's one of us."

The venom in her eyes was ripe. I tapped her chin so her attention was on me, not Ben.

Jaz looked up at Jude, "Is she fucking mad?"

He cleared his throat and glanced at Ben. "He was integral to your survival. And no, Sophia is not… mad," he smiled at me.

Jaz screwed up her mouth, paled further and fell back onto her pillow, "I feel sick."

I grabbed a damp cloth and dabbed her face and neck. She leaned her head against my shoulder.

"I got you," I said.

Her hand flopped against mine, and she closed her eyes.

An Alchemae rushed to her, "She needs to rest. Her body has been through enormous strain."

Enl'iel took over from me.

The Alchemae held a tisane to her lips. Jaz pushed it away.

"Come now," the Alchemae encouraged her gently.

Jaz sipped at it, screwed up her face and coughed. "I'm tired," she whispered.

Enl'iel lay her back down and tucked her in. She placed a soul stone on Jaz' chest.

Jude took her hand again, "Rest, young one. When you have gained your strength, you will receive proper, disciplined training. I will handpick someone for you, and then we shall war together."

A tired smile lifted the corners of her mouth.

"Until then, you will do everything you are told. Do you understand?"

"Yes, Jude," Jaz said dreamily.

Her next breath drew her away to her first psynostris.

My skin pricked with wonder, and my heart warmed with relief, but my gut churned with fear. My best friend was a descendant of A'vean. No longer a human, but someone who would save humanity.

She was one of my family.

Twenty-One

Jude, Brennan, Ben, Lorcan, and I made our way to the Zythros stone once I was sure Jaz was settled.

"You were pretty quiet back there," I said to Lorcan.

"I've never seen an Awakening or someone rise from the dead," he said. "She did both, and I'm glad."

I stopped and looked at him, "Really?"

"Yeah, I am. I can see now how strong she is and how important she is to you and also to…" he glanced at Jude. "I got her back now too, Soph."

Jude pushed between us. I forgave Lorcan and mouthed a *thank you*.

"What are your plans?" Jude asked. Despite his grim expression, there was a kinder note to his tone. He was a big softie under all the barbs.

"Well, dear Jude, Mona Lisa was very forthcoming. Brennan?" I held my hand out whilst Brennan fiddled in his pockets for his ever-handy phone.

"Why do you need one of those again?" Lorcan asked, rolling his eyes.

The smart phone burst to life. It popped melodiously as I typed.

"Because, dear disbelievers, Google and Mona have just shown us the next move on the chess board," I turned the phone to them. "Looks like it's back to France!"

With the phone cradled against my chest, I leaned into the Zythros stone. Its murmurings rumbled to life at my touch; there was panic and chaos in its hurried whispers, and confusion about what to do and where to go. Arguments across the nations chattered through its veins. They needed help, but I had a job to do; a job that would help everyone in the end.

We armoured up.

"Jude, Brennan, go find Gedz'iel and Koi. Join them and the Eloi. We need to bring everyone together and re-group so that we have a strong and united front when I need it."

They glanced at Ben and Lorcan. I crossed my arms and cocked an eyebrow.

"You heard that right. One good guy, and one sort of good guy with inside knowledge. I got this, don't worry."

I caught Ben's derisive sneer at Lorcan, who smirked with victorious satisfaction.

I balanced a red orb above my hand, "And I'm not too shabby with one of these myself."

Brennan smiled. Jude did not.

"I need two extra pairs of eyes for this trip, that's all," I said. "You two will make all the difference getting a strong force together. It's what you're trained for after all," I said.

"But…"

My mark flared, "Brennan, I'm well past babysitting."

Jude stepped forwards, "She's right." He crossed his arms. "You are a soldier of worth. This is a wise choice, a brave choice," he elbowed Brennan. "You must trust Sophia."

"Go get 'em, Princess," Brennan nodded at me.

Feeling truly supported and trusted was a first for me, and it was empowering.

Jude pressed his finger into Ben's chest. "There's something about you that urges me to believe in you, despite my gut instinct to rip your head off," he tapped on Ben's armour. "Honour her, and you honour yourself."

Pain flashed in Ben's eyes. Was he thinking of Neren'iel? He sighed and glanced my way, rubbing a thumb over his still-fractured knuckles.

Jude took a step back, "I see your pain. You want redemption as badly as the rest of us. You're tired of pretending to be something you're not. Be who you truly are. Release the darkness, brother. Nik'ael, Ben… whatever you wish to call yourself; be the Watcher that lives deep in your heart."

Ben's eyes reddened, "Thank you, brother."

Jude slapped him on his shoulder. "Good," he tightened his weapons belt and accidently elbowed Lorcan in the process. "Hmm. You've rid yourself of those baby curls. You finally look like a decent soldier," he tugged the thick plait running down Lorcan's head. "You could nearly scare me!" Jude wriggled his hands in mock fright.

"Yeah, okay, hands off," Lorcan smoothed his palms over the shaved scalp above his ears, his mouth a fine line of self-conscious annoyance.

"C'mon, guys!" I said. "Go. The stone is full of fear, we've people to help."

Jude and Brennan leaned into me for a K'ufili. Jude activated the stone and they were gone in a bright flash.

I showed Ben and Lorcan the coordinates one last time, "Got it?"

"Yes," Ben said.

Lorcan nodded.

In another surge of E'lan, we departed too.

We exploded out of thick, white clouds. The day was cool but clear below us.

We coasted over a gargantuan castle in the Loire valley. An immense expanse of roofline and turrets nestled next to the calm Loire River. The size of a small township, the castle's medieval beauty was incredible.

Lorcan pointed at the spectacular castle, "That's Chateau D'Amboise."

"You know the place?" I asked.

"I know a lot more than you think," Lorcan tapped his temple as he scanned the scenery.

"Sorry," I said. "I meant nothing by it."

He shook his head and smiled, "I know you didn't. No bother."

"Ben, find somewhere quiet to land," I said.

Ben took the lead. He peeled away from my side. Lorcan and I hovered in the clouds as Ben sunk lower.

"Why are we here?" Lorcan asked.

"That's where Leonardo is buried," I pulled Brennan's phone from my leg pocket.

"Bloody things," Lorcan mumbled.

"Yeah, well, it was handy for plugging in the latitude and longitude I found in Mona's eyes. Led me straight here," I swept my hand towards the castle and wondered what I would find down there.

Ben waved us down, and we swooped through the air. He crouched on the edge of a slate-roofed turret.

It was midday, and people were out. On closer inspection, they weren't just any people but armed military.

Ben indicated the soldiers below and held his finger to his lips, "Those guys mean business."

Lorcan and I nodded. I held the phone back up.

"Leo is buried in the Chapel of Saint Hubert," I opened an image of a small but ornate chapel, "You know it? It's somewhere on the castle grounds."

Ben shook his head.

Lorcan took the phone and held it between two fingers as though it were poisonous, he frowned then nodded t himself.

"Right, got it. This way," Lorcan moved off.

Ben and I followed him onto another turret. Its steep roof was slippery, so we frog-hopped across two more with a flap of our wings before landing on a flat, round part of the roof, which I imagined was the castle's Keep. On one side ran the river, where there was a smattering of army trucks parked on the road, on the other was a sweeping estate of luscious gardens. Pathways lined geometric, manicured lawns, a mash of wintery greens and browns. I followed the path of six guards, who marched towards the castle. They drew my eye to a church steeple not too far from where we were.

"Over there?"

The boys nodded.

An SUV pulled in, and Ben pulled me back from the edge. Two heavily badged, older military personnel exited and headed into the castle.

"Must be a base of operations," Lorcan said. "I'll conceal myself and keep a look out."

Lorcan shimmered into an army uniform and dropped onto the grass, his sword slung over his shoulder as it took on the shape of a rifle. He marched towards the church.

Ben pointed to a group of trees near the church, "Let's transfer behind those."

I took his hand, "Ready?"

He fingers curled tight around mine.

In a blink, we were sliding down a rough tree trunk. We slunk towards a set of double doors under the watch of a stone-sculpted Virgin Mary. Lorcan paced across the path a hundred feet beyond.

"All clear," he called into my mind. *"They are mainly inside the castle."*

I took in the ornate gothic chapel, "Seems quiet here."

Ben eyed a military helicopter that thundered past. "Could be because the world is currently going to Hell," he rattled the chapel's internal grill doors.

"Well, not if I can help it," I melted the lock and entered.

Ben smiled and followed me.

The chapel was tiny and vacant. Vaulted ceilings beset with arched rainbow-glass windows drew the daylight into the church. Soft beams of sunlight fell across a stone floor emblazoned with fleur-de-lis. No pews or items of significance other than a small wrought-iron fence underneath one of the windows. On the wall behind it were black plaques and something embedded into the stone floor.

I pulled Ben's hand, "Look over there."

It took only five quick steps and my feet rested on a cream marble slab with a circular effigy of Leonardo da Vinci's face at the top. He had a robust head of hair, a strong nose, and eyes that I just knew had been curious until the day they had closed for the last time. His name was in large lettering in front of them.

I fell to my knees and slapped my hands to my cheeks.

"First I steal the Mona Lisa, and now I'll desecrate Leonardo da Vinci's grave."

Ben squatted next to me, "Not your first grave, so I hear?"

I scowled at him.

He nudged my shoulder with his and snorted a laugh, "Nothing like making a reputation for yourself, Soph."

"Can you not?" I said, but we both smiled.

"So, why would he send you here?"

I sighed and recounted a clue.

"'*Behold! Mine life's love regards the way. Beneath mine atlas, two souls unite.*' Brennan thought Leo was referring to a book of maps," my voice echoed through the chapel.

"Don't see a library here," Ben looked around and shrugged "There isn't even so much as a bible, which is rather odd, don't you think?" he stood up, scanning the walls.

I followed suit, pondering the prophecy's lines.

"Let's look around," I said. "There's probably a hidden nook or something. They seem to like that kinda thing, just to make life difficult. Look for anything; an image, an inscription, or a latch. Whatever it is, it *has* to be here."

We circled the walls from different directions, our steps light, keeping our presence as quiet as possible. I ran my hands along the many angelic and demonic sculptures, which were so typical of this time in history. Fearsome gargoyles and avenging angels had once borne their judgemental eyes over a cowering, worshipping flock.

"Anything?"

"No," Ben was near the door, his attention outside rather than inside.

"Lorcan still out there?" I asked.

"Yeah, but more trucks are pulling up. Might want to hurry."

I stopped in front of a garish portrait of an angel stepping on demons' necks. The demons were pawing up from Hell. Most were skeletal with eyeless orbs for heads; spines and ribs crushed under the angel's feet. I ran my fingers over a skull and stopped at its neck. Beneath the vertebrae lay a dagger, a hidden weapon that the demon was reaching for. The handle rested just under the very first vertebrae of the skull — the atlas bone. My skin prickled.

I rushed back to the crypt, already drawing blood from my palm. I squeezed until a thick line of it dribbled to the floor.

Ben dashed back and grabbed my bloody wrist. "What is it?" his eyes were narrow with concern, confusion, or both.

"Atlas isn't a book, it's the classical name of the first vertebra. The atlas sits beneath the skull. I've got to open his grave," I was bouncing on the balls of my feet, excitement flushing hot under my skin.

"Huh. Clever." Ben nodded and peered at the grave, then back at my hand. "You making this your specialty? Kind of gross," he smirked.

"You're hilarious. Keep watch," I said.

Ben looked towards the door. "All good, according to Lorcan," he tapped his head.

I dropped to my knees and ran my fingers around the edge of Leonardo da Vinci's grave. My blood quickly clotted as it sunk into the hairline perimeter of the slab that separated his bones from me.

So far, nothing, not a rumble, not the slightest vibration. I sat back, staring at the marble, wracking my mind. I bit my lip, surely my blood hadn't lost its magic, surely, I hadn't made a mistake?

Ben pointed at the effigy of Leonardo's face, "Try there."

I pulled the already healing cut open, it stung, I winced, but I squeezed the skin until my knuckles whitened. Blood bloomed along the seam of sliced skin; I held it a few inches above the effigy of Leo's face. Droplets slid down Leonardo's cheek and into his mouth. It pooled below his nose. The colourful light from the stained windows caught my blood's iridescence. It cast a rainbow sheen over the sculpture. I spread my hand over the image and pulsed heat into it, hoping my energy might hurry things along.

I waited, rocking on my heels, hands clutched under my chin; impatience whipped my heart.

The marble slab began to rumble.

"Something's happening," I said. Excitement overtook impatience.

The effigy began to move. It twisted like a bottle top until it had rotated three hundred and sixty degrees. The grave ceased its quivering, the effigy sat quietly, nothing further opened or clicked or moved.

I curled my bloody fingers into my thighs, "Have I missed something?" I said more to myself.

"Sophia?" Lorcan whispered into my mind, *"Don't know what you've done in there, but there's a fog on the horizon. Hurry up."*

I bit my thumbnail, "C'mon, Leo, make this easy."

Ben dropped in next to me. "You need the whole grave open?" he ran his hands along its edges, his skin tinged red by my blood.

I chilled with the fear that Rogues would chase me away before I found what I needed. I sunk my nails and my dagger into the slab's edges, pulled and levered it, but nothing budged.

"I don't know!" I snapped with frustration. "Elizabeth's grave just opened when I ran my dagger around — oh, hang on!"

I slapped my forehead as though I was stupid and edged back to the effigy. I'd bled on it and it had turned, but it hadn't tasted my dagger. I drew the diamond point around the effigy. Nothing moved.

I took Ben's hands, "Let's see if we can…" I guided his hands under mine, pushing clockwise, our fingers interlocked and our power combined.

There was a click.

Together, we turned the effigy. It moved slowly, grinding against the five hundred years it had been settled in place. Ben's hands glimmered with power under mine. I added to it, a small pulsation with each push.

Lorcan appeared behind us, his disguise gone, his face flushed.

"The Rogues are just beyond the castle's boundary!"

"I can smell them," I said.

Ben and I pushed harder.

"What have you…" Lorcan halted mid-sentence as the effigy clicked again, and the disc came loose. We lifted it, a rush of stagnant air plumed out. We dropped the disc to the floor.

We peered into the black hole of Leonardo's grave; a perfect circle, the size of a large pizza. The thought made me hungry. I hadn't eaten in a while. My fingers curled over the edge, the air within the blackness below felt thicker, hotter, not at all inviting.

"That'll be a tight squeeze," I muttered. "Here," I unhooked my belt and passed it to Lorcan.

Deep breath in, deep breath out.

"Careful," Lorcan said. I nodded thanks and sat at the edge. I dangled my legs into the hole, toes curled in my boots at the prospect of what I was about to do… again.

"Wonder how deep it is?" I looked at both Ben and Lorcan, shrugged and lowered myself down to my waist. I kicked around with my feet, feeling for something to step onto. Hanging by my elbows, I was about to drop in when something caught my eye on the underside of the effigy, which lay a couple of feet away from me.

"Oh my God, it's there!"

"What?" the boys asked.

"Under the disc!" I pulled myself back up, "Look, there's something stuck und…"

Something grabbed my ankle and yanked me into the grave. I hit my head on the edge on the way down. Stars peppered my vision. I hit something solid but very much moving and rotten in the grave's stuffy darkness. I knew what it was immediately.

The Rogue flipped me underneath itself. Vile fluids slipped through my fingers as I clawed at its snapping jaw. Bony fingers dug into my shoulders, pushing me into the slimy ground. Slush filled my ears as I wrenched my face around to avoid the Rogue's bite. It chittered and snarled as it lashed for me.

I was fighting a corpse that could well have been Leonardo Da Vinci.

"Soph?" Lorcan yelled.

"Sophia?" Ben screamed my name.

"Stay there!" I screamed at the boys, but gagged when I breathed the fetid air.

With every movement, I smashed into the slimy sides of the crypt. I flushed light into my hands. The vile creature was nothing but bone, which afforded me multiple places to latch onto it.

Ben dangled his feet in.

"No!" I yelped. "Stop… any more getting… in. I've got… this!"

The corpse gnashed at me again. I dug my fingers into its eye sockets and pushed it away from my neck. I curled my fingers through its ribs while its skinless fingers clawed into my shoulders. I screamed through my teeth and ripped a rib bone out of its ribcage. It let go, the pain of its fingers ripping through my flesh excruciating. I flipped us over, shoved its skull into the slush. Thick ooze seeped through my clothes, as I pushed it down. The Rogue slowed as the mud sucked it deeper.

I pulsed more heat into my hands and punched the skull. I spread my wings, and the ceiling exploded. Daylight streamed in. Marble pummelled into me, but I didn't stop; ignoring the assault of the debris, coughing on the dust, I finished what I started.

Astride the thrashing Rogue, I sunk my fingers into the eye sockets and pulled, decapitating it. A scream of relief erupted from me as I sat on the bones gasping, horrified, exhausted.

Ben and Lorcan reached down to give me a hand up, but I shook my shoulders and pumped my wings once. Landing back on the chapel floor, I leaned onto my knees, heaving with exertion. Bone and stone fragments fell from my hair, I wanted to vomit, but I held it back, wouldn't do it in fort of them.

I groaned, "Any… more… out there?"

"You're hurt," Ben said.

I coughed, "I'm fine."

Lorcan kneeled next to me and plucked something else from my hair, "You're bleeding… a lot."

"I'm fine!" I snapped. I was pissed off at every single part of this endeavour.

A wave of dizziness rocked me to the side. "Actually…" I slumped onto my backside, "Sorry, I just…." My shoulders pulsed; pain clawed through them. The numbness of shock wore off and I felt everything. "Help me please," I reached for one of them, I didn't care who.

"You're okay, were here," Lorcan ran his hand over my shoulder as I healed a gash down my forearm. He picked up my hand and healed the wound I'd made with the dagger. It joined the myriad of other silver scars across my palm.

I smiled weakly and pulled my hand away, "Thanks."

Lorcan smiled, Ben offered me a hand up.

I took it, held it longer than necessary before I dusted myself off.

"I'll feel a whole lot better when I'm out of this place," deflection was my specialty in these moments. "Where's the effigy?"

We searched the rubble strewn across the floor; kicked clumps of marble and sludge out of the way. The place was destroyed, a sliver of guilt struck me, until Ben called out.

"Got it," he slid it from beneath a shard of stained glass. With shaking hands, I turned it over. On the flip side, right under the head where the atlas bone would be, an oval gemstone glowed quietly to itself. I held it up and smiled at the boys with relief.

"Beneath mine atlas!" I shook my head, plucked it carefully out of its niche. It sent my pendant into a flurry of excitement. The chain pulled towards the new gem. The gem, in turn, pulsed white and trembled between my fingers.

I held my pendant steady and brought them together. When they were mere centimetres apart, Leo's gem flew from my grasp and smacked into my pendant. They clung to each other like long lost lovers.

My new pendant spun, slowly at first but became brighter and faster until it was nothing but a white blur. Its energy was strong and strange, and triggered my mark into a power surge — a power that brought calm and new confidence. It slowed, the glow dulled, until it fell limp against the chain. It had doubled in size and sat warm in my palm.

"Well, that was… unexpected," I said.

Ben poked the pendant.

Lorcan pointed to the door, where fingers of fog made their way inside, "We can admire it later. Let's get out of here."

The pendant was heavier against my chest as I slipped the chain back over my head. I pulled out the phone again and double-checked the second set of coordinates.

We transferred with my hopes soaring.

Chapter
Twenty-Two

We landed into a run along a narrow pathway dug into the side of harsh limestone hills. A rugged treescape hugged their base. The ground was hard and slippery with frost and a light peppering of gravel. A brisk breeze whistled through the landscape.

I held out the phone and followed the compass. We were a quarter mile away and needed to go up. Flying would have been easy but too dangerous; a beacon for evil to follow.

"Power down," I said. "I don't want more Rogues if I can help it."

I followed the pulse of my reborn pendant. We took careful steps as the ground steepened and became icier. Urgency pushed me on, but I didn't want to risk more attacks.

I shielded my eyes from the glare of the falling sun, unsure what I was looking for. A bird cried above and landed on the handrail of a wooden walkway up ahead. I held out the compass and brought out the coordinates again.

We took off towards the bird. The path was two-people wide. I led until we crossed the walkway and stopped in front of a small arched cave. Security doors screened it. Trespasser warning signs hung from its vertical struts.

It was heavily signposted as a heritage tourist site.

Ben pulled at the handle.

He huffed and scratched his head, "Everything is always locked."

The one bonus of the world-wide panic was that tourist destinations were abandoned. We didn't have to conceal ourselves, which made things a little less stressful.

Lorcan sniffed around the door and tugged at it. "What is this place?" he read the information placard. "An excellent example of the best-preserved figurative cave paintings in the world," Lorcan frowned, looking the sign over again. "Interesting. It's called the Chauvet Caves."

I ran my hand along the rocky walls.

"Well, whatever it is, we need to go inside."

My pendant pounded so hard now that I had to hold it tight to keep it from ripping off my neck.

"I know this place," Ben said.

I swung around to him, "You have my attention."

If he'd been here, were other Daimon still lurking? Worry tapped the back of my mind.

Ben brushed past me and melted the locks with a sharp pulse of power.

"No powers, man," Lorcan protested.

"Calm down, it was only a spark," Ben pulled the handle, and the gate screeched open.

Being a tourist hotspot, there were industrial light switches just inside the door. A quick flick, and the entire place lit up in a sandy glow. Steel-trimmed wooden walkways skimmed walls that were painted with all manner of animals and figures. Coal lines of Palaeolithic horses and people stretched across the walls like an ancient Bayeux tapestry of prehistoric man. I stared in awe.

"Are you going to tell us how you know this place?" I asked.

"I sent a Daimon down here a long time ago," Ben responded. "Maybe five hundred years ago. It was supposed to extract intel from someone hiding here."

He walked on ahead, fists clenched by his sides, and peered over the balustrade. I leaned over the railing next to him. There was nothing but puddles below.

Lorcan hovered near the door to keep watch.

"Who lived here?" I asked.

He moved to the other side, looking left and right, "Leonardo, Soph."

"Here? He lived here?" I leaned back against the balustrade and crossed my arms, trying to imagine why one of the greatest minds of modern times, would have lived in a dank cave.

"Why were you interested in him back then?" I asked.

Ben scanned the art works, "He was just a person of interest who'd been associated with Queen Elizabeth, your grandmother. Ironic now. It's all sort of just falling together now, isn't it?" Ben peered over his shoulder at me, a shadow of a smile softened the seriousness of his face.

I pushed off the railing, grabbed my pendant.

"They lived during the same time period, long enough to associate. We weren't sure if he was important, but clearly," he eyed my pendant, "Leo was very important."

I followed Ben further along, drumming my fingers against my lips.

"You know, that makes sense," I said. "I've read a little about him over the past two days, and apparently, he disappeared for two years, totally unaccounted for. When he returned, his art and inventions weren't the same." I paused to admire the black markings of men chasing deer, "His art was more imaginative and frightening. He documented that he'd lived in a cave and had been tortured by visions of demons." I gasped, "You tortured him?"

I shoved Ben in the back before I realised what I was doing. He stumbled forwards.

Any anger fell quickly from his expression.

His hands flew up. "Listen, I delivered a long-dead Daimon here. I never touched the guy," his mark brightened around his eye. "He must have come across Rogues or something later on," he shrugged and kept his distance.

"Why would he be tortured? And why here?"

"He clearly was hidden here, for his protection, but obviously it wasn't hidden enough. Kasadya visited here a few times, okay? I heard he tried to frighten intel out of Leonardo, I know that much. He wouldn't have harmed him and ruined his chance to get information about the Kaladai. Knowing Kasadya, he would have terrorised Leonardo with bribes and threats. He was a murderous bastard, but not a stupid one," Ben said.

None of that made it seem any better.

"Kasadya never got anything out of Leonardo anyway, because a Watcher drove him away," Ben gripped hard onto the balustrade, his knuckles white. "This Watcher whisked Leonardo away and protected him from then on. We never heard anything about him again. No Leo, no intel on the Kaladai."

"Until he became a Rogue?" I grunted, wondering if that could have been him in the crypt.

He threw his hands up again, "If that was him, it wasn't my doing,"

"We can argue all day about a dead guy or get on with whatever we're doing here," Lorcan pointed towards the length of the walkway, annoyance in his tone. He bolted the entrance door and jiggled it to check it was secure, "You know Ben's done some bad shit, Soph, but you've vouched for him, forgiven him, and encouraged us to trust him. You need to leave his past in the past."

I pinched the bridge of my nose. "You're right," I wiped my hands over my face. "Sorry Ben."

Ben swept his arm out for me to go ahead, "It's okay, I understand. Let's keep going."

I squeezed his hand as we walked back to the main door. We started again, our searching new and deeply focused.

Small but powerful floor lamps shone up from the underside of the walkway. They highlighted the most well-preserved images of bison herds. I ran my hands along the balustrade. The shadows beyond the lights drew me in, and I paused between two lights.

The boys leaned in and squinted beyond the spotlights' reach. A shiver ran through my body, snuggled into my belly, and churned a dreaded chill.

"I think this place has seen more than I care to know," Lorcan whispered.

The light didn't catch the less palatable pictures, the ones that were inexplicable and horrendous. They were left in the deepest shadows, where human eyes couldn't penetrate. Shrivelled faces bore down from the upper reaches; Rogues in various stages of decay, some faded, some bold and frighteningly life-like.

"It must have been terrifying for Leonardo," I whispered

I followed the dreadful images until we reached a crossroads. My pendant pulled strongly off-track to the left, where the walkway ended and darkness enveloped the light. I threw an orb in that direction and jumped back when Belial's face blazed into view high above.

Lorcan brushed close to me, "Hell, I thought it was him too." He had a hand on his weapons belt and one over his heart. "You okay?"

I nodded as I studied the life-like painting. Every detail was precise, down to the two horns he had once possessed.

I shivered, "If Leo met him and survived, he must have been one strong human. I can't imagine being mortal and not losing it after encountering Belial, especially in those times."

"Leo was a little…" Ben circled his finger next to his temples, "From what I've heard."

I shook my head. "Can't have been too undone, he's left some damned clever clues for us," I pointed ahead. "My pendant's pulling this way."

We moved to the last foot of the walkway. A large sign warned not to trespass due to falling rocks. I jumped over the balustrade onto uneven ground. Shadows engulfed me, and my pendant pulled me into the solid darkness. I waved for them to follow. The thump of their feet echoed around us.

"Something's here, that's for sure," I said. "My pendant is about to rip my head off."

The air cooled significantly as the incline dropped quickly. The smell of calcified rock mixed with damp was heavy and stagnant.

I pointed ahead to where two smaller tunnels branched off from the main cavern. I flicked my hand and drew out a modest orb. Its dim light was enough to reveal hundreds of images around the smaller tunnel. Detailed etchings of flying machines and mathematical equations beyond my understanding surrounded winged beings. I kicked something and looked down to find scatterings of human activity. A cup, half a wooden plate, and dozens of coal nibs. Ben picked up what looked like a paint brush hewn from a twig. He turned it over a few times and dropped it again.

Above the waist-height entrance, all these things were under the watching smirk of an umber portrait of Mona Lisa.

"Looks like a clue to me," Lorcan muttered. "He must have spent a lot of his time here," he picked around the detritus.

Ben threw a skull at Lorcan, who caught it and growled.

Ben smirked, "Looks like one of his Rogue visitors."

"You're an arse."

Lorcan threw it back at Ben, who ducked. The skull smashed somewhere behind him. It calmed me to see them muck around.

Ben brushed past Lorcan and kneeled to peer into the arched entrance, "You ready to go in there?"

I squatted next to him, "Are you?"

I was really getting sick of dark holes.

"Angels first," he drawled.

His scent of ashes and spice was uncomfortably tempting. I turned away and crawled into the tunnel.

It narrowed and became claustrophobic. I grasped the uneven terrain of smooth rock and bit my lip, forcing myself to face the dark.

Lorcan squeezed in behind me, "You okay up there?"

"Yep. I think I'm… Yes, I'm out," I pulled myself out of the tight tunnel and threw a light orb up.

I was in a large inner chamber with a ceiling that soared way up into blackest heights. Two impressive alabaster stalactites, covered in concentric circles, plunged through the middle.

The boys stretched out next to me, hands on hips.

"Well, if that isn't my calling card," I pointed at the stalactites and their matching stalagmites. Water drizzled from them, a slow, mesmerising *drip, drip*.

I hopped across a fissure in the ground to reach them. My fingers trailed across their smooth rock and into the deep circular indentations. Lorcan walked around them, inspecting their glistening, calcified skin.

Ben rested a hand on the surface, "Can I read the last prophecy? I might be able to help."

I reached for my dagger, ready to accept Ben's help. Lorcan subtly shook his head, "Don't show him."

Ben ground his jaw and slapped the stalagmite.

"You said to let the past go!" I glared at Lorcan.

"I know, but..." Lorcan ran his hand roughly across his chin, thinking. Old habits and beliefs died hard.

Ben scoffed as though he sensed we were communicating, still unsure of him.

"Fine, work it out yourselves, but I know what this is," he said.

"What would Enli'el do?" I wondered to myself. No, I changed that quickly to, *"What should I do?"*

My fingers lingered on the dagger, growing tighter by the second.

Ben sat on a nearby rock, stretched his arms over his head, and leaned back looking all too care free. I waved him over.

"Are you sure?" Lorcan whispered into my head.

"Yes. Besides, I've got you. Everything will be fine."

"Don't you know it!" Lorcan reversed. "I'll watch the entrance," Lorcan wandered back towards the small tunnel.

Ben wandered over to me and raised his brows; no smile, no smart cracks, "Change your mind?"

"Give me your hand," I said. He looked surprised when I placed the dagger in his palm, "Forgiveness, right. That's what I offer you."

Ben curled his fingers around the blade. His hand glowed a little, and he took a deep breath. He walked to a large outcropping and paced; the dagger tight in his hand.

"Light it up," he said.

I shone my light through the dagger, and the prophecy projected onto the rocky wall. Ben ran a finger under *I'el doth balance upon the truth.*

"What does that mean?" I asked, my brows knit tight.

He stepped away and turned me around so that I was looking at the stalactites and stalagmites.

"Now, back away but keep your eye on them."

We reversed together. I glanced towards Lorcan, who was disappearing back through the tunnel. Had he heard something outside?

Ben guided my shoulders while I focussed ahead. He positioned me a little to the right.

"That's it, I think," he leaned over my shoulder and pointed at the largest stalactite and stalagmite. "Look at them. Position yourself until their points align."

"Got it. Now what?"

Ben threw a light orb behind the stalactite. It burst into a soft white glow and hovered, its light cutting through the shadows. He moved my shoulders a little more to the right. I checked for Lorcan again, but he'd disappeared.

"What do you see?" Ben's warm breath against my ear sent a shiver down my neck.

I cleared my throat. Another shiver ran down my neck, but for a different reason. My pendant thrummed at the sight.

Vitruvian Man stretched his arms on the wall behind the stalagmite and stalactite. From my position, the image nestled between the stalagmite and stalactite… balancing between them.

"I'el doth balance upon the truth," I whispered.

"How did you know?" I asked, heart racing.

"I've been around, you know. I'el is the balance of all things. He is truth, he is knowledge. On A'vean, at the entrance to the Great Throne

Palace beyond the White Mountains, there's a great sculpture of Him balancing on the universe as its creator and destructor. It looks almost exactly like this, except on A'vean, he balances between two great diamond shards. Looks pretty much the same to me from the ancient texts I was taught from as a child. There was little left to learn since the Fall, but that was one thing we were taught about."

I took a step forward. "If he balances on knowledge and truth…" I raced to the stalagmite, "It must be underneath!"

I hunkered over the stones. They were so earthly and utterly unimportant to the eye, but now I saw them in a very different light.

"Something's coming!" Lorcan's voice echoed somewhere within the tunnel.

I stared at my hands, rolled my eyes, "I haven't even bled yet."

Ben rushed to my side, "We've used the E'lan." He unravelled his wings. Their light illuminated the area further and provided a protective barrier for me. "Hurry. Lorcan's radar is spot on," He looked worriedly towards the way we'd entered.

I felt the shift; no fog, no stench, but a dark tug in the atmosphere. My fingers rushed all over the cool white stone, feeling along the circular etchings. The E'lan's panic quickened my every move.

Ben handed my dagger back, "You'll need this, I'm sure."

I snatched it and poked it into my palm below my thumb.

"Why not keep bleeding if they're on their way anyway," I urged my blood to run quickly, and it sizzled along circular tracks in the stone. Like my pendant, the E'lan pulsed faster, a rhythmic electricity in the air, tugged my hair, pricked my skin.

"Hurry!" Lorcan called, "I don't know what it is!"

A thunderous rumble reverberated under me.

"Can you make something happen faster?" Ben urged.

"Give me some space," I elbowed him back and willed a new surge of power to my hand. It coagulated the blood into silvery, ruby crystals, under which the stone developed cracks that spiderwebbed across its surface. "Umm…" I backed away, pushing Ben behind me.

The ceiling groaned, there was an ear-splitting crack and the stalactite fell towards the stalagmite. I lurched backwards into Ben. We ducked under his wings. They arched over us, deflecting the rubble. A white powdering blanketed the ground around us. There was a moment of silence when the stalactite's and stalagmite's points touched.

I crawled back to the geological marvels but pulled my hand back when the cracks on the stalagmite fractured open. It sent seismic rifts into the stalactite, which trembled until it fell and exploded on the ground.

I scuttled back under Ben's wings until the rocky hail had settled. We coughed on the dust, and I swished my hand in front of my face to clear the air. My eyes widened, "Wow!"

The stalagmite had opened up, blossoming into eight even segments. They started to slowly move inwards and outwards, pumping like a coarse geological machine that was winding itself up. It clicked and began to spin. "Look at that!" I said.

Ben's eyes were as wide as mine, a smile softened almost constant pain in his face.

"Sophia!" Lorcan called.

"We've got something!" I yelled back, "Hold on!" I pulled Ben's hand.

Ben hunched closer, "What is it?" Excitement hurried his words.

Unlike the panicked angst searing through my gut, the machine spun unhurriedly. The segments moved with a deliberate precision until something within it clicked again and the stone creation halted in suspended animation, wedges half open.

My pendant vibrated harder than ever. Its impatient pull stung where it dug into my neck. I unlatched it from my neck and held it above the strange device. I bit my lip when it began to glow. Blue, hints of pink and yellow emanated from within the pendant, a vibrant, nebulous glow that ignited a reaction in the stone segments.

Ben took my hand and quelled its tremor. We held the chain steady as the pendant and rock connected on a level I didn't understand. The segments moved again, fanned out; the grind of rock against rock like a grainy heartbeat. The pendant spun faster and drew the stone's core up and out of its centre. The movement halted, the grinding stopped, and my pendant stilled.

Ben pointed at the stone plug, "There's something under it."

I looked closer; something shimmered beneath the plug. I put my pendant back on despite its pulsing protests, I needed both hands for whatever I might find.

"Dig," I said excitedly.

Our fingers gouged into the ground and unearthed the rocky apparatus piece by piece. Ben flung the segments aside one by one until only the core was left. A rim of light emanated up from beneath it.

"You dig, I'll pull it out," Ben said.

The ground was harder the deeper we went. Sweat dripped from the tip of my nose. I found a sharp piece of debris nearby and sliced and jabbed at the earth to loosen it. Ben pulled and rocked the core back and forth. The light brightened underneath.

He fell backwards when the core slipped out of the ground.

My pendent fluttered. I reached into the tight hollow all the way to my elbow until my fingers hit something hard. I gripped it with my fingertips and retrieved a small, impossibly shiny object.

"Huh! Another box!" It sat snug in my palm, and I ran my fingers over it. It was plain chromious, simple and smooth without embellishments.

Wind rushed into the chamber, a short *whoosh* like the cave had taken a breath. I peered over my shoulder towards the tunnel, but Lorcan still wasn't back.

The ground rumbled.

"What the hell is that?" Ben yelled into the tunnel.

"No clue!" Lorcan's words were drawn out with a nervous lilt, "It's not Rogues though!"

Ben cupped my hand that held the artefact, "Please hurry. Sophia,"

His touch helped, and I had no idea why. The little container began to vibrate.

I curled my fingers around its edges to keep it safe whilst my pendant jiggled against the chain, matching its rhythm.

I felt the tingle of Lorcan's wings rustle the E'lan and heard the metallic echo of a sword being drawn. My stomach rolled; my hands shook until I couldn't tell if it was me or the box. The ground developed a rhythmic rumble that was almost in tune with the pendant and box.

"Go help Lorcan," I said.

"I'm not leaving you until we know what this thing is. He's more than capable."

"We don't know what's coming. Please, go check on him."

Ben squeezed my hand and tipped my chin up to his face. "I'm staying with you," his voice was firm, his eyes unrelenting.

I looked away first, and he dropped his hand.

The awkward moment was interrupted when the box shuffled around my palm and a new breath of wind rushed in, swirling debris around us. The thunderous pounding grew louder. My fingers twitched as static began to arc around the box. Ben held my forearm as its casing began to shimmer and shake.

It rose a few inches above my still-twitching fingers and spun. Its sides became liquid mercury and dribbled away into beaded droplets to reveal a spinning silver cage within. I reached for it, but it flew at me and thumped into my chest. I gasped and fell backwards, expecting blood under the bruising pain.

Ben pulled me back up, "You okay?"

He checked me over whilst the breeze settled. I patted myself down and wiped the stinging sweat from my eyes. There was no blood after all.

"Yes, I think so."

"But what…" Ben plucked at the pendant's chain. "Look at this," he held it up so that it dangled in front of my nose.

I drew a sharp breath.

The opal now sat inside a spherical capsule — a pulsing chromious cocoon that beat like a colourful gemstone heart and mimicked my own.

I took it between my fingers and sat back, bedazzled.

Ben squatted next to me, "What do you do now?"

I groaned. "More of the same, I suppose," I drew my dagger.

Ben winced. "Whoever decided this is a sick bastard," he shook his head and got back to his feet.

I pricked the edge of my palm. My hand was raw, and I resented every scar. Ben circled me and kept watch as I rolled the pendant over my bleeding palm. The gem flared at the touch of my biological PIN. A light beamed out of it, and I swayed in surprise. Its beacon bounced around the cave. It criss-crossed the whole space until it hit somewhere in the shadows to my left. More light erupted above a charcoal image of a large horse, rearing and wings wide.

I lowered the pendent against my chest and stumbled towards it.

"That looks like Grey."

The ground shuddered. Ben rose into the air and lit up, ready for whatever was coming. I freed mine, too, and hovered just above the unsteady ground.

I threw Kea's sword to him, "Use it if you need to, but look after it."

Ben swirled the precious weapon in an arc and ignited it with his energy.

Another rumble unsettled the ground. A regular thundering beat.

"Lorcan, get back in here!" I called.

He didn't respond.

"Lorcan?"

Still nothing. I couldn't focus on him as the ground's thundering beat became more reverberant by the second.

Ben and I circled back-to-back. New sweat drizzled down my face.

Lorcan finally flew in, his face flushed. He threw a fresh illuminating orb into the air and zipped in front of us, then behind us as he searched for the cause of the disturbance.

I faced the etching of the winged horse, "Seems to be coming from this way."

Ben turned back to the tunnel, "No, this way."

"It's coming from everywhere," Lorcan yelled over the cacophony. He circled the room and stopped by my side.

Metal screeched in the outer chamber where the walkways' footings rocked.

"Show yourself!" Lorcan said.

"You go that way, I'll go there," I said and we split up, each in a different corner.

I was drawn to the image of the horse, its proud head, the rearing hooves, the alert ears and smart eyes. The E'lan's tune felt softer under the image, its song melding with the rhythmic pounding. The sound reminded me of summer afternoons when my hair had streamed behind me, Grey galloping underneath.

There was an ear-splitting *crack*, and the image fractured. I lurched back as it slid off the face of the rock.

The wall exploded. I tumbled head over heels until my wings righted me. Ben and Lorcan landed either side of the gaping hole, their weapons lowered.

My hands flung to my mouth. I squealed with surprise.

A resplendent creature stood atop the crumbled mess.

"Hello, my friend. I've been waiting an eternity for this moment."

In all his stunning glory stood Grey, my Pegasus.

Chapter
Twenty-Three

Fresh acacia blossoms wove through Grey's soft mane. I buried my face in it, and he nuzzled into my neck. His warm grassy breath spoke of fresh mornings and blush sunrises, of memories of goodness. I twirled white strands of mane between my fingers, kissed his muzzle over and over. His fine whiskers tickled my nose, and I giggled. It had been months but felt like years.

Lorcan leaned in and patted Grey's neck, "Beautiful creature."

Grey snorted at him.

Lorcan backed off and rolled his eyes, "Sorry."

Ben laughed, "Don't get between Soph and her animals."

I laughed, too, and for a moment, contentment coursed through me.

"We must depart," Grey whispered into my mind. *"We have a long journey to make."*

Wanting to savour this moment, I clung to him a little tighter and ignored the E'lan's chatter until its song changed. Its essence held the strange tone from before, a dark bass that made me want to run. Grey tensed. He wrapped his wings around me and pulled me against his warm body.

"Hide," he nudged me with his muzzle. The air buzzed with something wicked.

Lorcan energised his sword, his eyes quickly sweeping over me. "Get out of here, Soph! Do what your beast says."

Grey hugged me closer, obscuring my view. Outside my safe haven, I heard swooping sounds like magpies dive-bombing in spring. I peered through a gap in Grey's wings.

"Get her out of here!" Ben yelled, his back to me, watching the thickness of new shadows that seemed to penetrate the cavern.

Grey struck out at something with his rear hooves. I pushed my way out from his warm protection.

Human shaped smudges dashed about above. They moved so quickly it was hard to tell how many. They swept down in pairs, struck with smoky wings, and slashed with clawed hands.

Grey's wing knocked one of the things away from me. It screeched like a hawk and thudded to the ground.

Grey circled me. *"Get on my back!"* his hooves clipped noisily as he aimed his wings at the attackers.

"Now, my friend…up!" Grey stamped impatiently and I hoisted myself onto his back and gripped with my legs as Grey double-barrel-kicked out behind.

Lorcan and Ben chased the shadows around the cave and away from me, their blurring light the polar opposite to the attackers' dark.

My pendant chilled and shivered as though it, too, was scared.

I held on tight to Grey's mane as he reared and struck another two. The E'lan in his blazing white hooves turned the creatures to ash before I could see what they were. The smell of burning flesh began to permeate the air.

Ben swooped in. "Stay with Grey, and get out of here!" he threw Kea's sword back to me.

I dug my thighs in for balance as Grey poured his hooves into the ground, snorting and tossing his head. I infused Kea's sword with power so it shone like a beacon. I held it up, trying to identify the creatures. Whatever they were, they held off for now, and I didn't fancy inciting them further. In the crevices overhead, orange eyes beamed down from the shadows. Six were circling overhead. They seemed very much like us, but not.

Grey pivoted on his back feet and kept his eyes on them. Ben and Lorcan flanked us.

"What are they?" my voice quivered.

"They look like hers," Ben seethed.

"They certainly…" Lorcan was cut off.

The ones circling overhead formed a V and dove down. Lorcan and Ben shot up, slashing their wings at them.

Grey arced a wing over my head. I flattened myself against his withers and sliced out to gut an assault to my right. The force unbalanced me, and I slid heavily to the ground atop the still-twitching body of what looked like a Watcher but smelled of blood, old and new. I rolled away and groaned in disgust. Grey's hooves smashed the torso, descending the creature. Orange and blue flames engulfed it.

There was another *thud* nearby. I hurried to my knees and spread my wings to lift off, but I slid in something. Sharp pain sung through my head and blurred my vision. Something swooped down from above. I rolled out of the way, glimpsing Ben overhead with a whip of light. It looked like slow motion. The sounds were dull, as though far away. But the metallic tang of blood in the air was raw and drew my senses back.

I pumped my wings to slide away from another body that fell heavily to the ground, but it smelled like a fresh ocean breeze. I froze.

"Lorcan?" I felt like I'd been punched in the chest.

I lunged towards him and grabbed a limp arm. His fingers curled weakly around mine, and he moaned. I hauled him into the shadows under an outcropping of rock, rolled him right into the wedge between the ground and the wall.

"Oh God, no! Lorcan, open your eyes!" I shook his torso. He didn't respond. I shook him a little harder, "Where are you hurt?"

Something swooped close to me. I turned and shot an orb at it, hitting its arm. Grey pivoted towards us and lopped its head off its shoulders.

Grey lowered his muzzle to Lorcan's face and nickered. *"Be quick, young one. We must leave this place,"* he rose back into the air and circled above me.

I ran my shaking hands over Lorcan's body that was slippery and wet. Blood pulsed from a hole in his chest guard. For a moment my entire body froze.

"Please, just be a scratch…" my fingers trembled back to life and I reached to unlatch his armour. He moaned, and his eyes fluttered. I pulled his chest plate away. "Ben!" I screamed as arterial blood sprayed into my face. A glowing elemental spear was still embedded in a large gaping wound. I pressed my hands against his flesh to stem the blood flow, and Lorcan moaned louder. "Hang on, Lorcan, I'll fix this," I knew I couldn't, but I wasn't about to accept what was pressed beneath my hands.

"Leave him!" Ben yelled.

A single creature chased him. Ben slashed its head away, and the body fell to the ground. Grey stomped into it.

Ben landed next to me and reached for my hand, his expression when he saw Lorcan was truth in a glance, "Get on Grey *now*!"

"No! He's gonna be…" I slapped Lorcan's cheeks, trying to get a response. "You can't do this to me!" his skin was cold and sour. I pulsed heat against deaths' grasp. Above, the chaotic screeches grew louder and wilder.

I glared at Ben, "Keep them away from us. Please, just give him a chance!"

Ben's eyes slid between Lorcan and I. He checked on Grey, who chased another creature into the air.

"I'll do what I can, but when I say *go*, you go!"

Despite what my heart demanded, I nodded.

Ben shot up behind Grey. A chorus of screeches followed.

"Hold on, please?" I flipped Lorcan onto his side. He groaned deeper. "Please Lorcan, I need to… I need you to know how sorry I am…" tears blurred my vision.

The weapon's glow revealed an even bigger wound in his back. My skin chilled. "Shit!" I snapped my head up, blinking my eyes clear, looking for whoever had done this. No vampire or Rogue could have used the E'lan to create such a weapon.

"There's a Daimon in here somewhere!" I yelled to Ben.

The power of Ben's wings was like strikes of lightning. The creatures dashed amongst his swipes. Bile stung my throat, their numbers were growing, and Ben was on his own.

The glowing weapon in Lorcan's chest faded, slowly, petering out, a dying ember, just like him. It had cut through his spine, macerated all his innards. My hands shook impossibly hard as they glided over the glistening flesh. Rib bones, raw and sharp, poked out of the wound. I bit my lip and curled my fingers into a tight fist, extinguishing the useless healing energy. This injury was beyond me and so was the opportunity to apologise for treating him so badly.

Tears of guilt and despair dripped from my chin, melded with his blood. I rolled him over and pulled him into my lap. I cocooned us within my wings while shivering at the sounds above.

"Lorcan? I… I'm…" I lifted his limp head, kissed his lips, and held him tight, "I'm so sorry, Lorcan. You deserved better from me."

His pulse was gone, his cheek cooling against mine.

"He's dead!" Ben shouted down, "Get onto Grey!"

Grey's hooves hit the ground behind me.

I hesitated, then lowered Lorcan gently back onto the ground and kissed his forehead, and gave him a last K'ufili, "May we meet again." He took a reflexive last breath and burst into blue flames.

My body moved like someone else was driving. I retrieved Kea's sword and scraped it along the ground, then swung it in a circle overhead. My skin trembled with anger, but this was well placed, and in my control. I pressed my lips together and swished my wings as I pulled myself onto Grey. I looked back at the blue flames that licked at Lorcan's remains and raised the sword.

"Go!" I shouted as fresh tears seared down my face. My skin trembled with fury.

Grey surged towards Ben and smashed through a cluster of five that had been flying in a figure eight. His front hooves knocked two out of control. I swung at another whose orange eyes widened with delight at the sight of me. The too-human face gnashed un-human canines at me. It threw itself at me, clawed fingers ready to strike. A deep, raw scream rushed out of me, and I swung at it, sliced its hands clean from its arms, and it fell to the ground howling. My attention caught on the shine of Lorcan's bones.

I urged Grey to the left to cut my eyes away from the sight and towards the other two that were heading for Ben. Grey flattened his neck to gather speed, and I leaned into his body.

"Hold on!"

We barrel-rolled. Grey's wing sliced a wing off one creature, but we missed the other.

Ben rushed towards us, casting orbs either side of us. I raised my sword and turned to strike whatever was coming, but it hit me hard and I fell from Grey to the ground. My vision whited out as pain gnawed at my spine. I raised my head only to have it slammed into the earth again.

Kea's sword still in my hand, I tried to get up. My eyes watered, I tasted fresh blood. I rolled onto my knees, woozy and nauseous. I stabbed the sword into the ground and pushed myself to my feet. The air above me moved. I peered up, blinking hard, and caught my attacker's swift movement as it lunged again. I swept the sword wide whilst the vile thing pulled up in front of me and seemed to weigh up how dangerous I was. Its amber eyes narrowed, and it sniffed in my direction. We circled each other.

An amused laugh echoed from the nearby shadows. I slashed towards the sound but spun back to the vampire, who was still holding back.

Sweat stung my eyes. My rapid breaths dulled the sounds around me. I held Kea's sword out front, my wings in constant motion. Ben was flying unsteadily, and Grey blurred as he kicked at each attack to keep us safe. My heart stuttered at the thought of losing Ben too. I slashed out again and sliced nothing but air. It had disappeared.

Something rammed me from the side as I was distracted searching for the other vampire. Kea's sword clattered to the ground. There was a flash of sunset eyes and hot breath as it crushed into me against the unforgiving rock wall. My amour whined as it deformed under the pressure. An urgent hand ran over my body and scratched my skin as it searched for something. I turned my face away from its fetid breath and tried to wrench free, but its other arm deepened its vice-like pressure on me. I headbutted it. It screeched and loosened its grip. I drew my dagger before the creature pinned me down again. I thrust upwards, twisted and shoved my blade in until it went no deeper.

The creature yelped and staggered back, grasping at its side. Its misty concealment faded. It fell to its knees and hissed at me.

It looked no older than twelve and utterly confused.

Its mouth quivered, and its eyes clenched from pain. I watched the child-like vampire grimace and snarl as I retrieved Kea's sword and cut off its head.

I leaned onto my knees and gasped. It would have killed me, but… it had been a child.

Ben landed heavily in front of me. Another body fell to the ground nearby. It wasn't dead but lolled under the pain of searing burns across its gut. Ben stood astride it.

He wriggled his fingers, "Your sword, quick!"

I threw it into his hand. He plunged it through the vampires' shoulder, pinning it to the ground.

"Who commands you?" Ben demanded.

The vampire screeched and writhed. It lashed its smoky wings, kicked at him, and hissed like the other had. It was all teeth and claws. Like the other one, it appeared to be a teen, it possessed an undisciplined pubescent face. Its eyes narrowed, and it cocked its head, like a dog listening for something.

Ben twisted the blade, "Who. Commands. You?"

The vampire screamed. It began to yelp a strange repetitive sound, a wild animal calling for its herd. The sounds above faded. The creatures Grey had been chasing fled into the shadows. The E'lan stuttered in my ears, its anxious sting adding to the chill swirling through my bones.

Ben pulled the sword out, "Had your chance."

He cut its neck. Red sprayed into Ben's face. Our eyes met, his wide and wild.

Grey landed nearby. With a flick of his back hoof, he kicked the body aside. His nostrils flared with a stallion's snort.

"I must get you away from here."

I threw myself at him and rubbed his neck, leaned into his warmth. The still air was calm and empty.

"That was one of Lilith's, wasn't it?" I asked, my voice thready and dry.

Ben's heavy eyes were lined with congealed blood. He ran his hand across his stubble, and his shoulders slumped as he squatted.

"I don't know how she could be breeding," he said, shaking his head. "Yeqon cast her out," he smoothed his hand over his head, his face smeared with the vampire's blood, like war paint.

"Well, what do we do about them?" I clutched Grey's neck while listening to the surroundings. Sweat pooled in the back of my neck. Apart from the E'lan's panicked buzzing, there was nothing.

"Listen to Grey," Ben said. "You need to leave. If Lilith's children are hunting you, things are so much worse than Yeqon."

My gut squirmed when fear flickered through Ben's eyes. He bit the side of his mouth. His stare held mine until he shook his head and pushed himself to his feet. His eyes constantly swept overhead.

"We'll need more than just us. We'll need Gedz'iel, we'll need everyone," he squinted into the inkiness. "But you need to keep moving. You're in more danger than ever."

Ben nodded at Grey. Self-preservation made me reach for Grey's withers, ready to see the back of this place.

Ben rose into the air. He spread his wings and pulled out a string of light, which curled around his hand like a whip.

"Get her outta here," he grunted through his teeth.

The E'lan rushed across my skin like a cool electric current. Something whooshed overhead, and I swung up onto Grey's back. Out of the eerie quiet, one of the vampires nicked the back of my neck, then it was gone. I screamed and grabbed my neck. My hand came away glistening red. Ben threw an orb high, but it revealed nothing.

Grey reared, and I held onto his mane for balance. I felt his pulse against my leg and the beginnings of a transfer. I breathed in his comforting smell without a clue where we were going. As his hooves left the ground, I reached for my pendant to hear its reassuring song.

It wasn't there.

I slapped at my neck as Grey's power increased. Through the haze of the pull to another place, I saw a shimmer in the distance.

"Stop! It's got the pendant!"

My voice was syrupy through the tendrils of the transfer, my limbs were lead and my heart and thoughts frantic. The pendant was part of the Kaladai; I couldn't leave without it.

I slipped off Grey and landed with a winding *thud*.

"Sophia!" Ben screamed angrily at me. As I scrambled to regain my senses, Ben scooped me up. I pushed him away.

"I need my pendant back!"

"We're outnumbered, Soph. It's too dangerous!"

Grey landed next to me. *"There will be another way,"* he nudged me with his nose.

I edged away from them, "You don't know that! I will find it, even if I have to kill all these goddamned vamps myself. I didn't go through all this just for them to bloody take it!"

The strain of anger pulsed in my temples. My nostrils flared as I searched for the culprit overhead.

"You can help me or not, but I'm not leaving without it!"

I glared at Grey and Ben whilst my hand slid to my weapons, Kea's sword a comforting weight.

Grey flew next to me, hindering me from rising higher.

"Grey! Out of my way!"

"No, there will be another way. This is not safe."

Ben coasted on my other side and pulled another twine of light from his wings.

"Not one breath of my existence is safe, Grey!"

Conceited laughter followed. My head snapped up.

Nephr'eus clapped as she fluttered down from above, enveloped by a vampiric consort, "Such fun!"

"What the hell are you doing here?" I spat the words like venom.

Ben growled deeply and inched closer to me. Grey screamed a stallion's warning at her.

She batted her long lashes. "Don't worry your pretty little face about a rather tawdry little charm. I've a vault full of lovely things you can have, all for you! Wouldn't that be nice?" her head tilted as she batted her eyes innocently at me.

I rushed at her but pulled up short, sword high above my head. She didn't flinch, just tracked me with her black, seductive eyes.

I urged power from the depths of myself, until it infused the chromious and turned my sword into a whip. I flicked it, and crackling power surged from it straight at her. Her blood-thirsty minions shielded her. Three dropped dead at her feet.

I screamed, "Coward!"

Ben grabbed my waist, but I elbowed him away. Grey also stayed close enough to keep me within the safety of his reach.

"What are you two doing?" My cheeks quivered with fury, "I need my pendant. She killed Lorcan, for the love of…"

"Dear, dear," her sickly voice trilled. "I did no such killing. Friends don't do such things," her hand fluttered to her chest, and she looked to her protectors for support. "Would I do such a thing?" she tickled the chin of the closest vamp. It winced at her touch. She wiped away a little iridescent blood that smeared its mouth and licked it off her finger.

"I'm *not* your friend!" I yelled.

Ben pulled my arm, "Enough. Don't poke a snake, and especially a viper like her."

I swung away from him and circled closer to her. My face burned so hard I though my eyes might ignite.

"Stay out of this, Ben!"

I summoned an orb to my free hand whilst trying to steady the shake in the other.

Nephr'eus' smile thinned, "Feistier by the day, hmm? Perhaps we aren't close, but I'm more your friend than Yeqon, I assure you of that."

The orb left my hand. Her vampire protectors absorbed it. One died from its impact and fell to the ground, looking almost peaceful in repose.

Ben hovered near me, but not in my way.

"What the hell are these abominations?" he asked.

"Hello again, lover," Nephr'eus bit her bottom lip and flicked back a curl. "So many questions, not enough answers."

"You won't leave alive this time," Ben growled.

"Oh, really? You'll dispatch me like my sister?" her eyes narrowed and slid to me, a mocking glint in them. "Will you have your little girlfriend get her claws dirty perhaps?"

She laughed. I cringed and drew new ammunition to the surface. Kea's sword sung with the energy.

"You won't be laughing when I throw you to the Pits of A'vean," Ben said. "Or, return the pendant now, and make your own way to the Hell of your making."

She pressed a hand to her lips, suppressing a laugh and then waiving us off. "Oh, I laugh at your blindness, the both of you. You never saw the forest for the trees, Nik'ael. Always focussed on the pretty little things right in front of you," Nephr'eus blew me a kiss.

I lunged ahead, my body shook with rage, "His name is Ben!"

"It is Nik'ael, is it not?" a deep voice called from the gloom above.

My heart hammered harder against my ribs, my attention torn between Nephr'eus and whoever this was. Shadows flurried about in the vicinity of the unsettling voice, which had a familiar ring. My hackles rose. A glint of red, a flash of white. Grey snorted and swished his tail as his ears angled forwards and then flattened. He zig-zagged in front of me.

Blue eyes glimmered down. Confusion whipped my heart harder. I raised my sword, the metal illuminated with power and my body humming as I infused it with more power. I pulsed an orb from it, but it fizzled away without having revealed the source of the familiar voice. I tried to sense its energy signature, but its noise was radio static.

Nephr'eus chuckled.

"Who are you!" I glanced at Ben, who shrugged. His face was contorted with confusion too.

E'lan whipped around us, attracted to my anger.

Nephr'eus laughed louder and clapped her hands to her face.

"Oh, poke the bear, my dear! Please do! I'm the least of your worries now," she laughed louder.

Ben nudged closer to me, "What are you talking about, Neph'reus?"

A deep laugh rumbled overhead.

"Who is it?" I asked, panicked by another unknown.

"I… I'm not sure. Stay close," Ben whispered into my mind. *"This danger is very different. It feels…"* there was a nervous shake to his tone, more than fear.

"Personal?" I whispered back.

Ben nodded.

The energy was so heavy, so very dark. It felt worse than Yeqon. Nastier than Nephr'eus. I gulped, tried to convince myself to stay and fight, but common sense prodded my bravado. My hands were sweaty; I had to adjust the sword twice to regain my grip.

A new wave fluttered above and disturbed the still air. Grey's stallion cries a damning warning to them. Ben urged me towards him.

"One of our own is up there," Ben said. "One of our own with Lilith's offspring and Nephr'eus. This is beyond bad, Soph."

I didn't resist when he urged me back onto Grey's back.

"But I still need my pendant," I said. "It's guided me for so long. I can't not have it."

"I need you alive more than you need it. Let's transfer somewhere, anywhere. We can regroup with Gedz'iel and come back at them with a force that'll spin their heads."

"But my..."

"We'll find it or work out something else. I don't know who that is up there, but we can't win this one, not here."

My fingers curled though Grey's mane.

Nephr'eus waved us off, "That's right, lovers. Flit away. Off you go, Petal."

Her vamps chortled and flapped their wings as though unsettled. "There, there," she cooed, and pulled one into her bosom stroking its face while smiling at me.

Grey flexed his head so one eye was on me. *I know where to go, and I am sure help will follow you there. Trust me, young one.*

I quivered with the fear of failure, but I acquiesced under the vile energy. My fingers were shaking when I gripped Grey's mane tighter. I looked up into the shadows, back over to Nephr'eus, and finally settled on Ben. Leaving a key piece of myself behind was wrong, but he was right. I was no good to anyone dead.

"We will find a way," I leaned into Grey's mane and whispered, "I'm ready."

Grey reared higher, and his gleaming hooves struck out. Purest wings pushed an updraft between us and them.

"Stop her!" the voice yelled.

Nephr'eus gawked between the shadows and us. Confusion ran through her conceited expression.

"Get them," she yelled, shaky and unsure.

Ben pulled a new whip of energy from his wings and lassoed it over his head, "Go! I'll hold them off!"

Vamps swooped towards us, their swift speed a frightening *thump-thump* as they sliced through the cool air and dive-bombed. Ben's slashes kept them at bay. His whip cracked to my left, and I turned to see a vampire's neck open only inches from me. Blood sprayed though Grey's wing.

Grey arced wide but dove to the right and lowered again, *"I can't find the E'lan!"*

He hit the ground in a gallop and jumped over the bodies. His hair was slick with sweat, which made it hard to hold on. A vamp darted in close. Grey dodged left, but its claws degloved one of Grey's ears. The bloody pink leaflet twitched with agony. Grey screamed and struck the vamp with his front hooves. It tumbled backwards twice but dove at us again, its horribly human face split by a garish fanged grimace. Grey tossed it up like a rag doll. Ben dropped down and cut the beast in two with a single slash.

He slapped Grey's rump, "Get her outta here!"

"He can't transfer," I yelled.

Ben knocked back four with a barrage of orbs.

Grey pumped his wings as he tried to grab hold of the elements.

I infused my hands and shared my energy with him, "You can do it."

Grey launched into the air again.

"Show yourself, coward!" Ben shouted.

"Close now," Grey whispered into my mind.

But the E'lan burned with a different chord; a deep, painful thrum as though we had hit a nerve.

Ben plunged down to us, keeping Grey's course clear. He held another orb aloft, its intensity illuminating the blood that coursed down his arm.

"Come on, beast," Ben called. "Protect her!"

Grey whinnied in frustration.

Ben's eyes bore down on me. Fear shimmered within them.

"What about you?" I dug my infused fingers into Grey, urging him to connect with the E'lan quicker.

"I'll find you, I promise," Ben's voice faded as he disappeared in the darkness.

Grey's nerves rippled under his skin. His body lengthened as he galloped through the thick air. The E'lan sparked with outrage whilst its gentler hands called us into the transfer.

"Got it!" Grey leaned into its pull. My gut twanged and pulled towards it. Ben shimmered in and out of focus. He darted around us, his hair a sickening death-red. Nephr'eus drawled in the distance. The cavern faded, but Grey still struggled.

"Nearly... there," his voice was pained, his muscles strained.

My pendant's call mixed with it all. I wanted to crush that Daimon. I wanted to find my pendant. But this wasn't about my wants, it was about the needs of the many.

The silence of the transfer's nothingness drew closer. I flattened onto Grey, his rapid heartbeat pulsing against my cheek. Comforting heat washed over my back—until his cry broke the fragile connection, and we fell. Blood spots hit me as Grey spiralled down.

I screamed as nails dug into my leg. Kea's sword fell from my hand. I slashed out with a wing and hit something, but the fall became dizzying. Grey's hooves thrashed as he struggled to regain his balance. A vamp flew through our scorching wings and exploded into ashes, but the swarm was growing.

Grey couldn't grasp the transfer whilst these things kept coming. Their frenzy increased with the blood pouring from my leg. Grey kicked to get away from the horde that kept nipping at our heels.

Ben whipped a vampire I hadn't noticed above me. I lurched out of its way and lost my balance, summersaulting over Grey's rump. I didn't have time to catch myself with my wings. I landed on my butt with a sharp jolt. I rolled to get back up, but something grabbed my waist. Ben's voice became a smothered howl. A thousand shadows plummeted towards Ben and Grey as strong hands hoisted me into the gloom. I tried to claw at it, felt skin split as I struck it, tried to transfer to Ben and Grey, but its fierce power didn't yield.

We stopped high above the affray. A hand slapped over my lips. I bit until I tasted blood. A throaty groan rumbled in my ear and the fingers clamped harder against my mouth. It confined my arms against my torso. My wings refused to release, to sear my captor away. They were strong, their core energy in tune with mine. Recognition tapped inside my head but refused to reveal a name. Was it another Eloi? Someone closer than that? It felt like the latter.

This was no vampire. Their wings ate the shadows away. Nephr'eus fluttered down from a ledge and strutted along the besmirched ground like a peacock.

"Oh, lovers, this is far too simple," she snapped her fingers twice and tutted. "Leave them be."

Ben and Grey shuffled back as the sea of vampires parted, both raw with wounds. The vamps nestled into a flock and folded their misty wings around themselves.

Heaving, Ben fell to one knee. Grey was lame in his front right hoof. He nudged Ben and lowered a wing to protect him.

I struggled harder. My captor clamped their hand harder against my mouth until I was suffocating. My eyes strained to stay on Ben; I heard better than I saw.

Ben coughed, "You've had your fun, Nephr'eus."

She laughed, "I still love my name spilling from your beautiful lips."

I tried to open my mouth, but my captor growled and readjusted. My jaw cracked, but I saw more clearly and the movement had freed my left hand.

Nephr'eus sauntered closer to Ben. Her renaissance skirts ruffled in perfect symphony with her cautious steps.

"Can't you just die?" Ben rushed at her.

They slammed into the wall, his fingers tightened around her throat. The vamps hissed, unsure eyes flitting amongst themselves, but they didn't move without Nephr'eus' order. My captor's heart beat faster with the excitement.

"She… will be ripped… in two!" Nephr'eus pointed her slender finger up at me.

Grey was airborne in an instant, eyes on me, searching for me.

Nephr'eus shook her head. "One move… and I promise…. her entrails will… decorate this place… like it's Christmas. Stop… this," she squeaked, and her eyes rolled back.

My captor chuckled, deep and masculine. His arm squeezed against my armour; the damaged metal sliced into my flesh. His hand loosened a little, and my lips quivered with anger against his rough skin.

The vamps pooled behind Ben and snapped at Grey's hooves.

I was too close to ending this war to let some traitorous letch ruin it. I wriggled my left fingers, breathed in through my nose as much as I could, and slammed an orb into his leg.

He growled. His hand jerked free from my face, and I twisted. "Get off me!"

My captor yanked my head back. "Do *not* do that."

I couldn't make out the familiarity in his tone. His energy was nauseating like Ben's had been. He pinched my lips together, a fresh metallic tang coated my mouth.

"Behave as I've had to," he breathed close to my neck, then his mouth rested near my ear. His voice sung of violence, a simmering anger between the first and last notes. "Do as you are told, it is, after all, what you were born for. Nothing more," he called down Ben. "Let her go, Nik'ael."

Ben looked up like he, too, recognised the voice.

Nephr'eus cocked her head to the side and smiled.

Ben hesitated. His arm shook with uncertainty and anger.

I squeezed my fingers into fists and tried to wedge them between us. My captor's heart thundered against my back. He hugged me closer, and a wing blanketed me… a perfect white wing. My blood froze.

"No. You won't do that!" he seethed.

My neck cracked as he yanked it back harder. I groaned from the pain; my thoughts called for Ben. My head was yanked harder again.

"We will have no mind chatter."

"Let …me go!" I managed through the pain of his grip, then I let my struggles lax. He readjusted my now floppy body; I formed a new, small orb. He wasn't too smart since he'd fallen for this twice. I twisted and cut the edge of my wing through his wing. He yelped and loosened his hold on my chest.

I rammed my elbow into his chest. He grunted and I smashed my orb into his thigh. He roared and doubled over. I relished the smell of the burn. I tried to wrench myself away, but he'd wedged me between his chest and legs. My arms, however, were free.

"Stop!" he seethed.

"What has Yeqon promised you?"

I pummelled my elbow into him again. My head swam when it fractured, but it caused him enough pain, too, that I could pull my torso free. I turned to uncover this monstrous traitor, but he remained in the darkness of concealment. He slammed me into the ceiling, and we smacked into a protrusion. Rock cracked under my face. I pumped my wings to push away, but he struck my back. Horrendous pain surged up and down my spine. A mind-numbing, consciousness-killing pain. I pumped my wings, but I was falling.

A temporary reprieve. Something caught me. A satisfied laugh. *He* caught me. Cool, musty air rushed against my skin before rock grated at my flesh again. A scream rose and petered away in my chest as I fell again. Dull sounds and warbled screams filled my ears. I felt cold. I hit another rock, and my vision blackened. He pulled me back up.

"How does it feel to be someone's plaything?"

My injuries dizzied me and rendered my limbs to jelly. My nerves numbed as though preserving me from the torture. Bile climbed my throat as my stomach lurched to release its contents.

He grabbed my arm and flung me across the cavern. I awaited the inevitable crunch. My heart beat slow in my temples, I opened one eye. White zoomed past and intercepted my tormentor. Ashes and spice filled my senses.

I clamoured for control, but only one wing obeyed, sending me into an uncontrolled spin. I pumped that wing harder, but I spiralled into an outcropping. Exhausted, I clawed at it as I slipped down its rough edge. Skin ripped off my fingers. White spots waltzed across my vision.

The rock shifted under my weight, and an ear-piercing *crack* followed. Breath rushed from my lungs as I plunged with it.

As I tumbled there was a blurred flash of my pendant, the dash of a shadow, and muffled thuds. I wasn't quite sure if I was still conscious until I hit something, but there was no pain, no breaking bones. Although I was no longer falling, I was still moving.

"I've got you," Grey whispered into my mind.

His reassuring heartbeat returned feeling to my arms. Grateful, I clutched handfuls of his hair. His hooves clattered on the ground, and I slipped into Ben's arms. He gently but urgently prodded my injuries. Grey sniffed me. He whinnied and snorted; his muzzle nestled into me.

"What have you done?" Ben yelled.

"Don't blame me, darling," Nephr'eus said. "I didn't lay a finger on her."

I blinked the fuzz from my moist eyes. The outer edges blurred like a dream.

"Who is he?" Ben's heart drummed hard against my cheek, his skin hot and salty.

My bleeding nose obliterated his comforting scent. I coughed through it and strained my ears.

"Settle down, petals," Neph'reus tended her flock.

There was movement. My left eye cleared. Nephr'eus' remaining vamps settled at her feet, licking their wounds and preening one another. She patted one on the head and smiled. Her black eyes on Ben.

"Who is he?" she looked up. "The sins of the past, darling. I did what was necessary. All I wish is for her to stop her little quest. Now, *you* will stop. She is incapacitated; I wish her no other harm. Find yourselves a little nest somewhere and do not seek the portal, ever. Is that not a simple request? The bloodshed shall stop… well, considerably lessen if you comply."

Ben nudged me, and my head settled into him. His warmth eased my brokenness. I forced my one good eye to stay open and on him.

He ran his hand all over me. A groan erupted from my lips at the healing heat.

"We have to get her out of here, Grey."

"Please do!" Neph'reus trilled.

"Shut up!" Ben's voice rumbled against my ear.

Grey's nearby steps pounded in my head.

"Who was it?" I whispered into Ben's mind.

"I don't know."

"Liar," Even my thoughts hurt.

"It doesn't matter now."

Ben ran his warm fingers across my lips. I groaned as the swellings succumbed to his touch. His hand travelled around to my spine. He gasped.

"What's wrong with me?"

"He…"

Fire erupted underneath me, along each tender vertebra. Agony forced a moan from my throat.

"What?"

Ben held me tighter, "He ripped out one of your wings."

I struggled against the razor slicing down my spine. My vison blackened from the shock.

"My, my! How tragic!"

Neph'reus presence lingered like a plague. The sound of her voice coupled with the devastation of my injury made my skin tremble, I had no energy left.

I squeezed my eyes shut, *"Get me away from her."*

Ben smoothed a hand over my eyes. I smelled my blood on them and breathed it in like fuel for my fire. When his hand fell away, my vision was restored. Ben lifted me up, ready to put me onto Grey.

Nephr'eus twirled and laughed. Her skirts danced a waltz about her heels.

She clicked her fingers, "Come, my little butterflies. Our work is done."

Nephr'eus sauntered closer. Her vampiric shadows gathered above her, a cumulous darkness billowing above and behind her as though she was the eye of a tornado.

"Come, come. Don't fret now, lovers. You've a wonderful future, I'm certain of it! No responsibility other than pleasing yourselves. Isn't that just divine?" she steepled her hands under her nose.

Clearer than ever, the vamps discarded their concealments. They were no longer just flashes of teeth and sunset eyes, but strong, sleek youths bearing the smoky wings of Daimon. Watcher in beauty, Daimonic in power. A hybrid of hellish heritage.

"What the hell has Lilith done?" Ben seethed.

"Exactly as you see, darling. She is expanding her family into a robust and effective support network," Nephr'eus tickled one under the chin. It tolerated her touch but pulled away quickly, its eyes mean and narrow.

"Who fathers these creatures? Yeqon cast her aside," Ben said. "I'm surprised she lives. Who is feeding her?"

I sensed Ben's apprehension as he folded one of his wings over me. The burn in my back surrendered to a frightening numbness. How would I fly and fight?

"I can't feel anything!"

His lips pressed onto my head.

"You will be fine!"

Images of Cael flashed into my head. *Pain… endless pain.*

How would I complete my mission with part of myself destroyed? I had no pendant, only one wing, and no hope. I remembered that Jaz had risen against the most impossible odds, and it pushed the negativity away.

Nephr'eus tucked a curl here, fluffed some lace there. "Ah, Nik'ael, it is a beautiful love story, one many years in the making, but alas…" she peered towards the ceiling and sighed. "I've no time to tell it." Laughter trickled through her lips and drew them into a satisfied smile. Her mark glowed. Her eyes dazzled within their darkness as a serene blueness returned.

She moved closer while the vampires licked blood off one another in a sick display of communal care. Ben stood and backed away with me. He laid me across Grey's back.

Grey carefully backed away from the threat. Ben would lead us to safety. Grey would take me where I needed to be.

I surrendered and let my eyes close.

I let my mind disappear into E'lan's embrace and floated into it on a current of peace. It bathed me in its warmth and lapped against my skin — a liquid light, a fluid and tangible amity.

A sweet giggle disturbed the beautiful neutrality of this place.

"Who's there?"

"It's me, pretty Sophia!"

Av'ael's delicate form emerged like an apparition. She ran on the tips of her toes and threw herself into me. Vast whiteness surrounded us. Nothing other than Av'ael was familiar.

"What are you doing here?" I asked. "What's going on?"

"Ooh, I've missed you!" Alabaster curls frizzed around her shoulders. Milky eyes resting upon rosy cheeks sparkled up at me.

"I've missed you too," I said. "Where have you been?"

"With Mumma. But you're here now!" She twirled and giggled. Mid spin, she stopped and wiped tears from her eyes. A pout crested her chin. "You're not meant to be here, Sophia. You must go back. You have a job to do."

"Where am I?"

She shrugged.

"Av'ael!" Her ever-intolerant mother appeared. "Again, disobeying me!" she wagged a finger at Av'ael and then at me. "I've had quite enough of this. You are perfectly fine, Soph'ael. You think you need your body because you've been conditioned into it, but you need nothing but your spirit. Pain is mortal, you are not. Flesh is weak, you are not. Leave my child alone and do what you were born to do," she leaned into me, her eyes stern.

"But how do I trust that part of me when I feel so broken?" I asked.

"If you cannot trust yourself, we cannot trust you," she lay her hand on my forehead. "I will show you a future where you have given in to your mortality rather than your truth."

I fell into an abyss of horror.

Agony gnawed at my soul like a rat feasting on a live victim. It was not my personal pain, however — it was the terror of millions. Desperate screams for help, for relief, cut through my mind.

Billowing thunderclouds, peppered with forked lightning, blanketed a desolate landscape. Foul mist skirted rows of blackened tree stumps. A red sun parted the storm, midnight silence at the peak of the day. Flocking birds flew around in a V formation. They fell out, preferring a new circling pattern. Birds of prey eyed a victim far below them. Lightning frequently struck the ground and revealed filthy people, malnourished and nearly naked. They clawed at the ground, trying to get under it. They dragged branches and bracken, slipping below, covering their burrows with whatever they could. More lightning revealed hundreds of mounds made from modern life's detritus—the building blocks of an apocalyptic world. To my right, someone rushed some stragglers into their burrow and pulled a large green freeway sign over the top as they disappeared inside. The birds circled lower.

Wind howled and thunder rumbled, an eerie movie of light and dark drenched with the smell of fear.

I floated amongst it all. Coarse chunks of concrete circled most of the mounds. Old tires weighed down tarpaulins used as flimsy roofs, a khaki sea swimming in junk and waste.

A hand wriggled behind an upturned car. I swum through the air, moving towards it.

"Hello?"

My feet touched to the ground. It was hot and uneven. The hand pulled away, so I rushed around the bonnet. "Oh God!"

The arm was moving because a wild dog was pulling at the torso.

I retched.

A pack of dogs milled about on the other side of the wrecked car, tearing into the corpse's belly. Its head lolled with the movement. A large portion of the throat was gone to the right of the windpipe.

The birds flocked faster, left and right. I retreated from the horrid sight.

Amongst the dreariness, a white butterfly flitted past my cheek and hovered in front of my face before heading towards a distant brightness. Happy to see the back of this horror, I followed it over and around a dozen decrepit mounds. Thousands of butterflies joined the first, a cloud of wings beckoning me towards the only two trees. Vines hung from naked boughs. The insects fluttered on either side, urging me inside.

With every step, the earth responded to my presence. Gems rose to the surface and left veins of diamond and opal behind every step I'd taken. I kneeled and picked up a handful of dust. It spilled from my palm, a fine glitter of emerald. I poked the ground, and a new opal vein magnetised towards it. As I pulled away, the opal rose from the ground as a workable element. I fashioned it into a vibrant blade of blue and pink with a smattering of gold.

A butterfly tickled at my cheek, reminding me to keep going. They swept the vines apart as they followed me in and coalesced into a human shape.

"Allow your mortal fears to rule, and your legacy will be thus," Enoch said.

He stepped aside to reveal a door-sized portal. Its watery blue-green shimmer became a clear window through which I saw a landscape — the same vista I had just traversed.

"There are no Angels of A'vean in this world," Enoch said.

The flock of birds landed, a dark sheet falling from the sky. The sound of their wings was a storm in its own right. They perched on the barren trees, but they weren't the vultures I'd thought they were. Sunset eyes with an equal measure of swirling A'vean marks glimmered towards their feasting grounds.

Horrified, I looked back to Enoch. He crossed his arms over his linen robes. Sadness moistened his aged eyes.

"Sweet Angel of thy Creator, behold the children of Lilith. Begotten of the darkest evil, stronger and more soulless than even Yeqon, they flourish through a lack of faith."

Through the portal's safety, the vampires saw me. They snarled and hissed, flapping their charcoal wings as they paced along their perches. Their angelic faces belied the beautiful danger they were.

Enoch entered the portal, making his way across the barren ground until he stood below the vampires. His old eyes sought mine.

"Cast away your worldly beliefs. They are no more than a mirage such as this," he moved farther away. "Soph'ael, child of I'el," he raised his eyes skywards. Thunder bellowed. Lightning forked in the distance. The blood-red sun glowed a sinister shade of death, "Save us."

And the vampires descended, tearing Enoch apart.

I screamed; the sound so bereft I thought it was someone else's. With my sword raised, I rushed through the portal. Lighting struck its tip, and the energy hoisted me high into the raging weather. Electricity coursed through my veins. Another arc snaked down from the heavens. I caught it with my other hand and brought both together. The opal sword hummed. Sparks crackled out of it and out of me. I moved on the sky's static, my one wing safely tucked away. E'lan was my propulsion, my accelerator, and my brake. It was my guide and my strength.

I was the energy of the universe.

The vampires scattered when I burst into their frenzied feed. Only a bloody puddle remained of Enoch. I vaporised the closest vampire with a swipe of my sword, and the rest fled into the billowing storm. I surged into it and hovered on my bed of elemental uplift to survey the world below.

I raised the weapon, and lightning kissed it once more. My mark seared to life — I was alive.

"I am Soph'ael, daughter of A'vean! Dare to cross my path!"

There was a pull in my gut as Av'ael's mother called me back from the terrifying vision. I blinked at the brightness of the strange, achromatic meeting place.

"Enough indulgence," she said. "I trust you can truly believe in yourself now?"

I nodded, still buzzed from the vision.

She scooped up Av'ael. "We will be here for you when the time is right."

Av'ael waved and tucked into her mother's neck. Warm light enveloped them. They dulled, and as they did it almost seemed as though Av'ael melted into her mother. They left fingers of light twinkling like stars. I fell back towards reality.

Chapter
Twenty-Four

My eyes flew open. Grey's warmth returned, and my pain was gone.

Ben and Nephr'eus were inches apart. Two vamps bordered her. Ben's fists were fury white, his wings holding him close enough to strike.

"White hair Nik'ael?" the honeyed poison of Nephr'eus' voice pierced the serenity that had overcome my pain, "I much prefer the Daimon you."

"And I'd prefer the descended you," Ben said.

Her vamps growled.

Nephr'eus pointed up to me and Grey, "Going to risk life and limb for that?"

"Are you sure, young one? I can transfer now."

"Yes, and then we'll get the hell outta here."

Ben glanced at us, "What are you doing?"

My strength had returned. Power rose in my gut like a phoenix.

I would treat Nephr'eus like Yeqon, let her ego be her ruination.

"Ready, Grey?"

His whinny reverberated through me. Behind the veil of his wings, I armed myself.

Ben beat his wings towards Nephr'eus. "You've all but killed her. Get the vampires out of our way and let us leave," he formed an orb in his hand.

The vamps hissed but cringed.

Nephr'eus casually inspected her red fingernails and pursed her lips. She then lurched at Ben and took a swipe at him with said nails. The vamps scattered as Ben caught her forearm. Her skin crackled like roast pork under his touch.

Her eyes rolled back, and she screamed, "Go die under a rock somewhere!"

Ben twisted her arm. Her cheeks blossomed, and a dewy sheen sprouted on her skin. She hissed through her teeth at the vamps, who settled on a ledge above her.

Nephr'eus swung a wing at Ben and sliced across his face. He stumbled and pinched the wound back together. Her other vamps jumped at the smell of fresh angelic blood, their nostrils flaring to draw in the enticing scent.

She swatted them back, "You'll eat when I tell you!"

She edged away as she tried to heal the bubbling flesh on her arm; one vamp dared to sniff at the roasty smell. Ben smoothed glowing fingertips over his own wound. All the while, they watched each other.

Nephr'eus swayed on her feet whilst Ben glowed from head to foot, an energy bomb ready to detonate in his hand.

I counted on her ego to give me time to power up. Grey kept his distance, and I used it to unravel under her nose.

Nephr'eus wiped sweat from her eyes with her forearm. "You wish me dead, Nik'ael? A little harsh, I think, coming from you. You've had your fun too," she glanced in my direction.

Ben winced. He didn't want me to know what else he had done as a Daimon.

"As I said, darling, it is quite simple from here on," Nephr'eus sniffed the nervous edge from her voice. Her black eyes alternated between Ben and I.

Nephr'eus batted her now-clumped lashes and urged a vamp to circle over Grey. I pretended to flop under his movements. I even moaned.

"Ensure your saviour refrains from her quest," she said. "All we want is a small square of the universe to ourselves. No I'el, no A'vean. We have earned our place on this planet. I'el has everything else, doesn't he?" she shrugged. "It really isn't much to ask now, is it? One destroyed piece of the Kaladai and an incapacitated saviour will be enough," she readjusted her injured arm and fluttered into the air. Her eyes twinkled, and her smile broadened, "I'm sure you can empathise?"

My fingers trailed to my neck only to remind me that my attacker had ripped the pendant away.

"That's not a bargain anyone this side of Hell will agree to," I croaked.

"She speaks!" Nephr'eus' eyes widened along with that fake smile. "One thought she was a mute, hiding in that creature's stink. Defeated and still rather full of ourselves?" she tapped a broken red nail on her bottom lip.

"Bide your time, young one," Grey whispered into my mind. *"Do not goad her. Her ego will bring her undone. The E'lan is clearing; we will be gone soon."*

"That's what I'm counting on, buddy," I replied.

Grey reversed; his wings folded over me. The vamps hissed with annoyance; they edged our way. It gave Ben more room to parley with Neph'reus while Grey was searching for the transfer. My body rippled with a surge of power.

"And what of the rest of us? To hell with us all is it?" Ben asked.

Grey's heart hammered harder under me. I flexed my raw shoulders. I had one wing, one immense goal, and one all-consuming strength. I knew now what would happen if Nephr'eus and Lilith had their way. Av'ael's mother had shown me their future. With new-found ease, orbs formed in my palms as though they knew they were required.

"The rest of you can do as you wish, I really don't care," Nephr'eus said. "Just stay out of our way."

The vamps licked their lips and cracked their knuckles. Their wings sizzled until their excited buzz was an uncomfortable resonance.

Ben flew higher so that he was looking down at her. Her smile melted into a sneer.

I groaned a little louder. Nephr'eus looked down her nose, eyes squinted in concentration, assessing that I was still incapacitated. While her attention was on me, Ben slipped his hands behind his back.

Nephr'eus dismissed us with a flippant wave of her hand, "Be gone. I wish to see the back of you both."

"All you will see is the back of this!" Ben disappeared.

He transferred behind her. Nephr'eus spun around, but he already had a whip of light ready. He lassoed it around her torso. She gasped and grabbed for it, singing her palm bloody. He pulled the coil away, and she twirled. A warbled scream caught in her throat. Her head lolled on her shoulders as her eyes rolled white. Her wings fizzled out, and she slumped to the ground.

The vamps didn't assist. They coasted overhead, chittering almost happily.

Nephr'eus scrambled to her knees, coughing and spitting blood, and tripped over her skirts. She fell onto her elbows and grabbed at her bleeding midsection.

"Help me, you fools! He's right there!"

Embers from her wounds caught light around her waist. Her skirts melted. Cinders caught on the draught Ben's wings created.

Nephr'eus patted wildly at the burns, gasped and sputtered, "Get them or I'll tell your mother how pathetic you all are!"

The vamps rumbled with displeasure and deluged towards Ben. He rose into the air, his wings and energy ablaze. The brilliance that shone within him was so powerful that I lost my breath. He drew the vamps into his wings. Four of them bit and clawed into him, dashed in and sliced his chest. One clawed open his healed cheek wound. He grimaced but kept their attention on him.

I pushed myself up, "I'm ready."

Grey reared and charged into them, all hooves, lashing wings, and teeth. I delved my hands into my remaining wing and fused the two orbs into daggers, then thrust them into a vamp about to dive at Ben's head. It clutched its chest and exploded into flames. The others fell away from Ben, eyes burning and wide as they licked his blood from their lips.

Nephr'eus screeched at the sight of me, her eyes venomous slits, "Kill her!"

She hobbled across the floor, a naked mess of burned flesh and wounded ego.

"Where are you?" she screamed towards the ceiling. "You coward!" She opened her wings, "I do your dirty work… now help me!"

"He's not as brave as you thought! Huh?" Ben despatched a vamp with a tidy blow of his wings. Most then retreated to the shadows overhead, leaving Nephr'eus alone, only a handful left circling Ben.

"You filthy snivelling runts!" her lips quivered under the strain. Spittle sprayed with her fury.

In the darkness above, a heart thudded with malevolent hatred as thick as anything I'd felt from Yeqon. He was still here.

I drew the E'lan into me, and its warm spring sizzled up my spine. I stretched my arms, orbs in each palm.

And I rose above Grey by pure will alone.

"Help Ben," I said.

Grey whinnied and thundered into the vamps, splitting them away from Ben. I glanced at Ben and pointed up. He nodded.

I wanted to know who he was. I wanted to destroy him.

Nephr'eus snivelled and scuttled against a wall. "So, you're invincible now?" she fumbled to steady herself and leaned into the pain of her wounds. She followed my gaze to the shadows above, "Show yourself! She's here for the taking — a buffet for your vengeance! Isn't that what you've always wanted?"

Who wanted vengeance against me? Who had I wronged that much?

Nephr'eus slapped her hand onto the ground, her coif in total disarray. The old me might have pitied her.

"I can smell your gutlessness!" she sobbed through her words.

"You going to let her have all the fun?" I called up to the shadows, hoping it would drag his sorry arse out for a fair fight.

His breathing quickened.

Ben hovered close by; arms crossed. He cocked his head to the side, "Seems you're on your own, Neph'reus. It's so hard to find good help."

Nephr'eus unravelled her fist. "I suppose *I* will have to do it then!" she shouted again at the shadows. Her energy rose as she pulled herself upright.

I turned quickly and struck with a whip just like Ben had. It coiled around her neck, and I reeled her in.

Nephr'eus dangled below me like a stunned fish, clawing at her throat. Tears sprouted in her bulging eyes. A dusky blueness tinted her skin. I hoped she suffered as Jaz had.

He stirred. Air moved — the draft of wings.

"Get out of my sight," I closed my hand, breaking the connection to the coil. Nephr'eus fell silently.

I closed my eyes and felt for the waves of air that lapped around the excited heartbeat above me. An all too familiar heartbeat.

"Watch her," I said to Ben.

I flew up, Grey to my right. Drawn to the steady pound of the familiar energy, I surged into the shadows and right into him. We hit the far wall, his disguised body cushioning mine. Bones cracked. Air rushed from his lungs in a pained groan.

I pinned him down with burning white fists, "Who are you?"

He groaned again, but I felt a smile under it.

He punched my sides. I arced back, but he flipped me under him. Breathing hurt. I struggled against his grip on my arms.

"A question you'll wish you never asked," he whispered.

Foreboding washed through me. Everything about him screamed familiar.

"Cowards hide," I said. "At least Yeqon is honest about who he is."

His fingers breached my skin, yet I bit the sting away. His breath smelled like sulphur tinged with the odours of healing, of cedar and lavender. Confusion ran through me like ice water.

"You have no idea what you're talking about," his murky concealment didn't hide the desperation in his tone.

"I've got better things to do than waste my time with a wannabe!"

I headbutted him and flipped us over until I was back on top and pinning him against the rock. My wing cast a wedge of light across his honeyed skin, dissolving his disguise a little. A strong jaw line, scarred and stubbled. The faces of Yeqon's lackies flashed through my mind, but none fit.

A deep, furious growl burst out of him. He punched my jaw, bringing moments of light and dark.

"Stop while you can," his whispers slid like needles down my neck.

My knee shot up into his groin. He yelped and slid down the wall.

I sank a few feet to heal my face. Something sparkling caught my attention — my pendant hovered in mid-air. It disappeared, then he reappeared right in front of me.

My pendant was around his neck.

"That would be mine!" I reached for it, but he had disappeared again.

"You learn the hard way, every... single... time," his voice raked at my memories.

He hit me in the back before I could turn around. Energy snaked around me until it locked me in its power, a python of light squeezing the life from me. His concealment strengthened until not even his outline was visible.

"You will never realise your purpose," he said. "Just as my life was taken from me, so will you suffer the blow of failure. It is a more tender pain to know you are a disappointment."

He released me. The static of his transfer followed me as I fell.

"No!" I screamed not for the fall, but for his escape.

"Sophia?" Ben caught me. "Are you okay?"

"I'm fine," I screamed into my hands. "No, I'm not!"

Grey landed nearby just after Ben, who lowered me to my feet. The ground was sharp and cold; exactly how my heart felt. Grey's breath warmed the cold failure around my neck.

"I lost it. He has the pendant," my nails bit into my palms. My eyes ached as I stared at the emptiness above.

"Who was it?" Ben asked.

"I don't…" I noticed streaks of blood across Grey. His rump was pockmarked with bite and scratches, "You're injured!"

He whinnied, "*I am fine.*"

Nephr'eus hovered a dozen feet from us, a limp and bloody version of herself. I sighed with disgust that she was still alive. Orbs filled my palms. Ben's lit as well.

She drew a blade from her wings and pointed it at us. "Keep your distance," her arm wobbled.

"Your dust will be nothing more than the grime under human feet," Ben taunted her.

Nephr'eus screeched, and they smashed together in an explosion of light and fury. She was so powerful still. Her elemental energy pulsed at Ben whilst she shielded herself with her wings.

"Cover me, Grey."

He stomped in front of me.

I kneeled whilst Ben dodged Nephr'eus' ammunition. I hurried, my fingers calling the stones' song up from the ground. The vein of pink and gold advanced like a vine as it followed my fingers. I teased gems from the ground into a weapon.

Grey side-stepped and stretched his wings; my secret weapon hidden.

My fingers pulled and rolled the molten opal. I stretched one end into a point and snapped the rest away. The remainder sunk into the ground. The opalescent blade drew a perfect red pearl, streaked with gold, to my fingertip. The E'lan burned stronger through my body with every passing moment.

Grey tossed his head and sniffed the dagger, "*That skill is rare, my friend. It will be useful.*"

Step by step, I skirted their war zone behind my hulking Pegasus, buffeted by his remark.

Nephr'eus pulled herself to her feet and lunged at Ben. They rose high into the air, then crashed to the ground. Nephr'eus matched Ben's every move. Despite her broken arm dangling by her side, her other released torrent after torrent of orbs, lashes, and deadly needles. Ben shot forwards and grasped her milky neck. Her wings sputtered out, and Nephr'eus fell. She skidded across the sweat-and-blood-dampened ground. Smothered in gritty gore, Ben rolled her over and sat astride her torso. She wriggled for a moment, then went limp.

The moment Ben loosened his fingers, Nephr'eus transferred behind him.

"I'll miss your lips on mine," she pulled a small blade from her undergarment and swung it at his throat. Ben spun; eyes wide as the blade sliced through the air.

Nephr'eus stiffened. Her knife sailed out of her hand and landed in a vamp's ashes. She stumbled, but her bulging eyes found me. Luminous blood trickled from her gaping mouth. A gurgle bubbled though the blood. Her legs gave way.

Her good hand clutched the spear I'd thrown through her throat.

I moved past Grey and past Ben, who touched his own throat in shock. I pulled my new weapon out of Nephr'eus and grimaced at the sucking sound. Her fingers quivered towards the wound. Her muscles spasmed.

I wiped the tip of the spear on my trousers and slid the clean blade into the space next to my diamond dagger.

"In another life, I would have healed you," I said. "Today, you rot in Tartarus. Say *hi* from Soph'ael."

I kicked her. Her eyes rolled back, and Nephr'eus exploded into a ball of flame.

Chapter
Twenty-Five

The delicate chromious chain dangled between Lilith's blood-red nails. It blistered her skin, and her fingers flinched from the pain.

The walls around them rumbled. Sulphurous vents hissed nearby.

Lilith held up Sophia's pendant, entranced by the chromious orbit around the opal. "Nasty little thing," she shrugged. "Pretty though, I suppose," she shrugged.

She draped it around her partner's neck. Welts erupted around his collarbone, calling a pained dew to his skin. He winced but let it be.

Her partner rested against a great rock pillar. Lilith scooped a wooden cup into a font to her left and sipped from it. She placed the cup to his lips. He took a thirsty gulp, and water dribbled from his mouth. Satisfied, Lilith smiled and threw the cup aside. It landed at the feet of an Afflicted, who picked it up and dashed into a dark tunnel at the far side of the cave.

Lilith kissed his lips, "You are the bravest of all A'veans, my sweet."

She ran her talons through his black-and-white hair. He leaned into her passion, hungry for love.

Lilith held his chin between thumb and forefinger. "I knew it was right to take you under my wing, so to speak," she trailed the curve of his jaw down to his throat. His fingers dug into the coarse rock behind him. She titled her head, "Worth all the pain?"

He nodded. A lusty moan rippled in his throat.

"There is no ecstasy without pain," she stared long into his blue-black eyes. A baby started to cry. His eyes slid to the infant swaddled by a hearth behind the font. Lilith sighed and picked up the babe. Its head bobbed against her chest until it found her breast and latched onto her. She cooed; her eyes shut. It bit through her flesh. She winced and sat on a wooden chair by the crackling flames.

"There, there," she cradled its head. Blood and milk trickled down her stomach, "The last of our new-borns, my love. One more to rise for us."

He ducked out of the path of volcanic steam and stopped in front of her. He watched the infant suckle. Love didn't wash over his face, but a forced smile lifted his cheeks. Lilith's eyes remained slim, watching his reaction. He prodded its cheek with the crook of a finger, and it snapped its ghoulish mouthful of teeth at him, annoyed at the intrusion.

Lilith laughed as it returned to her breast. "Oh, you two will get to know each other," she caressed its smattering of black hair. "Father will protect you. We only bite our dinner," she eyed the pendant. "Or anyone who gets in Mother's way," her satisfied smile reached her liquid amber eyes.

"What about Sophia?" his mark of A'vean flashed at her name.

"You wounded her yourself, and we have her pendant," Lilith said. "She doesn't possess what she requires to complete her mission, therefore, she is useless. She isn't even worth Yeqon wiping his feet on her anymore. I won't waste more of my children on her."

The chair creaked when Lilith threw her head back in mirth. The babe grizzled, biting harder, and a thicker trail of blood trickled down her cleavage as it sucked, "Yes, my little darling. And soon the world will offer you your fill of blood."

She noticed her mate's pallor. Even the firelight didn't bring warmth to his cheeks.

"Why are you concerned?"

He peered into the fire. "I worry about Yeqon. No one has seen him," he eased the pendant from one scorched area to another, his jaw tightened.

"My King? He is as good as descended," Lilith said. "We have our own children now, more than he ever had. We shall rule with the power of our offspring, not the disgusting creatures he dug from the earth. Our children are the new power, and I am Queen of Queens," she felt a heady rush, the thrill of a great future.

He smiled, but it didn't reach his watery eyes; her joy dampened.

Lilith caught the words *love* and *hate* tattooed on her knuckles as she readjusted the babe. She shivered as the letters brought another's face to her mind. Hugging her infant tighter, she blinked the memory away. The shadow of jealously darkened her partner's blue eyes. She bit her bottom lip and huffed. He had nothing to worry about — the one who had adored her long ago would gladly kill her on sight today. Gathering the child up, she rose to her feet.

"The past is just that now. Prepare the most mature children. They will need their wits, not just blood lust. No more new-borns."

Lilith lay the sated infant on a pile of animal hides by the fire and wiped the blood from its rosebud lips. It had grown to toddler size since its morning feed. That it grew faster than the others filled her with satisfaction. She kissed the infant's head, then stood tall and stretched her arms. Her bones cracked, and she moaned with pleasure.

"The last batch of our children have been a terrible disappointment," she said. "They made a mess and an unnecessary scene. I cannot tolerate pointless bloodshed. It is for food or defence, not for sport."

The small child settled into a fitful sleep. She kneeled and tucked it in tighter.

"The older ones are doing well, undermining Gedz'iel's army," her partner said. "He doesn't know who to send where first. All we need them to do now is focus on the humans whilst we follow her to the portal. She will still surely seek it."

Lilith walked to him like liquid velvet, her hands tender against his tense neck.

"And then you will destroy it for me?" she asked.

"With my bare hands."

She loved the way his chest muscles clenched when he was impassioned.

"And her? What is she gets under your feet again?"

He plucked at the pendant, which hummed in protest. His mark reacted to its anger, lighting a face of beauty beset with eyes of hate.

"Her pain will be greater than mine ever was."

Chapter Twenty-Six

Sleep hugged me like a protective mother. Psynostris pushed against my eyes as the world called me back, but for once, the timing had been perfect. After defeating Nephr'eus, I had needed it.

Cold air coaxed me awake. My senses tuned into every sound, smell, and vibration. Grey's warmth countered the bite of the whistling breeze, and I leaned deeper into the sweet comfort of his back.

"Good afternoon."

With a weary groan, I opened one eye a little. A flash of light blinded me.

"You are safe. Do not be afraid."

I opened my eye a little further, and realised the light was the soft glow of his undulating wings.

"Wake up little one, we are nearly there."

Tightening my grip on his soft warmth, I pushed myself up. The sharp sting of the freezing air shocked my eyes open. They watered as they adjusted to the temperature.

"Where are we?"

"I am taking you to the portal. We are nearly there."

I twined my fingers through his mane.

"The p-portal?" I stammered.

"The one and only."

"You know where it is?"

My heart drummed against my ribs. I wanted to feel fear and self-doubt, but elation and relief surged through me instead and tugged at my lips. I scanned the horizon. Nothing but a strange land lay beneath the thick cloud.

"I know the general area where it was. I arrived through it a very long time ago, after the fall. I was the last of my kind sent to Earth. Uriel charged me to await you and to help you when you arrived. It is my destiny to guide you there, just as it is your destiny to open it."

I stared across the points of his ears. My beloved horse — a part of I'el's plan. A part of I'el's utterly ridiculous, convoluted plan. My fingers curled in frustration. It all felt so pointless. Everything could have been so much simpler, but the point was to punish the fallen, and they had it endured well. How much more did I need to do to end that punishment?

Grey sped up as we began to descend, and I leaned into him. The clouds thinned, and warm sunshine shot through.

We banked right and dove. My stomach flipped and took a while to catch up, but I screamed with delight. Far below lay a sparse, brown terrain. The sight drew a torrent of memories to the forefront of my mind.

My nails were crusted brown with Nephr'eus' blood, my knuckles raw. I gulped but relished the success of ridding this world of another Daimon. My smile deepened.

Grey slowed and levelled. We circled towards pale etchings in the landscape. The chalkiness along the ground reminded me of the sweeping scar on Ben's jaw.

I sat up, "Where's Ben?"

I twisted around to see if he was following us. I hoped he was.

"He has returned to Gedz'iel to gather support for us."

My shoulders slumped.

"I told him how to follow. Now, hold on."

Grey let out a long, joyful whinny and sped along the enormous image below. The rush of the wind was exhilarating. I leaned right, and the air dragged through my hair as I absorbed the fabulous white lines that brought a giant hummingbird nestled into the landscape to life.

I squinted as I tried to place it, "I've seen that somewhere before."

"I am sure you have. Humans have puzzled over our guides for a long time."

I half laughed; half gasped, "They're the Nazca lines?"

"That is the human name. We merely call them our guides. They're ancient, even to me. I'el placed them here at the beginning of human time to guide us to the various portals. This one is significant as it points us to the last functional portal."

Grey spiralled down, sniffing for something as he skimmed the rugged landscape beyond the image. He was following the direction that the hummingbird's beak pointed to.

"What do you remember of the final prophecy?"

"Um…" I pictured the prophecy projected on the wall. "A child, a mirror in the earth, and a lion."

Grey dropped lower. The movement shifted my weapons, and I reached down to push the diamond dagger back a little.

"Oh, that's right!" I had Yeqon's dried blood on it. "And ichor of the devil! Do you know what it all means?"

Grey snorted, *"I am but a beast, my friend."*

Sun warmed my back. I stretched my remaining wing, and it felt good. A clear, blue sky capped the thickening horizon. The ground merged from barren grasslands into a lush treescape. Mountains draped with dense foliage loomed ahead. Once we swooped into the jungle's steamy embrace, the warmth waned into a sticky heat. Only fingers of sunshine penetrated the canopy. Birdsong ceased.

Grey hit the ground at a gallop.

He puffed, *"Your drop-off is not far from here."*

"My drop-off?" I wasn't happy with that statement at all.

"The portal's closest surroundings are just ahead. You will find your way. Have faith."

"Faith?" I muttered under my breath. What good would that do me in a freaking jungle?

As I grumbled to myself, the trees thinned and sunlight brightened the abundant verdigris that enveloped us. A foliage-dense hill bearded with masses of purple arose, perhaps six or seven stories of twisting branches and sapling offshoots. As Grey slowed to a trot, I noticed symmetrical stones peeking out.

"Is that a building?"

Grey nickered, *"Indeed."*

The towering structure was wide at the base and ended in a pyramidal point just below the tallest umbrella of trees.

Grey stopped. I slid off his back, my feet lost in a sea of strange, knee-high lavender. Its stems like succulence; its purple buds deeper and more pungently floral than I'd ever seen before. I picked a couple of buds and tucked them into my plait.

"This is it?" I waded towards the structure hidden beneath the vertical garden. Sweat ran down my back from the humidity.

Grey's soft footfalls followed close behind, *"You must enter the temple. You will find your way from there."*

The ground was cold compared to the humid air. I craned my neck and scanned the giant structure. Everything was so quiet, barely a breath of wind. Water dripped from overhead trees onto my cheek, it steamed across my mark.

I walked along the building's front, counting my steps. One hundred, and I was only halfway.

Grey yanked up mouthful of greenery and revealed a step.

"This is where I leave you."

I swung around.

He ground his teeth against the vines with soft, doe-eyed satisfaction. A leaf hung from his mouth.

"But you're here," I touched the soft black hair of his cheek, felt the vibration of his chewing. "Stay with me. Please?"

Sweat chilled my skin, but perhaps it was dread at being dumped in a jungle to fend for myself.

"You must enter alone. I will remain outside to guard against that," Grey flicked his head to his right.

Outside the perimeter of lavender buds, where the birds didn't sing and the sun didn't reach, a thick blanket of fog tried to enter. The lavender's dense scent hindered it, but the fog's stink breached the distance between us. A hundred feet perhaps; a hundred miles wouldn't have been enough.

"Rogues?" My fingers dug into my thighs, the hairs on my arms bristled with torturous apprehension.

The jungle remained pin-drop quiet.

Grey nudged me gently, *"It won't hold them off for long. Go before they break through."*

Shadows moved amongst the fog.

"They know you are here by the beacon of your unique energy. Yeqon trapped them out here a long time ago, when he tortured this country; they will be impatient and hungry. They will make their move soon, whether I'm here or not."

I glanced between Grey, the monument, and the fog, and pinched my nose to avoid the smell of rot.

"Follow the prophecy."

Grey nudged me forwards again and retreated to within a few feet of the fog. It wafted behind him, ready to swallow him whole. Protestations caught in my throat — time had long passed for any more of that.

I ran to him and hugged him, holding his warm muzzle in my hand. "Be safe."

He nuzzled my hand, then pushed me on.

I reluctantly turned away from him, uneasy and unsure of my way ahead. The diamond dagger in my hand comforted me. The new opal spear an extra reassurance. The energy of Kea's sword put a confident step in my movement. I breached the first mossy step and gazed up at the grandeur. I pulled more lavender and thick vine away to reveal a steep staircase camouflaged under the jungle's clutches. On the front face of another step, was the well-rounded etching of a sun. Further weeding revealed an ornate structure, which wasn't so scarred by time as to hide its ancient splendour. This was an impressive place for a portal…and I was here without a single piece of the Kaladai. Everything was under the Zythros stone in Kaymakli. A new sweat sprung across my chest.

"Grey?"

I spun around to find he was no longer there, and the fog was slowly burning across the nubs of lavender. My heart sank.

Deep breath in, deep breath out.

"Okay. I have no key, a crap load of jungle, and steps to somewhere," I leaned into my thighs. "Calm down."

The only way was forwards. I grabbed fistfuls of vine, and the fibrous rip echoed through the unsettling silence. Three more steps revealed themselves. The cool, mossy stone was slippery underfoot. I pulled at another clump and peeled it away from a stone balustrade that edged the stair case. A ghastly face roared up at me—a feline etching with its tongue rolling out of a wide maw. More tearing revealed another next to it.

"Lion Mountain?" I whispered, recalling the prophecy.

I peered towards the temple's peak and spotted a smaller building up top. The only way seemed to be up, so up I went with frequent checks on the fog. The foliage thinned the higher I climbed, and the staircase narrowed as the peak neared. Where the sunlight reached through the jungle canopy, bursts of delicate yellow flowers relieved the mass of green. The yellow blooms thickened as I dashed up the final steps.

I looked down to the base. The fog was at the first steps.

The dagger was tighter in my grasp as I hurried to a square building etched with hundreds of glyphs. My fingers grazed over them, drawing out a few emeralds. The carvings were weather-damaged, but it was easy to recognise winged gods hovering above bowing people. Some stood on the bodies of the lion-faced creatures. Around a corner, a larger winged creature held another by its throat. Next to it, a human was removing the heart of another and offering it to their horned aggressor, it looked like Yeqon. A disgusted groan rumbled in my chest. I stumbled back, not wanting to look at him anymore.

I walked around the temple, searching for... well, I didn't know. High above the jungle's roof, the land around it was vast, secluded, and ancient. Crisp, thin air cooled my skin. Sunlight licked the tree canopy, which barely reached the temple's uppermost steps. I was almost as high as the clouds. Leaning over a remnant of a wall at the building's rear, the perimeter was clouded along the ground. Rogues were marching fast, their shadows darting amongst the rank fog.

On instinct, I swapped the dagger for Kea's sword and pointed it at the heavens. Power surged through my arm and into the chromious, which hummed like a tuning fork as the light erupted into the sky. I sent my name along its current, calling my kin and telling them I was here and ready.

Someone giggled.

I spun, pointing the sword towards the sound, "Who's there?"

The weapon was loose in my sweaty palm, so I swapped it to the other hand and walked cautiously around the perimeter of the building. The E'lan was calm and quiet.

Another giggle from up ahead.

"Av'ael? Is that you?"

I turned the corner and was back at the front of the building. The long staircase dropped away behind me. Coarse gravel crunched under every step. Fresh uncertainty snaked through my belly; I wished someone was here with me.

A curtain of lush vines swayed in the breezeless heights. They draped across the middle of the upper building. Their gentle fronds beckoned me forwards.

"This way!"

It was definitely Av'ael's voice, but what was she doing here? And how?

"Where are you?"

The vines swayed again, and she giggled again.

"With my friend," her voice echoed as though she was far away.

The vines shimmied again, revealing a dark doorway hidden behind them. The leaves were cool and heavy, their stems curled snakes that knitted together. They gave way to sticky webs when I parted them. A small orb singed them away and I pushed into the darkness.

Lightless tunnels never led anywhere good.

My movements resounded along the thin corridor. The light from my wing, my face, and my sword illuminated a scenery of ancient life carved into the walls—morbid sacrificial snapshots of a culture lorded over by winged gods. The floor sloped downwards until it opened into an inner, perfectly square chamber beset with tall pillars in every corner. Sunlight cut through an oculus in the centre of the ceiling and shone on a large stone altar. Green fingers of vine cut the motes that swam through the sunshine.

"Over here!"

Av'ael was sitting on the remnants of a stone throne. She cupped her mouth to hold a giggle at bay.

"What are you…"

"Shh, pretty Sophia. The monsters are coming."

I ducked reflexively and peered up the corridor, but there was no fog yet.

"What are you doing here?"

She rolled her milky eyes, "Playing with my friend, of course!"

A quick sweep of the place told me there was no one else present.

"Who is your friend?"

Av'ael pointed into a tangle of vines that had taken possession of the ancient seat long ago. Thick branches of an unusual creeping lavender draped over the top of the throne. Its pungent but welcoming aroma was a relief to my senses and a reminder of home.

Av'ael bounced on her feet and clapped. "She wants to meet you," Av'ael pointed at purple tufts entwined with another vine, which had rather large clusters of sickle-shaped thorns. She pressed her finger against her lips, "She's hiding from the monsters too."

"I don't know what you mean," I said. "This isn't a safe place for you though. You must go home."

The vines at the entrance swished. Decomposition tainted the musty air. The E'lan's fine vibration fluctuated. Insects erupted from hair-line seams in the ancient walls, scurrying to the higher ground of the pyramidal roof. Shards of sunlight refracted off thousands of scales that hurried into deeper recesses.

Av'ael jumped up and down on the back of the throne. "Quick, before they find her," panic flushed her cheeks.

Alarmed by a prickly shift in the E'lan, I pressed my finger to my lips too, "Quiet, little one."

A thorn drew a few pearls of blood when I reached for the throne. The second its scent hit the air, the E'lan vibrated harder and the rotting smell intensified.

I shook my head and sucked on my finger, "Brilliant. Nothing like a bit of Sophia to draw the right crowd."

The sunlight had moved closer to the throne. There was something hidden under the barbs, tucked away behind the lavender buds. I reached in again and found something hard and dry. The leaves peeled away easily— I fell to my knees.

There, nestled within a floral tomb, sat the mummified remains of a child.

Thick black plaits draped over beaded necklaces. Little hands hugged leathered knees. It looked like a long-discarded doll, but it wasn't.

Some part of me forced my body back up to face the macabre mummy, "This is your friend?"

Av'ael nodded and anxiously sniffed at the air.

My eyes were glued to the corpse, my mouth fell open. *To the child who dwells beneath the veil, preserved by devil's poison.*

"The devil's poison is the lavender!"

Av'ael was biting her fingertips, "Quick!"

I peeled more of the foliage away, "Who is this?"

"Her name is Inkasisa," Av'ael beamed, but her smile lasted only a second. "They're coming, pretty Sophia!" she squealed in panic.

"What do I do?" I asked.

"She is stuck. She needs to go home to her family."

"Stuck? She's dead!"

Av'ael rolled her eyes again and slapped her palm to her forehead. "Of course, she is, but her *ghost* is stuck here. She had to wait for you so she can show you what to do."

Sweat ran down the sides of my face, "I don't know what that means." A thunderous pulse echoed in my temples.

Av'ael wrung her hands anxiously, "She will tell you. Ask her."

My hands cupped under my chin; my mind raced, "Umm…"

I smelled something other than rot. Relief flooded me.

Ben was behind me, a new sword in hand, wings wide, and dead serious.

"Do what she asks," he said. "No time for questions, just do it."

"Okay…"

I reached for the corpse but pulled back twice, unsure about touching the tanned remains. Shrivelled gums set small yellowed teeth into a gruesome smile. Little eyelashes glued hollow sockets shut. A bug crawled out of a shrivelled nostril. My skin prickled. When I plucked up the end of a braid, an electric shock sung through my body.

"Copacati!" a little voice called into my mind. Her language was new to my ears.

My hand quivered atop her dry forehead. I fell into the blur between realities as a vision swept me away.

Kea rose from a lake and padded across floating beds of reeds. An alpaca wriggled in her embrace. She lay it down at the shore, surprised to see a teenage girl who snuggled a guinea pig under her chin. The girl whispered to Kea, who drew back in alarm. She swept the girl up and flew over the circular mountain range that hugged the large lake. They landed in the shadows of the Incan throne room's far recesses.

A line of shaking humans moved towards a sacrificial stone, dripping with fresh blood, under the threat of spear and mallet. A regal couple sat on their stone thrones. Adorned in gold, they didn't move, didn't intervene. Heavy makeup blacked out their eyes, their lids hollow and closed as though they were blind.

Kea held Inkasisa close and covered the little girl's mouth.

"Receive, oh Lord, the riches of my people," a vacant-eyed priest, his lined face ceremonially striped with blood, plunged a knife into the chest of a very conscious victim.

Four other priests held the sacrifice down, one on each limb. Ululations of prayer drowned out his ear-splitting screams. A small crowd kneeled and bowed, and wiped their hands down their faces every time they sat upright. None opened their eyes.

Kea tried to cover Inkasisa's eyes, but the girl pulled Kea's hands away to witness the massacre.

The woman next in line fainted. Another vomited and was whipped for it.

The victim began to fit. Women dressed in loin cloths and colourful beads over their breasts placed stone bowls at his neck. The altar tilted back to encourage the blood to flow down veins carved into its surface. Blood poured into the receptacles whose handles were the ugly maws of Rogues.

The priest sawed through the rib cage, cracked the sternum and stretched it open. He removed the heart in a precise yet unenthusiastic manner and held it aloft. It beat twice before falling still, its life force trickling down the priest's arm.

"One life for many," the priest said. "May our lord and guardian Supay receive this gift as a token of our loyalty."

The room bowed and moaned.

"May he accept it and bestow protection upon our people."

Through an aperture in the centre of the ceiling, a beam of light shot down and burnt the heart to cinders.

Courtiers leaned in on either side of the royals and whispered to them. The royals nodded. A tear slid down the queen's cheek. Their tawny skin paled with the horror. The queen clasped the king's white-knuckled grasp on his throne's armrest. The victims were brought forwards, one dribbling, screaming mess after another. The queen brought a square cloth to her mouth to hide her retching.

Fog milled around everyone's feet. A bright light flashed through the space, which caused the crowd to shield their eyes.

Supay — Yeqon, appeared. Lilith clung to his side. He strutted around the room and glared at anyone who dared meet his stare. He struck the sacrifice with his trident, and the corpse slid to the ground in its own blood. Its flaccid arms trembled as Yeqon struck the ground again.

"You have not fulfilled your duty," Yeqon said. "Every full moon, you are bound to sacrifice the few for the many, yet my queen and children have suffered the pain of hunger for two moons. You think today's offerings will suffice?"

His gaze landed on each and every occupant.

Inkasisa was shaking. Kea snuggled her closer.

"You will see punishment for your disloyalty!" Yeqon bellowed, his lips

quivering with rage.

Gasps rattled the terrified silence.

Lilith preened herself and lifted the blood-filled bowl to her lips. Her sips were delicate, sophisticated. She spilled not a drop whilst the crimson liquid enhanced the fullness of her lips.

The king rose. "Lord Supay," his voice trembled, but his stance was proud. "Please, I beg your mercy. It is not easy to bring my people to their deaths. We must collect the wicked and criminal for this task, not the good and obedient," he bowed his head. "These days, my lord, my people break the law less for fear of..." he rolled his hands in front of his belly.

Yeqon puffed his chest out. His large fingers strangled his trident as his eyes darkened to jets and his nostrils flared.

"For fear of what?" he teased maliciously.

The king swallowed hard, licking dry lips, wiping a fulminant sweat from his brow. "For fear of the consequences my Lord. For us, mere mortals, mere lowly subjects, it is a terrifying demise," he bowed low, his queen reached for his hand, guided discretely by her court ladies.

Yeqon's' eyes narrowed; his top lip curled up.

"You feed my queen only the lesser of your people? Only the vile and repugnant?"

Yeqon circled the dead body and kicked it away. It rolled on its side, spilling clots of blood and entrails. Someone retched.

Yeqon sneered, "Is she not worthy of your best?" He shoved the priest aside. With his trident, he picked up the hem of the king's skirt, then flicked it away, "Your troubles are greater than fear of death, dear king. Your worries would be better placed with the survival of your very existence."

His eyes fell on the queen. Her ladies gathered near her, but he hissed at them. They screamed and backed away.

"A worthy meal for my love..." Yeqon smiled at Lilith, "Where would I find such a treat?"

He touched the queen's cheek. She gulped and held her breath. A black-smudged tear trickled onto her breast, and Yeqon's finger followed its trail. He lifted his finger to his lips, tasted her fear. He leaned in and whispered something.

The queen screamed. She shuddered and gaped. Tears fell from her sightless eyes. "No, I beg of you!"

Her trembling fingers found her king's hand, "Do something!"

Her husband seemed frozen.

Supay clicked his fingers, the sound sharp and threatening. A scream rung out. A Rogue appeared from behind a column, dragging a child by her arm behind it.

"Manko!"

A female courtier stumbled behind the Rogue, "No, please, she is but a babe!" Another Rogue smacked the courtier to the ground. Blood seeped from her skull. She didn't move.

The king shivered, "Not my daughter!" Anger flushed his fear from his cheeks. His neck stiffened, and his lips tightened, "I forbid it!"

Inkasisa screamed into Kea's hand. Kea's tears fell on the girl's head.

"You, forbid it?" Yeqon's sneer morphed into a sadistic deep belly laugh. He flung his arms wide and turned on the spot, "Anyone else agree with His Highness?"

Everyone averted their eyes.

Yeqon twirled his trident, "I should think you all know your place by now."

He spun around and speared the king though the chest. The courtiers wailed. One fainted by the king's slumped body. Inkasisa screamed again. Kea clasped her hand harder across Inkasisa's mouth, her eyes wide with shock.

"Who else forbids it?"

The queen slid to the floor by her husband's body. She moaned as her hands felt their way to his face. She turned it to hers; it shook in her hands. She wailed with the others.

"Not my king, no! Not my daughter!" her sobs were breathless and defeated. Manko kicked and thrashed at the Rogue, who threw her at Lilith's feet. She launched forwards and bit Lilith's calf.

Lilith kicked the child away, "Filthy vermin!"

Yeqon held Manko up by her plaits, "Who dares object to my wish?"

The shocked onlookers bowed as low as they could, shaking their heads and too scared to make a sound.

Inkasisa's lithe frame slid out of Kea's embrace, "I object!"

"Another child?" Lilith snapped, "Pathetic."

Inkasisa ran to Manko and punched Yeqon's legs.

Kea flew into the crowd. Cries of surprise and relief echoed from every corner.

"Copacati!" someone cried as she hovered above them, dazzling the room with her light.

Yeqon dropped Manko. She whimpered at his feet. Inkasisa scooped her up only for Rogues to surround them. Asbel and Ged'erel emerged from the shadows, their weapons ablaze.

Kea drew her sword and beheaded two Rogues with one swipe, but she was alone and quickly surrounded.

"You cannot do this, Yeqon," she said. "It is beneath even you!"

"Ha, ha, ha, ha." Yeqon clapped between each laugh, "Timing is so sweet."

Yeqon clicked his fingers. Pineme, Kasadya, and Ben lunged from the darkness behind him and pinned Kea into a corner. His hair and eyes were as sinfully dark as theirs.

Yeqon picked up his trident, "I can do anything I wish."

"Inkasisa!" Kea yelled, "Take your sister! Run!"

Inkasisa looked over at Kea through her wide, tear-filled eyes.

"You taught me to care about others," Inkasisa's cheeks were red, and her chin quivered. "You put yourself in danger for us and suffer for us. I will do the same for my family."

Kea lashed out at Ben, who was leading the charge. With one swift orb, he threw her to the other side of the room. Her cry was muffled as they chased her through the chamber. She tried to get back to the children but had Daimon on all sides. They backed her into the dark corridor and away from the children.

Inkasisa hugged Manko tight. "You will not have her," she yelled over the noise. "You will have me instead." Inkasisa stamped her foot in defiance.

Yeqon chuckled, "Well, well. A mere child, braver than a Watcher who runs in fear rather than sacrifice herself."

Lilith's eyes sparkled. She ran her tongue over her teeth and smiled at the chaos.

Yeqon leaned down until his face met Inkasisa's. Her little body shook.

"I choose who and what I want for my queen, young one," he patted her head.

Inkasisa shrugged away from his touch. She straightened and peered into his eyes.

"You don't know what you choose then. Manko is a runt, an outcast. My mother picked her off the streets as an act of kindness. She was flea-bitten and diseased. You don't want that. I am a true king's daughter. My blood is pure by *birth." Inkasisa pulled a little knife from her satchel and stabbed it into her palm. She winced but didn't make a sound. Rogues chattered in excitement, but Lilith cut them down with a flick of her nails. She wiped her fingers clean on the robes of the dead king and sauntered over to the child. Saliva pooled at the corners of her mouth. Inkasisa's hand trembled, but she raised her arm higher.*

Lilith snatched her up, "I'll take this one."

Her fingers dug deep into Inkasisa's arms. Inkasisa squeezed her eyes shut and bit her lip. She turned her head away from Lilith's mouth.

Lilith licked her upper lip. "A true princess," she smiled at Inkasisa.

Manko ran screaming out of the chamber. Yeqon raised his hand to let her flee. "Have your fill, my queen," he said. "We shall not be alone for long."

Lilith plunged her teeth into Inkasisa's neck and moaned as she gorged herself. Inkasisa jerked. Her eyes bulged, and she cried. She went limp, her hands swaying with the movement of Lilith's rhythmic gulps. The remaining humans gasped to themselves.

Yeqon ripped Inkasisa away from Lilith. He flung the twitching child to the floor and shoved Lilith aside.

The room flashed white. Yeqon ducked as the thwomp of weaponry pierced the still air. He backflipped, and an orb exploded where his feet had been. Energy daggers shot towards him. Ben deflected them with swift swipes of his wings and threw an orb at Jude. It crackled overhead only to be doused with a pop by a second barrage of Jude's daggers. Jude sliced the head off a Rogue and landed at the king's body.

The last of the courtiers ran howling for their lives. The vault quickly emptied.

The vision faded and changed.

Jude spat on a pile of Rogue ash, "They are gone for now."

Inkasisa lay across Kea's lap. Her heavy tears fell onto the child's pale skin.

Kea kissed Inkasisa's black hair, matted with blood, "Sweet child, I failed you." she sealed the wounds on the girl's neck. "Her pulse is too weak, Koi. I cannot save her."

Koi walked through the mass of bodies. The fog faded at his ankles. His eyes were heavy, and he rubbed at his knuckles as though trying to wipe something away. He kneeled and lay his hand on Inkasisa's head.

"We have both saved and condemned her," he said. "Lilith has left her poison

in her veins. She cannot ascend with such blackness, yet I cannot rid her of it. Her soul is trapped here," he closed his eyes and sighed, letting his hand fall back to his side.

Kea cried and held Inkasisa's head into the crook of her neck. She rocked as she caressed the limp child. "I've got you, sweet one," she kissed the side of Inkasisa's head.

Koi rubbed his face, "I should have killed Lilith long ago when I had the chance. She is an anomaly that confuses the laws of nature. She will see my justice, Kea."

Koi took Inkasisa from Kea's embrace, swaddled her in his arms, and whispered into her ear. He lay her down on the throne. Kea draped her in the weeping lavender blossoms that fell through a window.

"I have whispered her into sleep," Koi said. "Saving her soul is beyond any of us while we are bound to Earth. It is a task for the Earth-born."

"We do not know when the Earth-born will live," Kea said through fresh tears. "By the word of I'el, Koi, she could be trapped like this forever," she kissed Inkasisa's head one last time.

"A long while, yes. Forever, no. She will rest sooner than you believe."

They turned to see Uriel. He was beset with purest wings of light. His resplendent armour rattled as he strode forwards and scooped up the child from the floral nest. Kea and Koi bowed in surprise and relief. Jude kneeled at Uriel's feet.

"Rise and be witness."

With a father's gentleness, Uriel settled Inkasisa into his embrace. Her slight frame almost disappeared within his enormity. Her skin paled further in his light. Uriel's long hair fell over her and shielded his whispers. Inkasisa twitched twice. His mark shone brighter than any Watcher's. A capsule of light burst out around Inkasisa and faded. He lay her back onto the throne, wrapped in the sweet aromas and soft leaves.

Uriel turned to the three Watchers, "Children of I'el, raze this city. It shall be Lilith's feeding ground no more. Move these people to safer lands." he glanced at Inkasisa, and his hard face softened. "Her destiny is now entwined with your redemption. She will be at peace when you are at peace."

I returned to the present and cried for the brave girl, whose remains lay before me; a victim of evil and time.

Chapter
Twenty-Seven

"You were there that day!" I hissed through my teeth.

Ben felt too close to me after the vision this young girl had gifted me. I was shaking from a surge of hatred for him. Witnessing him with Yeqon had churned my gut. I forced myself to look at him. His jaw was tight and his nostrils flared, but there was no rage in it. His eyes spoke of shame as they reddened around the edges.

"Yes," he whispered and let his head fall.

My fingers dug into my temples, and I breathed deeply to push vengeful thoughts away. I'd made my peace with him, but not with his deeds. How much more would I discover? How much could I forgive?

The smell of rot brought me out of it. Fog billowed where I kneeled. Its tainted fingers touched my skin and drew back as though testing what I was. I burnt it away with a flick of my wing; just a touch of its energy vaporised the foul gas.

Ben kneeled next to me, not too close but close enough that ashes and spice pushed back at the darker feelings.

"I will pay my penance, Soph. I have always accepted that the time would come," he rubbed his still-broken hand.

I swallowed hard, "I know that."

My attention swung back to the remains in front of me; I couldn't fathom what his penance would be.

The anger and sadness fell from my thoughts for the moment.

"But now, we have to move forwards, not dwell in the past," I flicked my head for him to move closer. "Where are the others?"

Ben moved in and examined at the corpse. His nose crinkled.

"They're coming. War has broken out in the northern hemisphere. Missiles have been launched."

My mouth dropped. He nodded and cast his attention back to the little figure.

"Gedz'iel is arming the humans with chromious artillery. Kristen and Thomas have been deployed to the Russian forces to guide them against Rogues. Fighting the vampires is another matter; Brennan and Jude are churning out new battalions as quickly as they can."

I was relieved to hear that Kristen had recovered enough to return to duty.

I grabbed Ben's wrist, and he froze, "What about Jaz?"

Av'ael clapped, "Pretty Jazzie, pretty Jazzie."

I'd forgotten she was there.

The tension left Ben's body. He shook his head with a wry smile and chuckled. I let his arm go.

"She's, ah… She's embracing her true self, you could say," he said.

I smiled a little too. That would be Jaz.

The E'lan shifted with a familiar buzz on its current.

"Speak of the dev…um, angel. Where are you, Brennan?" I sensed him close by.

He appeared behind Inkasisa's throne. His eyes lacked their usual spark.

"Rogues are halfway up the pyramid," his voice was dull. "Hurry with whatever you're doing."

I could barely look at him, his loss too evident in his eyes.

"I'm so sorry about Lorcan," I wrung my hands like it would wash away my guilt over his death and the hurt I'd left in Lorcan's heart. "I should have saved him."

Brennan sighed. The light of his wings cast an ethereal halo over the throne. His energy softened.

"I don't blame you," Brennan said. "Lorcan let go of his mortal life to save you, as was intended. If anyone should feel guilt, it is me. I made a sport out of mocking him," his lips tightened. He blinked hard to contain his misery.

I bit my lip to stop its tremor, "He was so brave."

I reached out to Brennan, and he rounded the throne. He hugged me, grief hammering in his chest.

"Under it all, my brother was incredibly brave."

Av'ael bounced, "Quick!"

I pulled away, "Okay, Av'ael."

"What? Who are you talking to?" Brennan squinted at where I was staring above the throne.

I forgot that, most of the time, only I saw Av'ael.

She giggled and glimmered visible.

"Whoa!" Brennan said, "You again!"

Av'ael waved, "Hello!" her smile rapidly waned. "Help pretty Sophia, please?"

Brennan followed my attention to Inkasisa.

He clicked his tongue, "Well, that's a bit Halloween. Who or what is it?"

I welcomed the hint of the old him, ill-timed though it was.

Ben pointed to the door, "Doesn't matter who it is."

Something crawled through the curtain of vines.

"Running out of time here," Ben threw an orb at Rogue's head. It screeched and erupted into flames, "Just make the dead kid help us get out of here!"

Brennan fanned his wings behind me. Ben pulled a coil of light from his wings and paced by the entrance, lashing it through the air.

My heart galloped wildly. "What do I do, Av'ael?" I stood and peered around the throne, "Av'ael?" I threw my hands up in the air. "Of course, she's gone again."

Ben snapped his whip, "We'll all be gone if you don't sort that thing out!"

Brennan flew over my head and cast an orb into the distance. He somersaulted over something, slashed down with his sword. I smelled the burn of rotten ash.

I ducked and focussed on every morsel of intel that I had. In the vision, Koi had said only I could draw the darkness out of Inkasisa, so I hesitantly probed the remains. My fingers unenthusiastically ran the line of her body. I gently tugged the foliage away, hoping for a sign. The prophecy had mentioned devil's poison and Inkasisa's head rested beneath a lavender cluster, which was toxic to Daimon and protected her from them. In that I felt confident.

Brennan looped overhead and crashed behind me. I didn't dare look over my shoulder as the chittering of Rogues assaulted my ears. There was another screech and the crackle of flames.

"I don't want…. oh shit!" I yelped.

I'd knocked the mandible out of place, it fell to the left. With fumbling fingers, I attempted to push it back, just as two thick, hairy legs emerged from the mouth cavity. I quelled a scream as a yellow banded tarantula surfaced, angry to be disturbed. I froze as it bared its inch-long fangs and raised its front legs in threat.

The fog was thickening again around the throne. The chittering outside was much closer. Ben and Brennan were grunting and swearing behind me. The warrish sound of their weapons pinged around the room.

"Stuff it!" I grabbed the spider by one furry leg and flung it aside; it skittered away behind the throne.

A horrified shiver stuck in my chest as Inkasisa's mandible hit the floor and cracked in two.

"Sorry," I ran my shaking fingers all over her remains, looking for anything that might tell me what to do. I noticed a dark patch of tanned skin where neck veins would have coursed. It was a bite mark if ever I'd seen one.

The room was filling with gag-worthy fog. I slapped my hands to my face, "Think! Damn it, think!"

I ducked when Ben flew over me to chase something. He slammed into the floor.

"Any time now would be good," he groaned.

The glow of an orange flame lit the rear of the throne. A foul miasma obscured the door and reminded me that Yeqon's long-ago-laid trap was rising fast.

I rested my palm on the ancient neck wound and closed my eyes. I thought about how I called up positivity in myself, how I tapped into the E'lan, and concentrated on the opposite — a prickly, noxious, painful energy.

The nausea hit, but I clamped my hand over the wound. I forced my eyes open so nothing would escape my attention. I gulped, and it burned my throat. Flesh desiccated between my fingers. The tissue flecks floated in a dark liquid of evil, something different to a Daimon or a Rogue. It was thick like oil and smelled like a sewer. It sunk into my skin, burning like fire. It lasted only a few seconds, yet it felt like hours of bone-deep pain. The poison made its way through my body until it settled in my stomach like a stone. I clutched the arms of the throne as I retched and vomited. The corruption extruding from Inkasisa was as bitter as it was dark.

Blinking away the tears of discomfort, I stared at the oily pool on the floor and spat out the last of the taste.

"Copacati?" a youthful voice called, "Is that you?"

A young girl, perhaps thirteen, smiled at me. Inkasisa was as real as I was, not an apparition. She squatted on the throne, head tilted left, eyes wide as saucers.

"You're not Copacati," she frowned, wriggled out of the squat position and leaned towards me. Lavender sprigs clung to glossy black hair.

"I'm Sophia. Copacati is my friend. I'm here to help."

Inkasisa's hand traced my chin, but she yanked it back when Brennan fell into the chamber with two Rogues on him. Ben beheaded one whilst Brennan incinerated the other.

Inkasisa screamed and launched into my arms.

I hugged her tight, "It's okay. You're safe with me." She smelled of lavender and leather and spring air.

"Are you a Cloud God?" she squeaked into my neck.

"Um… yes, I guess I am," the thought was strange, but that was how she would have seen angels.

The slit of sunlight from the oculus dulled. A Rogue crawled in through the aperture, its bony fingers like nails on a chalkboard as it clawed across the ceiling.

Inkasisa screamed and burrowed into my hair, "If you're here, then the devil, Supay, is close," she slid from my hip and grabbed my hand. "Come quickly," her slight arms yanked mine to follow her behind the thrones. She pushed at the largest one, grunting and puffing. "Open it!" she indicated for me to copy her.

I pushed. It didn't budge.

"Getting outnumb…"

A red orb exploded and cut Ben off. The air tinged blood red.

Inkasisa's many wooden necklaces jangled. Sweat glistened on her olive skin.

She pointed at the rear of the throne, "Here!"

The dying red glow revealed engraved concentric circles. I was relieved to see something so familiar and simple. I drew my dagger and nicked my thumb, careful to preserve Yeqon's blood on its tip.

The moment it touched the smooth indentations, the ground rumbled. The throne trembled and began to move.

"Ben! Brennan!"

Inkasisa and I pushed at the heavy seat, but it ground along at painfully slow pace. Brennan hovered over our heads. He fired orbs towards the doorway and shot arrows of light at the oculus whilst the throne revealed a dark recess. Stale, warm air blustered up — air that was alive with E'lan.

I gestured to Ben and Brennan as they fended off the slobbering fiends. Descended Rogues erupted everywhere as they sped to Hell. Another one dislodged its arm to enter through the roof. The bone fell into the hole by my feet. I backed towards the first step down into God knew what with Inkasisa tugging at my hand. I fired an orb at the Rogue. With immense satisfaction, I struck its neck. Its head burst into a black smear against the roof, and its remnants rained onto the sacrificial altar.

A loud *crack* followed where I'd damaged the roof. A thin line spider-webbed across it. Dust sprayed into the already clogged air.

The boys arrived, heaving for breath and still firing orbs towards the doorway. The Rogues kept coming.

Brennan peered at the hole, "In there?"

"Yes, another dark hole in the ground!" I rolled my eyes, not happy about it either.

I breached another step, sent an orb for the doorway as more bone-white Rogues entered. They exploded into dust; the chittering of more screeched outside.

Inkasisa pulled me down the steps, she did a double-take at Ben. He lowered his eyes and waved at us to rush.

Brennan hurried into the dark next to us, "This feels familiar."

I threw orbs ahead to light the way. They revealed a carved tunnel a good six-foot-wide and at least eight foot high. Its smooth walls were unadorned, its paved floor damp. Faint drips echoed in the distance.

"I'm waiting until this closes," Ben yelled. "Go on ahead. You don't need these things down there too!"

I wanted to hesitate, but that was emotional. It was stupidity. Ben could and should look after himself, and Inkasisa's enthusiasm was increasing.

Inkasisa jerked on my hand, desperate to pull me along. I glanced back to where the cold scrape of stone on stone echoed along seams of variegated rock as the throne closed off the tunnel. The tunnel shuddered after a dozen muted thuds. Ben was fighting alone; my throat closed a little as I followed Inkasisa and left Ben behind.

We ran.

Koi's voice boomed down the corridor and sent a shiver of relief through me. I thanked I'el, he'd heard my call and Koi found me.

"Keep going!" Koi yelled.

Within seconds, he was by my side along with the smell of ashes and spice. Another wave of relief. Ben was here too.

The ceiling shook. Gold-veined quartz streaked the ground like a runway lighting strip.

"Good to see you, Koi," I said.

I took Inkasisa into my arms and lifted off the ground. Brennan and Koi coasted next to me along the strange tunnels. The sounds of the Rogues gave way to something altogether different.

I slowed when I felt far enough away from the thrones and landed. The others followed suit.

"Quiet," I ran my fingers along a finger-wide quartz vein. A subtle hum emanated from it. "Do you hear that?"

The walls tremored.

Brennan scoffed, "I think I'el could hear that."

"No, the whispers," I followed the quartz until it forked up the walls. I pressed my ear against it. Inkasisa also leaned in.

I gasped, "There's something inside the wall."

Koi placed his ear to the wall, "It's the souls of the fallen," his face lit.

"What?" I asked. "What do you hear?"

With each whisper, the gemstone seams in the walls pulsed brighter. They dulled at regular intervals like gentle conversations. The whispers were too soft to understand. My erratic, over-excited heartbeat enough to drown them out. I strained to hear them, I needed to know who was there.

"The Cavern of Souls was said to dwell somewhere near where the old palace once stood," Koi murmured, resting his cheek against the cool stone. "A miracle on Earth," he closed his eyes and breathed in slow and deep. "I believe we have found it," he smiled and curled his fingertips against the wall. The quartz blazed brighter.

I pressed my ear closer, felt the cool under my hands. The voices grew louder, more urgent, but they were still muffled. I moved along the wall. The voices followed me, louder with every step I took.

I looked into the dark tunnel, "I think they want us to follow."

Brennan's eyes were wide and his mouth slightly parted as he trailed his fingers along the quartz. It glimmered under his touch. His lips peeled up in a tiny smile. Ben did the same.

I stepped a few more feet ahead, feeling their soft buzz in my fingertips.

A *bang* rang down the tunnel from where the throne had closed us in. Thuds and scratches followed. Inkasisa clung to me. The tunnel shuddered.

We flew, following the quartz. I kept one hand on the wall. My touch set the stones ahead alight and cut through the darkness. The floor inclined down, and we dove with it until it narrowed and forced us into a single line. I took the lead, Koi was behind me, then Brennan, and Ben in the rear.

The whispers elevated into an insistent call. We rounded a corner into a large chamber and touched down.

Neat, squared walls rose to an ornate ceiling of glittering crystals. Thousands of icicle-like projections, whose brilliance reflected our light into a myriad of colours. The quartz veins conglomerated into a single white sheet, which fanned wide to one side and engulfed the entire wall. It flickered to life.

The whispers were much louder here, audible without me touching the wall. We took a moment to take in the sheer iridescence.

Inkasisa wriggled her fingers at the wall, "This is the place."

The whispers stopped. It felt like the earth was listening to us.

Brennan touched my elbow, "Be careful."

"Follow the child," Koi said, and Ben nodded.

Inkasisa pulled me to the wall. Her smile was a beam of triumphant sunshine.

She lay her hands on the stone, "You do this."

Shadows swam within the stone.

"Be careful," I picked her up and checked her hands to make sure she was okay.

"Do not be afraid," Koi said. His eyes were fixated on where Inkasisa had been.

He moved to the wall and glanced over his shoulder at me. His eyes flickered with joy, then moistened with sadness. He placed his hands and forehead against the seemingly alive geology. His fingers splayed wide, and he breathed deep. The strange shadows were drawn to him. They swirled close, then pulled away. One separated from the others. Its tall, featureless shape sharpened into a humanoid form as it walked closer to Koi.

My mouth went dry. I don't think a breath passed my lips.

"I've not been here in a long time," Koi murmured. "Not since the fall."

Ben and Brennan leaned into the wall as well, their marks bright. Human shapes skimmed past them like schools of fish, stopping as though testing who they were and whizzing away again.

Three people-sized silhouettes settled in front of Brennan, Koi, and Ben. Like liquid shadows, they mirrored their movements, leaning into the stone from within.

We had found the Cavern of Souls. All those gone before, right in front of me. I wasn't sure if it was reassuring or just dammed frightening.

I felt the E'lan's peaceful pull as a gentle warmth washed over my skin, a calm that felt like love.

Inkasisa bounced up and down and pulled me to the others, "You too, you too!"

I felt like an intruder. My hand was on my heart as I followed her one tentative step at a time. The closer I came to the wall, the stronger the E'lan radiated an elemental pull I couldn't resist.

I leaned in next to Koi. The moment my skin touched the stone, thousands of voices erupted in my mind.

"She is here!"

"We are saved!"

"Blessed be the Earth-born."

Dozens of hands pressed against the inside of the stone. Bright blue eyes fluoresced on the faces of these shimmering angelic forms. The power, the deeply emotional connection hit the very core of my soul.

I relaxed, no longer feeling like an outsider, and leaned my whole body against the tingling wall.

There were so many voices, but one called my name louder than the rest. My heart flipped. Their form moved closer until I felt her energy as clearly as my pulse. Her hand pressed against the wall, mirroring mine.

"Sophia?" her voice was a shock and a balm to my battered soul.

"Kea?" I smoothed my hands across the surface, trying to find a way in. Trying to understand what this was, how she was there, how I was here, "Is that really you?"

She grinned, "Of course it's me, kiddo!"

Words were thick on my tongue, "What, um… this is… how did you get in there?"

I traced the shape of her hand. Kea's fluid, ghostly form was a glimmering angel in contrast to my pink fleshiness.

"Is this what…" the words caught in my throat.

"Death looks like? Yes. For us, anyway. My body is long gone, but my soul has remained here. I've been waiting for you, and here you are. I knew you'd make it, kiddo."

Her fingers traced my face, from the place within a place. It was an incomprehensible dimension that melded with the earth's elements. My mouth hung in awe, then I smiled, so happy to see her again.

"Are you okay?" I asked.

"Of course I am. A little miffed that dammed Asmodai fooled me. Bit embarrassing really."

My smile waned. I leaned my forehead against the wall.

"I'm sorry I couldn't save you."

"Oh, but you have. You're here, aren't you?" Kea shrugged, "When I arrived here, my memories returned. This is the place, Soph. Somewhere nearby, the portal is ready and waiting for you." Kea slapped her hands within the stone. The mark on her face glimmered.

"Where?" I looked left and right.

Kea laughed, "Not in here, silly! But somewhere close. You go slay that portal, okay?"

My smile faded again, "You're not going to help?"

"I'm a little caught up, hon. Can't get outta here until you bring this all home, you understand?"

I nodded. They were stuck here until the portal freed them. They couldn't walk the Earth in their angelic form, it would have been too shocking and dangerous for humanity.

The walls rumbled, and the E'lan spiked with a warning to move on.

"You got this," Kea said. "Get outta here. Reunions are for when wars are won."

She faded and melded into nothing, as did the shadows the others had spoken with. My heart sank, but I sniffed back my emotions when the walls shuddered again. The others, too, wore muddled expressions as they stepped back from the wall.

"We're close," I said. "Come on," I hauled Inkasisa onto my hip and floated up.

"Soph'ael?"

I shuddered to a stop.

I'd never heard that voice, yet I knew it, I felt its familiarity in my soul. My feet touched the floor again, and I set Inkasisa down. My heart thudded, my face flushed hot, I felt dizzy. The nearby drip of water seemed louder and matched my heartbeat. Ben put his arm around my shoulder. It felt heavy as he guided me back to two shadows that emerged out of the opaqueness.

My heavy arms were liquid. My hands took hours to land on the wall. The moment they touched, I was shocked back into reality. Tears blurred my sight. I couldn't blink them away fast enough.

"Mum?"

A soft smile lit up her oval face. Energy pulsed around her like a halo. She looked like an angel to me.

"Daughter?" said a deeper, yet still-soft voice.

"Dad?"

The word barely made it out of my dry mouth.

"Is it really you?" I asked softly.

They nodded and touched the wall. I saw the gentle curve of my mother's lips and the strength in my father's eyes. My palms rested against theirs.

"I… I missed you. I…" my throat constricted. I spread my arms against the wall, emulating a hug. It was far from what I needed, not enough for the ache of loss in my heart.

Anger at the unfairness rose; I clawed at the quartz that separated us. An irrational rush surged through me.

"Open it!" I yelled, "Get them out!"

No one responded. My anger tipped into desperation.

I ran my hands frantically over the stone, which pulsed brighter everywhere I touched. There was no latch, no crack to hitch it open.

"Open this damn thing!" I screamed.

"Be calm, daughter," my mother edged closer, but not close enough for me or for that vacant ache deep in my heart.

"We cannot be free until you have opened the portal," she said.

I tore at the wall, "Damn this fucking place!"

The earth rumbled as I cried.

Inkasisa hugged my leg.

Ben rested his hand on my shoulder, "There's no room behind there. It's solid quartz. Their souls move within it, they are part of it." he squeezed my shoulder, "There is no door to the Cavern of Souls."

Despite everything, his voice still tipped something in my heart. As the tremble in my lips calmed, I rested my hand on his and leaned into it. But then I looked at them again, at their serene forms, and anger fizzed through my veins again. I shook Ben off.

"I want them out of here. They're *right there*. I've never had them in my entire life!"

I fired a dozen orbs at the wall, but they ricocheted off the quartz like bouncy balls. I worked up a sweat. More souls rushed to it. A hundred fascinated eyes peeked out.

I drew a red orb and wound my arm back. Inkasisa squealed and ran into Brennan's comforting arms. The glowing orb flickered on my palm as I heaved for breath, my skin pins and needles.

"Daughter, desist," my father spoke insistently. "We are safe, you are not. Finish your journey, then we will be united."

I smacked my hands together and screamed at myself as I extinguished the orb. My fingers entwined until the skin was white. I held them to my face which burned with every emotion.

I squeezed my eyes shut to push the tears away. I ran back in and leaned into my father's image.

"I've missed you all my life," I sobbed. "Please... how do I finish this?"

I crumpled to the floor. My parents kneeled with me.

"My sweet, beautiful Soph'ael," Mother's words were liquid love. "We had to bear more than most in losing you, in never knowing if you survived. Just thinking about the evil that hunted you long before you ever existed nearly broke our souls. You will finish this because you are our daughter and because you are I'el's chosen. You will succeed because you are you."

"But..." another sob escaped me. "I've..." I sniffed and wiped my nose on my sleeve. "I've done so much. I followed the prophecies, and I've come so far, only to lose the Kaladai."

"Nothing is ever truly lost," a woman said inside the wall.

My parents retreated. They bowed as another woman floated forwards.

She kneeled, "Dear child of mine daughter, your heart remains closed."

I took a sharp breath, "Grandmother?"

Her tranquil face was inches from mine. I touched the wall again, a barrier to all that I wanted. Her hand mirrored mine.

"What you seek has always been within your grasp," she said. "All that you require awaits you before your unseeing eyes and your unbelieving mind."

She spoke such confusion. She sounded like Enoch.

I shook my head, "But my pendant... your pendant... I lost it," I patted my chest, failure ran cold through my skin.

Queen Elizabeth smiled, "And it will find you again, just as it found you once before."

"What about the Kaladai?" I asked.

"And still the Earth-born dwells in mortal faithlessness," a new voice echoed behind me.

Reluctant to lose sight of my family, I left my hand pressed to the wall, peered over my shoulder.

Koi bowed, "Master Uriel."

Ben and Brennan followed suit; Ben held his head the lowest.

"Rise," Uriel ordered. His commanding voice reverberated above the ongoing vibrations that shook the earth.

I held my breath and turned back to my parents and grandmother, but they were fading.

I banged on the wall, "No! No, come back! Please?"

My legs felt weak, I struggled to stand up. Tears streamed down my face, a lifetime of yearning, of lost love, melted away into the rock.

"Don't cry, pretty Sophia," Av'ael's voice drew me away.

I wiped the tears from my face and raised my eyes. Uriel was gone, Av'ael in his place. She swayed left and right in that coy, childlike way. Her hands clasped behind her back.

A glance behind me drove home that my parents had vanished.

I pulled myself back up and wiped my eyes, "Where have you been?"

She giggled and shrugged. She swayed from side to side.

Koi's eyes were curious, "You know this child?"

I nodded. Av'ael beamed a broad smile his way.

"Strange little thing, you are," Brennan said to her, still looking around for Uriel.

"Where's Uriel?" I asked, a semblance of control returned to my words, and my muscles regained their strength.

"Not a clue," Brennan said. "Uriel was here, then *poof*... Av'ael was in his place."

Ben's jaw clenched; his eyes followed Av'ael's every move.

Inkasisa looked on, excitement brightened her eyes, delight blossomed her cheeks.

"I can help you, pretty Sophia. I've always helped you. Here," Av'ael produced my backpack.

I gasped and rushed to her, "Where and how did you get this?"

I plunged my hands into my bag. The Kaladai cogs were inside, along with the original scrolls.

Av'ael giggled and skipped around me.

Koi peered inside at the bounty. He smiled and nodded with satisfaction. "Well now, that was most unexpected."

Av'ael stopped in front of me with a proud smile.

"How did you get this from under the Zythros stone?" I asked.

"Mumma got it," Av'ael rolled her eyes and put her hands on her hips. "Even though she thought you should have got it yourself," she puffed out her lips. "She's so bossy."

"Where is your mother?"

Av'ael's mother appeared out of nowhere behind Ben. There'd been no transfer buzz in the E'lan… she was simply there.

Ben stepped aside, paling as she passed him.

"I am here," Av'ael's mother said. "And this is the final time I will tolerate your insolence, child! I've told you to leave her alone!" she shook a finger at Av'ael. "Quickly now, your time is over. The darkness comes our way," her voice was taut. She met no one's eyes but Av'ael's. She wriggled her fingers impatiently for Av'ael to come to her.

Av'ael sighed, "I'll miss you, pretty Sophia."

"What do you mean?" I reached for Av'ael, but she skipped to her mother.

"Where are you going? How did you even get here?"

Koi stepped between me and the mother, "That's what I'd like to know too. Who are you? How did you come here with this child?"

He rubbed his fingers together. Sparks arced, ready to form an orb should he need it. I took his hand and quelled his stinging energy with the healing warmth of mine.

"I know them," I said. "It's okay."

Koi didn't take his eyes off the mother and her angelic-faced child. "Who are they, Sophia?"

The ground shook. Fissures webbed across its width. I floated up to avoid toppling over. A torrent of water rushed to freedom; an ever-growing flood drowned the slope of the floor.

Av'ael's mother stepped over the torrent and released her wings, "Enough!" she flashed her eyes at Koi.

Av'ael jumped up… not into a loving, motherly embrace, but rather her mother absorbed her, as though Av'ael had run through a veil.

I gasped as Av'ael and her mother merged into one. Their forms elongated, shimmered and pulsed until they reformed—

Into Uriel.

He smiled at me like we had shared a secret.

Koi and Brennan fell to their knees, but Uriel focused in one direction and narrowed his eyes at Ben. Ben didn't look at Uriel as the others had. Uriel moved to him. Ben winced as the light of Uriel's wings spilled across his body.

Uriel lay his hand on Ben's head and closed his eyes, "It will take more than this to redeem yourself, Nik'ael. Rise, and be the great Watcher you once were."

Ben complied, but still couldn't reach Uriel's eyes. He massaged the fracture in his hand again. I wondered if he would ever let it heal.

Uriel looked back at me, "Rise as darkness falls, Soph'ael. Make haste before the father, the mother, and the son of evil descend this world into a Tartarus never before imagined."

He turned away and threw a blinding white orb ahead. He pointed towards it. It exploded into brilliant fireworks. He faded as the tunnel glowed.

"Wait!" I rushed through the fizzing heat of his remnants.

"He's gone," Koi said. "Do as he says. Darkness isn't coming, it's already here," Koi turned me around, shoved me forwards, "Go!"

I ran towards Uriel's' light. I chased it down the tunnel, leaving behind the conundrum that was Av'ael. The others joined me, and we flew away from my parents' resting place. Inkasisa clung to Brennan, squealing with delight. We ducked and weaved around stalagmites and stalactites the deeper the tunnel sloped into the earth. Uriel's orb zoomed on ahead, and I was thankful that I had a real helping hand for the first time.

Ben swooped under me, "Who *was* that kid?" his wings grazed the walls, drawing out a new glow of quartz.

"Av'ael," I said. "She's the child who visited me so often. She was my friend, sort of."

"Never seen her," Ben said.

"I have," Brennan shouted from behind me. "Knew she was NQR!"

The tunnels lit up the gemstone veins that raced ahead, our guiding light.

"What is she?" Ben asked.

It dawned on me that she'd always appeared generally when no one else was around. The only people I knew had seen her were Jaz, Brennan and Matias.

"She never existed," Koi answered for me. His wings shadowed me overhead.

Uriel's orb disappeared and we took a sharp right, relieved when I still saw it in front of us. The tunnel narrowed. I moved ahead, and Koi fell behind.

"How did she bring me the Kaladai if she wasn't… real?"

The earth groaned; more cracks raced us along the walls.

"She is Uriel's conscience. I have seen it before, when we warred on Satanos. Innocents dwelt there, believe it or not, and some of us struggled to abide by I'el's will to eradicate everyone. When there is turmoil in a soul, it can split to, satisfy its conflicting emotions. Some felt conscience-bound to split themselves, I suppose. …" Koi veered left at a fork, following the orb, "They were compassion and duty-bound halves. The compassionate half would warn of what was coming, the duty bound half constantly tries to reign the emotional side in," Koi moved a little further ahead of me now.

We bore left at another turn.

"But isn't Uriel…" I started.

"A hell of a lot more important than us? Yep!" Brennan called. He sounded farther away than before.

"An archangel has every chance to be conflicted when discharging their duty, because more often than not, their duty is a bloody one," Ben said. He coasted in next to me, "Like Gedz'iel, Uriel chose to remain connected to Earth to help where and when he chose. He tried to help me once," Ben's eyes met mine briefly as we swerved a hard right into colder air. "He's obviously been helping you, but has been in crisis with his conscience and his obligation to I'el. He and Gedz'iel risk retribution from the Throne for their interference," Ben said.

Brennan whistled, "Tough gig! Who is the son he was talking about?"

Koi grumbled to himself. The mention of a third enemy hadn't eluded me either.

"Well, I suppose we'll find out soon," I said, recalling the veiled enemy at Chauvet Caves.

I stopped when the tunnel ended abruptly. Uriel's orb hovered in front of a large basalt slab with a concentric quartz circle in its middle.

I lowered myself and shuffled my wing back. The nub of a new one wriggled along with it.

Brennan landed in front of me, "A door?" The orb was beginning to sputter out.

"Of course," I grit my teeth. "I'll be bled dry soon."

The earth shook. I pricked the tip of my thumb as water cascaded down the icy ground in slippery sheets. I held my thumb against the quartz, and my blood coursed through the circular striations. The quartz pulsed. Light shone from within it.

Just like in the Australian sanctuary, the door lit up with hundreds of stars. Smatterings of gemstones twinkled to life inside the stone.

"Pretty," Inkasisa whispered.

I was in awe of I'el's power over the Earth, its connection to me… to everything.

The walls shuddered again. The time between each rumble was lessoning. Millions of years of geology ground against itself as the walls strained to retain their secrets.

Something crashed behind us. Fog rushed around the corner like a foamy wave and lapped against the walls. The clawing and scratching of bones against rock sounded close. Rogues had made their way in.

"I've had enough of this!" as the fog thickened into a putrid ashen film around my ankles, I drew energy into my hands and pointed at Brennan. "Keep Inkasisa safe."

He slid her onto his back so he could hold his sword without hurting her. She clung around his neck, a little doll.

I thundered past the boys towards the chitter of the dead, whose echo deepened as they edged closer. I wouldn't wait for them to catch me anymore. They could run from me instead. I drew Kea's sword and infused it with the angry heat in my arms until it shone like a neon beam. I peered around the corner into a smoky haze.

"Don't look," I called back to Inkasisa.

She squealed and pulled Brennan's hair over her eyes. Ben flanked Brennan's right and Koi his left. I swung around, I didn't need a constant nanny service at my heels.

"Stay there," I ordered with an authority that surprised me. "Protect the door. Don't let them get to it."

They looked nervous but fanned out, holding their positions. I held up my sword and breached the corner, waiting for the first stupid Rogue to show its rotting face.

One... Two... Three...

I rushed headlong into the fog. A dozen or so Rogues crawled towards me along the walls like insects. They screeched with excitement when they saw me. These were ancient, long-dead things with their skinless skulls and needle-point fingers of ashen ossification.

The closest one dropped off the wall and launched at me with an open maw. I struck Kea's energised sword through its ribcage, incinerating the Rogue on impact. Stinking ash stuck to me. I coughed it away as another slithered around my feet. Five bony digits clung to my ankle. I stamped on the forearm, leaving the hand to quiver and fall from my foot. My sword high, I plunged it into the corpse's spine. Another explosion of orange flame and a moment of quiet followed; I heard only the odd scrape of an unsure limb hidden in the mist.

"Come on! Is that it?"

To my right, something moved. To my left, a chittering hiss. I smiled, held the sword with two hands, and burned more power into it. I cut my index finger along its searing blade and let my blood take its time to hit the ground. They could come to me to meet their destiny.

"Mmm, yummy," I teased. Four shadows, like ghosts on a moor, moved closer and gathered in front of me. They snapped and snarled, unsure before my power, but desperate for a taste of me.

"Soph?" Ben breached the corner.

"Stay back!" I yelled and when he disappeared, I threw an orb up to clear the air. The Rogues backed away a little. The odd piece of Incan jewellery rattled against their bones; their burial attire long disintegrated. They hesitated when I didn't run and gurgled amongst themselves, their teeth grinding in their skulls.

The smallest one jumped. It ran straight at me on all fours and met the smooth sweep of my blade. Another two charged. One sunk its teeth into my thigh as I plunged the sword into the other's skull. The pain was bearable as its few teeth were old and worn. It tried to chew, but only a trickle of blood ran from the wound. The pathetic creature fell easily away when I punched it with the sword's handle, fracturing its skull. I felt strong, and I was pissed off.

"That's the last taste of me anyone will get!"

The last one gnashed its teeth and clenched its fingers, cracking and popping with every movement. Its eyeless sockets seemed to see me as it tilted its head and followed my movements.

I jutted the sword at it and pointed it at my bruising leg, "Come on then. You've waited long enough."

Its mouth quivered. It clicked its teeth as it ogled the trail of blood seeping through the cotton.

I stepped closer, "If your master were here, you wouldn't dare resist." I pulled a sliver of energy out of my good wing.

It cowered and slipped on the mounds of ash. As my blood pooled around my toes, it edged forwards, its hunger fighting with its instinct to survive certain death, so to speak.

In the distance, the tunnel rumbled again. New scraping echoed far away. More were coming, and I was out of patience.

I flew up to just below the ceiling and fell onto it with a powerful cut to the left. Bones shattered under the chromious bite, scattering in every direction. The skull remained intact, however, and rolled around in a circle before it stopped by my right foot. Its mouth bit at me, pathetic in its desperation. I grimaced as its arms, hands still attached, pulled themselves through ash and bone to find each other and then sought the head. It was trying to put itself back together, an abomination that defied the laws of nature. I watched it with a sick fasciation.

My foot fell hard on the snapping skull and the arms fell still.

Returning around the corner, dragging the tip of Kea's sword along the ground behind me, I felt like thunder. I sheathed it hard into the belt as I stared at the door, hands on hips. Hopefully, it would be the last goddamned roadblock.

I felt the heaviness of everyone's attention behind me.

Peering over my shoulder, I smiled wryly.

"What? You never seen a girl be the hero before?"

Chapter
Twenty-Eight

How long do you stare at a wall of rock and wait for something to happen?

Not long, I decided. Koi held the diamond dagger aloft for me and the prophecy beamed onto the wall next to the gem-crusted door.

Inkasisa climbed back onto my hip.

"What more can you tell me, little one?"

Inkasisa stared wide-eyed at the words, which were impossible for her to understand; she snuggled in.

"The Cloud Gods lived in a palace on the lake. Copacati visited me on its shore. Their city was destroyed when the monsters came. You must go there, but it sank into the lake," she nodded and twirled my hair.

Ben ran his finger under the script, "What does this say? The shapes are familiar, but I can't make them out."

"Earth's mirror within the lion's keep where old angels dwell," I answered as his eyes narrowed in thought.

Brennan pointed up, "Well, we've found the Cavern of Souls where ascended angels live, they're old I suppose?" he scratched his head in thought. "We're below Lake Titicaca. Water reflects, like a mirror. I suppose that could be it?" Brennan shrugged and squinted harder at the script.

"Hmm…" I bit my lip. "What is the lion's keep then?" I muttered.

Inkasisa bounced on my hip, "Lions live in the mountains. They protect the lake." she grinned. "They even lived with Copacati in the floating palace!"

"Hmm, okay. The lions kept the lake safe, and the angels lived in a palace on the lake until it sank…" I readjusted her on my hip. Where did the portal fit into all this?

Koi tapped his finger to his lips, his eyes in the past.

"I remember that place," Brennan said. "Didn't know it had anything to do with a portal though."

Ben pursed his lips, "None of us would remember any connections to the portal. Anyone who lived here after the fall would have done so with the portal right under their noses. Ironic, huh?"

Koi's eyes brightened as he stared at the swirls and dots, looking for meaning where only I could.

"The floating palace was our place of congregation to keep abreast of events across Earth," Koi said. "Gedz'iel resided there. Many vulnerable people were in this region, and he protected them until…"

"Until Yeqon took too much interest in it," Ben said.

Koi nodded. The smile of his earlier recollection faded from his eyes.

"What happened?" I asked.

Inkasisa gripped my sides and buried her face into my chest.

"Kea collapsed the city," Koi answered. "As the child said, it lies abandoned at the bottom of the lake. We concluded that the indigenous communities would be safer if our energies weren't attracting the Daimon. This is one reason why most of us began living underground permanently."

Inkasisa's lips quivered. "They did not leave us," she narrowed her eyes at Ben and tightened her mouth into an angry pout.

"I've seen what they did," I smoothed her hair gently, kissing her head. Her memories still vivid in my mind.

"He tormented everyone. He caused the fall of our empire," Inkasisa whispered angrily towards Ben.

Ben lowered his eyes.

"Do you remember him?" I whispered into her ear.

She nodded and dug her nails in.

I glared at Ben, "Make this right." The ground shuddered, "And make it quick."

Ben doused his wings and kneeled in front of us. The white of his hair, the blue of his eyes, the collection of tears that pooled in his lashes. all these things made her grip relax and my heart clench.

"I'm sorry for what you saw and for what happened to you and your family. I will make amends, I promise," he said.

Inkasisa rested her wary eyes on him. She slipped from my hip and put her forehead to his. His breath hitched. Another rumble reverberated through the tunnel, and she climbed back into my embrace.

The water under our feet rushed a little faster.

I refocussed on the door, "Okay. Ancient city, lake, mountain, and hopefully a portal."

The concentric circles pulsed a faint light and the door remained alive with gemstone imagery, but it hadn't budged an inch.

"Could we not go overland and down through the lake's surface?" Brennan asked.

A piercing *crack* echoed, and a deathly funk filled my senses.

Brennan swore under his breath, "More of the bastards."

"Does that answer your question?" I asked. "I saw them at the temple's base; Grey was holding them off as best he could. Heading back out there would be like running straight into a slaughter house."

"She's right," Ben said. He tracked back into the direction we'd come from. "We... Yeqon left many here to scare the people into submission. They'll make it down here, but slowly," he ignited his wings. His sword glimmered in his hand as he peered around the corner.

Brennan and Koi followed Ben.

"Do you know more?" I asked Inkasisa.

"'Return the city of the Cloud Gods. That was whispered into my memories," she fiddled with the wooden beads around her shoulders. It reminded me of Enl'iel and myself and our pendants.

I placed Inkasisa behind me and sent her running to Brennan.

"Back up farther. I'm going to try something."

I rubbed my hands into a fiery heat. Whilst my feet numbed in the torrent, my hands burned a satisfying white. I formed an orb. I rolled it to basketball size, wound my arm back, and threw it. The orb hit the stone right in the middle of the blood-filled circles.

Nothing happened.

"Cover her eyes," I called to Brennan, not wanting to blind Inkasisa.

I created an orb in each palm, weightless fire and high hopes, I slapped them together. The tunnel flashed a brilliant white. I heaved the giant orb into the same spot, which resulted in an extension of the cracks that had already spider-webbed the walls. The leak spread, and more water gushed in.

Fog eked around my ankles again, mingling with the rising tide.

"Damn it!"

I read the prophecy again. Perhaps now was the time to use Yeqon's blood? I scraped my dagger against the quartz circles. A high-pitched *ting* followed as it deposited the dried cells that had once flowed through Yeqon's veins on top of my own. I smeared them together, mixing our bloods into the circular indentations.

"Okay, guys, watch out. I'm not sure what will happen."

I spread my fingers; they fluoresced more brilliantly than the quartz. With my palm on the bloody etching, I pulsed it to meld light and dark together.

The congealed mix blazed orange and blue, the heat too much even for me. I jerked my hand away as a tiny blue-and-orange flame traversed clockwise around the circles like a flame to dynamite. I backed away and took Inkasisa into my arms, covering her eyes with my hand. Thin smoke trailed up towards the centre of the circles. An earthy burn overwhelmed the Rogue stench, but the fog thickened rapidly.

I pointed behind us, "Can someone check up there?"

Ben and Brennan disappeared around the corner. Koi stayed with me, mesmerised by the goings-on.

Less than two breaths later, Brennan's voice boomed urgently back down the tunnel, "There's hundreds of them!"

The familiar blasts of orb weaponry echoed along the tunnel. Rogues chittered and gurgled between blasts. Inkasisa squealed.

"Go help them, Koi."

He opened his wings. "I'll be a mere thought away," Koi dashed around the corner, and the battle sounds intensified.

I shuffled. What would happen first? A deluge of Rogues, or the door opening to let me out?

Water leaked around the edges of the burning circles, and the flame changed to a brilliant white. Sparks sizzled as water flowed down the rockface. The flame reached the centre and disappeared within the rock. A crack, then two, splintered out from the middle. I took a step back.

"Guys?"

I didn't like the idea of these leaking walls when there was a lake above my head.

The boys' blasts must have drowned out my voice. I tried to send my call to Koi's thoughts, but I didn't have a chance.

Lake Titicaca exploded into the tunnel. A raging torrent filled the space in seconds. I spun head over heels under its wrath, shocked by its frigid bite. The freezing flow pulled Inkasisa away.

I screamed as my head breached the frothing water. Huge chunks of the wall tossed through the water and threatened to crush anything in their path. Light flashed around me… the boys. Bones scraped past me… Rogues. The current hurled the Rogues around like Halloween dolls and ripped them apart.

The water stilled as the pressure equalised. I adjusted my sight to the pitch dark and found Koi first. He took my hand. Ben swam up from under me, and Brennan floated in the vast opening the explosion had left. The musty tunnel air bubbled away in soft, muted pops as the water submerged us completely.

I couldn't see Inkasisa.

"Where is she?" I whispered into Koi's mind.

He shook his head. I dove to the opening, dragging him along, and peered into a sheet of utter darkness. I swam back around the corner, where I flicked floating Rogue remnants out of the way. An icy pain speared my heart. I squeezed Koi's hand hard. Inkasisa was gone.

Ben and Brennan's light illuminated the vastness of the lake beyond. I swam over to them. Ben grabbed my elbow and pulled me through the opening. I looked up, hoping to find Inkasisa swimming around, but instead, there was a strange twinkle like the night sky. Innumerable dots of light pinpricked the aqueous void. They floated along a gentle current; watery gemstone motes skittered amongst pale paths of light from the sky.

Ben pushed me forwards, *"Let's go."*

I spun back towards the tunnel, *"We can't leave her here to die all over again!"*

My blazing wing lit the sand bed far below. The surface was too far away for a little girl to have held her breath long enough.

Reality punched me in the gut, a fucked-up assault that tore me down.

Koi's light warmed the cool water as he moved closer, *"Our time here is done, and so is young Inkasisa's."*

He pulled me around and inclined his head to the crook of his arms. There, curled up like a sleeping baby, were Inkasisa's tanned remains, just as I'd found her in the temple.

My cry of pain hurt in my chest. I reached forwards and touched a black strand of Inkasisa's hair.

"She is as she was, only you have freed her soul now," Koi whispered into my mind.

I shook my head; tears couldn't flow in this watery hell.

"Honour the child who waited half a millennium for you. Her soul has departed; she is at peace."

Koi smiled. I couldn't, but the thought of her being at peace released the clamp in my chest.

I mourned our brief encounter and thanked her. Koi let her go, and her little bones drifted away into the great oblivion of Lake Titicaca.

Twenty-Nine

Sparkling motes tickled my skin as we followed the current that had claimed Inkasisa's remains. Pure silence and cold gnawed at my bones. The belly of the lake seemed endless. The reaches of far-away daylight warbled across the surface and diluted the water into a breath-taking aquamarine as we rose over a ridge. It was like being on the other side of a mirror. Was anyone or anything looking down at us? I hoped to I'el that it wasn't Yeqon or Lilith.

We crossed a deep canyon and glided along a sand bed rich with the archaeologies of lost civilisations. Urns were plentiful. The hollow remnants of a boat, thick with barnacles, and collapsed stone columns criss-crossed the sediment. Coated in algae and worn from the current, a large building lay snug against the sand, gripped with water weeds. A mostly shattered gabled roof sat sideways along a palatial archway draped in thick seaweed. Pyramidal spires, roads, and the stony faces of winged beings peered up from the depths in various states of decay.

Colourful schools of rainbow trout scattered at our approach.

"What is this place?" I asked.

"It's the lost City of Light Inkasisa spoke of," Koi answered. *"Our floating palace."*

I used my good wing to propel me ahead. A pale light streamed from inside the arch. Those sparkly motes darted towards it against the current as though with sentient purpose. I followed.

"Keep up with her," Ben said, and Brennan was at my side in an instant.

"Do you remember this place?" I asked.

"Sort of. I never hung out here much, too posh for me. Kea loved it though," Brennan answered.

"Keep an eye out, okay? Who knows what's lurking down here," I said, the strange place tugged at my nerves.

Brennan gave me a scout's salute.

I followed the microscopic lights through the arch. The space behind it was small; the lake had long-ago swallowed most of whatever the arch had led to. An array of gemstone images along sunken walls was similar to those in the library back home. They were faint until I wiped away a thick layer of slime and my touch ignited the glowing symbol of I'el — an enormous and dazzling star surrounded by thousands of smaller stars.

"You okay in there?" Brennan asked.

I glanced back to see all three draped in the seabed greenery and looking at me with intense interest.

"All good. Just keep the dead things away, please?"

"You're okay for the moment, Soph," Ben whispered.

Koi's eyes shone with nostalgia.

"Come in, Koi. Help me make sense of this."

He rubbed at his knuckles like this place dredged up memories, then he hugged his arms around his chest.

"Are you hurt?" I asked.

He shook his head, slow and liquid under the water pressure, *"I don't like the cold. It bothers me."* Koi was lying. The closer we got to the end of this journey, the more unsettled he became. He was quieter since Yeqon had disappeared and Lilith had entered the conversation more. I didn't know why, but let it go, it wasn't the time to dig up his business.

He ran his hands along the walls. His light frightened away an octopus, which scurried into a narrow fissure.

"This was a transport room," Koi whispered. *"A great Zythros stone once stood here. Perhaps that is what we should search for?"*

I nodded in response.

Ben glided into the ruins. His eyes didn't light with surprise, and he moved around with the ease of familiarity. As usual, he added little, rather, he ran his hands along the walls as though reminiscing and stopped under I'el's star. He winced and shook his head.

I followed the little lights, which were still flitting around. I supposed I was looking for another circular thing to bleed on as well.

Ben suddenly sped outside. A rush of dull thuds drew me out. What new aggressor had stepped in my way? Koi pushed through the archway first. I peeked out after him, and saw a brilliance like no other.

Watchers and Eudaimonian soldiers, emblazoned with the light of E'lan, floated in the waters of Lake Titicaca, an arc of protectors. Some faces shone brighter than the others.

I forged my way towards Jaz. The reverse of her old self, she hovered ethereally by Jude's side. Her sassy strength and conviction shone through the mischievous twinkle in her eyes. Her signature short hair wisped like the soft fronds of dandelion.

We embraced.

"Holy... I mean, Jaz! Look at you!"

She excitedly gesticulated at me.

"What was that?" I asked.

Her face soured, and she pursed her lips. Jude settled her temper with a sharp sideways glance.

His mouth quirked into a half smile.

"Her impatience prevents her from melding her mind with others as yet," he held his palm up to pause her. She tugged impatiently at his arm. He rested his mark against hers, and she calmed.

"She would be able to achieve more, and more efficiently, if she were more even tempered," he said.

"You have your hands full then, Jude," I responded.

He raised his brows, *"More so than with you."*

I took it as a compliment and scooped Jaz' hands in mine.

"You can hear me?"

Jaz nodded and dug her fingers into my palms.

"Be careful, please?"

She rolled her eyes and nodded, pointing down at a dagger and a sword on her belt. She made an *A-OK* sign, clearly impressed with her deadly haul.

"That's a lot of nasties to give her, Jude."

He smiled at Jaz, *"She's got the temper to use them too."*

Enl'iel floated closer, eyes earnest with worry.

"Go do your duty, Sophia. Do not worry yourself with us. We are your shield," Enl'iel took my hands from Jaz, she clasped them tight. *"We heard your call, and not too soon either. These ancient lands are teeming with death."*

This wasn't news to me; I had smelled it when I first arrived.

"Have you seen Yeqon?" I asked.

She shook her head. *"Worse, a scourge of vampires. It is like the world's end. Our numbers are depleted, all our resources low. Humanity is at a grave crossroad."*

"So I've heard."

I looked at the ruins, then up at the sky's pale shimmer. The weight of the world was heavier by the moment.

Enl'iel pulled away from me.

"We have your back," Enl'iel swept her arm out to emphasise our kin surrounding the ruins. It was reassuring but shed no light on what I needed to do.

I returned to the ruins. The light of my companions guided me, their intensity bringing out a brighter vivacity to the sludgy stonework.

Ben followed me and glanced back at Jaz, *"She looks…"*

I pulled seaweed from a statue, *"Amazing."*

We swam to the left of the archway, where thicker mounds of various sizes and shapes awaited our attention.

I reached for his hand, *"She will forgive you one day."* I wanted to take it to reassure him but pulled back before we touched.

"I hope you will too," Ben swam ahead towards something glinting behind softly swaying foliage. I kicked my legs harder to catch up. We pulled at the weeds, and he glanced at me with the blush of excitement on his face. I wiped away a green film to reveal smooth, faceted stone.

My heart hammered, *"Is this a Zythros stone?"*

"*Yes!*" Ben dug at the base of the hibernating monolith. I called the others.

Relief swept across Koi's face, *"Praise I'el. This is what we need."*

We clawed sediment away from the base, cleaned as many crustaceans off it as we could until we exposed a vast, pointed pinnacle. I leaned in and put my ear to it. Deep inside, the whirring of an elemental life force pounded like a beating heart.

I floated a foot away, *"It's alive!"*

It was dull, lacking the light of the others, but it was pulsing faintly with life. It looked like a larger version of the Kaymakli stone, *"I think I need to turn it on."*

"Bring it back for us," Koi said.

My palms rested on the cold diamond surface; my skin magnetised to the stone. It ignited my hands itself as it sucked my power into its core, a nauseating pull. A tiny light awoke in its centre and began to pulse.

It was draining. It wanted too much.

"Help me, it's too strong," I whispered into the others' minds.

All three put their palms on it and focussed as it drank from us. I felt their effort, saw the strain on their faces. I grew dizzy. The others paled but kept going. The stone's heart beat stronger, its multispectral coloration a rainbow that strengthened and grew every second.

Brennan fell away and sank into the sand. Ben relented next.

Koi collapsed next to them, *"We aren't strong enough. You have to finish this."*

I felt a heartbeat short of collapse, too, but I kept going. I imagined myself connected to the stone and didn't let my skin leave its surface. If I hadn't been in water, I would have been drenched in sweat. Every muscle burned, but I focussed on its growing heart. Mesmerised by its pulsations, I hugged the great stone, lay every part of myself on it. When I'd been a nurse, I stuck with my patients and worked myself to the bone. I'd gone home and collapsed, knowing that my pain had eased theirs.

At some point, I fainted. When I came to, an immense pressure pushed me against the Zythros stone. I couldn't move, only felt its strong whispers under me.

Daylight and fresh air hit me, a shock and a relief, yet I was still moving, but not by my own doing.

I was shaking violently with the rumbling ancient city as it rose from within the depths of Lake Titicaca.

Chapter Thirty

The enormous structure settled atop the foaming waters whilst I clung to the Zythros stone like a barnacle. The noise was a deafening waterfall until the ascent ceased and the soaked turrets, walls, and alleys gleamed in the daylight. Fresh air hit my cool skin. Heavy clouds banked in the distance. The afternoon sun balanced atop distant mountains. I slowly pushed myself up, legs astride the stone.

Water lapped at the base of the immense floating palace, a football field-sized sandstone masterpiece of antiquity. High above sea level and hugged by mountains, Lake Titicaca was the angels' home on Earth; a laugh of delight rolled from my throat.

Brennan clambered up between two pillars onto a jetty, sodden and shaking out his hair. "Holy Mother of I'el!" he coughed, spread his wings, and hovered. "For once, I've got no words," his hands were on his hips, his face a picture of wonder.

Ben and Koi emerged next and stretched their weary muscles.

I pulled a thick wad of seaweed from the side of my head.

"You both okay?"

"Fine," they said in unison.

I slid from the stone and landed next to them.

Ben smirked at me. "Way to go, Earth-born," he smiled wider and ran his hand through his wet hair.

"Thanks," I wandered about the amazing City of Light.

Excitement roared through me, "I can't believe that just happened!"

We all gazed at a pillared causeway leading to a great arched door set into a high wall. The domed roof of another building behind it capped its edges. The Zythros stone, a beacon for travellers, was set on a dais about fifty feet from the jetty.

The other Watchers breached the lake and settled around it to protect the city's perimeter. It was strange to see my kind out in the open in broad daylight, their wings alight. That they were out in full power because of the grave threat we faced doused my thrill almost instantly.

I homed in on Jaz, who looked every bit as intimidating as Jude.

"Bren, where's Enl'iel?" I asked.

"Don't worry, she's back on dry land. Medical back-up. She's brought Alchemae with her."

I sighed with relief as the Watchers turned and faced the mountains around the lake. They raised their heads as two fighter jets appeared and disappeared in a deafening streak overhead. Their sonic boom felt like doom.

Koi edged closer to me, "This is what it has come to. Humans are forced into war against Lilith's plague."

Blips of light accompanied the jets, and twelve Watchers disappeared with them. A distant flurry of explosions followed.

"We are helping them out in the open?" I asked.

"Human leaders have always had an A'maggedon plan with us," Koi said. "We are bound to help them if they are at risk of extinction. Now is that time."

"Probably their most powerful time in history, too, just as long as they don't use their nukes," Brennan said.

"None of them are allowed to detonate," Koi said. "Gedz'iel made sure of that."

Two more jets scattered a flock of birds that had come to rest in the floating city's safety.

"Let's keep going," I drew my diamond dagger and recalled the prophecy.

"*A'vean's light shall rise,*" I muttered the clue and climbed up three steps to the Zythros stone. I rested my hand on its smooth surface. Warmth radiated out of it.

"A'vean's light… I am the Earth-born," I circled it, felt its indentations, heard its whispers, "It's always been my blood, my light." I placed both palms against it and leaned my cheek onto it.

I turned to the others, "I know what I have to do. Like at Stonehenge, I think this will show me which way to go."

Brennan hovered above the jetty between the two pillars, his eyes glued on me. "Go for it, Princess."

Ben and Koi rose into the air and flanked me as two more fighter jets scrambled overhead. Thunder rumbled in their wake. The clouds had thickened and dulled the sun's hold on the day.

Ben nodded at me. "I'm right behind you."

I wished I had my pendant. I had been so sure it would guide me through this.

The diamond had warmed considerably before the sun disappeared. Its touch was comforting, the glow of its core entrancing. I leaned into it and released my wings; the new one was steadily growing and reached half as far as the other. I felt a stir in my gut, let it roll and build before I drew it up. It was no longer a sting or a burn, but a powerful, supernatural extension of myself. I breathed out and let the stone drink it up. It took all that I gave it until its pull ceased and it dulled to a coal-black.

The warmth in me turned cold and I held my breath.

The Zythros stone burst back to life. Every facet exploded with a light that reached far into the surroundings. It crashed through me, hot and invigorating, and eradicated my moment of dread. Giddy, I tumbled back. I felt every pulsation as though they were a part of me.

Opaque white fingers probed the dusk landscape like spotlights and came together in the centre where they fused into a single thick beacon that forged a path between two islands in the lake. A deep, electrical hum, which blinked rhythmically above the two landmarks, hit somewhere far in the distance beyond.

I floated into the light, feeling drunk on its energy.

"Look at her mark!" Ben said.

"Give her space," Koi sounded far away, but I knew he was mere feet away from me. "She is experiencing something we cannot."

I closed my eyes.

"What is she doing?" Ben asked.

"Don't know," Brennan responded.

I floated onto my back, stretched out my arms, and listened to the stone's voice. It felt like my own pulse and sounded like every breath I took. Its ancient language whispered deep into my soul. Ashes and spice drifted into my senses, and a hand slid into mine.

"Soph?"

I opened my eyes and met Ben's concerned stare.

In a determined voice that seemed a totally different me I said, "I need to go with him."

I let Ben go and delved deeper into the light to listen to the secrets it was sharing with me. In my mind, I saw the portal — a shimmery mirror amidst a large stone façade.

"Follow me," I said to no one in particular.

I was drawn into the centre of the beam, surrounded by the soft cooing of a language so basic, so primal, it seemed to meld with my DNA. I was so infatuated with its song that I was barely aware of the bag, heavy with the Kaladai. I tied it around my belt, not wanting to lose anything else. As I began to coast along the light, I saw Koi and Brennan flanking me outside with Ben underneath its brilliance. Dozens of Watchers dotted the air around me. They followed, accepting what I was doing, or what was being done to me — I wasn't sure which it was.

Through the gentle buzz in my ears, I heard people speak.

"There is the Isle of the Sun."

"And the Isle of the Moon."

The beam drew me over the two small isles in Lake Titicaca.

"Over the moon and across the sun…" I murmured… the prophecy was alive.

The light tugged at me faster. Its heat streamed over my body like a warm embrace.

Across the reed-clogged banks, buildings appeared.

"Juli," floated from my mouth.

Arched churches dotted the modest township nestled under bare hills. A group of Watchers descended towards a military barricade across the town's centre. Fires burned in and around the town.

"That isn't good," Brennan's voice was like honey.

Heavily armed soldiers were pacing outside a cathedral. There were no citizens to be seen.

"They're bunkering the township," Koi sung as we soared over the domed building.

"Yeqon?" Brennan's voice was an angry soup.

"Not this time," Ben's fear cut through my contentedness. My eyes cleared, and the reality of what that statement meant prodded me wide awake. It wasn't Yeqon who would be a problem for me from this point, it was Lilith and her vile children who wanted the portal destroyed.

My guiding light stopped over another ridge. It burned into the flat face of a damask stone edifice, fringed by smooth red boulders and draped in the same weeping lavender. My Zythros light charred its centre. The pungent smell of singed lavender filled the air. I reluctantly let the comfort of its light go and coasted over to the unusual geological formation. Bilious clouds capped the structure; a mere shred of cerulean sky remained. The ground was dry and hard, a ruddy hue with a scrap of grass here and there.

The area was deserted.

Ben was by my side. His eyes followed the light and furrowed at the door-shaped depression that the light carved its charred design into.

Tiny Keepers spun within the beam where the light hit the rock. They worked on it like a labour force, engraving it in circular motions with great precision.

The edifice was three or four stories high and at least as wide. A breeze fanned the foliage overhead.

I touched the wall. The light evaporated, as did its beautiful song. All that was left was a large circular singe in the middle… a huge concentric circle.

Koi leaned into the cool stone and closed his eyes, "By the grace of I'el, it has been here all along. Invisible under our watch yet within our grasp. The locals have called this the Gate of the Gods for centuries. They believed it was how the cloud Gods travelled to Earth," he brushed his lips against the stone, took a deep breath, and…Koi hugged me.

"It must be the original portal," Koi rested his head on my shoulder. "Finally, *finally* our penance will end."

I felt a tear on my shoulder and his body relax. His fingers gently clung to my back, and I clung to him. The warmth from his wings a fatherly comfort. He had endured so much more than I, so I steeled myself to be the strongest version of myself. I told my heart to calm the hell down, chastised my buzzed brain to chill its panic.

I was about to change the world.

"Koi, it's okay. I know what I need to do."

He pulled away, "I'm right by your side, daughter of A'vean," he gifted me a K'ufili kiss and bowed.

Ben glanced around, "You got this?"

The Watchers surrounded us. Jaz and Jude were closest. She pumped her fist and winked at me. Enl'iel had reappeared with five Alchemae, heavy with supplies. She nodded, and they retreated to a bank of boulders to my right.

I smiled, "Yeah, I do, Ben. I've got this. I've got all of them, and I've got you."

I turned away and brought my diamond dagger out once more.

High-pitched thunder drew my eyes skyward as six more fighter jets zoomed past in a V formation. I sensed Watchers take flight to follow. The E'lan was screaming in the wake of the aircraft, but I held my hands still and kept my wits in check.

"One last bite!" The blade slid silently across my palm and it slapped onto the still-hot char marks. For a moment, as it did in the Prime Scroll Chamber, my palm seemed melded to the circle as it verified who I was. This time, I went with it rather than panic. With Ben, Brennan, and Koi's reassuring energies behind me, I relaxed into it until the circles released me with my blood crusted into the burn.

A deep grind shook the ground. The charred circles began to shine with a blinding glow.

It finally happening! The thought rolled over and over.

A loud *crack* split the circles. Four fine fissures webbed out from it; two above, two below, like a giant X. As the cracks furrowed, the circles moved. The middle ground out first, then back in. The second slid out over the first and then back in. The largest did the same until all were pumping like pistons, slowly grinding against one another as they opened the fissures wider. The fissures reached the rock's edges, and the movement ceased.

All was quiet until another booming *crack* made me jump—the face of the doorway had sheared away, its rubble at my feet.

The boys lit up their weapons.

"By the word of I'el," Koi whispered in wonder.

Ben hugged me and wrapped his wings around me, "You've done it, Soph!"

We froze in this embrace for a moment, and for that moment, I wished everything else away. Then I forced myself to let go of what I never wanted to let go of.

"Not… quite yet," I said.

His face was flushed, and I turned away to hide my own blush.

Where there had once been ordinary stone, there was now an engraving of Vitruvian Man. It was so precise; it couldn't possibly have been hewn by anything but modern technology — or something far more otherworldly and wonderous. It must have been ten feet high. There was an indentation in the middle of his belly. Its outer edges appeared like a cog. Within was an oval protrusion atop an axel.

And surrounding it all was the swirling perfection of A'vean script.

I trailed the indentations, "They're numbers."

"Sophia!" Jaz called, her voice rich with alarm.

A grey fog drifted along the ground behind them. I'd bled, of course they had sniffed me out.

I glanced up at the ever-darker sky, pissed as hell, "Not once would you make this easy!" I yelled at I'el.

I undid the backpack and passed the smaller cog to Koi, "Here, hold this."

I slid the largest over the axel. Its teeth perfectly sunk into each slot. With my ear pressed close, I heard something inside. Not a hollow or mechanical sound, but something akin to the voice of the Zythros light.

I wriggled my fingers, "Can I have the next one?"

Koi placed it into my hand, his breaths heavy with the anticipation.

The second slid into place. The little carving of Vitruvian Man on the cog sat snug but sideways.

"What now?" Brennan asked.

"I'm not sure," I bit my fingernails as I looked everything over a dozen times.

Nothing happened, not even when I touched it or squeezed a last drop of blood onto it.

"Koi!" Jude bellowed.

I peered over my shoulder to see him mustering Watchers towards the fog. The stench had reached us.

"Leave me," I said. "Keep everything away so I can work this out," I glared at them and flicked my hand, "Go!"

Koi hesitated but sped to the other Watchers with Brennan and Ben in tow. They checked back on me as they flew off. A spot of rain fell on my cheek.

I puffed the foul tinge of death out of my nose and focussed on the great image. I tried to turn the cogs, but they didn't move an inch. I shut my eyes and thought till it hurt. How could I activate them? There was shouting in the distance, but no change in the E'lan. No confrontation with the Rogues yet.

"What's missing?" I asked the wall.

Was the circle of hundreds of A'vean numbers a code? An icy chill ran down my neck—I had never been great at math.

The gleam of the small Vitruvian Man on the cog drew my eye. His splayed position, arms and legs askew and his palms wide open. He was a perfect match to the larger one on the rock. I kept touching the metal and felt tiny etchings on his palms and feet.

The first orb of war exploded behind me. The pressure had just become suffocating.

I read out the letters engraved on his hands and feet.

"L… I… V… I… D."

The ground rumbled. Thunder arced across the sky.

"For God's sake, give me a break!"

I repeated the letters multiple times. Were they parts of words?

I punched the wall, "Leo, why couldn't you make this easier?" I ran my hands around the sphere of symbols surrounding the larger figure, felt the sweeps, the points and curves. "Hang on…"

The first bolt of lightning blighted the horizon and flashed over a symbol just as my fingers skimmed a character that resembled the mathematical symbol of Pi. It was the number fifty in A'vean language. My fingers slid back over the L on the small Vitruvian image. I slapped my face…the letters on the small Vitruvian man were Roman numerals.

"Shit, shit, shit!" my hands shook, "Here, um… Here…."

I touched four A'vean numbers in the sequence of the Roman numerals. Luminous, glossy crystals erupted from them, one by one. I touched the A'vean symbol for 'fifty', then 'one', then numbers six and five hundred.

I jumped back to take in the full picture.

The livid creator of the prophecy, didn't refer to I'el being angry, but the Roman numerals for representing those numbers.

"Thy livid creator shall turn into A'vean's embrace… Clever!"

I tried to turn the cog so the numbers of the small image dialled up to match the larger image, in line with the A'vean numbers. It remained stuck.

"Come on, damn you!"

More lightning crackled, and blazing orbs lit the encroaching dusk. Bright flashes zoomed across the sky.

I heard Rogues chittering. Fog reached my ankles. I stamped it away.

"What do you want?" I punched the wall again, and it shook along with the ground.

The Rogues grew louder.

I clenched my head and felt for my pendant out of habit. My eyes returned to the Kaladai as I remembered a part of its design. My fingers sunk into the oval depression in the centre of the axel. It was the same shape as my pendant.

I clasped my hands over my mouth, "No! How did he know?

"Educated guess."

Spine-chilling fingers clawed at my heart. The voice from the cave.

I spun around. No one was behind me, just the silhouettes of the warring Watchers.

"Looking for this?"

My head snapped skyward. Rain blurred the person on the ledge above me. I shielded my eyes so I could see him.

I couldn't move. I couldn't breathe.

"Not… you!"

Rik laughed, "Why not me?"

Anger and betrayal boiled inside me as his blue eyes narrowed at me with scorn. I'd cherished those eyes the first time I'd seen them.

"Rogues are coming," he said. "I'd scatter away if I were you."

He twirled my pendant around his finger. My lips quivered with fury. My heart broke.

"That's *my* pendant," I stretched my good wing, encouraged the new one, and balled my hands into fists. "Give it back!"

"And lose all I've created?" Rik shook his head. Lightning flashed across the short crop of his dark hair. "Oh no, sister. I've worked too hard and suffered too long to just throw it away."

Pain burned in my chest and my heart.

"I don't want to fight you!"

"Accept your lot, sister, just like I accepted mine. The curtain has fallen. It's time to leave the theatre."

The rain became torrential and blurred Rik's smirk. I quelled my orbs and followed my pendant's trail as he looped it over and over in his hand.

Then, quite suddenly, I laughed, "You can't be serious. You? Of all the monsters, *you* want control?"

Rik's self-satisfied smile waned. He crossed his arms and tucked my pendant under them. His blue eyes darkened to an ugly shade of Daimon.

Orbs itched in my palms.

"Are you kidding me?" I asked. "After all I did for you? You're my brother!"

He smiled a beautiful, dangerous, victorious smile. He jumped down from the boulders, landing in the growing puddles with a splash.

"Saved *me*?" Rik pointed at his chest and looked behind him like I meant someone else.

"I saved you from Yeqon," the words were bitter and difficult to utter through my teeth.

He checked over his shoulder again, but we were alone.

"I beg to differ. What you saw was what you needed to see — the game of a lifetime played for both yourself and Yeqon. All to keep you at the right place on the chess board," he bowed.

I wiped the rain from my eyes. He stared at me without blinking, like an utter maniac. I stepped back towards the portal's thrumming energy, which was teased by the glow of my pendant dangling just behind Rik's elbow.

I threw an orb at him. He was fast, faster than I'd ever seen him.

He'd been faking it all along.

I withdrew my sword and threw the second orb at his feet, not wanting to destroy the pendant. He side-stepped and smiled harder.

Rik whistled between thumb and finger, "Nice try. Those are big weapons, sis, but mine are better." Two bodies fell from above and landed in a squat. They rose by his side.

"Meet your nephews, two of them, anyway. The rest are otherwise engaged," he glanced overhead.

My blood turned to ice. In the storm's flashes, hundreds of dark-winged creatures flocked overhead, heading towards the battle.

"They're *your*… children?" I couldn't process it, didn't want to.

His vampire wingmen flexed their murky wings and looked at me like I was an entrée.

"Our children!"

I didn't notice where she came from, but Lilith's arms oozed around Rik's bare waist. She rested her head on his shoulder and slowly kissed at his neck. Her eyes didn't leave me.

My sword and jaw slackened, "You're with *that*?"

Lilith pecked again at Rik, "Did you hear her? Such an insult."

He turned his face and they kissed passionately. My stomach flipped and all the guilt I'd felt turned to bitterness.

I pointed my weapon at his head. His sons hissed; Lilith hushed them with a wave of her hand. Rik traced her face with my pendant.

"As I said, sister, we have a role in this great game. This is mine. It has been since Lilith rescued me from Yeqon."

I slipped in the mud and grabbed for the wall to right myself. The movement put the vamps on edge.

"I saw them torture you!" I said.

Lilith's shrill laughter was cut short by more thunder.

"I have prepared him from his youth, my sweet," she batted her eyes at him like she was as innocent as an angel. "I have trained and guided him so he may have an eternity of pleasure. Yeqon was his pain, I am his pleasure," Lilith flicked her auburn hair across her shoulder.

"Yeqon was a means to *our* ends," Rik said. "We kept him busy. He fed my queen, sustained and energised her as we created our own family. Now, we are complete."

Someone screamed my name, but the rain obliterated the source. *"Who is it?"*

The downdraft of vampire flocks pushed against me. They swarmed left and right overhead as they waited.

I saw Enoch's vision right before my eyes and infused my sword with energy until it shone.

"What have you done?" I demanded. Rik laughed at me.

"Now that I've assured my future, Sister, you can step aside. I gift you one chance to make your own way in the new world — a thank you for showing me kindness, even if it was somewhat misguided," he looked me up and down and leaned into Lilith's lips again.

I lunged and struck one of his vamps. It screeched and grasped at the slice across its throat as it fell.

Lilith screamed. She threw Rik aside and leapt at me. I swept my sword at her feet, but she jumped over it and dove over me. I slid forwards, straight at Rik, but he was a well-trained warrior, who had merely hidden under the guise of an abused captive.

He arched back, hovered on his wings, and kicked me in the face. Stunned, I slid back in the mud. My head hit the base of the portal. Black spots scattered in my vision, and my surroundings dulled. In the background of my stupor, the growl and screech of Rogues edged closer. Their stench was so sour that it pulled me back from the brink of unconsciousness.

Rik leered over me; the pendant tantalisingly close. He dangled it above my nose. His wings swished over me like an angry cat's tail. To my left, Lilith licked her lips. Her child right next to her, a wild, untamed hunger in its eyes.

The portal hummed behind me with my sword just out of reach.

In my mind, I called to anyone who was listening. I hadn't expected my brother to betray me at the last hurdle or at any point in my life; if I moved now, I was dead.

Ben and Brennan flashed overhead, slaying through the vamps.

Lilith pushed her other son on the attack, "Kill them, you imbecile!"

The vamp surged up at Ben.

Lilith backed away whilst Rik pinned me down. One of his wing tips pierced my shoulder.

"Always so stupid, aren't you?" his lips paled against his teeth.

I screamed through the pain as Lilith sung a haunting tune — a soft repetition of notes that drew her flock together above us in a congealing mass of blood lust.

Brennan's pale face flashed overhead. I squeezed my eyes shut and opened them again to find Ben circling the vamp Lilith had set on him.

My sword was just inches away. I reached for it, but Rik pushed harder, and I screamed louder. Other Watchers joined Brennan and Ben. They dove into the mass of vamps as I struggled against my evil brother. The mud helped me slide around enough that I kneed him in the groin. He jerked back. I grabbed my sword and smacked its handle into his temple. He went down roaring and grabbing his head.

"You will regret that," Rik growled.

"I don't think so."

The sky was ablaze with orbs. Blood tainted the rain.

I rolled over in the sludge and pulled myself to my feet as the vamp chased Ben past me. I stumbled but found my balance and urged power into my sword. Rik rose too and flexed his muscles, his teeth clenched.

The vamp that had been after Ben slapped into the ground between us. Mud splattered over my face. Ben landed on its struggling torso and thrust a sword down through its shoulders.

He arced his sword, "You might want to run now, you fucking coward."

"Don't look so shocked, big brother," Rik sneered. "It's nothing *you* haven't done."

"I've done my share of bad shit, but I'd never breed with vermin," Ben glanced up at Lilith, who had distanced herself from us, surrounded by a horde of her children.

Ben rushed forwards and swiped at Rik. My pendant swung in Rik's grasp as they hit the ground and rolled around in the mud.

Lilith's frightening song still hung in the air; her children amassed by the thousands. Brennan raged in and out of the mob.

Blue streaks shot up where Watchers fell. I couldn't do anything but follow my pendant. I needed it, there was no other way.

Rik and Ben were wrestling. Grunting and swearing. Ben pulled Rik up by the hair, but they slipped back down. I edged around them, hoping to get a clean shot at Rik. Ben slipped. Rik fell on top of him. I raised my arm, about to stab my brother in the back, when a thump to my head floored me.

A female vamp flipped me over and clasped her hands around my throat. My sword was still in my hand, but it was sucked away by the claggy mud. I clawed the vamp's face and pushed against her razor-sharp teeth. They sliced into my palm and excited her into a frenzy. I let her bite, grunting through the pain, and rammed my other hand into the mud to call on the earth for help.

I drew on the energies that flowed beneath us. The sludge became gritty, then hot, and then firm. It melded into a weapon, and I held on tight. I dug my fingers into her face and jabbed the fresh gemstone dagger into her eye. She sank. I sat up and slashed her throat.

Ben and Rik rolled in combat. Watchers and vamps screeched closer than ever. I could barely hear my own thoughts through the chaos but my pendant's gentle song called me through it all. I crawled towards it amongst the feet of fighting angels and vampires, keeping my sights on Rik and Ben. They fell to the ground, lost in the sea of blood and mud. Glimpses of the pendant dazzled here and there.

The battle rose and fell upon air and land around me. The vamps were shot down like vultures. They crashed into Watchers, pinned them to the ground and gnashed for their blood. The Watchers were fast, but the vamps were just as quick and numbered us two to one. The Rogue fog began to retreat.

I needed to be invisible to get another shot at Rik, so I withdrew my wings and powered down. I clambered through headless corpses and past an eviscerated belly. I was stood on and kicked as I tried to get back to the portal, where I saw my pendant fly with every sweep of Rik's arm. Every part of me ached. I saw the glint of Kea's sword a few feet away. I reached for it amongst the flurry of legs, and a foot crushed my wrist. I quelled a scream and drew blood to my lips as I tried to stay unseen. My hand swelled and my fingers numbed, but I pulled the sword free with a grunted yelp despite my best efforts.

Ben slammed down next to the portal. Rik fell on him, his wings obliterated in the fight.

A twitching vamp with its face burnt off fell next to me. It stank of old blood, but I hauled it over my shoulders. I slipped under its weight, using it like a cape. Sweat melded with rain. My legs burned as I pushed against the mud, rain and battle. The corpse's head banged against mine. The filth and vamp's sickening drool coated me. No one paid attention to me and that's what I needed.

Rik dragged Ben deeper into the battle away from the portal again. I followed. They disappeared for a minute or two, so I trudged in the general direction.

The corpse was getting too heavy. It slipped to the ground, and I fell with it. Overhead, my pendant glimmered under Rik's wings. Ben was right behind him as Rik headed back towards the portal—running away from Ben. He truly was a spineless weasel.

I dug my heels in.

Rik ducked out of sight into the mash of vamps.

"To your left!" Koi shouted.

Ben dashed left and I followed, faster with every stride.

"Lilith!" Rik screamed, "Where are you!"

Crashing thunder pierced the screeches of battle. Ben and Brennan soared overhead. Along with Koi, they scouted for Rik and blasted orbs at any stupid vamp that dared get in their way. What they didn't see was me — and I was right behind Rik. The surge of bodies banged him left and right. His side was bleeding. The vamps gave him a wide berth, their eyes only on Lilith above who sat on the intertwined arms of two of her children like a queen on her throne.

"Destroy the portal!" Rik screamed at her.

She smiled down at him…and did nothing.

Ben found Rik and dove.

Rik turned to flee, straight into my blade. I held it firm as it lodged deep in his stomach. His mouth gaped with shock. He reached for it, and as he did, my pendant fell from his arm. I caught it. I held the dagger a second longer, forcing him to look me in the eyes. His were bloodshot, watery, and tinged black. I shoved. He fell to the ground.

I transferred to the portal. The pendant was like jelly in my fumbling fingers as I fitted it into the centre. It needed to snap in just the right way, but it slipped and fell. I reached for it, but my knees went weak at a painful, stinging thud in my back. My fingers tingled; I couldn't reach the pendant. I clawed myself back up the portal whilst a metallic taste filled my mouth and fluid dribbled down my chin. My hearing dulled. I leaned into the rock. The soft beat of my pulse intensified. My whole body I was trembling. My stomach spasmed, and a strange warmth blanketed it. I looked down at my abdomen.

Someone screamed.

There was scuffling somewhere behind me and a gravelly, angry voice. It was familiar, but I felt too weak to worry who it was. I clawed at the portal, willed the pendant off the ground, but numbness gave way to a pain so great I couldn't call for help.

I dabbed at my stomach. My hands came away bright red. It looked wrong.

"That's what happens when you don't take the gift horse, sister."

I winced. I didn't want to look too closely at what was wrong, but my neck was weak and my head too heavy. I couldn't fathom the appearance of my chest guard, which was peeled open like a can.

I laughed inside when I saw it. It had to be a joke.

Rik's blade still pulsed with power, frying away my blood that smeared along its length.

I tried to dab at my chest, to heal the gaping hole, but no energy came to my hands.

"No power of this world can repair that, sister," Rik's breath was behind my ear, the only warmth I felt as I began to shiver from the cold of death.

The energy blade dissipated, and my blood flowed faster.

"We all have to make sacrifices," Rik said. "This is yours."

I flopped against the portal and turned in agony to face him, my vision blurred. I slumped to the ground. I managed to open my eyes just in time to see Rik wind his arm back, ready to strike again.

The hit didn't connect. Instead, Rik rose into the air, arms and legs flailing. Yeqon's silhouette shimmered in my dying vision, Rik dead on his trident.

"He was a poor excuse for a son."

Chapter
Thirty-One

The puddle was a dark, unpleasant red. It filled a muddy footprint, fed by the driving rain.

A foot splashed into the bloody puddle. A light fog surrounded the black boots. The lingering smell of Rogues added to the bone-chilling cold that gnawed its way through my limbs. I didn't hear the fighting anymore, just saw darting shapes here and there. Light and dark. Where was Ben?

Coughs racked my chest. Yeqon rested his hand on mine and held it over my wound. When he withdrew it, his eyes were wide at the crimson glove that now covered it.

"And all is in place, Earth-born. It is a shame it had to end like this for you."

Something bright caught my eye. Yeqon held Kea's sword.

Was I already dead? Was I dreaming? I felt light.

I closed my eyes and awaited the blow that would stop this nightmare.

Coarse fingers took my hand, "Take it."

Something small slapped into my palm.

"Finish it. Prove your worth."

I opened my eyes again. It was so hard to move my eyelids. Moonlight flared behind Yeqon. His face inches from mine. A strange fascination sat in his black eyes.

"You have all you need; a prophecy, a key, and plenty of your blood," Yeqon smeared some of my blood across my cheeks with his thumb, then drew it across his own. "Don't disappoint me now. I did save you from your bastard brother, after all."

A gut-wrenching screech interrupted my nightmare. Vamps flew down in a nasty, unnatural umbrella carried on Lilith's distress. She fell on Rik's body nearby.

"What have you done!" Lilith screamed at Yeqon. She tried to gather Rik's smouldering remains, but the flames of descension already licked at his flesh, "Stop him from descending!"

Oblivion called for his flesh whilst death tugged at mine. I mourned that I'd failed everyone whilst I closed my fingers over the pendant. The portal was above me, and a simple rock it would stay.

Yeqon thrust Lilith away with his trident. She rolled out of his reach and hissed. The flap of the vamps grew louder. The smell of the Rogues wasn't nearly as frightening.

Where is Ben?

Yeqon stamped his trident into the mud and ignited its points.

"I am outnumbered, Soph'ael. You have one chance to open the portal," Yeqon put Kea's sword into my other hand and curled it into a fist. "Make yourself a worthy martyr."

Lilith screamed some garbled words and began her song again.

Where is Ben?

Pineme and Ged'erel burst through the vampires. My vision clouded. I clenched the sword and tried to use it to pull myself upright, but there was nothing left of me. One of them pulled me by my hair towards the portal.

"It will be done, one way or another," Ged'erel said.

He dragged me through the cold slush, bumping me over bodies and across rocks.

"Sophia!"

"Ben," I whispered into his mind.

Ged'erel dropped me. An orb exploded; its energy warmed the chill on my skin. I reached for it by rolling one arm across my body. A flash of white wings. A Rogue's head rolled in front of me. I vomited blood.

Ben fell to his knees and scooped my head into his lap. Overhead, Brennan and Koi flung red and white orbs to keep Yeqon and the Unseen at bay. I tried to shake my head, tried to tell them to stop, but my voice had dried up. The pendent burned in my palm, thrumming the only life into me. My pulse was so weak I didn't feel it anymore.

"Shh," Ben hugged me into his warmth. He ran his hands over my body, trying to heal me. "Koi! Help me!" he screamed.

I felt Koi's presence but didn't see him.

"Stay with her," Koi said. "I'm going for Yeqon."

The light of Watchers shone in the edges of my vision. More orbs popped, and the Rogues' chitter lessened. They sounded farther and farther away. Yeqon bellowed for back-up.

Fear welled in my throat, and I wanted to flee from it. I was scared to die.

I clasped the pendant just enough that it wouldn't fall out of my palm. It hummed a little louder, and I felt the tiniest spark of energy.

"Stop," the word spluttered out through bubbles in my mouth. I coughed hard, and the pain in my chest returned.

"Shh," Ben said.

I didn't see him; looking was too hard.

"Stop… touching me… Stop…"

"Brennan, help?" Ben sounded like a child who was unsure of what to do.

I pointed one finger in the direction of the fighting, "Don't… fight… him…"

"Don't worry. We've got them surrounded."

I shook my hand, "No… Helping… us… Yeq… help… us…" I coughed again.

Ben pulled away a little. I wanted him closer; I wanted him farther away.

"Koi, look!" Brennan yelled, "Yeqon is fighting the vamps!"

His shadow swept past me. Ben tensed against me.

The thunder of feet and the swish of wings told me they had realised that Yeqon was fighting Lilith's army to keep the portal free for me.

The pendant thrummed harder. My heart thumped faint in my temples.

I managed to turn my head, but everything was in slow motion. I felt like I was in a movie, not really me but someone else.

I grunted towards the portal, "Up…"

Ben tried to help me, but I would end this on my terms.

I sucked in a breath and squeezed the pendant. It gave me enough to push Ben away with a flick of my shoulder. My head lolled.

"Don't… touch me."

I fell forwards. Mud splashed into my mouth. I crawled in a circle, slipping and holding my guts inside my belly as I dragged myself towards the gate. Ben was right behind me; I heard his distress in every trembling breath. His orbs knocked vamps out of my way. I crawled over their death twitches; some eyes still had the fading gleam of life.

Lilith was screeching in the distance. The ground hardened as stone replaced mud. Kea's sword became my crutch; its strength would be my strength.

I heaved for life giving breath, dug deep for the last of myself. I stopped and thought on those gone before me. Dash had given his life for Eilir. Jaz had nearly died for me. Poor Lorcan had died in a filthy cave so that I could be here now. Dearest Esme, the first and hardest. And then there was the vision of Earth being Lilith's dominion.

Kea's sword scraped on the stone as I pulled myself to my feet. Pain peppered my vision. I pulled a latch on my armour, and it fell away. The relief from the pressure gave me a boost towards the gate—a rhythmic *bang, scrape, slide, bang* as I stumbled along.

I reached the portal. Its hum was annoyingly uncaring. My dying went on, but I leaned against the rock and slotted my pendant into the Kaladai. With slippery, bloody hands, I turned it. The sound must have been louder, but all I heard was a dull *clunk* as I twisted the arms and legs of Vitruvian Man to dial in the numbers fifty, six, one, and five hundred.

My knees gave way, and I fell into someone's arms.

"My sweet love," Ben's tears were fire.

The E'lan was singing a song of joy. The portal rumbled.

I smiled, and took my last breath.

Chapter Thirty-Two

"She's dead!" Ben screamed at the sky. "She's died for nothing, you fucking bastard!" he sobbed uncontrollably whilst he held Sophia's body against his.

Enl'iel ran through the Daimon, no care for herself. "Oh, my beautiful child!" she wept, one hand on Sophia's forehead and the other over her own breaking heart.

Ben couldn't look at her, "I've failed her."

"No, *they* have!" Enl'iel spat in the direction of Lilith's vamps.

Ben watched them dive for the Rogues, ripping their heads off and sucking up their rot. Lilith squealed delightedly from in the sky.

A few feet from Ben, Yeqon shook with rage and bared his teeth. Ben glared at him; his neck tight with fury. He wanted to gut the Daimon.

"She's dead, and you've got nothing to show for it but a bloody rock and a fuck-load of death!" Ben yelled at Yeqon.

Lilith floated higher and laughed, "And so, it will be done," her shrill voice trailed down. "My reign has come to pass!"

With a wave of her hand, she and her flock disappeared.

The shocked Watchers stopped and stood stock-still. Yeqon, Ged'erel, Pineme, and the last of their Rogues glared at their momentary allies, who were now trapped between them and the quiet portal. No one moved. Yeqon licked his lips. His eyes fell to Sophia's corpse. He thumped his trident into the mud, and his army ran towards her.

Ben scooped her up and backed away against the whirring portal. Koi, Brennan, Jude, and Jaz roared and ran to them. Jude flew up and slashed down with his sword. Two skulls exploded. Jaz wielded her longsword like a pro, cutting a Rogue in two. Brennan and Koi led a dozen Watchers as they pushed the rapidly depleting Rogue army back. Yeqon screamed at the undead to push forwards, but he saw he was outnumbered.

"Retreat!" Yeqon bellowed.

Pineme and Ged'erel flanked him when he flew a hundred feet away. They settled on a rock cluster, a handful of Rogues at their feet.

Ben had rarely shed tears in thousands of years, but this was Neren'iel all over again. His eyes glazed as he kissed Sophia's bloodstained hair.

The Watchers formed a barrier of protection in front of Ben.

Jaz was sobbing, "I can't look."

Jude hugged her into his side.

Jaz fell to her knees next to Ben, "Don't you fucking dare do this to me! You have no right to die! I lived for you!" she shook Sophia's chest, unfazed by the gaping wound.

Jude tried to pull her back, but Jaz elbowed him away and spat at Ben's feet.

"You're just as responsible as they are!" Jaz screamed. Jude pulled her back into his embrace.

Ben hugged Sophia closer, he kissed her hair, ran his fingers along her bloodied cheeks, "What do we do now?" he choked on the words.

"You place her into my hands."

Ben looked up through bloodshot eyes to see Uriel, a light in the darkness. He floated down from the Gate of the Gods. Everyone dropped to their knees.

"Nik'ael, give me the Earth-born,"

Ben's mouth tightened as Uriel reached for Sophia. A new tear slipped from his face onto hers.

He slipped her into Uriel's embrace and collapsed. Enl'iel drew him into her arms.

Koi kneeled and lowered his head in shame, "Master Uriel, we have failed her and the Throne."

Uriel laid his eyes on every survivor. Even Yeqon received his attention.

"None of I'el's faithful have failed, and neither has the Earth-born. She has fulfilled her destiny," he lay her body at the portal's base. "Soph'ael, daughter of I'el and born of this earth, come forth!"

The E'lan shifted. The dead night air prickled with static and made the group shiver.

Uriel held his hand above Sophia. A light emerged from her chest wound. It rose and curled around her body. It shifted to Uriel, who cupped it in his hands and offered it to the portal. Her light surged towards her pendant's swirling energy. They touched.

And the world stopped.

A colourful light hugged me, welcomed me and called my name. I followed it, happy to be rid of the pain. It sped past me, or did I speed past it? It was soundless. There was no feeling to it other than that it felt right.

Its colours became so fast they blended into white, and I burst out of it into a forest of diamonds. Twin gemstone mountains glittered beneath rushing waterfalls, the most beautiful sound I'd ever heard. I moved towards them, then between them. I wasn't walking but carried on an invisible current. Gilded buildings of equal size dotted a vast horizon in neat rows along perfect paths. Crystalline trees, whose beauty was indescribable, bordered them. Two suns sat fat and close in the sky, enormous orbs of ambient light and gentle heat. They glittered across a silver lake. It drew my eye to a diamond palace of such enormity, there would be no comparison on Earth — for this, I knew, was not Earth.

I found myself inside the palace. Its walls were supported by hundreds of columns hewn from clear diamond. Its ceiling the open sky with planets and stars as adornments. It felt strong and ancient. A moon with a glorious halo sat in its middle.

"Do you have more to do on the planet named Earth?" the moon asked. Its voice was genderless, neither loud nor soft.

"Yes," I answered.

"Will you uphold the ancient laws? Will you let the indigenous peoples develop freely and of their own will?"

"Yes."

"Do you wish to offer redemption to any who have wronged the laws of A'vean?"

"To Nik'ael," I answered Iel's final question.

Chapter
Thirty-Three

Yeqon watched the portal come to life. His heart thundered with victorious thrill.

"Stand by, Ged'erel. Wait."

Ged'erel and Pineme flanked him with a dozen Daimon either side of them. A handful of Rogues snivelled and slobbered behind them.

The ground moved, and a smile spread on his gore-splattered face, gore that included Sophia's blood. He ran his hand across his stubble and took a moment to enjoy the sight of it.

A loud *crack* emanated from the portal. An animal howled in the distance, and a Rogue gurgled at the sound. Yeqon watched with unbridled intrigue as the rock disintegrated. The Vitruvian Man crumbled into nothing. A massive, watery jet exploded from the gate. It drew in Sophia's remains and anything else in its path. Yeqon sucked his teeth with his tongue, a small twinge of regret at the waste of her.

Nik'ael screamed at the torrent whilst Koi held him back from its cutting rush. Nik'ael struggled in Koi's grasp; it satisfied Yeqon to see him suffer all over again. He had been a waste too.

The portal's thunderous wave raged out across the landscape, a physics-defying snake of ethereal fluid that roared along its path before the flow slowed. Yeqon waved his trident for his depleted army to retreat. The waters stilled, and it idled quietly above the ground, its light ebbing away the landscape's darkness. Yeqon marvelled at it. An incandescent rainbow curled through its core and retracted with a sudden rush. It snapped back to where it settled as a shimmering mirror — a portal to another realm.

Yeqon's smile broadened until his cheeks dimpled.

"Now?" Pineme asked.

"No. Wait until they're consumed by it. Then we shall strike."

Yeqon stared into the wafting shimmer and smiled as his A'vean memories retuned.

Koi was talking to Uriel.

Ged'erel spat at the ground, "Archangels!" he screwed up his face. "Pretentious."

The night had stilled since Lilith had vanished. That bitch would pay. Yeqon would no longer take in unwanted dregs, no more outcasts. Once he controlled the portal and had access to the universe, he'd take only the best of the best.

He cocked his head forwards to hear Uriel's overdramatic speech. He wasn't disappointed, chuckling to himself.

Uriel spread his arms wide. His wings shone brighter than the full moon.

"Children of A'vean, ready yourselves!"

The Watchers drew their weapons. Yeqon straightened. Pineme and Ged'erel growled beside him.

"Now?" Pineme asked.

"No!" Yeqon snapped, pointing at Uriel, who drew his golden sword. "You might want to watch his every movement or he'll send you straight to Tartarus? He can do that, you imbecile!"

Pineme sneered, but fear washed over his eyes.

Uriel's eyes were as bright as stars as he raised the sword and scanned the Watchers.

"On this day of A'maggeddon, I join you, my brothers and sisters. This world will be born anew, free of its darkness."

"We will see about that," Yeqon muttered.

Uriel thrust the golden sword into the ground. Everyone swayed back. A rumbling came from within the portal. A shadow, small but growing by the second, dotted its centre.

Yeqon's eyes widened.

"What is this?" Ged'erel asked, the gravel of his voice unsure. He rubbed his temples. His mark glimmered and faded under a bloody, swollen eye.

An ache pierced Yeqon's forehead as more of his memories returned. One of his Daimon shot into the sky, too weak and too gutless to face the final act. His entire army became unsettled as they, too, remembered. Another Damion fled into the night. Pineme shot an orb after him, and he smacked into the ground.

Yeqon slammed his trident into the hard earth, "Hold your positions," he tossed souls from his satchel into the fissure he'd made.

"Something's coming!" A Watcher shouted in the distance.

Yeqon's attention shot up. He narrowed his eyes as she pointed at the watery portal.

"Make way!" Uriel called.

The rumbling turned to a thrum, which became deeper and more pronounced — a string that plucked at the Earth's core and released its inner baritone. Yeqon felt its strength under his feet as a new fog rose.

"Yeqon? What is he doing?" Ged'erel asked impatiently.

Uriel walked a path between the Watchers and edged them to one side.

Koi pointed at Yeqon who shook his trident and roared; they would see, as well as feel his power.

Yeqon hit his chest, "When the undead rise, we take the portal."

Others mimicked him, but not Ged'erel and Pineme.

"Strike now!" Pineme growled impatiently.

Yeqon grabbed him by the throat, "You wish to ruin me now? We are on the precipice! Shut your mouth, or I will sear it closed for you." he held the burning points of his trident just under Pineme's throat, then shoved him away.

Pineme bared his teeth and wrapped his hand around his bow.

"Save it for Uriel," Ged'erel murmured.

Yeqon growled and stirred the fissure with his trident. The first new Rogue was rising. Sweat beaded on Yeqon's brow—they weren't quick enough, and Uriel's behaviour worried him. He threw another few souls into the small abyss. He needed just a few more for cannon fodder.

Uriel widened his arms to push the Watchers farther out. He left a wide path between the portal and Yeqon.

Yeqon sneered, "He's making a pathway for me? How kind."

Four more Rogues clawed out of the ground. Yeqon's heart raced as the portal's waters rippled. Its colours darkened. Shadowy movements became faster and closer. Yeqon had used the portals more times than he could count, but this… he had no idea what A'maggeddon would bring. He only knew that he would take it straight back to I'el.

A reverberating horn blared. Ged'erel drew in a deep breath.

Pineme took a nervous step backwards. More Daimon fled. Yeqon kicked two Rogues into submission in frustration at his dwindling numbers.

"Yeqon, you know what they are?" Ged'erel sounded scared for the first time that Yeqon could recall.

"Yes, I do," his eyes sparkled with intrigue. A garish smile spread his lips.

Two angels emerged from the portal. Long golden horns in their hands, they took up places on either side of the portal. They blew their horns, and their deep resonance boomed out into the night.

The Watchers' attention was on the messengers of A'vean.

The Heralds blew their horns louder, a rhythmic warning song.

"Get back!" Uriel commanded.

The horsemen emerged, three High Angels on their Pegasi — Raph'ael on a horse as black as the night; Gabr'ael on a steed of desert red; Mich'ael on a horse as white as snow. And lastly, a rider-less beast as golden as the sun galloped through the portal. It whinnied and thundered to a stop before Uriel, who jumped on its back. Their weapons glimmered with gold and silver so pure, Yeqon couldn't look at them.

His smile waned.

All four horses reared, their eyes sapphire, their hooves aglow with the power of the heavens. The Watchers fell to their knees.

Yeqon gulped. His hands slipped on the trident.

Ged'erel stepped away, followed by Pineme. Yeqon's chest heaved at the sight, but he paid his comrades no mind. He was shaking with rage at the scene ahead.

"You can all die on this shithole then!" Yeqon walked forwards alone. He glanced back to find his gutless kin had spread their wings, ready to flee.

An ethereal voice sung across the sky.

"Spread across this wretched world," Gabr'ael called. "Cleanse it of its filth. Help us and Soph'ael, I'el's highest of high servants, to restore the good and the true."

The four horsemen parted, and a fifth horse exploded from the portal. It was the largest of the Pegasi, jet black with a shimmering white mane.

It carried Sophia.

Chapter
Thirty-Four

Rebirth was instant and painless. I emerged from the portal empowered and with such strength I felt weightless. The night had cleared. The air was still cold but electric with the stronger E'lan.

The shock and relief of the many eyes before us gave me more strength.

I smiled down at Ben and saw the pain leave his eyes. I held up my sword and squeezed Grey. He reared, his warm breath steaming in the night. I found Brennan in the crowd and winked at him. I urged Grey on, and he pranced away from the portal. Raph'ael, Uriel, Gabr'ael, and Mich'ael flanked me.

Moonlight paved a path from the distant lake all the way to the portal. A lone figure walked along it towards me. His movements were raw and hesitant as though Yeqon had never really believed he'd make it this far. Fog followed behind him, but it was thin and carried the shadows of only two Rogues. The Unseen stayed far behind him. Retreating Daimon streaked across the sky.

Jude rushed out of the crowd. Jaz and a dozen others followed him, wings ablaze and aiming for Yeqon.

"Stop," I called. "Let him pass."

Yeqon hesitated, but his greed for vengeance overwhelmed his sensibility. He should have run like the others. He looked left and right, his trident high and his chest wide.

All I needed was patience, because Yeqon had none of that left.

Grey was on edge and stamped his feet. I circled him around back towards the portal.

"Steady, my friend," I soothed him.

He whinnied and stretched his wings.

I smiled at Mich'ael, and he nodded. I dipped Kea's sword into the portal's plasma.

The Rogues arose from Yeqon's fog. He screeched at them, and they rushed towards us — skinless bones running on all fours. Gabr'ael's and Raph'ael's beasts reared and stamped them into dust.

Yeqon roared. He fired orange flames from his trident's points, spread his wings, and clenched his teeth with wild eyes.

I raised Kea's sword, "Move out!"

Our beasts stepped aside the portal's path. I threw my weapon at Yeqon, and he skidded to a halt when it landed inches from his feet.

He shook his trident towards me. "You! You were just…"

The Earth's thrum cut him off. The sword quivered in the ground, its plasma energy bubbling the mud around it. Electric sparks rans along the wet earth and reached towards the portal. Blue and orange crackles danced into the portal's mirage.

"And that, Yeqon, is how you train an ordinary girl."

His eyes bulged.

The portal's explosion carved a path of fiery plasma energy towards Yeqon. It scorched the sludgy ground into hardened stone and vaporised him before he could take flight. It burned across the landscape and eradicated his lackies who hadn't yet run far enough.

It retracted into the portal with a crackling *pop* that echoed off the distant mountains, and returned to its calm, watery appearance.

I smiled, not for Yeqon's death, but for everyone's freedom.

Uriel turned his Pegasus to the portal, "It is time for redemption."

He threw a golden orb into the portal, and a brilliant pure-white beam shot out of it into the world. Its light bounced off the earth's geology, lighting up miles ahead.

Grey rose above the clouds, and I waved for Ben, Koi, Jude, Brennan and Jaz to join me. Raph'ael, Mich'ael, Uriel, and Gabr'ael followed on. Ben flew silently by my side. For a while, we watched the beauty of A'vean's power crisscrossing the globe. There was no need for words—the Earth and Av'ean showed us their combined might. Its beam reached out to all the dormant portals and reactivated them one by one—Stonehenge, Göbekli Tepe, Carnac, Avebury, and the Gate of the Gods. Five portals for the five horsemen of A'maggeddon. Each ancient gate launched its guiding light to the stars to invite all back in. They opened an ancient power that wiped out all that Lilith and Yeqon had created.

Our beasts followed the beam at incredible speed. Koi flanked my other side as we spanned the globe. We rejoiced as the portals came alive. Watchers entered from other worlds through every portal across every continent to renew the Earth — no raising the dead, no burning in Hell, just restoration of what had come before it.

Grey and I headed for Kaymakli to make sure all was well, but my mind lingered on Lilith and her whereabouts. As we flew over the many countries, I witnessed long-raging wars end in an instant. Persecution amongst man stilled as Yeqon's lies were wiped from man's memory. The universal truth returned the moment I had opened the portal. Humans remembered that they were all one and the same.

Grey landed on a hill not far from Kaymakli and ripped out a mouthful of grass. Koi and Ben landed next to me. The others looped overhead.

"We haven't found Lilith," I said.

I was worried about the damage she could inflict before we hunted her down.

Koi peered across the Turkish landscape with his back to me, his body rigid, "I know where she is."

"Where? I'll deal with her," I said.

I glanced at Ben. The rush was the same.

Koi sighed into his hand, "No, Sophia, I must deal with her myself." He ran his fingers over his head.

"Look at me," I said. Grey nuzzled Koi's chest. "Why?"

He turned to me and circled the letters on his knuckles like Ben always rubbed at the break in his.

"Are those markings a reminder of your mistake?" I asked.

In the distance, the night sky erupted in a pink-and-blue supernova that spat out millions of shooting stars.

"What was that?"

Ben flapped his wings twice and landed on one of the fairy chimneys. He threw his hands in the air, "The middle realm has released."

The colours flashed over his white hair, lighting a rare joyous smile.

I was dazzled by the sight, "That's every human soul?"

"All the ones since the fall," Ben said. "They're free now."

I hoped Esme was up there somewhere and happy.

We watched the dazzling sight for a short while. Ben explained they would search for a portal to return to A'vean and the life it held beyond the Earth.

"That's so beautiful," I said.

Grey snorted as he relaxed too. Ben landed back next to us.

Koi had remained quiet.

"I know you have pain too," I said to him. "Let me help you for a change."

Koi held his hands over his face and sighed again. When he finally looked at me, his eyes were heavy and his mouth thin.

"I need to right a horrible wrong. Best I show you."

"Okay," I said. "Let's go."

We were all fallible; I had no business questioning Koi. Now was the time for redemption, and I would help him get his.

Göbekli Tepe was close by. We landed quietly, and I left Grey to graze nearby.

Koi pointed at the centre of the sunken ruins. Tall sandstone columns decorated with animal reliefs shimmered under its reignited portal. There was movement in and out of it. Watchers and souls sped up and down the highway between A'vean and Earth.

I smelled the distinct odour of old blood. "Lilith?"

Koi nodded. I peered worriedly at the portal.

"She can't use that," he walked ahead and pointed down. "Underneath. Its where we lived once upon a time," Koi's fingers wound together; his voice thin. He lacked his normal exuberance.

Ben pointed at an eviscerated corpse near a set of stone steps that led down into the ground.

I kneeled. The throat had been ripped wide open.

"She is desperate," Koi said.

He pointed for us to go down the well-worn steps. They brought us through a rough-hewn archway into a bland subterranean space. It was snug with three smaller arches that led into different tunnels. We had to bend to fit through the entrance.

As soon as we'd followed Koi into the middle tunnel, I heard her wailing.

We stepped around several body parts in our way; I shuddered when I stepped on a finger. We entered a small pitch chamber. Koi threw an orb at the ceiling.

Lilith was huddled in the corner, snivelling to herself. Angry, I moved towards her, but Koi put a hand out to stop me.

"Let me do this, Sophia. Please?"

The pain in Koi's eyes stopped me. Ben reached for me and I took his hand.

"Okay, but we're here for you."

A piece of me broke for Koi. He had carried this pain and guilt for a very long time.

Lilith sobbed. "Come to gloat?" she looked shambolic.

Koi took two steps forwards, "Why would I do that?"

"Why wouldn't you finally get your revenge? You've won!"

She pulled at her hair and screamed. Koi waited for her to stop.

Koi held up his hands in peace, "I don't want revenge."

I arched my eyebrows. I'd expected Koi to descend her on sight, but then again, this seemed more personal. I felt like a voyeur, so I kept my distance and my mouth shut. My fingers wound tighter in Ben's.

Lilith threw her hands up, "What then? Shall we go back to old times?"

"You know that can't happen," Koi said.

She edged against the wall and thinned her amber eyes at me.

"Of course not. You were always too pure, weren't you? Like her! Too good to enjoy the life we could have had!"

She held her fists to her chest and rubbed her knuckles over and over, just as Koi had the habit to do.

"You left me," Koi said. "You chose the darkness."

Lilith laughed hysterically through her sobs. She bit into her knuckles and ripped the flesh off.

"I was not to know what would become of me because of him! This is his doing, his fault!"

Her bloody mouth dribbled. The dry ground absorbed the blood pooling around her.

"You cannot erase what you have done," Koi said. "You chose him over me because he indulged you. You chose darkness to indulge all of your desires."

Lilith sniffed. She stood and straightened, attempting to tidy her hair and her pride.

"And what is wrong with desire?" her eyes slid between Ben and I.

"All Yeqon did was use you and turn you into the monster you are," Koi said.

She screamed, balled her hands into fists and shook them at him. Koi held up his hands.

"Love," he lifted the left, then the right. "Hate. With you, I had both, wanted both. I nearly lost myself to it. I've kept these to remind me, just as I know you did."

Lilith looked at her own knuckles, emblazoned with the same words.

"Once, there was a part of you that cared about how these made you feel," Koi said. "They spoke to the human conscience you no longer have."

She hissed at him, but rapidly withered before our eyes.

"How long since you fed?" Koi asked.

"Isn't it obvious?" she fell to her knees and pulled a clump of loose hair from her head. "Too long, Koi. Help me. Please. I don't want to die," she gripped the hairs between her fingers and cried.

Koi circled the chamber and checked inside two urns.

"What are you doing?" Lilith snapped.

"Ensuring you have no sustenance left."

Her eyes bulged, "You wouldn't be so cruel." she crawled towards him.

Koi turned away from her and ushered us out.

"Humans have a wonderful concept called Karma, Lilith. This is yours. Here you were born, and here you shall remain."

She screamed, choking on herself. I heard her scramble after us, but with nothing to feed on and being as ancient as she was, she failed quickly.

There was a heavy thud as she fell.

"Koi! My love, don't leave me here!"

We left the chamber she was in. Koi pushed a boulder across the entrance, sealing her within the earth.

It didn't feel victorious.

We stood outside until her screams waned.

I placed my hand on Koi's arm, "I'm sorry. I can't imagine how hard that must have been. Are you okay?"

"Yes," his shoulders relaxed, and he nodded. "I'm finally free. If there had been any possibility of forgiveness, I would have searched the universe for her, but evil swallowed her whole," he nodded with a finality and turned for the steps.

We walked back to the beautiful glow of the Göbekli Tepe portal. Its hum kept the night's insects excited, and its light melded with the moon's trail across the ground.

Koi glanced between me and Ben, "And what about you, Sophia? Your journey has been painful too."

I sighed and took Ben's hands in mine again. I turned to him. His fractured knuckle was still red and swollen. He looked at the wound, and I carefully rubbed over the swelling.

"When you've dealt with your pain, come back to me."

He tightened his grip, "I'm not sure I ever will, or deserve to."

I smiled at him, "Well, I'm to believe we've a long time to wait it out."

"Soph, I…"

I put a finger to his soft lips. "Just go make amends. Right what you've wronged. Do what you need to do. I'll be waiting," my eyes stung. "Always."

My heart was breaking, I wasn't sure I'el would ever let him back. I worried about Tartarus, too, but forced a smile, my fingers circled the back of his hands.

I wanted to hold him forever, to protect him from the pain of his redemption, but he would never heal that way. Our marks connected with the softest K'ufili. I breathed in ashes and spice and held his scent hostage in my memory. I let go of his hands, and he retreated into the portal.

Ben waved me goodbye and slipped out of my life, perhaps forever.

We watched his light meld with the portal and fade.

Koi took my hand, "I returned from the darkness. He did it the hard way, but he did it, and he did it for you. I'el will be merciful."

Koi and I hugged. Our losses were different, but our shared pain was a comfort.

We took our time journeying home, lost in our thoughts. When we arrived in the Dandenong Ranges at the break of dawn, we embraced again.

Koi smiled, "Well then. Haven't we had a journey?"

"Yes. Yes, it's been, um…" I shook my head, unsure how to put it together in a word or two.

He bowed and placed a K'ufili on my cheek. "It's been an honour, Soph'ael. Now, let's find somewhere to make tea, and then we had best rescue Jude," he laughed. "Jaz is more than he bargained for."

I laughed too, "I expected nothing less."

We transferred back to my old home, wandered past the chasm where the sanctuary had imploded towards the ruins of my house. The morning sun warmed my back, and a kookaburra laughed nearby. I breathed in the fresh aromas of the bushland. Grey dashed past me to a large clump of grass. There was a peaceful hum in the air, a calm tune to the E'lan's melody.

No more fog, no more fear, no more hiding.

No more being afraid to be me.

Given the choice, I would do it all again.

Epilogue

The rolling pin prodded its doughy charge into submission. The kettle bubbled and clicked as I sprinkled currants across the pastry.

"Tea, Alfie?"

"As sure as my next breath," he called from outside.

My old boss from the Miss Marples Tea rooms, Alfie, was painting the new balustrade a deep burgundy and staining the hardwood to resemble our old home.

I poured him a strong brew and stirred in a generous scoop of sugar. With a shortbread biscuit on the saucer, I took it outside.

"Looks wonderful," I said.

He sipped the steaming tea, "Sorry it's taken so long, darling."

I waved him off. "What's a year here or there? I have all the time in the world. And besides, there was that rather large hole to deal with first," I kissed the top of his head. "I'm just glad to see my old home reborn."

His eyes moistened and wandered off into memory.

"Joan would have loved what you've done," I said.

She had passed away from complications of her hip surgery. I hadn't been able to say goodbye whilst I saved the world from destruction.

Alfie nodded, focussed intently on me, "She would be so proud of you, with what you've done and such."

He never spoke of the revelation, of the world's awakening from its ignorant slumber. He just accepted it.

"Can I smell something burning?"

I slapped my hand to my forehead, "My Eccles cakes!" I ran back in, hoping Enl'iel wasn't home yet to laugh at my errant baking skills.

The hot tray slid across the shiny new kitchen bench — I'd grabbed it without an oven mitt, "Ouch!" I yelped.

There was snuffling near my feet.

"Don't dare you laugh!" I dropped a blackened piece of the pastry to the ground for my new best friend, Storm. He wagged his tail as he barked at the morsel and nosed it around the floorboards.

I laughed, "Well, thank you. It's that bad, eh?"

I threw the ruined pastries into the bin and peered out the window. Maybe I should just buy some from the bakery.

I watched Alfie wander towards the new shed. The sky held the shimmer of the portals, which was still a breath-taking sight. The world was safe, humanity at peace.

I ran water in the sink and swished soap around until it was satisfyingly bubbly, but felt compelled to stop what I was doing. I turned the tap off but held on to it.

The E'lan changed from a whispering current to a heart-racing torrent, but only for a moment. It settled back into its peaceful cadence as the soft fall of cautious feet padded behind me.

My chest tightened. Dizzy, I let the tap go and held on to the edge of the bench instead.

"If you're hungry, I just burnt the Eccles cakes," I said softly.

Storm barked. He threaded through my legs; his puppy hackles raised.

"I hear charcoal is good for digestion."

His voice stole my breath. I felt him move closer but kept staring at the panorama of eucalypts past the grassy mound that covered what had once been an angelic sanctuary. My heart thrashed against my ribs.

"How's the hand?" I asked.

"Ready to be healed."

His breath was on my neck, I bit my lip. My skin warmed in a way it hadn't in such a long time.

Storm squeezed though my feet. His little nose sniffed my visitor's feet, he began to lick his toes.

"He's like Shadow," Ben's voice rocked through me.

"Yes, he is," I whispered with not enough breath. "I miss him terribly."

"I missed you."

I closed my eyes. I didn't want to open them in case it was a dream.

His arms slid around my waist. The scent of ashes and spice was a thing of the dark past. He now smelled like sunshine. I took a deep breath and turned around.

"You look…you look so…"

"Not like a Daimon, I hope?" Ben's lips pulled into a coy half-smile. His eyes had lost their pain and shimmered the vivid blue of a Watcher. His long hair was white and sleek.

"No. Not like a Daimon."

"That's a relief!" he prodded his cheeks playfully.

I took a strand of his hair between my fingers. It was soft and thick. "Suits you."

A brief silence brought forth all the discomforts of unanswered questions. I dropped his hair and leaned my hands against his chest.

"Ben, I…"

"Ben doesn't exist. He is a figment of a life I want to forget. Please, Sophia, call me by the name my mother whispered into my ear. Call me Nik'ael."

I looked into his eyes. His hands slipped into mine, and our fingers entwined like they could never be parted again.

"You want to know what happened while I was gone?"

"I need to."

Would he stay or had he returned for Neren'iel? It was a selfish thought, but I couldn't help it.

"Neren'iel moved on a long time ago," he said. "She is happy, and I am happy that she found happiness. Neren'iel gives us her blessing."

He squeezed my hands a little harder, as though he was scared he would lose me.

"That is, well… does she have something to bless?"

Nik'ael held his breath. I held mine too. I needed a moment to gather my thoughts and to believe in happy endings.

I pulled away from him and walked outside. I grabbed a cob of corn from the barrel by the back steps and whistled. Grey half galloped; half flew from the back paddock.

Nik'ael laughed, "The beast is still here?"

"The beast can hear you," Grey whispered into our minds as he munched.

"He wanted to stay with me," I said. "I couldn't leave this place either, too many wonderful memories. Many have stayed. I suppose like me, they are used to being here and want to enjoy the Earth without Yeqon and Lilith."

Grey whinnied and trotted away to munch on Enl'iel's new roses.

"She'll kill you if you eat those again!"

He snorted and bit off another before he galloped to the pond for a drink.

Just us again. I heard Alfie tinkering in the shed. I sat on the top step where the lavender grew thick and lush.

Nik'ael joined me. Our legs touched. His broken knuckles rested in his lap.

"What happened on A'vean?"

He sighed and ran his hand through hair.

"Did you suffer?" I wanted the answer to be *yes* and *no*. I wanted him to have been held accountable for all he'd done, but I couldn't bear the thought of his pain.

Our eyes met.

"I faced the Throne and asked what I could do to deserve love again," he cupped my cheek, and it felt like home. "I asked what I had to do to deserve *your* love."

His eyes travelled over my face; his thumb trailed my lips. My heart raced. My thoughts scattered.

My love, the man who would always be there, gave me his hand to heal. I ran my power gently over his skin.

"What did you have to endure?" I whispered.

"Everything," he watched my fingers knit his fractured hand back together. "I gave I'el everything so that I could return to you, and give *you* everything."

My breath hitched. I put his healed hand back in his lap. He raised it and looked at it in wonder as he stretched his fingers, enjoying the freedom from pain.

"Nik'ael," I looked at him. "What did you have to give to I'el?"

He lifted the hair next to his mark to reveal a thumb-sized scorch mark. I touched it, and the depth of its power sent a shockwave up my arm.

"I must forever watch over the Earth, never to return to Av'ean." He placed his hand over mine and pressed it onto the mark, "One thought of the darkness and my soul will be extinguished, as though I never existed."

A rush of fear ran through me. Could anyone ever be that perfect? Could he really have eradicated all that he had been as a Daimon? It felt unjust to have that hover over him forever.

My fingers traced I'el's mark.

"It's what I deserve and what I'd give to be with you, if you give me the chance?" his eyes wore the fear of rejection. My hand travelled down to his lips, he closed his eyes, tears slipped from them. "I wronged you deeply, Soph. I know I'll need to earn your forg…"

I kissed the words away. I let the hurt close, sealed off old wounds and opened my heart. I pulled him closer, not allowing a breath of air between us. Salt mingled between our lips from his tears. I kissed them away with soft pecks and nuzzled into his neck.

"I love you whether you're Ben, Nik'ael, or whatever."

Nik'ael stood and pulled me with him. He plucked a handful of lavender, which no longer burned him, and threaded it through my hair.

"You saved me," he said. "Every time I looked into your eyes; you saved a piece of my soul."

He glanced at the clear summer sky and released his wings. I followed suit. We soared high above the mountain ranges that I'd grown up in and stopped to admire the new world — or rather, the old world reborn. Hand in hand, we took in the horizon, which was studded with Watchers guarding the people of Earth.

"It began like this," Ben took my hand and pulled me close. "And this is heaven on Earth."

For the first time, my heart was content.

The End

Thank you for reading
The A'vean Chronicles

If you would like to read my other books,
please scan below for links

ACKNOWLEDGEMENTS

To write an entire book series has been something I never imagined I could achieve only a few short years ago. As a lover of sagas, I now appreciate with so much more depth of understanding the energy and work that goes into creating something from nothing. To all the authors who've inspired me over the years, I thank you.

None of this would ever come to fruition without the amazing help and support of others. Writing is not just about an author and an idea, it's a village of people raising a manuscript together.

To my amazing editor, Sarina Langer, I can't put a value on what you've taught me. You've corrected some amusing typos in the many, many versions of my manuscripts. You've been kind and understanding and helped me develop Allegiance and Redemption into works that I truly believe befit the vision I had for my story. Thank you for your friendship, your funny commentary and for being an author I admire as well.

To Beverley Lee who helped with reading and guiding the story's development. Yes, there were many clenching of knuckles! Ha, ha! I kept the knuckles on the rarer side for the final product. Your support as an author I admire, and as a friend has been invaluable.

To Julia Blake who again read through with her finest-toothed comb and picked out errant typos, your help is unquantifiable.

To Becky and James Wright, of Platform House Publishing, you have made my books, things of utter beauty. Redesigning all my covers and formatting the manuscript more beautifully than I could have imagined. Thank you so much.

To Kat of Katart Illustrations, a whole series of gorgeous character art & the original covers imagined from your mind, purely from a few Dm's from me. Your art is incredible and lives on in the new versions. Thank you for bringing my characters to life.

To Joanne Middlemast, you were the very first person to read a very raw version of Allegiance and Redemption before they were re-written. Your feedback is gratefully appreciated and thank you for tolerating what must have been a million typos.

To my family, Chris, Kristen, Thomas and Ava, it's been five years of me rambling on about Sophia and Daimons… thanks for putting up with it all.

About the Author

G.R. Thomas is an Australian indie author. An avid reader since childhood, it has only been well into adulthood that pen was put to paper to capture the stories that have always been her mind.

In between working as a theatre recovery nurse, being mum to three beautiful children, wife to an ever-supporting husband and running a hobby farm, writing is the passion that glues a very busy life together.

Follow me
Please keep up to date with what I'm up to on social media.
Instagram: @grthomas2014
TikTok: @grthomasindieauthor
Facebook: G.R. Thomas Author
Website: www.grthomasbooks.com

If you enjoyed this or any of my other books, please leave a small review on Amazon, Goodreads, or wherever you prefer to review the books that you enjoy. Reviews are the gold dust that make books sparkle and are forever appreciated by authors.

Thank you for reading Redemption.